COYOTE

GIGI MEIER

BALBOA.PRESS
A DIVISION OF HAY HOUSE

Balboa Press books may be ordered through booksellers or by contacting:

Balboa Press
A Division of Hay House
1663 Liberty Drive
Bloomington, IN 47403
www.balboapress.com
844-682-1282

Because of the dynamic nature of the Internet, any web addresses or
links contained in this book may have changed since publication and
may no longer be valid. The views expressed in this work are solely those
of the author and do not necessarily reflect the views of the publisher,
and the publisher hereby disclaims any responsibility for them.

The author of this book does not dispense medical advice or prescribe the use
of any technique as a form of treatment for physical, emotional, or medical
problems without the advice of a physician, either directly or indirectly. The
intent of the author is only to offer information of a general nature to help
you in your quest for emotional and spiritual well-being. In the event you use
any of the information in this book for yourself, which is your constitutional
right, the author and the publisher assume no responsibility for your actions.

Cover created by Just write. Creations

Print information available on the last page.

ISBN: 979-8-7652-3198-2 (sc)
ISBN: 979-8-7652-3197-5 (e)

Balboa Press rev. date: 11/11/2022

CONTENTS

DEDICATION PAGE

Mom and Dad,

You have always been my biggest cheerleaders and strongest allies. From listening to all my wild ideas, reading sample stories, and letting me yammer on about my dreams. Thank you for instilling a strong work ethic, fierce independence, and unwavering ambition to achieve everything I have ever set my sights on. From Brunhilda Plotz in the German helmet to GiGi Meier in homage to our German heritage.

Chapter 1

"Faster! Faster!" Mom screams across the cab of the truck. Her panic is palpable as blinding lights bear down on us. Sweat rolls down my neck and into the collar of my white shirt, now smeared with dirt and blood. My heart pounds through the palm of my hands while I grip the steering wheel. My foot jams the gas pedal to the floorboard as prayers chant through my mind.

Please don't die.

Please don't die.

Please don't die.

We race across the desert floor at breakneck speeds, tossing the girls around the back and filling the cab with their screams. Dust envelops the windshield, making it difficult to see the remanent pavement of a long abandoned road.

Shots ring out, clinking into the truck's armor. Their vehicle, the one I stole.

"Shit! Get down!" I scream in the mirror, seeing three trucks barreling behind us. "Come on, come on!"

Adrenaline courses through my veins. My arms lock, trying to maintain control of the steering wheel, shaking wildly in my grip. My thigh strains under the pressure of my foot, flooring the accelerator. I catch a flash of Mom's hand on the dashboard, bracing herself against the rough terrain. The tires skid on the sand, sending another round of screams into the tense air.

"Oh, my—" Mom murmurs.

"Hold on!" I jerk my foot off the gas and turn into the spin to careen across the desert. The force of the spinning truck spews vomit across the back and fills the cab with a stench. My stomach turns, and I gag.

With all my strength, I grip the inside of the wheel, fighting to turn the tires against the mountain of sand collecting under them as gravity slows us down. If I flip this thing, we're dead.

A circle of light illuminates the truck. Mom prays. I curse. The whirl of the helicopter blades drowns out the roar of the engine fighting against the mounting dirt. Clinking bullets litter the armor covering the top of the truck, eliciting more screams from the terrified girls in the back.

"Get down! We gottaaaaaa—"

The truck slams into a rock formation, throwing everyone to my side. Dust and debris swirl outside the windshield, blocking any visibility. The violent force of the crash rams Mom into me and my head against the side window. Pain rockets through my skull, and my vision blurs. Mom's mouth is moving, but I do not hear her.

I shake my head, squinting my eyes to focus and pulling on my earlobes. She yanks on my forearm and points to the passenger side before opening the door. I nod, understanding we must make a run for it.

She slips out the side and immediately disappears. Fear prickles my skin. Knowing there is no place for it, I shut it out and crawl across the seat to sink into the thick sand.

A partial headlight burns in the darkness, spotlighting the pit the swirling truck created. I glance beyond the pit and see it. In the dark distance is the ominous beacon in the night, bringing a heaviness to my heart.

"Mom!" I turn toward the girls and gasp at the chopper's searchlight dancing across the landscape. Our only chance of escaping the coyotes is to run. Run fast as hell to the gates of Hell. "Shit! Hurry!"

"Go! Go! Go!" I point, shaking my hand at the scantily clad girls scrambling out of the back. "Run!"

The sounds of the helicopter jolt them forward, past my waving hands. Mom grabs the smallest one's hand, and they run into the dark desert. The others are older, not by much, and equally underweight, yet their fragility doesn't stop them from sprinting across the terrain.

"Run!" I glimpse the six headlights of their trucks descending on us.

Dirt collects in my boots and weights down my steps. Ahead, Mom slips, and the little girl tries to help her up. My arms pump faster, and my lungs heave to get to them in time. I shove the little girl toward the women. One of them runs back to scoop her up before running again.

"Go! Save yourself, Sammie," Mom yells while stumbling to get up.

"No! I'm not leaving you!" Together, we push out of the dense sand, my hand gripping hers, convinced I am breaking every bone in it as I drag her behind me. "Faster!"

We dart from cactus to dead bush, a dangerous game of zigzag while the chopper flies overhead. The searchlight misses us but casts enough glare to show the girls clustered against the centuries-old stone.

Mom falls with twenty feet left, taking me down with her. "Go, honey! Just save the girls!" The chopper's twirling blades swirl dust into a sandstorm around us, sucking the oxygen out of the air.

Mom chokes on the sand. I cover my mouth with my sleeve and wrap my other arm around her waist to dislodge us. "We're almost there, Mom."

Her brown hair swirls around her face, and I am not sure she hears me until her fierce brown eyes connect with mine. With blood pumping through my heart at triple speed, I tug her close to me. Together, we sprint through the curtain of sand, dodging bushels of tumbleweed until we reach the bottom of the fort. The beam soaks the stone walls in light, causing the girls to sink further into the shadows of the abandoned gun turret. The little girl lunges into Mom's arms as we huddle into a crevice.

"It's okay," she murmurs while shielding the little girl from the roaring truck engines.

I crawl past them, feeling my way over the rough stone.

Come on.

You got to work.

My hands tremble, searching the rock of the lower fort for the inlet containing the lever that will save our lives. My breath is barely above a pant as my cheek presses into the dirty wall. Cuts litter my fingers, and an occasional sting registers a new nick until I find it. With my fingertips curled around the rusty metal, I tug with all my strength.

It does not budge.

Please. Please. Please.

I shift farther over to gain leverage and repeatedly tug, praying it doesn't break until it finally gives, causing me to fall on my butt. I wait for an alarm or siren to announce our unfortunate arrival.

It has been five years. He's got to have installed some sort of security system. But nothing, no sound, no sirens, and no alarms. I breathe a silent thank you to the universe. My gratitude is short-lived when the shouts of men wielding machine guns cut through the spotlights in search of the girls.

"Over here," I whisper, reaching for the first one to guide her through the entrance, then the next, until I feel the small trembling hand. Giving her a reassuring squeeze, I pass her through to awaiting arms and mutter, "You're safe," knowing we are a thousand steps from safety.

Mom is last, pausing long enough to flash a look of uncertainty before she disappears into the darkness. Hair prickles around my neck as the shouting draws closer. A flash of boots crunching the dirt a few feet away propels me to activate the lever and dive into the dark as the trap door groans closed behind me.

My body sags against the wall of the damp, musky cellar. My heart is beating in my throat, and my lungs are clenching with adrenaline. A brush against my thigh makes me jump out of my skin until a loud whine ricochets off the ancient walls.

"Tiberia?"

Astonishment coats my parched throat as slobbery kisses cover my hands in the dark.

Is she still here?

Oh my God.

Her whines get louder and louder as she jumps on me.

"Hush, girl."

I squat to wrap her in a hug and dodge her relentless tongue. Cooing in her ear to quiet her does the opposite. She is too excited and howls in happiness. The girls scream, lost in the blackness, going from one predator to another until light floods the cellar and blinds us all.

The room erupts with men in black fatigues pointing guns at the girls, and their screams are deafening. I bolt from my position on the floor with Tiberia to push through the huddling girls. The guns shift when I reach the front, all pointing at me. I raise my hands to show I have no weapons.

Sweat blazes down my temples, and fear coils in the pit of my stomach. My breath is harsh, panting like a rabid animal as I stare into the empty eyes of our new captors. They can end us without contemplation or concern.

Deep snarls rise on my right, and a stealthy Tiberia stalks into my peripheral vision. A gun shifts to her. The movement causes the girls to cluster closer to me. I slowly lower one hand to touch her ear.

Her snarls roll one after another, unyielding as my fingers slide to the back of her neck to grip her fur. I don't dare break eye contact with the men, even as one looks past me to leer at the poor girls. His mouth curls, filling me with disgust.

Footsteps echo off the stone floors. Fresh cologne surges into the musky space, and those familiar eyes fall on me.

"Well, well, well. How you say?" His face is sinister, full of contempt. "Ah, yes. Look what the cat dragged in."

We lock eyes. He's bigger than I remember, darker, and more menacing. His dark suit clings to his muscular body, and power radiates off him. That once beautiful face has a scar intersecting his eye, and I can't help tilting my head to wonder what happened. A new tattoo snakes around the side of his neck and slithers into his black dress shirt.

A shadowy beard coats his clenched jaws, bringing out the pink of his lips. He never used to wear a beard. His eyes, which used to hold reflections of me, are hard and cold.

"Maximiliano." His name falls from my lips like an unanswered prayer.

His mouth twists, pleased with his effect on me. He saunters forward, shrinking the space and the girls' sobbing heightens. I glance over my shoulder to hush their fears, knowing it will have little effect. Mom steps forward when he pulls my chin to meet his gaze, and two guns move to her.

"Don't touch her," Mom demands, standing beside me and moving to touch him. His men inch closer, the threat unspoken, and her hand drops to my shoulder.

"Mama, I presume?" His voice is gravely low, unconcerned, and unwilling to call off his men to help us poor, defenseless women. Anger stirs in me.

"Leave her alone. She doesn't know."

"Still a fierce *gatita*, I see." His accent stumbles across the words. My heart aches at how much I once loved it. Now, the familiarity stings. "But you can't make demands." Mom's hand trails down my arm, catching my hand to hold and conveying our unity.

He lets go of my chin, and I raise it in defiance.

"True, but I didn't expect our paths to cross again."

It's the truth. The mission didn't go as planned.

"Ah yes, this noise, shall we call disturbance, is because of you?"

He steps back, pointing to the ceiling, and the steady burr of the helicopter is getting louder by the minute. I look around the empty racks that once held unspeakable things in this room and release Mom's hand.

"Yes."

"You know I like the peace and the quiet, yes?"

I meet his stare. "Yes."

"And this, gatita, is not peace and quiet now, is it?"

"No." I shake my head. With a flick of his wrist, his men lower their guns and stand down. I inhale a shaky breath, feeling a small amount of relief.

"I need a few hours, and then we'll be gone. You'll never see me again. You can have your peace and quiet back."

"*Niña traviesa*, what have you done? These *cochina bambinas* and the *anciana*? What are you up to?" His tone is both accusatory and mocking. He already knows. I don't know how, but I'm almost sure he does.

Cat and mouse was always his favorite game. He loves having an advantage over people. Thrives off control and indebtedness. He must relish me being the one to owe him now.

"They're too young, Maxie."

I hope using his old nickname would favor me, but seeing his sneer, I know I made a strategic mistake. He abruptly turns and walks toward the cellar entrance. I shoot Mom a weary look, which she meets with a concerned one.

"You want something from me now, and years ago, I wanted something too." His words carry the gravity of the situation. He won't let us go. No, there will be a cost. There always was.

Nothing in his world has changed in the last five years. Mine is vastly different from the impressionable girl I used to be. Tiberia's nose bumps my hand, and I raise it to pet her head. When he finally turns around, he's disgusted at the sight. "You even turned my dog against me."

His dog? Is that how she is still alive?

He suddenly whips his gun out of the holster hidden beneath his suit coat and points it at Tiberia. The girls scream, and Mom jumps, but I fall to my knees in front of her. I shield her fluffy body with my petite frame, putting my head directly in front of the barrel.

"No . . . please. Don't kill her," I beg, throwing my arms out to hold Tiberia back and pray she doesn't lunge at him. Her renewed growls rumble through her chest and vibrate my back. "Tiberia, down girl."

His calculating eyes stare at me, and I whisper, "Please." His barrel hits my forehead, and I close my eyes. If this is how he wants it to end, then so be it. I don't stand a chance against the dark, violent world he lives in. I am nothing but a mere desert flower in this dry wasteland he calls a life.

His harsh laugh rings out in the silent room. The cold steel is no longer pressed against my clammy skin.

"Always saving the world. I will let the dog live. Let the anciana and cochina bambinas leave."

"Thank you."

I breathe, shifting to wrap my arms around a growling Tiberia to calm her. I wipe my watering eyes in her dusty fur before using her body for balance to stand.

A pounding on the door sends a collective gasp into the air.

"Please, Maximiliano," I beg, and he knows why. Those calculating eyes stare into my light green eyes for several agonizing seconds before he raises a finger to one of his men. As the soldier retreats, I glance at the narrow passageway to the old stone staircase hidden from the fort's grand hall.

The air is smothering, and the tension is thick. I don't know what he meant when he said we could leave. Does that mean leave after the heat dies down? Or does he plan to turn us over to the coyotes? Or will he allow an old friend safe passage to the local authorities?

Nervousness swims in my stomach, causing me to feel nauseated, but I must ask. I step forward, reaching my hand out. I need to know. Do we make a run for it and risk getting shot? Or can I trust him to hide us somewhere in his compound?

"Maximiliano?"

He views my hand scornfully, and I tilt my head in a silent plea. I know I'm pushing my luck at this point, but it's all I have left. No ideas, no escape route, no backup plan. Just hope and a prayer. Six women, a young girl, and God help me, Mom, depending on me for their survival.

"The old wing, gatita. Not a sound."

His ominous warning rings to the danger I have placed him in. He hates precarious positions, and asking him to hide us puts him directly in one.

"I'm indebted."

I speak the words we both know are true. His dark eyes slowly scan my body, lingering on his once-favorite parts before returning to my eyes.

"Yes, you are. Now go."

Chapter 2

His tone communicates both a promise and a threat. If I wasn't in so deep. If things had gone according to plan. If a hundred things were different. I could 'what if' the rest of the night, and it wouldn't change reality.

I wait until Maximiliano saunters out the cellar door to nod at Mom to follow. Wordlessly, she slips past me, holding the little girl's hand. I wrinkle my nose when I get a whiff of sweat and spicy cologne from one of the men. To think what they would have done to these girls. I shudder.

"Go, go." My voice is low as I gesture for them to follow. They cluster in the middle of the passageway. I stand at the end, blocking the men from passing or grabbing at the girls. It's dark, nearly impossible to see, and the smell of the dank air is hard to take. Tiberia's tail brushes the back of my leg, and I find her head to acknowledge we're in this together.

With little light and the men grunting their dissatisfaction behind me, I need to lead us through the maze of the tunnels that lie ahead. I whisper soft instructions as I pass each girl, hoping to dampen their fears by giving reassuring touches to their arms. I learned long ago that there are only a few benign places to touch abuse victims without triggering their trauma.

Tiberia pushes past me, acting as a guide for our group. When I get to Mom, we share a look that says a million things. But now is not the time for words. It's the time for actions, swift ones.

With Tiberia leading, we move quickly and quietly through the tunnels to the old wing. He once told me about the old fort, the romanticized version. It was one of few that survived the Pancho Villa attack.

The sad irony of this property is that it once housed a nobler cause. It was the unofficial headquarters for General Pershing and his troops to execute the President's order to capture the elusive old villa.

The thick stone walls, unlit hallways, and dusty wood floors enhanced the eerie mystic of this old treasure. Too bad it had fallen into the hands of a wealthy cartel kingpin that uses humans as pawns in his drug operations.

Maximiliano Maldonado.

I had heard his name many times over the years, related to several violent acts that I suspected to be true. I wasn't a witness to them when I knew him except that one day. What I saw was beyond comprehension, and I left. That was over five years ago.

I blink away those old memories, wanting to shake them right out of my head, when the tunnel curves, revealing a light at the top of a creaky old staircase.

Out of one danger and into another.

Tiberia takes the stairs two at a time, her fluffy tail sending a slight breeze into the stale air. I look at Mom, checking to see if she needs help, and the little girl squeezes tighter to her side. She nods, conveying she's fine, and I whisper, "Wait here." I climb the tapering staircase, keeping a hand on the wall for balance until I reach the tiny landing.

The brass handle is tarnished, and the door is covered in cobwebs. Even as light peers through the cracks of the door frame, it seems like it hasn't been opened in years. Regardless of how much I rattle the handle, it doesn't budge. I lean the side of my body against the carved panels, hitting it repeatedly with my weight until the door finally yields with a protesting groan.

A rush of cool air caresses my hot cheeks. When I peek around the corner, I see a series of wood doors. Turning back, I motion for them to ascend and see the little girl helping Mom up the stairs.

Tiberia shakes out her fur, a small howl escaping before she pads down the dimly lit hall to scratch at one of the old doors. I cautiously follow. My fingertips gather dirt as I drag them across the dusty wall. Tiberia is vehemently scratching at the last door on the right. I raise my hand to stop Mom and the girls a fair distance behind so I can investigate. Tiberia's whining grows more insistent.

"What's it, girl?"

The palm of my hand rests flat on the door, leaning my ear close to see if I hear anything. After a long silence on the other side, I grasp the door handle and swing it open. Tiberia barrels past me to chase a rat scurrying along the baseboard.

Tiberia's toenails clack on the wood floors, and her furry tail wags as she scampers after the rodent. I remain in the hallway when Mom and the little girl join me. Our eyes lock, and I mutter, "A rat."

She glances at the little girl watching both of us.

I proceed into the room, seeing a shadow of a lamp on a table, and turn the knob. It casts a dim hue against the faded plaster walls. Sparse, I remember him saying. The only furnishings are a full bed, a chest of drawers, and a wooden chair. That's fine. It will do for tonight.

Before Mom can enter the room, Tiberia runs out with a tail sticking out of her mouth.

"Let's hope that's the only one," Mom says, her face a mixture of exhaustion and apprehension.

"Yes, let's. I remember there being two bedrooms in this corner of the wing, with an adjoining bathroom through that door. We can sleep three in a room. I can't imagine the beds being too comfortable, but it beats taking a spot on the floor." I muster a paltry smile before investigating the other bedroom and hoping there are no rodents in it.

I walk through the bathroom door. It's tiny and dusty. When I turn the faucet handle, cold water gushes out. The little girl rushes into the bathroom to cup her dirty hands together and drink the water. Not ideal, yet who knows when they last had food or water.

With the light from the bathroom shining into the other bedroom, I see the same setup. A bed, dresser, and chair, and thankfully, no rodents. It's not much, but it's far better than the girls' dungeons. Although Maximiliano is as much an enemy to these girls as their coyotes, I can't help silently thanking him for his benevolence tonight. It could have been so much worse.

I walk across the room to turn on the lamp when Mom asks, "How do you know him?"

I stiffen, sitting on the bed to look at her beautifully weathered face. Where do I begin? How do I tell her she wouldn't be here without him? As much as I hate that his drug money saved her, I can't say I hate him for it. He saved her then, and he saved us now.

"It's a very long story. There's another room, not connected like this, down the hall. We won't all fit in here." I want to escape her scrutiny, and she allows it with a reluctant frown.

"When we get these girls settled, you're telling me everything."

I hold her gaze, a test to see who will break, and a groan loosens from me. After all this time, maybe she deserves to know, or at least know, what we are up against.

"I know."

She taps the door frame and leaves the room when the little girl gasps.

Chapter 3

I sit with my head in my hands, staring at the floor and thinking about tomorrow. We're safe for now, or at least the few remaining hours that make up the night. A blessing and a curse. Time to rest and time to think is a dangerous combination.

She wants me to tell her, and I should have before, but now is not the time. I need to use this time to plot our next move, not skip down memory lane. Maybe if I tell her some, not all, then she'll help me figure a way out of this mess.

What do I tell Maximiliano when I see him? That I need safe passage out of Columbus? That I need his security detail to accompany us to ensure the coyotes don't intercept us on the road out of here.

And his words. They are both a promise and a threat. What will it cost?

A soft wisp of fur brushes my arm, and a nose plunges between my hands to swipe a kiss across my grimy face. Disgusting, considering she had a rat in her mouth.

"Tiberia," I whisper. "How are you still alive?"

A low whine rises from her, causing me to smile. She is thinner, with a smattering of mud and grim on her coat, but at least her lively spirit is still intact. I sit, scratching behind her ear when I see the little girl peering around the corner at us.

"Do you want to pet her?" I motion for her to come over. "It's okay. She's friendly."

She disappears around the corner, so I wait for her to feel brave enough to try again. It takes a few moments, but she eventually enters the room. Sensing the little girl's apprehension, Tiberia sits against my leg and waits. Her tongue hangs out of her mouth, and she looks back at me while I continue petting her.

"She's a good girl." Tiberia swings her head toward the little girl, causing her to halt halfway across the room. "It's all right."

Tiberia's presence is comforting and calms my nerves. Animals are known for that, but I never thought it would be the case in this situation. The little girl eyes me and eyes the dog, unsure what to do.

"Her name is Tiberia. What's yours?"

In the smallest, sweetest voice I have ever heard, she says, "Mary."

"Mary, that's a beautiful name, and you know what?"

She steps closer. Just two more, and she'll reach Tiberia.

"What?"

"Mary is Tiberia's favorite name in the whole wide world." I smile at how precious she is. To think what those men wanted to do to her. It makes me want to hurl.

"Can you pet her for me? My hand is getting tired." I pretend to rub out a hand cramp. It's the perfect thing to say to convince her to come over. Tiberia rewards Mary with a rub of her head against her tiny body, almost knocking her over. Mary squeals with delight when Tiberia kisses her face.

"She loves you already," I say, and she mimics the scratches I was giving Tiberia.

"I love her too," Mary whispers into the dog's fur. I look away, blinking back emotions. Mary sits on the floor, throwing an arm around her furry body and leaning into the dog. It's sweet and innocent, but at the wrong place and time. She should do this in her bedroom, safe at home. I clear my throat and stand. "Can you watch her for me? In this room?"

"Okay."

"Tiberia, stay." I point, and Tiberia slides to lie on the floor. Mary scoots closer to run her hand through her fur.

I pass two girls in the bathroom, dipping their hands in the water to wipe the grim from their faces. The rest are sitting on the bed, dazed and exhausted, with haunted eyes. They are filthy, hair matted and covered in dirt. The scraps for clothes provide little coverage and protection against the cold desert air. The thin blanket covering the mattress won't help much, but they should stay warm enough in this old drafty place with three to a bed. Most are barefoot except for the little girl.

They will need medical attention immediately. The physical cuts and an infected branding on one girl's hip oozes puss. The invisible damage will take longer. PTSD, nightmares, and years of therapy. A very tough road ahead for all of them. A set of empty eyes befall me. I smile as a gesture of empathy and an acknowledgment of something I don't have words for.

"Mom, I'm going to look at the room down the hall." I point to the hallway and cross the tiny room when her hand taps my shoulder. Mom's ominous look lets me know the conversation is happening sooner than I want.

"Okay," I murmur as Mom whispers instructions to the girls. She's quiet until we get to the third bedroom.

"Start talking."

"I don't even know where to start." I open the door to the third room. It's tiny. No bigger than a broom closet, with a mattress shoved against the wall and a lamp carelessly sitting atop a stool.

She sits on the edge of the bed. A small groan escapes her tired body, but she's otherwise alert and ready for story time. Lovely.

I sit at the top of the bed, ignoring the squeaks of the mattress springs to slump against the wall. My head falls back, and I close my eyes. The sting of exhaustion is instant, and the relief is short-lived when I open them to tell her.

"Do you remember when you were in Seattle getting treatment?"

"Yes, when you started Miles for Medicine," she says, scooting further onto the bed. "The first trip?"

I pause, thinking back to how I thought life was so complicated at that time. I promised Mom I'd stay with her brother in Texas while she received treatment in Washington. However, sitting around doing nothing while Mom fought for her life in an experimental cancer program didn't seem right. Here I was healthy doing nothing, and Mom was sick doing everything.

When I got the idea of grabbing my skateboard and posting my journey on social media to skate my way to Mom, it went viral. Soon people were donating money, offering their homes for me to stay along the route, or feeding me in every town I passed. What started as a sad and lonely journey grew into something bigger than me and formed my foundation, Miles for Medicine.

"No, the second."

Her eyebrows draw together, deep in thought. I dread what she's going to say.

"Nothing happened . . . or did it? What are you not telling me?"

I clench my jaws, willing them never to open again, and return her stare. Regret settles in. I should have told her before. I lied to her for years. Will she forgive me?

"Well?"

I relent.

"Something happened. Toward the end of the trip, I stayed with a *friend* for several weeks." Her stare is unwavering, so I continue, "I got sick, Mom, really, really sick."

"No one told me. Ardy, Will—"

"I begged them not to. I blackmailed them not to."

"Those mother—"

I hold up my hand because I am solely to blame for this deception, not them.

"Mom, it's not their fault. You had that relapse and weren't responding to the new treatment, and I couldn't tell you. I couldn't let me . . . be the death . . ." I stop, swallowing hard against the lump of emotions in my throat, and she swiftly moves to hug me.

"Oh dear, never. Never think you'll be the death of me."

And yet I might be the death of her tonight.

A hint of lavender hits my nose. I close my eyes and lower my chin to rest on her shoulder. I don't know how she still has perfume on when all I can smell is my body odor. She rubs my back, and I know I must continue because she deserves to know the truth, even as the guilt weighs on me. I pull out of her embrace to stand, pacing the room to release some of the nervous energy collecting in my veins.

"Anyway, I collapsed somewhere near to here. Dehydration, heatstroke, and all the rest. One minute I am admiring the red rock, and the next, I am waking up in a fluff of white bedding I thought were clouds. I thought I had died until the most beautiful face I had ever seen appeared in front of me. It was him. They said he sat with me day and night the first couple of days. I don't remember any of it. I couldn't figure out if it were day or night, where I was, who he was, or even who I was. It was odd, Mom. The hallucinations, the dreams, all of it."

"I ask you a question. Is my accent too heavy? You don't understand?"

He moved with grace and sensuality, making no sound when his dress shoes crossed the polished wood floors.

"No, no. Your accent is beautiful."

"You consider me beautiful, señorita?" Amusement coats his words.

I blushed and was mesmerized as he walked a slow circle around me in his grand foyer. I turned to maintain eye contact. Ardy always warned me never to put my back to anyone.

"No, not beautiful. I didn't mean that. I—"

"So, I am ugly, yes?"

Is he kidding? He doesn't have any ugly spec of anything on him.

"No, stop. Can you stop?"

18

The circling made me feel like I was on a merry-go-round, and those things always made me hurl. Coming downstairs from that cloud bed, I felt better, but his odd questions and circling me like prey made me lightheaded and nauseous.

"I ask simple questions, señorita. My English not good like you, but they are easy, no?"

He didn't stop circling me. I waited till he passed me to walk over to the staircase. I plopped down on the step and propped my elbow on my knee so my hand could cradle my head.

"You are ill. Come, we go up, and you rest."

I wasn't sure I could make it back to my room, so I laid full length across the step.

"Señorita, you no lie here. Get up." He rested his shiny dress shoe on the step below mine. I could probably see the reflection of my face in it if I leaned closer.

"No, it's okay. I'm taking a break, so you know, step over me if you need to go up. Or go back to where you came from. I'll be fine right here. Leave me here to die."

"Oh my God. I can't . . ." She covers her mouth, and I look away, continuing to pace the room.

"The guys later told me that they radioed for an ambulance, and due to the remoteness of this area, he was the closest to help. He had a doctor here." I decide to leave out why he has a doctor living here. "He and Ardy got along, and I trusted them to keep me safe. You know, at eighteen, we know nothing."

I stop pacing, waiting for her to take it all in. I didn't know anything at eighteen because I thought I loved him and that he loved me, and that was enough. What a fool I was.

"So, you were here and not with that Molly girl?"

"Correct."

"And he didn't hurt you in any way? You'd tell me that at least, even if you kept all this from me." I go to object, and she waves me off. "You had your reasons, and I see they were valid to you at the time, but here I thought my girl was safe and didn't need me when you needed me the most." She chokes with emotion now, and I step toward her.

"Mom—"

"No, I get it. We were too worried about each other. Please continue." She drops her hands into her lap, slowly rubbing them together, and I assume that's her way of dealing with her nervous energy.

I shrug, not wanting to say anymore because, at this point, it doesn't even matter. We must think about what happens at daylight.

"That's it. We spent time together while I was recovering, and when I was better, I left. He donated a million dollars to the foundation, but I didn't learn that until later. I had to finish the trip, and you were counting on me. I felt the online world was watching me, and I had that big sponsorship with Meier Boards."

"My dear." She stands, coming to hold my hands in hers. "I wish you told me because we could have done something else to get that money." Her expression shows regret, and I hate that. It intensifies my guilt.

"No, Mom. I wouldn't take it back. We can't take it back, and those trips supported the foundation that led to this. If we're able to save these girls, then all the choices from the past put us here, which is still the right thing to do." It's the absolute truth.

"You're a remarkable girl."

I half smile. "We'll see how remarkable I am tomorrow. Got to get us out of this mess first."

"That may be true. However, you have me this time, and we're in it together." She squeezes my hands and smiles. Five years ago, I decided not to tell her the trouble that haunted me here. Tonight, I told her enough for a tiny piece of guilt to break away from the encapsulated hurt surrounding his memories.

"Yeah."

Her hands fall away, and she steps back to leave. I want to say one last thing that won't change our situation but needs to be said.

"Mom?" She stops, turning in my direction. "I love you."

Her face brightens, and that beautiful smile I have seen a thousand times appears again. "I love you with all I am."

A couple of moments pass before she turns and leaves the room. I hear her left foot drag across the floors, a remanent of the stroke she suffered when she was at her sickest.

"And with all I am."

I sit on the edge of the bed and wonder if 'all I am' is anything at all.

Chapter 4

No regrets.

It's always been my motto because life is short, and Mom almost died twice. That motto provided me with an odd satisfaction to justify the decisions in my life. I never did like digging around in the past. It was a cemetery of old dreams, cobwebs of plans gone awry, and tombstones of people who betrayed me. No good ever came of pushing past the creaky gates to visit the graves of poor decisions, locked away secrets, and long-ago loves.

Yet, I find myself exactly there. Wandering through the prickly brush and swiping the dirty arches of the stones while the moon dances with the dense clouds. Like the cemetery, this fort is death. The same heaviness penetrating my soul now is the same when I visit the graveyard of my past.

Maximiliano was the beautifully sinister mausoleum in the center, covered in dead vines that stained the once white marble, and reached out to grab me in my nightmares. Nightmares that haunted me for months after I left this place.

A sigh loosens from my chest, no more prolonged panic attacks from the dark place where he reigns free. That's the magic of therapy.

Compartmentalize the pain and deal with it later. I kicked that pain can down the road as far as I could until I landed in rehab. Another secret kept from Mom and another tombstone residing in that cemetery from my past.

A noisy yawn in the doorway has me looking over to see Tiberia entering the room and a timid Mary following. Her hand is buried in a tuff of white fur. I realize she needs Tiberia more than Tiberia needs me.

"Thanks for taking care of her." I pat the bed for Mary to sit next to me. Tiberia takes it as her invitation to jump on the bed and stretch across the center of the bed.

"Silly dog, do you want to come up here?"

Mary's eyes light up, and she crawls onto the bed to lie between the wall and Tiberia. She buries her head into the woolly fur with only a tiny hand seen stroking Tiberia's fur. Dirt pools on the bedding and dust particles float in the air. Both girls are calm and content. A blessing right now.

Watching this beautiful innocence is bittersweet. I wonder how Mary got here, to begin with, and I hope she will be well cared for when she returns home.

"My dear, have you seen—" Mom stops when she witnesses the two snuggled together. "I should have guessed it."

"Mary's babysitting Tiberia for me, aren't you?" Mary peeks her head out from the fur long enough to nod and buries it again. "There you have it."

"So, sleeping arrangements? We're going to keep her with us," Mom explains when one of the girls appears behind her to whisper something in her ear. "But not the dog. She smells and frightens a couple of the girls."

I thumb the two already on my bed. "They can stay with me, not planning on getting any sleep anyway." I stand, and Tiberia starts to move too. "Stay."

"Okay, I'll be with the rest of the girls since you have her." Mom leans against the doorframe, her hair a mess and exhaustion all over her face.

"I have her, and the smelly dog will alert us if anyone is around. Be sure to lock the doors. I know no one will go wandering off, and I'll come to knock on your door in a few hours. Hopefully, we'll get out of here at first light. Not sure how yet, but I'll figure it out."

Mom musters an encouraging smile, for my sake or hers, I don't know. Most likely for all our sakes.

"Okay, let's get some rest. Things will look brighter in the morning."

I always loved that saying. It was Mom's favorite, even though no bone in my body believed her.

"Yeah." The word escapes with my breath.

Mom is slow to move off the doorjamb, and the girl behind her catches Mom's elbow to help. Such a small act of kindness, yet it speaks volumes about the caring heart of the girl wearing scrapes of lingerie. I wish those sick bastards would see these precious girls as more than a commodity to buy, sell, beat, and resell. What the hell is wrong with this world?

I cross the tiny room to watch them shuffle arm in arm down the hall. Guilt washes over me. I should have lied to her about this. I should have never gotten her involved. I lied to her about so many things, big and small. Why didn't I lie about this rescue mission? I didn't, and I should have when it mattered the most. I will never get over what this has done to her emotionally and physically. The danger I put her in . . . I hate myself that much more.

I continue watching until they cross the threshold, the girl looks back, and we hold each other's gaze until her head dips. An understanding of sorts, and I appreciate that. I respect it. Maybe she and I are somehow alike, wanting to help and needing something to care for simultaneously.

Their door creaks closed, and the metal latch echoes down the quiet hallway. I glance over my shoulder to see Tiberia and Mary, fast asleep and plastered together. I know I made the right decision risking it all for this mission. I hope I can see it through tomorrow.

I close our door, latch the bolt and lie on the edge of the bed.

Exhaustion seeps into my bones now that the adrenaline has subsided. My eyes sting with fatigue as I stare at the ceiling—my mind races with memories of him.

"It's not your choice. I say get up, and you get up. It's, how you say, a command," he literally commanded as he said the command.

"Look, I'm sure the man speaks in your country, and the little woman scurries off. But here in America, where we are the last time I checked, women don't have to listen to a man's 'command.'" I lifted one hand to use air quotes because the other hand was currently shoved into my stomach to prevent me from hurling all over his shiny shoes. *"So, go away and leave me here to die. 'kay? Okay. Good talk."*

I would have feared his red face if I hadn't felt so lousy, and he wasn't so utterly gorgeous. But as it was, I couldn't care less because I decided I was not moving until I was sure I could hold my vomit until I got to my room.

"You no know who you deal with. If you did, you would kiss the ground I walk on. Now get up and go to your room."

His accent was getting stronger and thicker, making his threats sound so freaking sexy that I couldn't take them seriously.

"I don't care if you're the King of England. If I move, the only thing happening to the ground you walk on is my vomit all over it. You go, and I'll eventually make it to my room. Okay, Your Royal Highness?"

He murdered me with his expression. At least my belly couldn't bother me if I were dead. I buried my face in the wood steps and blocked out those jet-black eyes.

That controlling jerk swooped down and snatched me off the stairs. Not in that romantic Hollywood movie way, where the hunky leading man carries the lady in his arms to safety, but in that sling-me-over-his-shoulder way. His muscular shoulder dug into my stomach, and I slapped my hand over my mouth. Don't throw up.

"Niña estúpido. No hablar conmigo que en mi propia casa."

I tried not to hurl as he jogged up the stairs to the landing.

"I'm going to hurl."

I warned him. Well, a one-second warning before I vomited down his back and butt. He stood as still as a statue. I would have been embarrassed if the retching weren't so forceful and smelly. He muttered harsh words under his breath. Once done, I wiped my mouth on a clean part of his shirt.

He bellowed out a long line of Spanish. His deep voice vibrated my stomach. Oh no. I cupped my head in my hand and shushed him. "Ugh, please be quiet. Your yelling hurts my belly."

It didn't work. He yelled louder. The vibrations rumbled through my stomach and started an avalanche of vomit. His arm locked over my thighs and his hand rested on my butt. It was not a sexual advance. He didn't want me to move and make a bigger mess.

But I had to get off my belly because hanging upside down was making it worse.

"Put me down."

"No, señorita. You liter my floors. We stay. They come and clean us up."

I smile at that memory, thinking how bold and idiotic I was then. Just a punk kid who thought I had seen it all from skateboarding all over God's green Earth. I was clueless, but damn if I didn't have guts.

Some days I am that girl. Most days, I am not. Tonight, I don't know who I am. Optimistic that we will get away or realistic that there will be a price to pay. Nothing is ever free or granted without strings attached, except his sponsorship those years ago. I never did ask why. It never occurred to me as I had plenty of donor servant hearts trying to help me save my mom.

Everything in his world is about money, threats, extortion, and deals. It doesn't add up. He was benevolent once and asked nothing in return. Benevolent again tonight, but will he still ask for nothing?

That thought turns my stomach to stone, and a prickle of sweat breaks out on my forehead. How far does benevolence go a second time?

Chapter 5

I don't remember falling asleep until I am jostled awake by the giant hand of a gruff man dressed in black fatigues.

"What the he—" I blink back the light falling across my face from the hallway. The doorway is crowded with two other men, holding guns across their bodies, and glaring.

"Get up."

"Where are we going?" I know I am in no position to demand information but risk it anyway.

"He wants you."

He. Of course, he wouldn't wait until the first light to talk. He'd demand to see me on his time. I strain my ears, and at least I don't hear the steady buzz of the helicopter. I do owe him for that and a lot more. Too much more.

Tiberia's snarling vibrates my side, and I place my hand over her snout to calm her. I don't want her waking up Mary and frightening her.

"Hush," I harshly whisper and let go of her nose. The snarls grow lower and quieter but continue.

"Stay." I point to the bed. She shifts, putting her back to Mary, which causes the little girl to roll against her furry body. Thankfully, she doesn't wake up.

His meaty hand wraps around my bicep, hauling me out of bed and shoving me toward the door. "Go."

I open my mouth to smart off and snap it closed. *You're not in a position to argue.* I chant to myself as we traverse the dark corridor, him at my side and the other two guards behind us. I have no idea why he sent three highly skilled mercenaries to get me. Not like I could escape them or this compound if I wanted to. I tried once. It was difficult with my security team.

He stops at a stone staircase, different from the one that led us down here. When I look at him, he tosses his head to indicate I should go up. I pause, see the first five or six steps, and the rest disappear in the darkness. I shake my head, looking into the face of a killer and knowing he could technically end me if he wanted to but won't with Maximiliano waiting.

"I'm not going up there."

No sooner were the words spoken than a hard thud hits my spine. The pain takes my breath away and floods my eyes with tears. The unexpected force shoves me forward, and I thrust my hands out to break my fall. The bottom step cuts my shins and sends shooting pain up the front of my legs. My tears drip onto the stairs, and when I glance back, I see the soldier adjusting his gun.

Arguing ensues between the ringleader to my side and the soldier behind me. I cough, sucking in air, only for it to wheeze in my lungs. The pain from my spine still radiates across my back before the gruff soldier yanks me off my knees and drags me up the dark staircase.

His hold is suffocating the blood flow to my arm. When we reach the top, there is a wood door adorned with ornate metal carvings and a loud brass knocker that bellows into the quietness when the ringleader hammers it. Daring a look behind me, the soldier that hit me and his companion vanished into the darkness.

Anxiety courses through me as we wait, sending my mind into overdrive. Do I plead my case first? Or let him start so I can get his point of view and then appeal to him that way? Playing it by ear seems the worst idea, but if I had his angle on things, maybe that would be wisest since we are not on friendly ground. He made that clear.

I know this much. Once he sees what his men have done to me, he will have their balls. The thought makes me smug. On the other side of this door are their punishment and my savior. I shift on my feet, standing a little taller, and my captor notices by squeezing my arm until it burns.

The door is flung open. I am thrown forward with such force that I land on my knees, hitting the stone so hard I'm sure both kneecaps are busted.

Harsh fingers grip my lower jaw and squeeze until I flinch. His boots are pointy, laced with carved steel at the end. This is not Maximiliano. The man wrenches my chin, and that's when I see the face of a dragon. His teeth are jagged with a couple missing. Pox scars mar his skin, but the hatred in his eyes makes me shudder.

Always the eyes. His are black and cold, looking through me rather than at me. I have no idea who this dragon is, but he makes my heart race and my skin clammy. He's the face of torture and death as I watch the satisfaction in his eyes when he crushes my jaw tighter, and I cry out.

"That's not too much for the fearless warrior." My eyes dart around the room for Maximiliano. Who is this guy? Is he one of the traffickers, and Maxie is handing me over to them? "Don't look for him. It's you and me right now, so let's have a little fun."

I am repulsed at his innuendo and claw his wrist to get out of his painful grip. He sneers, curling his cracked lips around his nasty yellow teeth. It's the most sinister thing I have seen. He digs his fingers further into my face, his long, filthy nails cutting my flesh. I reel back my boot to kick him in the leg with all my might.

He immediately releases my face and stumbles back. I scramble to the wall behind me, readying myself to fight. His face darkens into pure hatred. His eyes are wild and crazy, and the thick vein in the middle of his forehead pounds outward from the skin. He's a grotesque sight.

"You've made a big fucking mistake." He barrels toward me, and I dodge him, running to the opposite side of the bare room. I'm fast, and I must use that to my advantage.

He swirls, hands out, stalking toward me, and I try to distract him. "Where is Maximiliano?" It's a slow dance, him closing in on me while I decide to fake left so I can move right.

"Not fucking here." He lunges, and I duck right, narrowly missing his hand as his nails scrape across my skin.

I feel the sting on my arm, but I keep my eyes on him. He starts the slow creep toward me, and I back up to the wall again, hoping to stall until Maximiliano gets here. Surely, he didn't order this. "You can't hurt me. He'll kill you."

A sinister laugh fills the room, exposing more rot in his teeth, and a cold sweat blankets me. He lunges, and I dart left the same way as him. I don't even see the right hook coming until it connects with the side of my head, knocking me to the ground. The ringing in my ear is eclipsed by the pain ricocheting through my skull and into my jaw.

"Fuck," I groan.

He's on me in an instant. I protect my head with my arms and get a hard kick into his shin when his steel toe boot hammers my unprotected side—searing agony bursts through my body.

"Not so brave now," he taunts.

I writhe in pain, unfurling my body and exposing it to another vicious kick to my stomach. I can't breathe. I can't cry out. I can't do anything because my body is on fire. I cannot protect myself from blow after blow raining down on me. Blood explodes from my throat as he lands a kick to my left kidney. I scream and try to drag myself to safety.

"Who'd you think ordered this, *perra?*" His evil laugh ricochets off the walls. I can barely push onto all fours when another strike to my ribs crumples me to the floor. I nearly piss myself.

"He . . . n-no . . ."

His fingers weave into the back of my hair to hoist me up. My hands claw at him, fighting his searing grip, trying to scalp me. His kerosene breath fans the side of my face as his slimy tongue licks my cheek. "I like this."

With all the strength I can muster, I drive my elbow straight into his gut. He groans, punches my temple, and blood swirls in my head. Black dots dance about my vision, and my eye immediately swells.

Before the mercy of sweet darkness overtakes me, I see Maximiliano's dark eyes boring into mine. A final blow shoves me unconscious, and the last thought that registers is that *he* ordered this.

Chapter 6

"*He's an ass, Will, and I warned him. I felt sick and laid on the steps. He got all militant on me, ranting and raving in Spanish. You know I don't understand that. He threw me over his shoulder like a sack of potatoes and bounced me up the stairs. It serves him right, he's now covered in vomit, and my stomach feels better.*"

"*Well, do me a favor, either behave or stay away from him. A sweet little señorita offered me a go, and I'd like to hit that happy trail before we hit the trail.*" *His smile was wide and bright, and he wiggled his eyebrows for emphasis.*

"*You're a pig.*"

"*No, I'm a red-blooded male wanting to interact with your supporters.*" *Will was the most prominent country boy I had ever met. Even though I tried to fire him half a dozen times for pissing me off, he was one of the best on my security team.*

"*You stink, so grab a shower and stay out of trouble. I'm not answering my phone after 7 p.m. tonight, so don't start any fist fights you can't finish. I'm not on again until 9 a.m. tomorrow, got it?*"

He stands in the doorway of his room, his shoulders almost touching both sides and wagging his finger in my face.

"*But that's over twelve hours. What am I going to do?*"

"*His blue eyes twinkled, and his grin split his face. "Fourteen, and I plan to take full advantage of every second. I don't know, play Twister with your new friend.*"

"*First of all, eww! Second, he's not my friend. Third, that's a child's game I don't play. Fourth, whatever, go. I'll call Ardy to hang out with me.*"

"*Afraid not. Ardy crossed the border with some guys from his security team. They're doing the same thing as me. Be good, so we all can get laid, except you, apparently." He chuckled.*

"*Ha ha. You're so funny. I forgot to laugh.*"

"*What're you, twelve or eighteen? Now get going, you stink.*"

He laid a quick kiss on my head before he turned to peel off his shirt and throw it on his bed.

"*I hope you get an STD tonight.*"

"*Don't even joke about that.*"

A faint knock on the door echoes in my slumber, forcing me into reality. Did Will forget something?

My bed is so comfortable, and I'm tired and sore. I don't want to leave the cloud I'm floating on.

Whoever is at my door will disappear if I stay silent. Moments pass, and the silence wins by pulling me back into my dream world.

Chapter 7

Light touches feather across my face, and I wince from the tenderness. My head feels like a balloon, stretched to capacity, and aching under the strain of holding my brain. Even my eyes have a pulse of their own, swollen and burning, refusing to open.

My lips are tight, cracked, and stinging as I swipe my tongue across them. A cool cloth blots at the chapped skin, bringing temporary relief, and a moan escapes.

I raise my hand, searching for the owner of the light touches, only for it to be caught and lowered to the soft linens.

"Mom?"

My voice croaks, dry and hoarse from the rawness of my throat. I lift my other hand. The same thing happens, caught and lowered to the softness and then the heaviness of covers being nestled under my chin.

With all my energy focused on opening my eyes, a sliver from my right eye reveals an elderly Hispanic woman hovering over me. She wipes the cool cloth over my face, effectively closing my eye, and I exhale at how refreshing it is against my warm skin. She gently blots the left side of my face, and I wince, turning my head away from her touch.

The slight movement pushes a lump of swollen skin from the corner of my mouth against my teeth. It smarts, and I feel a big gash on the inside gum when I explore with my tongue.

I take a deep breath and am met with a stabbing pain from my left rib cage. I stop and hold my breath as I wait for the pain to recede. My head hurts like a motherfucker. My chest feels like an elephant is sitting on it, and I'm pretty sure I broke my back because each inhalation burns between my shoulder blades.

Looking around, I see that I'm lying in a bed, but not the cloud bed from before. This bed has a tapestry of colorful threads woven into a scene I can't make out. The room is more luxurious than the one in the old wing and unfamiliar to me.

Is this another room in the fort? I know I may not have seen them all the first time, but I don't remember this one.

The walls are brown stone, a different type of rock than those at the fort, and a set of French doors is open with long sheers blowing into the room. The air is heavy with the smell of salt.

"Where . . ."

My throat is dry. I swallow my saliva to coat it and clear the hoarseness to start again.

"Where . . . where am I?"

I shift my gaze from the billowing drapes to the old woman, noticing the deep wrinkles in her face are like a roadmap of time and experience. She smiles a toothless grin and pats my forearm, the only part of me that doesn't seem to hurt. Her voice is soft and soothing, but I don't understand her.

She motions to a glass of water she is holding, and I try sitting up, but white-hot pain rockets through me, destroying my progress toward the liquid. I ease onto the pile of pillows behind me to catch my breath.

The old woman sits on the bed beside me, and with great care, she slips her hand into my tender hair. She cradles my head, helping me rise to meet the glass and take a few sips. The bit of water is like raindrops on the desert floor. Refreshing and not enough.

Questions litter my brain.

Where am I? Where are Mom and Mary? The girls? Is everyone safe?

I want answers. I need them.

How many times did he hit me? I couldn't remember where his fists connected or how often the dragon's boots struck. The aches and pains all over my body tell the story. I recall trying to slither away until he dragged me by my hair, wanting me to see Maximiliano's eyes burning into mine before finishing me.

He did this to me.

He let this happen.

No, he ordered it because his men would never have acted alone. He controls them as tightly as he controls everything in his world. If he didn't want me to get beat, I wouldn't have been.

Maximiliano wanted this. He wanted to put me in my place and make me pay for the sins of my past. He is a bastard for beating a defenseless woman for seeking refuge from traffickers.

"Water."

I open my good eye and see her bringing the glass back to my lips. We start the process over until the pain from my ribs protests too much and negates the necessity of the liquid relief.

She lays my sore head against the soft pillow, and I breathe as shallowly as possible to minimize the movement of my ribs. Closing my eye to rest, I hear the caw of seagulls and the sound of waves in the distance, lulling me to sleep.

Chapter 8

I knocked on his bedroom door, knowing he'd answer, unlike Will, who ignored me in the middle of the night because he slept like a dead person.

It took a few seconds before I heard the lock. "It's 2 a.m." His voice was raspy, squinting against the hallway lights always on in His Royal Highness's old mission.

"I'm scared," I whispered, looking over my shoulder. "I thought I heard screaming." My hands gripped the folds of my robe, drawing it closed.

"I hear nothing." No sooner were his words spoken than when a faint scream traveled down the hallway to both of us.

Fear gripped my heart, and I leaned closer to his open door. "Did you hear that?"

"It's probably the wildlife out here. It's pretty remote, kid." He yawned, rubbing the sleep from his eyes. "You're always like this in new places."

"Please, Ardy?" I take a step forward. He wordlessly shook his head and stepped aside for me to enter. It's dark, nearly black in the room, and I run for the bed before he closes the door.

"Your Mom would kill me if she knew you did this."

The bed dipped under his weight.

"First of all, I am an adult. Second, we're not like that. Third, I can fire you if you don't—"

"Shut up and go to sleep," he grumbled across the bed. I wanted to continue my list of reasons but was smart enough to stop for fear he'd kick me out. Then I'd really freak out in this scary place.

"Are you Mexican like His Royal Highness?"

"Kid."

"Don't kid me. I don't like your room. It's too dark." I turned my back to him and closed my eyes to calm down. "And too scary."

He groaned in frustration while scooting closer to me. "Put the pillow up," he huffed.

I shoved a pillow between us. His heavy arm draped over my waist and pulled me toward the pillow. The weight of his muscles and knowing he guards my back always made me feel safe. "I'm from Cuba."

"I thought you're a Marine?"

"I was. Now go to sleep." His finger pokes at my stomach as a warning.

"Can you be a Marine and not an American? I me—."

"Get out."

"Night, Ardy."

The pounding of little hammers in my skull wakes me. Even before I open my eyes, my hand lifts to rub my temples.

My good eye pulls open, expecting to be alone and not expecting to see him sitting in an armchair by the French doors. If the bandages around my midsection weren't immobilizing, I would jump up and beat him to a pulp. I settle for closing my eye and blocking him out.

"Gatita, it's good to see you awake."

Several replies run through my mind.

Get out.

You bastard.

I'll kill you when I get the chance.

How could you do this to me?

Why did you do this to me?

Unable to decide which ones to mutter, I resort to none. I can't read his mood and his tone is empty of inflection. I can't risk another beating if I say something sarcastic. Saying nothing is the safest bet.

"What? No begging? No negotiating another favor that jeopardizes my operations?"

His thick accent causes my eyebrows to furrow, concentrating on the words he's pronouncing. Although he seems to have added verbs and transitions in the last five years, his words remain heavily accented. It takes a moment to adjust to the cadence I once adored.

Begging? No, look where that got me.

Negotiating? I didn't think that was what I was doing when I asked for safe harbor for the girls, Mom, and me.

Jeopardizing his operations? Hardly. He's untouchable and probably has every politician in my country and in his country on his payroll.

My fingertips trail over my enlarged temple and swollen ear to land on the puffiness that engulfs my left eye. I feel the stitches in my hairline, and I grimace when I move some strands away from my face. It's all tender to the touch.

I know he's watching. He always did. Let him. Let him study the pain twisting my face and the damage caused by his man. Let him feel guilt or remorse or something over the violent attack his former lover suffered under his charge. Hopefully, he'll feel something for what he has done to me.

My hand drops from its exploration, and I lick my cracked lips, seeking relief from the tightness pulling at the skin. Even though I am exhausted, I need answers and force my right eye open. He's staring at me as I had hoped and wanted. If he could read my thoughts, they would say, you're a dead man when I recover.

"Mom . . . the girls?" My voice cracks, my throat drier than my chapped lips.

If they were safe, then this is all worth it. It was always worth the risk. There was no other choice.

"Returned."

One word. His answer brings a sudden panic, and my lungs hollow, taking my breath away. Returned to the traffickers?

I search his beautiful, tan face, hoping to find the answer to my question. Please have done the right thing, Maxie. If you ever felt anything for me, please have gotten them to safety.

"To the authorities, as you requested."

Relief washes over me, and I exhale loudly. Closing my eye, I whisper, "Thank you." It's all I need to know right now. It was all worth it. Mom and the girls, little Mary, are all safe.

Even though I'd love to know more, love to know where Mom is and how she took the news of leaving me behind, I doubt he'd share. I doubt he'd concern himself with such details, deeming them insignificant.

Poor Mom must be out of her mind with worry and fear. I hate that. I hate him for doing that to her.

And the girls, I'd love to see the girls safely under the protection of the federal agents and eventually reunited with their families. I would have liked to bear witness to the happy ending to this tragedy, but he robbed me of that as well.

Being a man of observation, action, and minimal words, he'll never explain how everything occurred. He'd never give me the satisfaction of knowing the entire story. For that, I hate him again.

The room falls silent. The stillness brings forth other sounds. No imagined seagulls or ocean tide from earlier. This time, I hear the buzz of crickets and assume it is night from the darkness in the room.

I hear a quiet rustling and open my eye to see him shift positions. His long leg drapes across his knee, and his hand plucks at the tufts of the armchair.

"Where?"

"Where are we?" he clarifies.

His accent is as sensual as I remember it. No wonder I fell for him so quickly. That voice, the thick wavy hair, and chiseled face, not to mention his godlike physique. He is the epitome of strong and sexy, especially with the new scar stretching from his temple into his hair. He grew more alluring and mysterious in the following years.

"Mexico, by the coast."

I forgot what I asked—lost in my former lust for him.

"Why?"

My fingertips go back to exploring the damage on my face, tracing my eyebrow, and feeling a neat row of stitches. I try to press my nail under the line to satisfy the itchiness.

"Do not pick. It will scar."

Now he cares. Ironic.

He lowers his chin and intensifies his stare to warn me to stop. I want to argue, but I do neither and let my hand fall to the covers.

"Good, gatita. Keep your hands off, less damage."

I close my eye, humming in agreement to be pleasing when I want to daydream about the various ways to kill him. I try to shift off my aching back, only to feel a sharp pain steal the air from my body and elicit a loud moan from my throat.

"Careful. You should not move. You are in pain."

My patience with him stating the obvious and not acknowledging his role is fraying. A few more choice words and I'm likely to snap. I squeeze my eyes and bear down, trying to find a more comfortable position.

"You need help. I will get the *curandera viejo*."

I hear him rise to his feet and raise my hand to stop him. He stares at me while I stare at him.

"Why the beating?"

His dark eyes travel my injuries with the slow meticulousness they used to undress me. I thought I saw a spark of something that used to be there, but I am mistaken when he turns and walks out without a backward glance.

He didn't answer that question or the one before it. I don't know what coast or why and I certainly don't know why the dragon beat me. Now he will never tell me. I close my good eye and wait for whomever he is getting.

Chapter 9

I doze off in the time between him leaving and a man wearing black-rimmed glasses pricking at my hip. In a strange twist of irony, I'm forced to trust a drug lord not to drug me into oblivion or turn me into an outright addict.

That vague thought pushes into my fuzzy haze, and I smile, knowing he's taking care of me again in a small way. I snuggle deeper into the blankets, oblivious to the danger surrounding my sudden presence back in his world.

I float in and out of consciousness, seeing things that might not be real. The first is his fingertips stroking my cheek, and the next is my head lying on his scarred chest while his tattooed fingers twirl my ginger curls. My brain is mixing memories and current events, weaving them into new tales that I can't figure out if they are occurring or not.

The hall was empty when I peeked around the corner. I jogged down the spiral staircase until I hit a massive foyer with arched wood doors leading to sweet freedom.

Pulling open the door, I set off some alarm that blared like a submarine getting torpedoed, and I froze. Heavy footsteps befell me, and I laid my forehead against the ancient wood. Don't be him. Don't be him.

"Señorita."

Just my luck. I dragged my head off the door to turn and face him and three other men dressed in black.

"Y'all going to a funeral?"

He didn't crack a smile at my joke, nor did his funeral processional—tough crowd.

"Why you leave? I told you rest. You make mess all over me."

"Yeah, we've already been over that, remember? But no worries because I won't be your problem anymore as of tomorrow. So, I'm going to head out and explore for a bit. Okay?"

I turned my back to him and pulled on the door handle when a raven tattoo stretching across the top of his hand narrowly missed my face to close it. I shifted, shooting him a dirty look over my shoulder. He didn't move his hand or body, which was far too close to me.

"What you mean, no problem tomorrow?"

If he weren't such a jerk, that accent and his broken English would make me melt into a puddle of turned-on-ness. But as it were, I couldn't see past his cultural discrimination against women.

I sighed, tried to keep my temper in check, and simultaneously be a reasonable adult.

"I'm leaving tomorrow. And before I leave each place or town, I snap a few pictures for my scrapbook. It's kind of something I started on my first trip, and it turned out cool when I put the album altogether. Plus, I usually post them online so people following me on my social media can see where I am. I haven't posted in a few days, you know, since I was sick, so people are worried and messaging me." There, I completely over-explained everything, and he probably didn't understand it all. Most people I stayed with didn't block me from leaving their house nor questioned me for leaving.

"No one told me."

Because I didn't have to.

"I know. I decided in the shower. Thank you for your hospitality and taking care of me and all that, but we got to get back on the road. People

are counting on me, so if you will please move your hand?" I surprised myself with my patience and restraint.

I tried to open the door with his Hulk hand planted against it, but it didn't move, nor did he.

"Seriously, move your hand."

"No."

I shoved myself against his body to move, but he didn't budge. I glared at those onyx eyes, and his funeral processional advanced as if I were an actual threat.

"Will they take me out because I touched you?"

"They could."

"Look, Johnny Cash, if you and your men in black could leave, that'd be great. Then I can ignore you, you can ignore me, and we'll never see each other again after tomorrow. Good?"

"Who this Johnny Cash?"

"What? You don't know the greatest artist of all time? You know what? Doesn't matter. Move."

"No. My casa. I say no."

"Mi casa su casa. Now move."

I rattled the door handle like ten times and nothing. Then I kicked the door when I wanted to kick him. I was about to launch into a full-out tantrum when I heard another set of footsteps.

"What'd I tell you?"

I whirled around to see Will frowning next to the men in black.

"Will, I've shown incredible restraint and even patiently explained myself, but he won't let me out."

"She said you leave tomorrow," he answered when it was not his turn and was not the reason for our little standoff.

"You big fat liar, that's not what it's about." I throw my arms in frustration. He's so far under my skin that it reminds me of a nasty, itchy tick. "That's not it. I wanted to go outside, snap pictures, and call my mom. If this place weren't wired like Fort Knox, none of this would have happened. I'd be outside getting a little sun, and this guy would do whatever he and that funeral processional do around here."

Will wiped his hand over his face and turned to address His Royal Highness. "I'm sorry for her behavior. She's a lot to handle sometimes and—"

"Will? Seriously, whose side are you on?"

Seriously.

"She needs better handler."

I moved from glaring at Will to glaring at him.

"Rude. I don't need a handler. That's not true." That arrogant jerk.

"You volunteering for the job?" Will offered, and one of his men snickered at my expense.

"Possibly."

Then all eyes landed on me, and I screamed in frustration.

"Ughhh, why are men such pigs?"

"Señorita, you—"

"No, you're done. Don't say anything else to me." I shoved my finger in his face. "Will, get me out of here. I know you and Ardy are supposed to get laid tonight, but I can't stay here another minute with him. I'll make it up to you. Please."

"No, you no make up to him," His Royal Highness says to me, "You no have sex with him."

You could have heard a pin drop. By the look on Will's face, he was as astonished as I was. Did His Royal Highness tell me I couldn't have sex with my bodyguard? So many things were wrong with that statement. Will's mouth opened and closed a couple of times, so I took this one.

"First and foremost, how dare you! Second, eww! Third, who the hell do you think you are? Fourth, I'll have sex with every man in this room except you. Fifth, how dare you!"

I wanted to keep my rant going, but those five points summed it up.

"Señorita. This mi casa no su casa. You stay here. You do as I say. Not what you say. I say no sex for you with anyone."

I took three steps to my right and then four steps away from all of them and bellowed the longest, most frustrating scream my lungs could generate. It was grotesque. Will was the only one that covered his ears.

He had gone entirely mute as the situation had spiraled out of his control. If anyone needed a handler, it was that Latin asshole, not to be confused with the other Latin men in the room that hadn't said a word this entire time.

"Will, I'm packing my shit and leaving before I officially lose my shit. That was a preview." I made it a point to stomp each step as hard as possible when I went upstairs.

Chapter 10

The man in glasses interrupts my swirling dreams of His Royal Highness with pricks to the sides of my body. When he comes, the pain goes away, and the dreams return. Sometimes, the toothless healer and her cooling cloth appear. She's gentle, murmuring over me until I fall asleep.

Other times, it's Maximiliano's beautiful face twisting into the face the dragon. When he arrives, I scream and fight with every blow to my body. Then the pricks come, and I surrender, floating to the past. Where Maxie and I learned about each other, learned from each other, and became one under the summer sun.

The cyclical process hurdles me into a vortex of fantasy-laced truths and mumbled confessions from calloused hands that loved to touch me.

I yelled and kicked the dirt. When that wasn't enough, I clutched handfuls of desert sand and threw them into the wind. I moved to rocks and searched for the largest ones to hurl at his imaginary head. I scraped and scratched every loose piece of terrain and threw it at a dead stick of a tree that I envisioned was him. I worked myself into such a slick, sweaty mess that I plopped down on a rock and held my head in my hands.

"*Señorita.*"

"You've got to be kidding." I've had stalkers before, creepy dads, and overly excited brothers, but this . . . this took the cake. "Can't you leave me alone? Let me die out here in the desert. The vultures will appreciate it."

"Come, the sun too much for your pale skin." I dropped my hands and squinted at him. His hand was extended. It was an admirable effort if it came from anyone else but him.

"When you finally let me out of your stupid casa, I couldn't call my mom, no signal out here. Are you happy now? You probably already knew that, though, didn't you?"

I ignored his hand and pushed up from my rock. It was jagged and hurt my butt anyway. He was right about the sun. It was burning the top of my shoulders.

"I no happy. I want you here, not leave tomorrow."

"Wait, what?"

He turned and walked toward his giant fortress in the middle of nowhere. I fell in line beside him.

"Really? You don't seem to like me, so why do you want me to stick around?"

"I never say I no like."

Seriously?

I used the back of my arm to wipe the sweat from my forehead. "You don't come right out and say it. It's the way you treat me. Like a prisoner instead of a guest."

He reached into his pocket and pulled out a gray cloth. When he handed it to me, I gave him a puzzled look. "To wipe the heat. I have no guests. I, how you say, not friends."

That was considerate of him. I swiped the cloth over my entire face, which helped with my near heatstroke. "You have no friends, or you're not friendly?"

"Yes."

Okay. I chalked that one up to the language barrier because that was an either-or question. *Not a yes or no question.*

"So, you're lonely?"

"Yes."

Got it. I dealt with lonely people all the time on the road. Several times I had to carry the conversation. People were star struck, which made no sense because I was a kid that rode a skateboard. Or people were shy, quiet, or lonely. Lucky for him, I was none of those things.

"You're in luck because I have a ton of friends, and I make them easily. I'll be your friend. Is that what you want?"

"Yes."

His dark eyes studied me as we walked. It was unnerving.

"I'll be your friend if you stop bossing me around. Friends don't do that and certainly don't tell each other whom they can and can't have sex with. Understand?"

"I no like him and you together."

"Good, neither do I. He's my bodyguard, that's all. Him and I having sex is gross, and I blame you for ruining my mind with that disgusting thought."

"He's disgusting?"

"Yes, very."

I smiled at him and watched the corner of his mouth twitch. Ahh, close enough to a smile. When we were almost back at the fortress, I tugged on the sleeve of his dress shirt and gave him the sweaty handkerchief back.

"Hold up. I want to take a few pictures. I do this wherever I go, so it will always be with me."

"You take picture of me?"

"If you want."

"No."

"That's fine. Some people like having their pictures taken, others don't. It's no big deal."

I wandered away from him and opened my camera app to snap pictures of the desolate landscape surrounding his home. I bet it got lonely here. Not like he could run into people at Starbucks or the gym. I *wondered how he gets groceries. I was pretty sure Amazon didn't deliver out here.*

After taking a few dozen pictures, I saw him staring at me again. Doesn't he know that's rude? When I caught up to him, I asked.

"Why do you watch me so much?"

"What you talking about?"

He walked us over to the door, where we finally escaped the blistering sun and lingered in the shade of the fort's roofline.

"You stare at me. Like you're trying to read my mind or something. It's kinda weird."

"I no weird."

"Yeah, you kinda are. You stare, drop the verbs from your sentences, and boss me around."

He looked away as if he was thinking about what I said. His eyes squinted before returning to mine.

"I no understand you."

"My English?"

"No."

He looked away again, squinted harder, and struggled.

"Am I weird?"

His eyes lit up. Bingo. I was weird. Well, thanks for that.

"Yes."

"Weird how?"

"You scream and sit on the floor like child."

"Oh well, there's that. But you wouldn't let me out here, and I wanted to be outside. Understand now?"

"Yes."

"But that still doesn't explain why you stare at me."

"You hard like a book."

I couldn't decipher what that meant.

"What?" I shook my head because I needed more to go on.

"Like thick book. It hard. Take time to read."

"Like the Bible? It is hard to read and understand, depending on what version you get and—"

He frowned. "Not Bible. You, how you say, American woman, say everything. Different. Señoritas say nothing."

I raised my finger and needed a minute to process or a translator. Yes, a translator would have been the better option, but with none around, I took a stab at it.

What did I know?

I was weird, hard like a thick book, and American. Oh, and I said everything. Señoritas said nothing. Weird book, American, talked too much, not like señoritas. I snapped my fingers at my revelation.

"I got it. I talk too much, more than other women because I'm an American. No, wait, you're American too, so that doesn't match. American with a super thick accent but um, give me a second, I feel it's close." He continued staring and didn't volunteer any new words or insights while I rambled on, left to figure out his riddle. "Okay, I'm hard like a book but not like Bible, and I take time."

"Señorita."

He moved closer, and I held my hand up to stop him.

"Ah, I understand." I laid my hand on his chest, and his muscles twitched in response. I ignored it after how hard I worked on my analysis. I placed a hand on my chest and patted myself first. "I'm hard to understand. Not language, but actions. And I'm weird because I say what's on my mind like American women do, but not like the women here. If there are any, I haven't seen any. Are there some here? Never mind. Not important." I patted his chest next. "You stare because you don't always understand me, so you watch me for clues. Like solving a mystery."

My hands fell away as I smiled at him. That took some time, and a translator would have solved it in two seconds, but it was worth it. His mouth twitched again, and his chin dropped to look deep into my eyes. It made me antsy and uncomfortable.

I motioned to go in because I wanted to escape. It was blazing hot, and his scrutiny made me even hotter. He held my elbow, desire evident in his eyes when his lips descended to mine.

His eyes closed. Mine stayed open, not believing this was happening.

His plush lips nibbled at mine and beckoned for a response. Even though I was surprised, I succumbed to my curiosity and desire and closed my eyes. I wanted to feel every part of this kiss if I was leaving tomorrow. His hand rested against my neck, and his thumb stroked my heated skin. Blood rushed to my head, and my pulse throbbed under his caresses. Nervous to touch him, I tentatively raised my hand to touch his chest. He grunted with satisfaction and covered it with his own.

His tongue traced my lips, and I darted mine out to greet him. An invitation for more, he pulled me against him and expertly slipped past my lips to drink me in. I didn't know if it was the heat outside or between us, but I felt warm and dizzy.

He slid my hand around his neck to deepen the kiss, and I moaned. I had never been kissed like this before. I yielded to his experience and leaned into him as I wanted this kiss to last forever.

His head twisted, and the new angle plunged his tongue deeper until I felt little flickers against the roof of my mouth. I shifted onto my tiptoes for more, but he retreated as sweetly as he started with a light kiss on my temple.

"No leave tomorrow." He held me and wrapped a ringlet of my hair around his finger. My face was buried in his crisp dress shirt, spritzed with the best cologne I have ever smelled. "I want you. We're friends, yes?"

I leaned back in his arms and grinned. "Friends don't make out as we did."

"Lovers do."

Chapter 11

My body is clean with fresh dressings around my ribs, and my hair is soft and brushed. All without my consent or assistance. It must have been incorporated into the spiraling pattern of drugs, dreams, sleep, memories, and personal care.

Days bled into nights until time lost all meaning. The only concept of it entering my conscious thought is to watch the billowing sheers framing the veranda doors. If they are blowing, it is daytime. If they are not, it is night.

The toothless woman remains stationary on the left side of my bed while Maximiliano bounces around the room. Sometimes, he is in the armchair by the French doors. Other times he hovers over me, and currently, he is sitting on the bed beside me.

I couldn't differentiate if he was real or a fragment of my hallucinations. Often, I'd reach out to where I remember him last or where I thought he was in the room. Sometimes, my fingers connected to interlace with his. Other times I'd reach and grasp the air.

After an eternity of foggy obscurity and bewildering memories, the haze lifts. I open both eyes, blinking back the brightness of a sunny day. My fingertips dust across my face, assessing. The swelling is gone, and the stitches in my eyebrow are removed, with only a smooth line in its place. It must be a scar now.

The lump on my temple is healed, and the same silky smoothness from my eyebrow is also in my hairline. Running my tongue over my lips, they are soft and smooth, no longer cut and cracked. My teeth feel clean, and a minty taste lingers on my tongue. It is as if they kept me in an incubator to heal, and I am waking renewed.

Looking around the room, I am alone with the bedsheets bunched at my waist over a crisp, white cotton nightgown. My hands slide against the sides of my body to stretch, and the only hint of lingering damage is a dull ache on my left side. I kick the covers to the end of the bed and see skinny stick legs poking out from the bottom of my nightgown.

Wow, I've lost a lot of weight. I pull at the lace hem, raising it to see the delicate panties that aren't mine. I sink back, embarrassed that *He* or the old healer put such intimate things on me. I cringe and wrinkle my nose.

My stomach is concave, my hip bones are protruding, and the left side shows faint traces of feathery scars from where his steel-toed boots cracked my ribs.

He didn't want me to see this. That's why he drugged me. Or to keep me from making scars. Isn't that what he said, or did I dream that? Do scars even matter to him? He has so many. Would it matter to him if I had some? Or did he drug me to help the healing process? If that's true, it's the least he can do.

I lower my nightgown, letting intrusive thoughts of him infiltrate my mind. I'm too engrossed to notice his silent entry into my room until I feel the weight of his stare. Looking up, I see a deep frown on his face.

"You lost weight."

His voice holds sadness, the only sign of emotion on his stoic face. He steps further into the room and swings the door closed behind him. The space shrinks with his commanding presence, and I pull the covers up to my neck. He's already seen me at my worst, my most vulnerable, and I hate it.

"That happens when you keep someone drugged for God knows how long."

"It was necessary for you to heal. You are better, yes? No pain?"

I think about his question. No, I have no pain, just achiness, dullness, and phantom remnants of painful memories.

"Yeah, I do feel better. Just stiff."

"This is good." He saunters to the French doors, opening them, and a warm puff of air engulfs the room. "The curandera viejo says sea air is good for healing." He turns to face me.

"The curo andy veejoe?" I stumble over the Spanish words, and the corner of his mouth twitches in amusement.

"You are cute, like puppy." Not an explanation, although it justifies why they seemed open most of the time. It doesn't explain why I must get better. If he didn't want me to get hurt, why did he allow it in the first place?

"I'm having a hard time remembering what was real and what I hallucinated, but why did you have him beat me in the first place? Was it to make me suffer from before? From when you and I were . . ."

Lovers? I can't say the word aloud. It carries far more meaning than I care to admit.

Those gorgeous dark eyes reflect the bright sunlight. Before all the drugs, I asked him this question, and he did the same thing he's doing now. He moves from the doorway to stand tall and proud in front of me.

"Diego, how do you say, took matters into his hands."

Diego.

That is the name of the dragon.

But did he take matters into his own hands? I frown, debating on if that is true or not. Maxie was never a liar. Well, that's not true. He lied about everything except us.

But is he lying about this? His men didn't take matters into their own hands. They didn't move a muscle unless he commanded it. And who is the dragon anyway if he doesn't follow what his leader says?

"But—"

"No buts, gatita. He is dealt with."

I press my lips together to stop my knee-jerk reaction to protest and demand answers. Not knowing what to expect next, I need to be cautious with every move I make. I don't want to push him and get hurt again.

"I will have pozole sent up. You eat all of it. No hunger protests." Hunger strikes, same difference.

He closes the distance between us at an alarming rate, and I shrink back in fear. He frowns at my actions and holds my chin, turning my face and then tilting it to the side. Whatever he looks at seems to satisfy him when he grunts and levels his face to mine.

"Don't fear, gatita, I no strike you. I take care of my possessions."

I can't help the shock that registers on my face at being called his possession. He was always arrogant, controlling, and powerful, but this? This is a different level. This is merely stating a fact. The corner of his mouth curls, and his thumb brushes the curve of my cheek before he releases my face.

Possession? Surely, he doesn't mean to turn me out, have me doing the same thing I rescued the girls from. Panic grips my stomach and crushes it into a ball of fear, dread, and nausea. God above, please help me if that is what he plans.

He turns away, stopping to fiddle with a tiny camera mounted in the corner of the room. Well, I'll be damned. He's been watching me the whole time. No wonder he knew when I was awake.

"Um, Maximiliano?"

He turns, silently gazing at me to acknowledge my question.

"Is there a bathroom I can use?"

"Why?"

Is he serious? What does he think? I'm going to escape through the bathroom window after waking from a drug-induced coma? Yes, probably, especially now that I know what he intends to do with me.

"Because I have to pee."

He doesn't answer immediately, choosing to study me as if he has mind-reading capabilities.

"You not wearing the *pano del bebe*?"

I blink and stare. He doesn't blink but still stares. Pano del bebe? Well, bebe is baby and pano? Pano? I got nothing.

"Pano?" Baby pano. Pans for a baby?

"Yes, pano del bebe. You not wearing it?"

"Huh?"

"Diaper, are you wearing a diaper?" Anger laces his tone. Unless they make diapers out of fancy silk, I'm not wearing one.

"No." I purse my lips. What else do I say?

"Show me."

"What? No!" We are not like that anymore.

"Now."

He takes two long strides to stand beside the bed and yanks on the covers, locked in a death grip under my chin. Embarrassment or stupidity keeps me defiant and not compliant. His face tinges pink in anger, causing that new face scar to ripple when he draws his brows together.

"Gatita, let go."

"No way. It's bad enough you want me wearing diapers. I'm not showing you my underwear."

I tug at the bedding, but I'm fighting a losing battle with the difference in our strength. He thrusts his beautifully chiseled face into mine.

"Yes, I want you in diapers so you don't get up and delay the healing. If you wear something else, they are not from me."

The shock stops me cold, and I freeze. I'm thoroughly creeped out by wearing diapers. However, learning he didn't supply the delicate lingerie lying against my soft flesh is more disturbing.

He takes advantage of my hesitancy to sweep back the covers and whip my nightgown up to reveal the soft pink and blush panties.

He rants in his native language before whipping out his phone and slamming it against his ear. At the end of my bed, he is yelling and pointing at me. Unsure of what is happening, I scramble to grab the covers across the bed and bury myself under them.

His call ends as abruptly as it begins, and he turns that fierce, predatory gaze on me. I duck under the covers as if the delicate linens can protect me.

"Off."

With only my eyes peeking out from under the blankets, I stare at him, not knowing what he wants.

"What?" I squeak.

He pauses next to the bed.

"Take them off."

He holds out his hand, snapping his fingers impatiently, and my mouth gapes instead of my fingers obeying his command.

"Uh . . ."

I don't want to wear something he didn't buy specifically for me, but I don't want him to see my privates either. How long have I been out of it? I'm sure I am not properly scaped down there like I prefer.

"Gatita, you take them off, or I will."

His threat jerks me from my hygiene worries to a new set of them. Would he do it? Is this an idle threat that he's blowing out of proportion? If he didn't give these to whoever was taking care of me, then who did? Deciding he's been patient enough, he flings back the covers and goes to touch my nightgown.

"I got it." My hands clamp down on either side of the clothing, stretching it across my legs to cover more skin. "Can you turn around?"

"No."

Somehow, I knew he wouldn't be that cooperative.

"Please?"

He lunges toward the fabric, and I swat his hands away.

"Okay, okay . . ." I gaze into those glistening orbs to see him staring at my nether regions as if he has X-ray vision. Biting my lip and lifting my hips, I hook my fingers into the band on the panties without raising the hem of the nightgown. It turns out harder than it seems, and for every tug down, the cotton rises. "Almost . . . just about . . ."

He grows impatient, and his hand dives under my nightgown to whoosh the panties off in one second flat.

"Was that hard?"

I'm shocked by the speed and precision he has them off and stuffed in his fist. He could win a gold medal for the fastest panty removal of all time. It's probably how he gets women into his bed. I shove my knees together and tuck the fabric around my legs to prevent other unexpected intrusions.

"Ah, gatita. You no need to hide what is mine. We both know what a beautiful rose you are."

My face heats. I can't decide if I am angry that he claimed ownership over my body or embarrassed by the name he used to call my privates since the curtains matched the drapes.

"It's not yours."

Childish, I know, but I can't help it. No part of me is his. My heart used to be long ago, but no more.

His hand suddenly cups my mound. The heat radiating from his palm seeps through the cotton and is strangely delicious. Wetness pools between my thighs, and the unexpected response from my body is confusing.

"Wrong, this is mine. I was the first. I am the last."

I don't know what to say. I lie there immobilized by his hand, possessively holding my stuff while processing his words in my head. Is he my last? Does that mean he's not putting me to work like the others? My relief is temporary as a new thought pushes through.

Does that mean I'm not getting out of here? Eventually? Never? He can't be serious.

I have a life, and people depend on me. I can't stay here. I must check on the girls and Mom and continue with the organization I founded. People know me as a celebrity and an influencer. I have a platform that helps women, lots of women. Women who can't help themselves.

"I can't stay here."

I push his hand away, crawling to the opposite side of the bed until his strong hand circles my ankle and stops me.

"You will and are."

Panic sweeps through me, and I vehemently shake my head. "I can't, Maximiliano. I must get back. You must take me back to the States. People count on me and—"

"No, you cause me trouble and take away peace. You are going nowhere."

He drags me across the bed, and I fight to keep my nightgown down.

"No, Maxie, I can't stay. I won't stay. I have a life and a foundation. I do good in the world, and this . . ." I wave my hand around, hoping to distract him, but he tightens his hold. "It's not good. It's the exact opposite of good. It's bad and illegal and—"

"Enough."

His voice is steel, and his fingers tighten painfully around my ankle, threatening to crush the fragile bones. I lean toward him, pleading with my eyes and my hand touching his bicep. It flinches underneath my fingertips, and I use this slight advantage to put my other hand over his, trying to get him to release his painful grip on my ankle.

"Please, Maxie."

"Enough. You break into my home, disrespect me in front of my men, and demand favors for girls I could have easily sold off if I were a coyote. I spare the anciana, heal you, and now you spit in my face with your save the world crap. You look down at me, mock my power and position with your *ojos de cachorro*, and now you demand to go? No, gatita, no. You are here because I say so. I, Maximiliano Maldonado, say so, not Maxie. I say you stay. Enough."

His heavy accent emphasizes the words he fights to keep in English, so I'll understand. He makes me sound like a selfish brat with his offending words and angry tone. My mouth opens to beg for forgiveness when the door bursts open, and the old healer is being tossed in by one of his guards.

He lets go of my ankle and throws the panties in the healer's face while erupting into a long line of explosive dialogue. He points at me, and all eyes follow. I draw the thin fabric around my body and slither over to the covers to bury myself in them.

She stoops to retrieve the undergarment and holds it, letting slurred Spanish tumble from her foaming mouth as the guard shakes her by the arm.

Maximiliano's face is murderous, and I see a side of him I've never witnessed except that night long ago. He is even more dangerous than he was five years ago. I feel overwhelmed that a small thing like underwear could set him off so easily.

The voices get louder and faster, and I cringe behind the covers, not understanding a word they are shouting at each other. The guard sneers and the healer pleads with clasped hands until Maximiliano backhands her across the face. She lands with a hard thud against the chest of drawers, and the panties fall to the floor. Her hand cups her red cheek, and tears cloud her eyes as the guard hauls her to her feet.

I fly off the bed and scurry between them in time for his open palm to slam across my cheek. The sting sends a thousand needles over my skin.

I'm speechless. He struck me. Tears flood my lower lids, and snot drips out of my nose from the force of the impact. His eyes barely move from mine to his man, and I know why. He can't show weakness. I already made him look weak to his men. He won't let it happen again.

The healer murmurs behind me, praying as her hand touches my back. I raised my chin, letting him see the tears as they trickled down my heated cheeks. I harden my expression to match his and deepen my voice.

"Maxie is dead. You're Maximiliano Maldonado."

I glare into those hardened black gems, wanting a reaction that doesn't come. I should have expected no less from the infamous kingpin. He submits to no one. I turn my back to him, wrapping the healer in my arms and crushing her bony body to mine. I steal a glance at the guard, and he glares impassively.

This is his world. Cruel, violent, and downright evil. I don't know why I thought he'd be merciful. His world, the one he carefully built into the biggest drug cartel in the world, is without mercy, grace, or kindness. The empire that bears his moniker is synonymous with the dark underbelly it serves. I should always expect the worst if I'm to survive in this place.

I slip us away from the two men and sit her on the edge of my bed. She's shaking and murmuring, and I see a glimpse of rosary beads wrapped around her frail neck. I'm not deeply religious and don't understand what she said, but my assumption of prayers for safety in this volatile situation is probably it. I give her another hug and rub her back before I stand to pick the panties off the floor and place them on top of the bureau.

I feel his eyes on me the entire time, but I decide I will no longer meet them. I will not give him the respect of looking him in the eye until he earns it.

He rattles commands in Spanish, and I see his man give a curt nod and leave.

The healer raises her bony hand to my cheek to examine the damage, but I clasp it in mine and gently squeeze it.

"It's okay."

I want to feel the sting of loss. I want to feel the loss of what once was between us. I want to feel the validation that I was right to walk away from him five years ago. I want to remember that even when I had regrets and was tempted to return to him, I was right to break my heart and follow my morals.

What would my life have been like if I had stayed? I would have become hardened to it and all its wondrous treasures. I would have become him, and that's the most revolting thing in the world.

Another set of prompt commands has her flying off the bed and fleeing out the door, leaving us alone. I keep my eyes lowered, focusing on the crease of his pressed dress pants as they come closer to me.

"Look at me, gatita."

Damn him.

I pick at the lace on my nightgown, forgetting the thinness of the fabric and having given the guard a peep show of my naked silhouette.

"Now."

A long breath seeps from my dejected body, and I slouch to look at him.

"It was an accident."

It becomes harder and harder to hold his gaze as the water blurs my vision, and I drop my head. My lips tremble, and my eyes twitch, holding back more tears welling out of nowhere. When the teardrops fall onto my lap, I sniff as softly as possible.

I hate his world. It's ugly, tragic, and hopeless. I hate that it's all he knows and will ever be. I hate being trapped in it and forced to follow his rules or pay the price—too much hate.

He steps forward, slipping his hand into my hair and cupping my head to rest it against his muscular thigh. It speaks volumes to me. He is not entirely heartless. Maybe it's his way of ruling over me, but I take it as a sliver of his regret.

His fingers stroke my scalp, gently massaging it the way I used to like, and the tears flow harder. I close my eyes and press my face into his leg, wanting nothing more than human compassion and reassurance. His muscles flex, and his body tightens, uncomfortable with my overwhelming need to be held as I held the healer.

His hand pauses, pressing my head tighter to him and letting my soft sobs fill the room. It is intimate and beautiful, a deep understanding that I am what I am, and he is what he is, and the space between is worlds apart.

A sharp knock at the door rips apart the moment and catapults us away from each other. His heavy steps cross the sunny room to open the door to a servant holding a food tray. He steps aside and allows the young woman to pass, communicating where to set it down.

"You will eat outside, on the veranda. The sun will do you good. Don't think of jumping. You might survive, but you'll be in this room longer than you already have. You will eat everything. You are skinny and look like a *niño*. That's not good, no?"

I shake my head, understanding what he meant when he used the double negative.

He relays his instructions to the girl because she picks up the tray and walks past the billowing drapes to deposit it on a table outside.

"The bathroom is through that door." He pauses and points to a door on the other side of the bureau. "I will supply your clothes and necessities now that you are up. Be good. I'll be watching." He motions to the camera.

The girl appears back in the room, waiting for further instructions since she doesn't leave immediately. I cast a curious eye from him to her, seeing her flush under his scrutiny. Ah, she likes him. Yes, I was once that girl. Too bad she hasn't learned the world is full of devils. Him being the biggest.

"Do you need help?"

My gaze returns to him, and my head tilts at his question.

"In the bath—" he clarifies.

"No, no. All good. Uh, *bonito*?" I wave my hands as a no across my body to reinforce my answer, and the girl giggles.

"*Bien*." He shoots the girl a disapproving look, and her giggles immediately stop. He says something else that has her scampering away.

"Bonito is pretty. Bien is good."

"Oh, then I'm bien."

"*Estoy bien*. Means I am good."

"Estoy bien, *gracias*." I smile, remembering to add that at the end of a proper greeting. His stare penetrates me, and I let my smile fall, feeling silly for acting so accomplished. I look away, wondering how long he will stand there, and stare before he finally leaves.

"*De nada.*" I look back at the dark eyes and see the corner of his mouth twitch when I furrow my eyebrows. "It means you're welcome."

"De nada," I whisper, trying to commit it to memory and the other random words he mixes into our conversation.

He grabs the panties from the bureau and stuffs them in his pants pocket. When he grabs the handle and opens it, I ask the question that started it all.

"Maximiliano, where'd those come from?"

He stills but doesn't turn around. "Diego. This door stays locked, and only I have the key now, gatita."

I shiver at the mention of his name again, knowing firsthand what he is capable of. Then I realized the dragon was here, in Mexico, with me. He put them on me. He was with me when I was drugged, helpless, and at his mercy. Maybe being locked in won't be so bad if it keeps violent dragons out.

Chapter 12

I t all makes sense, the camera, his explosive words, and the violent backhand to the healer. Did she let Diego in? Did she fail to protect me? I'll probably never know. And now Maximiliano is the only one with the key? Who had it before? If Diego was in here, who else was?

I shiver, hugging myself as I walk across the room to go to the bathroom. I click on the light, basking the room in a soft glow. It's small and cozy. The feminine cream colors contrast with the masculine fieldstone walls.

My fingertips caress the smooth marble countertop and dip into the carved sink. The bathtub is large and luxurious, which would be nice for long baths with a book if I weren't a prisoner. As he said, he provided everything except a mirror.

There is no mirror mounted on the wall. Probably because I could smash it and use it as a weapon against him or his men. Come to think of it, is there anything I could use to protect myself if Diego were to sneak in?

I turn to stand in the doorway and survey the bedroom. It's both luxurious and sparse. A bed with fine linens, a huge wood headboard against the wall, nightstands bracketing it, and lamps atop. The only other furniture is the heavy bureau opposite the bed. Otherwise, the armchair he languished in while I was hallucinating was gone.

Knowing I am being watched, I don't want to make it obvious that I am looking for weapons. Casual as I can be, I saunter to the bureau and open different drawers to see neatly folded stacks of clothing.

The top drawer has a Spanish-English dictionary, which I flip through before putting it back and closing the drawer. I turn around and lean against the bureau, and it doesn't move. I glance at the decorative legs and see small bolts going into the floorboards. The same bolts are on the bed frame as well.

The nightstands are open at the bottom, with no drawers and the same bolts. Crossing over to a lamp, I pretend to straighten the shade, and sure enough, it doesn't move—neither the shade nor the lamp.

They bolted everything—a room for prisoners.

"This sucks."

Feeling dejected, I walk across the room, past the sheer drapes I've watched countless times, and my breath catches. The view is stunning, with deep blue water drifting in low waves and skimming the beige beach below. I cross to the veranda's edge and lean over the carved stone railing to see hundreds of jagged rocks below.

This is what he meant by saying I'd survive if I jumped, but I'd break every bone in my body. He's thought of everything. Then again, a person doesn't get to his position by leaving things to chance. No, he's always calculating and planning.

I search the coastline for other houses, but there are none. Does he own all of this? I straighten and turn, looking up at the bright white compound far more prominent than his old mission in New Mexico. He always called it a casita, and I once looked up the word. It meant a small house, and I thought how odd of him to call it that. After seeing this fortress by the sea, I understand why. In comparison, it is a casita. I wonder what he calls this thing.

The day is warming up, and although the breeze is strong, I can't sit out here without shade. He forgets my fair coloring burns instead of tans as he does. I'm sure he doesn't own a can of 100 SPF sunscreen, so I pick up the food tray and sit in the doorway's shade. This compromise allows me to feel the sun's heat without being directly in it.

Sitting cross-legged on the floor, I balance the large plate and wide bowl of pozole on my lap. My stomach growls at the aroma, and I realize I am famished. I haven't eaten in how long? I'm surprised I haven't passed out by now. Dipping the homemade bread in the broth and putting it in my mouth, I moan. He always had the best cooks.

Taking it slowly, I savor each bite while watching the waves trickle in and out. The bread and soup are delicious, but the portion sizes are far too generous. There is no way I can eat all of it, not after my stomach has shrunk from lack of food. I eat half of the bread and soup, leaving the fruit plate untouched to drink my water. I'm beyond satisfied.

I stand to toss pieces of bread in the air to the seagulls and laugh at their attention-getting antics. It takes five minutes to share it with my friends, and when I move on to the fruit, they don't eat it. After three failed attempts, I launch it over the balcony and watch it fall into the rocks. If the tide rolls in this high, the fish might eat it.

Depositing the tray on the bureau, I grab the comforter and pillows from the bed to create a makeshift mat on the threshold of the French doors. It's too hot to cover up, and thankfully, the shade from the roofline keeps the sun off me. I look at the sky and watch the white, fluffy clouds drifting across it. I listen to the steady roll of the ocean tide and the seagulls squawking above.

It is peaceful. I see why he has this fortress by the sea. It suits him. This is as remote as the casita. If circumstances were different, I could be anywhere. I could lie near the ocean in Belize or New Zealand, looking at this same sky and hearing the same sounds.

Is this how he unwinds after ordering hits or smuggling drugs into America? Is he human enough to need downtime like the rest of us?

I smile at my ridiculousness and switch to lying on my side to gaze between the slates of the stone pillars of the balcony to the horizon beyond.

How long have I been gone? Will he tell me if I ask? Poor Mom. She must be out of her mind with worry. I'd have ulcers if he kidnapped my daughter. I love her, that woman. After all the shit she's been through, all I have put her through, and this is how I show my appreciation by taking her on a dangerous mission and getting myself carted off by a drug lord to another country. The guilt makes my stomach turn. Will she ever forgive me?

I look at the sky. Please don't let this cause her cancer to return. Please send her comfort and peace that I will return to her. I don't know how or when, but I will see her again.

What about the girls? Not the ones Mom and I rescued, but the other units, thirty girls in total. Did they all get out or just mine? I could ask Maximiliano, but would he know? I want to believe him that he returned Mary and the teenagers because the alternative is too horrific to fathom.

Reaching for the sheet, I drape it across my hips to keep the breeze from climbing up my legs and fanning my private parts. I stretch and adjust, moving around to lie on my stomach. My cheek still hurts from his slap, and lying with it against my bent arm is not helping. Content by a full belly and warm temperatures, I doze off.

"I'm coming," he yelled at the top of his lungs before swinging the door open with a towel around his hips and one drying his hair. "I should've known. What'd you want?"

I stared at his naked torso, and a fleeting thought of how sexy his washboard stomach was passed through my brain before I squeezed past him to enter his room. "We kissed, Will."

"By all means, come on in." He slammed the door and turned to me. "And what're you yakking on about?"

I looked over at his unmade bed and straightened out a section of the comforter that I hoped didn't have semen on it. "First of all, I don't yak. I communicate. Second, is there semen where I am sitting because it feels wet on the back of my legs?"

He rolled his eyes and threw his towel at my head. "I should say yes to get you out of here, but I knocked over my water. Put the towel down and spill your guts so I can get semen smeared on a bed somewhere in this place."

"Eww!" I folded the towel and laid it on the corner of the bed before plopping on it. "You know this is all your fault."

"What's my fault?"

"He kissed me and asked me to be his lover."

"Good, you'll be getting some tonight too. Now get out." He was flexing his biceps in the mirror above his dresser and making his chest muscles pop up and down.

I tilted my head because he said the craziest thing I had ever heard. Sleep with a stranger. "I'm not doing that. Are you nuts? I don't even know the guy. You said it yourself. Girls like me want our first time to be special with someone we love. Remember?"

"Unfortunately, with you, I remember too much. Why can't you bug Ardy with this? It's his turn. I already had my psychotherapy session with you this morning and again when you set off the alarms. Which you owe me an apology for."

"What? How?"

"Wasting my time and hurting my feelings."

"Whatever, you don't have feelings to hurt. Now, what do I do?" I moved off the bed because I think the water had seeped through the towel and got my butt wet.

"Seriously, work this out with Ardy. I'm zero-to-two, and I'd like to even up the score. Make him explain the birds and the bees to you."

"Tell me, or you're fired." I pointed my finger at him, and he grabbed it to bend backward. "Mercy."

He released it and smiled. "You can't fire me like the sixteen times you've already tried."

"Willlll." I touched his arm and immediately let go because he was half-naked.

"Jesus, I don't get paid enough for this shit. It's simple. Either you do, or you don't. You must decide if he's special and all that crap or if you want to wait for someone to love you, which will take forever in your case, Ginger."

"You're no help at all." I stomped my way to the door. "And don't call me that."

"You're like a gnat, always buzzing around and tempting people to hit you." He tossed over his shoulder on his way to the bathroom. "Bug Ardy from here on out. I'm done with your nonsense."

"Ardy's not here, and you know it. I hope you get two STDs tonight." I whipped open his door and slammed it as hard as I could.

Chapter 13

I counted the meals as days—three meals a day, like clockwork. For the first three meals, I stared at the cracks in the ceiling and ruminated on how I got here. The next meal, I ate and moved my bedding and pillows to the veranda, choosing to sleep under the stars rather than under his watchful camera. The following forty-seven meals were spent alone and trapped with my thoughts.

With my soul hanging by a string, he returns. It is late, well after midnight, by the moon's placement and the constellation of the stars. I am perched on my favorite chair, leaning forward to rest my chin on my arms as they drape over the railing. I've spent hours watching Mother Earth's power all around me and feel so insignificant to it all. It's my favorite part of my day, in awe of her quiet yet forceful beauty.

Then he's here, lurking in the shadows behind me. I wouldn't know of his sudden reappearance if it wasn't for his musky cologne.

I don't move a muscle.

I simply take a page out of his book and remain silent.

"It's beautiful. At night when the world is still and calm. It's as it should be."

He slurs his words, his accent thicker, and I realize he has been drinking. I've never seen him drunk or not in control. As much as I want to turn and look, I refrain, holding myself back to reinforce the fortress around my heart.

His dress shoes clack on the veranda as he leans against the railing. I see him out of my peripheral vision and take in the handsome cut of a black tuxedo and the crisp white shirt against his tan skin. He's more breathtaking than ever, and I clear my throat to focus my gaze on the ocean's tide, counting the seconds between the waves.

"What happened?"

Chills prickle my skin, not from the cool night air but from his question. Is he asking about now or then?

I don't know.

I can't answer.

I will say goodbye. He will too.

"You wanted me. You loved me once. And then you go. Why?"

I did. I said it, and I meant it. But that was a long time ago. A lifetime ago.

"Gatita?" The vulnerability in his raspy voice causes me to catch my breath. "Why?"

Why did I want him, or why did I leave? They are both equally essential questions. He lost the right to both answers when the dragon beat me, and he brought me here.

I exhale, seeing him edge closer and wondering if he is a happy, sad, or violent drunk. I'm guessing sad by this conversation.

"Was it because of what I do? Who I am? Are you ashamed of me?"

He's mixing tense, referencing now when we are nothing when he should reference then when we were something.

"Why you don't speak anymore? The women, they say you don't talk. Don't study the book in the drawer. You smiled at me. When you thanked me, you smiled like you used to do. And I said you're welcome. You whispered it. It was cute, like puppy when you use the wrong word. Now you don't use any words at all."

That damn lump forms in my throat, and stinging tears flood my eyes. My chest constricts, and the high wall I spend days building around my psyche is tumbling down. He edges closer, his vulnerability on display, and I swallow a sob.

"Are you sad, gatita? Do you need something to love now that you don't love me? Will that bring you back? Will that bring your voice back? Will that bring your fire back? If I give you something precious to love? Will you come back to me?"

I can't hold back the sobs as my shoulders shake and my lips tremble. Hot tears race down my cold cheeks and collect under my chin. His strong fingers grasp my face, turning it to meet his, and in the bright moonlight, I make out the shadow of his eyes. He wipes my tears, presses my head to his hip to stroke my hair, and shushes my wall-destroying sobs.

"That is what I will do. Tomorrow, I will bring you something to love, and you will return to me like before, yes?"

I nod, trying not to get my snot and tears on his tuxedo but desperately needing the physical touch and comfort he is offering. His hand caresses my hair until my crying stops, pulling on the curls to tilt my head back.

"Will you move back to the bed?"

I gaze into his eyes and shake my head. I can't be in front of that camera, not again. He threads his hand back into my hair and pulls me against his hip.

"Tomorrow, you will go back to bed. Part of our deal. No sheets on the ground. No more sleeping all day and staying out here all night. You change it back. And eat more. You still look like a niño, but you're mi niño. Eat breakfast, shower, and be ready in the room, not out here, and then I give you a gift."

I nod, pressing into his body, and he grunts.

"Words tomorrow. No more shaking heads."

He keeps stroking as he talks until he's distracted by something and stops.

"I like it longer, more to twirl. We'll get there."

74

I bit my lip at what I think he is alluding to. I hope not. My poor heart is barely surviving. I hope to be rescued or somehow escape, not remain here with him forever.

He's already proven himself untrustworthy time and time again. I will trust him as far as tomorrow and his gift. But if he betrays me again, I will jump from this veranda and suffer the damage he said before. If I make it unscathed, I will run the shoreline until I find a house. Any house, and if they bring me back to him, so be it. If they don't and I make it out of here, I will get my life back.

"And gatita, if you don't do as you're told, I will kill it right in front of you, and everything changes."

My blood runs cold, and my tears stop flowing because the devil has arrived. Yes, this is the true man I know, not the memories of long ago. This is the drug lord, the leader, the stone-cold killer that murders people. Yes, this is el diablo.

I slowly extract myself from his hip and fingers, looking at my hands clasped in my lap. There are no words for his threat. Thankfully, they don't have to come until tomorrow. Tomorrow, I will choose my words wisely. Tomorrow, I will raise these lifeless eyes to his and do everything he demands. Tomorrow, I start to plan my escape.

"Goodnight, gatita."

He stands there waiting for my response, and I remain silent, waiting for him to leave. His sentence should have had an equally upsetting reaction, but I'm not talking to my Maxie. I'm talking to Maximiliano Maldonado, el diablo.

I nod. Wishing he had said his goodbye.

His warm hand pets my head and sweeps down my back before he steps into the shadows he came from. I resume my previous position in case he is watching. After several long minutes of letting the steady hum of the ocean's tide thunder against his words swirling in my brain, I assume he is gone and back to the life that warrants a cartel leader wearing a custom-made tuxedo.

How does he do this? He saunters in, gives me hope, and dashes it simultaneously. Why do I keep falling for it? It's another round of cat and mouse where I lose. And he wins. He always wins. Always his terms, rules, and consequences if I don't play as he expects.

Tomorrow, well actually today, since it is after midnight, he wants words and the old me. Well, I want the old me too. I want my life back. I want to get out of here. I want Mom.

"God, tell her I'm sorry. Tell her I should have listened. Tell her I really, really love her."

My voice cracks from lack of use, but I can't keep my prayers silent any longer. I have to say them out loud, so God hears because they carry more truth, meaning, and heartfelt love now.

Hearing a flicker behind me, I twist around to see a burning flame lighting a cigarette. He never left. I see his face for a moment before the flame extinguishes. It's as if he wants to stare at me without being seen. That's fine. Let him watch. I'll be back on camera in a few hours.

I see a puff of smoke drift into the atmosphere above him, and it's the only indication I see beyond the orange flame. I turn around, draw my knees to my chest, and pull the blanket over me. The occasional smell of cigarette smoke reminds me he's still there. He makes no noise and no attempts to resume our discussion, and I'm grateful for that. A small act of kindness from him.

My thoughts are a cyclical blend of regret, despair, worry, contemplation, and gratitude. I regret the choices I've made in my life, which bring feelings of despair. I worry that I'm depressed and won't have the mental strength to do what I must do when the time comes. I contemplate my feelings and actions, categorizing the rational ones from the irrational ones. When they are properly categorized, I pick the rational ones and sift through them to be grateful for the good things that have happened and thankful for all the bad things that could have happened but haven't.

Closing my eyes and taking in the heavy salt air, I feel his hand brush my cheek. I even out my breathing and remain still, hoping he thinks I'm asleep.

"Wear a dress tomorrow."

No such luck. Then he's gone, slamming the door and locking it from the outside.

Why a dress?

Curious, I flip back the blanket and walk across the veranda to step inside my room. Moonlight streaks across the floor, and hanging from the top of the bathroom door is a white sundress with pale green stitching around the boat-shaped neckline. Sitting on the floor are expensive wedges.

I exhale at what feels like another loss—controlling what I wear. How much more control does he need? Hell, I don't have any left to give. He has it all.

Resigned to my fate, I walk past the dress to brush my teeth and go to the bathroom before settling into bed. I don't bother showering or washing my face since I'll be doing that in a few hours. I turn off the bathroom light and straighten the bedding he walked over, as evidenced by his dirty shoe prints.

Why didn't I think of it before? Grabbing the blanket, I dangle it over the edge of the railing to see how far it is to the jagged rocks below. It doesn't even touch the tip of them. If I tied the bedsheets to the blanket and made a rope, I could escape.

Yes. That might work.

Snatching the blanket from the railing, I toss it on my makeshift pallet before sitting to arrange my pillows. Once everything is straight, I lie, looking up at the sparkling stars and plotting my escape.

Tomorrow night. Yes. One more day, and then I'm free. For the first time in a week, I smile.

Chapter 14

Sleep eludes me, fitful and restless. When I finally fall asleep, the breakfast tray is being carried in, and I groan in protest. Doesn't the dictator know it takes time to switch a schedule? No, because that takes forethought and consideration for others, neither he possesses. He snaps his fingers or barks into his phone, and people run to fulfill his commands.

I contemplate hiding under my pillow and faking my death, but I'm pretty sure that one of his poor victims has already attempted that ploy. God rest their soul.

The door closes, and I wait for the sound of the proverbial lock. Yep, there it is. I'm alone until he comes or sends someone for me. A dreaded sigh escapes my lungs, and I drag myself from the floor.

Being the faithful prisoner I am, I do as I am told by picking up the pillows and tossing them across the room to land on the mattress. The sheets and comforter are next, and I wind them around me on my way to the bathroom. My shower is hot and long, and I am taking my time to get ready.

I tighten the belt on my robe, fully aware the camera is recording my every move before stepping out of the bathroom. I peek under the metal cover and see one of my favorite dishes, huevos rancheros smothered in red chili.

Thank goodness I like spicy food because I'd starve if I didn't. The food is fantastic, but I had to tap out on a few dishes because they set my insides on fire. Plus, I've made no requests of el diablo this far, so I'm not starting by asking for a bottle of Pepto.

I take the platter to the veranda and sit in the chair. Starting on my breakfast, I think about what he said last night. *Something to love.* What does that even mean?

He said I didn't love him anymore.

That's true. Five years ago, I left the man I loved. I left him with my heart and didn't ask for it back.

And come back to him? I am back. I'm right here, where he keeps me day after day until he decides something else. What more does he want from me? My soul? Probably. Doesn't the devil collect souls? Keep them on a chain around his waist that hangs from his cloak.

Deciding I had pondered on him enough, I set the dishes on the tray, retrieve my undergarments, and lock the bathroom door behind me.

Once dressed and ready to go, I slip on the wedges and practice walking around the bathroom. They feel tight and restrictive after living barefoot since I got here, but they are my size and very pretty.

If circumstances were different, I might have felt beautiful. I would have gotten a manicure, a pedicure, a blowout, and wore makeup. Here, I feel plain, look plain, and am plain. Exactly how he intends it to be.

The loud knock on the bathroom door induces an arrhythmia, and I almost fall off my wedges.

"Gatita, you better be ready."

I take a deep breath, hold it for three seconds, and then let it out. I wipe my sweaty hands on the bath towel and slowly open the door. I bite my bottom lip and hold on to the door handle to steady myself.

Something strange happens when we stare at each other. He

breaks eye contact to look down. His eyes travel from my lips as I nervously nibble them to do a full body sweep up and down. I try not to fidget, feeling suddenly vulnerable in these nice clothes.

"Take the shoes off."

I look at him and frown.

"Time for words, gatita."

"Why?" I sound like a dead frog and clear my throat. "The heels, I mean. You don't like them?"

"No, you're tall. My gatita fits here." He measures a mark against his chest, signifying where the top of my head usually falls. These three-inch wedges make me five-foot-eight, and I like the height advantage. "Not here. Take them off."

I nod, and he catches my chin. "Words, no shaky head."

"Right."

Upon hearing my confirmation, he releases my face and waits for me to remove the wedges. I release the door handle and hunch over, trying to unbuckle the straps without tipping over. He offers his hand, and I stop to look at it. I can't keep him from touching me, but I will not willingly touch him.

I shake my head, and he stuffs his hand in his pants pocket. Once I get the sandals off, I place them on the counter. He snaps them up, spins on his heel, and crosses the wood floor with heavy footsteps. I scurry after him as he launches one into the ocean.

"What're you doing?" I can't believe he did it. I cup my hand over my eyes to block out the sun and stare at him.

His thick, wavy hair blows in the breeze, and his eyes squint when he looks at me. "I told you, gatita, too tall."

He launches the other. It sails through the air, hitting the water with the tiniest impact, bobbing twice before sinking below the surface.

"Get shoes on. Barefoot is for beggars and *mujeres embarazadas*."

"My jur what?"

"It means pregnant woman."

He turns on his heel to walk inside.

"Oh." Well, that's chauvinistic.

"These will do." He points to a pair of flat brown sandals. I retrieve them and sit on the edge of the bed to strap them on. When I finish the last clasp, I twist to see my French doors are closed. It's weird seeing them closed after having them open for so long. I open my mouth to ask why when he volunteers.

"They stay closed. For now."

"But not always, right? They can be open sometimes."

I feel panic rising in me. He can't cut me off from the only thing that keeps me sane. He can't make my jail cell smaller.

"Closed."

He locks them with a key I didn't know they required, and I fly off the bed, nearly in tears.

"No, you can't. I'll die in here. I need the outside, the air, the ocean, and the stars. You ca—"

"Gatita."

He watches me with a curious gaze, and I don't care. To him, it's silly. To me, it's everything. I was going to escape tonight. I measured the bedsheets last night, and it might work. If he locks them, I cannot escape. I'll be stuck here longer.

I can't.

"No, I've been good, haven't I? I don't cause trouble. I eat what you bring, and I wear what you provide. Don't take this away. Please."

He is silent as I stand in front of him, begging.

"I did what you said. I cleaned up my bed, I'm talking, and I even ate a lot. Look for yourself." I fly over to the tray and lift the cover to show him my empty plate. "Don't take the veranda away."

"Enough." His face is cold and emotionless, as always.

I race back to him. I can't lose this. I've lost so much. He controls everything. I've got to get out of here.

"You want me to beg, I'll beg." I drop to my knees and clasp my hands together. I hate that it's come to this. I hate myself for my loss of pride, and I hate him for turning me into this. "Please,

Maximiliano, please let me keep the veranda. This room is not enough for me. I have nothing left. It's gone. Please leave me the sun, moon, stars, birds, and ocean. Please give me that."

Tears fill my eyes, and I know it's another round of cat and mouse, but I can't lose this. My soul will wither if I can't get out of the room.

"Get up."

His voice is harsh, and his onyx eyes are angry. I don't understand. Isn't this what he wants? I crawl closer, hunching to beg over his shoes, and I'm disgusted with both of us.

"No, say I can have it. Please Maximiliano Maldonado. Please."

"GET OFF THE FUCKING FLOOR!"

A dam breaks within me, and I cry hysterically, lying on the floor in my new white dress. I curl onto my left side, resting my forehead on my arm as my body heaves and shakes. I'll never get out of here. He'll never let me leave.

"Why? Why do you . . . h-hate me?"

I cry even harder, my chest burning with hurt and disappointment. He's breaking me down, and I'm letting him. I hate him. I hate el diablo and Maximiliano Maldonado and every other side of him. His cruelty is insurmountable.

He plucks me off the floor and dumps me on the bed.

"Why?" I raise my tear-stained face to him. "Are you punishing me? Do you want me to suffer for what I did? I was eighteen and naïve. I still am. I don't . . ." I fall back to the bed, crying another brutal wave into the pillow until I feel his warm palm on my back.

His face is stern, and his eyes are cold when I sit. "No, please. Don't touch me now. Don't. I can't feel hope. Don't be kind because all you do is rip it away. You take, and you take, and I have nothing. I have nothing left to give. You took it all. You want my words. You want my voice. You give me nothing. And you ask for everything. You want me back? You said last night you want me to return to you? How? How when I am already dead and gone?"

My lips tremble, and my voice is shaky. I don't know what's left to say. He reaches for me, and I shake my head. I move to the middle of the bed, knowing he wouldn't get on it with me. I've also watched him, and he avoids it at every opportunity. He won't even sit on it.

"Gatita, come to me."

He stands as close as he can get, motioning with his hand. I shake my head. He wanted words. I gave him words. I can't handle much more. I don't want him to give me hope, which he is trying to do.

Before I speak, I scoot to the edge of the bed, the furthest point away from him.

"You give me hope and then rip it away. I was a fool the first time you hit me, and I was a fool last night. Say goodbye to me and let me go," I plead, threading my hands into my hair to pull my curls in desperation.

"No." He drives his fist into the wood headboard and shatters it on impact. "No, goodbye. No!" His tone is harsh, his stoic face darkens in anger, and his eyes are the blackest I have ever seen. "You stay with me. You look at me with love, not death. You share my bed. You did. Five years ago, you did. Then you leave. You left me." He rips his fist out of the wood to hit his chest, splattering blood across his white dress shirt, and fresh tears blaze down my cheeks. "You break me. Maxie is not dead. You are not dead. We are not dead. No goodbye."

He's struggling to control his anger while not flipping into his native language. His accent is strong, his sentences are choppy, and the message is meaningful. His muscular chest is heaving, pressing against his tight shirt, and the scar at his temple pulses. He doesn't notice the blood smattering his pristine shirt as his fist remains coiled against his breastplate.

I'm struggling too.

I'm trying to stop the flow of loving memories we once shared compared to how differently we look at each other now. He's right. How could I have not loved him back then? He was strong and commanding. His presence filled the room, and I was enchanted.

He was bold, and so was I. We matched wits. He threw back

everything I dished out. It was intoxicating. It didn't matter that he was older than me, so much older than me. It only added to the allure. He was the forbidden fruit, and I was tempted. Same as the first mother caved to temptation, I did too. I selfishly indulged. I bit the apple and am now dealing with the devil.

"Come here."

He points to a spot on the bed in front of him. I wipe my face and nose with my hands, trying to calm down the same as he's trying to do.

"Don't hit me."

My fingers twist into the front of my dress, but I don't move. He turns and yells, hands flying as he paces and rants in Spanish. The speed and cadence would sound beautiful if it weren't so scary. I push against the headboard, fixing the buckle on my sandal as it digs into my skin.

"I will not strike you."

His voice is deadly, and chills run down my spine. El diablo is in force. He turns, walks back to the bed's edge, and points again.

"Here. Now."

I want to stall and think of a way out of here. I want to escape and burn this place to the ground before I go. I hate it here, this prison on the coast. His prison. But I can't. For now, I can't, but one day, I will.

I wipe my face, swallow that familiar lump in my throat, and crawl to him. I won't look up. I lost again, and it is humiliating. Lowering myself to cry on his shoes. If I go crazy, it will be his fault. I hope by then, el diablo will feel guilt.

His hand brushes my hair, pushing my head into his thigh. I stiffen, not expecting compassion.

"Why do you fight me? It could be good. Like before. If you follow, it will be good. But you're like scared gatita. You hiss and bite and claw and cry. Look at me."

His fingers curl into my hair, cupping the back of my head to look at him. His face is calmer, less scary, and I exhale in relief.

"No more. No more."

I nod. Feeling another part of me break off and float adrift in the sea of losing me. We can't be like before. I don't even know the bold, sassy girl I used to be. She's dead, replaced by this pathetic shell of a woman.

"Words, gatita, no shaky heads."

"Okay."

"Come."

He steps back and holds his hand out to me. I promised I would not touch him, but I crawled to him like a dog. I can't even keep promises to myself.

"No more fights. Come."

He shoves his hand closer to my face, and I slip mine into his. His palm is warm and dry. The skin is rough and calloused, and a memory flashes from another time when those worn hands traveled my body. Back then, he was perfect.

"Good."

He changes our fingers, interlacing them as he pulls me to the door. My mind bursts into many thoughts. He's holding my hand like we used to do. What does it mean? What do I do? Hold it back? Give him the dead fish? I don't know.

When he opens the door and walks through, he tugs on our joined hands, and mine tightens on instinct. He grunts like he used to do. But grunts meant many things, happy, disgusted, unamused, or irritated. What does this one mean? Satisfied? Satisfied that he won, yet again?

Chapter 15

Where are we going?

With Maximiliano, I do not know. My palms sweat, and my stomach churns with nervousness.

He leads us down the stairs, guiding me to stand in front of a huge iron and wood door. He is so different from last night, yet I am too. More broken.

"Remember what I said. You don't do it. All of it, I kill it right in front of you."

His face is so close to mine I lean back and stare into those onyx eyes.

I remember. "Yes."

"Good. Open the door."

He tugs me in front of him and releases my hand. I hate that I enjoy holding it and soaking up the scraps of his compassion. I peek over my shoulder at him, but he gives nothing away. Releasing a breath, I slowly open the heavy door.

The loveliest thing I have ever seen is shaking and howling right before my eyes.

Tiberia.

That crazy Siberian husky is about to rip the arm off the guard holding her leash. She jumps up on two feet, fighting against his grip and yippie barks fill the morning air. I collapse to the floor and throw open my arms.

Maximiliano orders her release, and she launches herself at me. I wind up flat on my back with her lying on top of me, wiggling and squirming. My hands block her relentless kisses, but she noses through and douses me in slobber. I laugh and cry and hug her as tight as I can. I bury my face in her fluffy mane and thank God for keeping her safe all these weeks.

Maximiliano speaks again, and the guard pulls her off me, much to my dismay. Our reunion is cut short when he snaps the leash on her collar and pulls her back outside. She howls and howls while being dragged away. Twice she lunges, almost taking the guard by surprise to get back to me. I scramble out the door to calm her.

Hugging her again, I praise what a good girl she is and how happy I am to see her. I know she doesn't understand, but seeing her has brought meaning back into my life.

"Where is he taking her?"

"A bath. I had it flown in this morning, and it stinks. You train it. The dog will not knock you down again, yes?"

I smile, a genuine smile, and the first one I give him in weeks. I smile with all the happiness in my heart. Then I turn back to her and rub her ears.

"You don't stink, do you? Not at all. Be a good girl." I give her a bunch of kisses, and a cleared throat behind me must be the signal because the guard wrestles her away despite her noisy protests.

I watch him struggle with her, laughing at her silly antics when I feel fingertips tickle my arm to pull me to my feet. Even if it is at him, I will not wipe the smile off my face. His face is a stoic mask, and the only movement is a gentle breeze nipping at his hair.

When he broke off a piece of my heart upstairs, he captured it and returned it to me outside.

I push myself into his body, wrapping my hands around his

narrow waist and lying my cheek against his chest. I am both surprised and overjoyed at this blessing. He is right. My precious is his precious. I need something to love, and I will love her.

"Thank you! Thank you! Thank you!"

His arms are slow to hold me, but eventually, they do. I squeeze him as tight as I squeezed Tiberia.

"De nada."

I bask in the warmth and strength of his body. It had been so long since someone held me like this. I wasn't ready to let go. I wanted to stay in the circle of his arms and be told everything would be all right. Things are different now, and we're not like that anymore. My arms loosen, and I clear my throat before awkwardly stepping back to look at the dry soil.

"Come. We have things to discuss."

He turns and strolls into the house. I quickly survey the land, seeing miles of the same desert terrain leading up to the mountains in the far distance.

Damn, this is desolate. My only hope is to get to the mountains. If I leave in the middle of the night, I could make it to the mountains without being detected. From there, not sure. It depends on what's on the other side of them.

"Gatita."

I jump, turning my head to see him staring, and I scramble into the foyer to wait for his instructions.

"All desert, blocked by sea and mountains. Good for me and bad for my enemies. Very bad for *mi gatita*."

He knew. He knew I was surveying the landscape to figure out potential escape routes. His black dress shoes enter my vision, and I feel his fingers under my chin. I know what's coming next.

"Don't do it. You won't make it. I will kill the dog and then kill you."

I jerk my head out of his grasp and step back, the air seeping out of my lungs.

"You want to ki—"

"No, I don't want. But I will. You leave me again, I will."

Chills run down my arms, and I shiver, hugging myself. "Oh."

"Come."

He turns and strolls down a new corridor. I half jog to keep up with his long legs until he stops in the kitchen doorway with several women preparing food. They stop and immediately look at us. I want to hide behind him but decide to stand tall as if I belong here. If I'm never going to escape this place or get murdered for trying, I might as well try to make friends with these ladies.

"You will feed it here. Wash bowls when done and put them over there." He walks and points under the watchful eyes of his employees or servants. Do drug lords have servants, or are they kidnapped prisoners too?

"This door goes to the sea. You can take the dog out there. Follow the path. I own all the land so you can walk it, but not far. We will watch you all the time, everywhere you go."

"Yes."

"You teach it manners. I don't like animals in my house. Don't ruin it, gatita."

"Can she stay in my room? When we're not outside? It would help with the training." My hands twist into the folds of the dress, hoping he says yes.

He scowls, his jaw clenches, and he stares into my eyes. I don't flinch. I raise my chin to make it more comfortable to stare straight back. We're in a standoff, a battle of wills I hope to win.

"Gatita."

"Please? You already took away my veranda. Please, Maximiliano?"

I clasp my hands in front of me, trying to be as sincere as possible and not give him a tone about the veranda since that was a complete disaster.

"Two days. I don't like what I see, and it's outside in little house."

Looking down, I smile. I finally won. I finally, finally, finally won. I would jump with joy if I didn't feel his eyes piercing into the crown of my head.

"Gracias," I whisper.

It takes a moment or two, and then I think he doesn't hear me. "De nada."

My smile widens as I look at the colorful tile floor.

"De nada," I murmur to myself.

Everyone needs someone to love.

I had said that to him once, and his stare burned me. I had no idea about the weight of my words, spoken by a naïve fool, and yet he kissed me so passionately after. That kiss was the one that lost me to him, or perhaps him to me. I am not sure.

"Where did she come from?" I asked Maxie, gazing at the little black and white ball of fluff, biting my fingers as I bounced her like a baby in my arms. "You're soooooo cute. Aren't you cute?"

He grumbled under his breath, and when I looked over, he wasn't happy. "It got into the truck when my men were in town. He didn't find it until back here. I don't like it." He scowled at the wiggly husky that flipped herself over to crawl up my shoulder. Once she could see, she was content to let me hold her.

"He doesn't like you," I continued in my baby voice. "'Cuz he's a grumpy pants. Isn't he?" Her fur is soft, bursting out in all directions from her body, and I buried my face in it. "Mr. Grumpy Pants is what we'll call him."

"I no like the way you talk to it." My eyes caught his over her fur. Impatiently, he flicked his wrist to look at his watch and motioned for the guy to retreat. "I no like animals."

"Shocker." I walked toward the shade of the courtyard for the little bundle of energy to cool off. He complained as he trailed behind me. I chuckled when I saw his irritated expression. "Everyone needs something to love, Maxie."

His stare burned into me for a few long seconds until he abruptly grabbed the scruff of the puppy and dumped her in the dirt. His hands cupped my face, his dark eyes reflected my wild curls blowing in the breeze of the New Mexico desert, and his lips descended to mine to give me the most passionate kiss of my life.

Chapter 16

Reality draws me back when I hear an urgent conversation going back and forth between the ladies. My head darts up to see a couple of them pointing at us, mainly me. He fires back, and they seem to be shouting by the pace and volume of their Spanish.

He jerks my arm and then whirls me around. His hands are heavy on my shoulders, yanking my hair to the side to inspect my neck. More words are exchanged, and I couldn't be more confused.

"What? What's wrong? Is there something on me?" I freak out. "Is it a bug? Is there a bug on me?" I swat at my hair and shake my dress, trying to reach around to feel my shoulder blades.

"You're bleeding. They thought it was me, but this is dry," he replies, pointing at his bloody shirt.

I immediately stop my freak-out dance and look from him to them. "I'm bleeding? Where?"

I look at my arms for cuts but don't see anything. One lady points at me, sounding insistent and signaling with her hand.

"Down."

He points to a small puddle of blood, and I jump back. I don't feel hurt. I'm not in any pain. What did I do?

"I don't—"

"The dog."

He retrieves a gun from a holster hidden under his pant leg and charges down the hall.

"Wait, Maximiliano. It wasn't her. She did nothing!" I scream, racing after him and yanking his arm to stop, but he shakes me off.

"It hurt you. When it lay on you, it hurt you. Now it dies."

Fear surges through me.

"No, please don't do it. Please. She didn't hurt me. She's a good girl." I run past him and spread eagle against the door to block the exit. "Please don't kill her. She was excited to see me. That's all. Look at me. I'm not hurt. She didn't hurt me. Don't kill her." I clasped my hands in a prayer position at my chest.

He walks straight toward me, and I brace myself to be tossed away. I didn't expect him to pull my dress up and look underneath.

"You are bleeding from the womanhood, yes?" he says, fisting my dress in one hand while his gaze flickers from my privates to my eyes.

Shocked, I freeze. I always had an irregular period, but . . .

"You look." His tone is matter-of-fact, yanking the hem higher for me and the rest of the world to see.

"Er . . ." Horrified, I tug the dress out of his fist and turn around, carefully lifting the edge against the door to see what he sees. "Um, yes," I squeak, snapping my dress down and crossing my legs before facing him. He stoops over, putting his gun in the holster, and I want to run back to my room.

This is so embarrassing and gross. Ugh, I bled in front of him, the ladies, and on the kitchen floor. As if him ripping off my underwear weeks ago wasn't embarrassing enough, this is mortifying.

"Good means you can make bebes." He raises his chin, adjusting his shoulders back and appearing proud.

I'm speechless. Absolutely speechless.

"*El cuarto de baño* is here."

I blink, not moving because I understood part of what he said, but not all of it. His fingers slide under my elbow, and he escorts me into a cozy powder room tucked under the stairs. At least we agree about needing a bathroom.

"Take them off." He shoves us inside the fancy little room.

"What?" I hesitate. His accent must be too thick because I'm sure I didn't hear him correctly.

"Take them off. Now."

He pulls out his phone, rattles off commands while staring me dead in the eyes, and then holds his hand out.

I'm still stunned.

"Gatita."

I smile and then smack his hand like we're high-fiving, anything to avoid extending this pride-crushing experience.

"Why do you do that?"

He rubs his hands together, unsure and feeling for something.

"I gave you a low five. It's like a high five, but your hand was low and not up like this." I raise my hand and slap it to demonstrate. "I did a low five." I moved my hand and showed the low five. He stares, unamused.

"Gatita."

"But they're bloody, and it's gross. And private. Like super duper private," I justify, shaking my head to convince him how private this is.

"You think the fertile blood of mi gatita is gross? Do you think I am scared to hold the start of life in my hand? You deny what is mine, yes?"

"Um, well. No, because look at . . ." I motion to his shirt covered in blood, which hasn't bothered him, not to mention the blood he spills from others, so no period blood would not bother him. "But it's private. Not for your eyes. Only mine."

His dark eyes glitter, pausing for a moment, and when I exhale, he grips the neckline of my dress and rips it down the middle.

My jaw drops, my eyebrows are in my hairline, and I go mute. He smirks, and I rush to grab the tattered sides of my dress to wrap them across my bra and panties.

"Don't you ever say it's not for my eyes? This is only for my eyes. Only me." His fist pumps into his chest again, and in all that male bravado, I glimpse myself in the mirror over his shoulder. What I see reflecting is shocking. I push past his shoulder to stare at me.

I'm hideous. My skin has an ashen gray hue, and dark bags hang underneath my dull eyes. I bunch my dress in one hand and trail the other over the hollows of my cheek. My face is gaunt and sunken, forcing my cheekbones to be too angular and harsh. As skinny as my face is, it looks chubby and plopped on my thin, gizzard neck. I can't remember a time I looked so sickly.

I touch my hair and pull a ringlet like he used to, but it doesn't bounce back. It's darker and heavier, like my life. I bite my lip to keep it from shaking as tears fill my eyes. My gaze falls to my dress, and I drag it open. A sob catches in my throat. I knew I had lost weight, but seeing my body from this angle, I look disgusting.

His chest brushes my back, inching closer to me, and our eyes meet in the mirror.

"Why don't I have a mirror in my room?"

His chin lowers, setting his piercing gaze on mine.

"You don't need it." His voice is husky, with a bit of sadness matching the sadness stirring in me. My teeth are yellow from the drug use and lack of proper nutrition. Weeks of returning food, staying up all night, sleeping all day, and giving up on life are clear on my face and body.

"That's why you said I look like a niño."

"Yes."

"Oh," I mutter, fully understanding what he was seeing, his way of trying to intervene. He saw me losing myself even before I did. I can't tear my eyes from this horrible sight, even as the tears drip onto my cheeks. "Can you go, please?"

"Gatita." His hands cup my shoulders.

"No, not this time. No gatita. Please. Can I be alone? For once?" I shrug, trying to get his hands off me, but they tighten.

"Why?"

94

I tilt my head and look him straight in the damn dark eyes.

"Because I'm sad. Because I don't want you to see me like this. Because I don't want to see myself like this. Don't you get it? Don't you ever feel sad?"

"No."

Of course, he doesn't. El diablo doesn't get sad. You must have a soul to feel sadness.

"Why you feel sad?"

"Look at me? You said I look like a boy. What girl wants to hear that? What girl wants to look like this?" I explode, clutching tissues out of the container and no longer caring that the flaps of the dress hang open for him to see.

"You're not a boy. You bleed like a girl. You cry like a girl. You're a girl."

Why do I even try with him? Is it the language barrier, accent, or because he's a man and I'm a woman? Why can't he ever understand me? Hell, he stares at me enough. He should know exactly why to every question he could ever ask.

"Maximiliano, please go."

"No, you are sad, yes?"

"Yes."

"And you are girl, yes?"

"You already said that," I say flatly.

A headache is brewing at my temple, and I rub at it because I don't know what cat and mouse game this is now. Nor do I want to play it.

"Then why I go? I told you, this is mine. Sad, boy, girl. I don't go."

I shuffle around to face him, too disgusted to keep seeing glimpses of myself in the mirror every time I answer him. I blot the wetness from my cheeks and compose myself before explaining this to him. I don't even know why, but I'm tired from upstairs and angry that he threatened to kill Tiberia and me if I try to leave, and I need him to understand one stupid thing about me.

"Okay, you sell cocaine, right?" I ask, sniffing my nose.

"Why you ask?"

Ughhh. I'm not a federal agent.

"Let's pretend you sell cocaine." I use air quotes to add to the point I am making.

"Pretend is better."

"Right, you pretend to sell cocaine. Big shipment coming. But instead, you get marijuana. You can't sell marijuana. It's not what they want and what you paid for. That makes you upset? Angry?"

"Yes. I kill them." He grunts.

"Uh, okay, pretend kill. You remember what I used to look like?"

"Yes."

"I used to have chubby cheeks and nice skin. My eyes were happy, and I weighed more. I didn't look sick. I looked happy and fit. And now, I look like this. I looked like cocaine back then, and now I look like marijuana. Do you understand why I'm sad?"

He cups his hand under my chin and pushes it higher, bringing our faces closer. "You are heroin. Addicted first time." His thumb brushes my lips, and I freeze. Cat and mouse. This isn't real. It's another round of cat and mouse. Don't react. "I no like what I see. I see sad, sick boy. I want the happy, mean girl back."

He parts my lips, stroking the bottom with the pad of his thumb as he leans in. His warm breath fills my lungs, and his cologne's faint muskiness fills my senses. I search his face for any sign that this is a game, but as always, it's unreadable.

"She here, but no. She changed, but the same."

When his thumb stops, I hold my breath and wait for him to back away. He doesn't. He descends, and my eyes close. His lips feather across mine. They are soft and inquisitive, reuniting with an old friend. They feel so damn good, like before, and I relent, letting him push past my barriers to kiss me. It's brief, merely a passing hello amongst former lovers. When his lips leave mine, I crave more.

"She was mine the first time, is now, will always be."

His thumb caresses my jaw, and his lips follow, dusting kisses across my cheek. I know this is wrong. I know in my soul that this is wrong, but my self-esteem, confidence, and sorrow want to feel wanted by someone else, even if it's the devil himself.

"Kiss me, gatita."

His accent is strong and husky, kissing a trail of sensual kisses down my neck. I'm lost, wanting more and needing none. His fingers slip around my back, pulling me against him as his tongue licks the column of my neck.

A faint tap on the door startles me, and my eyes fly open. He reluctantly pulls away, muttering under his breath, and my fingertips touch my swollen lips. I look away, confused by his sensual kiss and his soft touch.

I can't let that happen again. I won't let it. No, this will mean something to me and nothing to him, causing another part of me to be lost to him. He's not to be trusted.

"Gatita, I'm opening the door."

I glance over, noticing he has straightened his shirt, and I nod, turning my back to the door.

"Ready."

The door opens, and his deep voice rumbles in contrast to the soft voice of the healer. Bless that woman for all she has done and keeps doing for me. Their exchange continues longer than I expect, and when I peek over my shoulder, she smiles at me before he slams the door in her face.

"She brought you things."

"You don't have to be so rude to her." I turn around and frown. Grandma pads. Ugh. I haven't worn them since I accidentally got my period at church and had to get one from my friend's mother.

"What's the face?" He ignores my comment about his behavior.

Do I debate with him about pads versus tampons? Sigh, no, no way. I reach for the box and pop open the lid. "It's nothing. Bien."

He snatches the box out of my hand, holding it away, and I merely glare at him. "Estoy bien, not bien. I ask again, why the face?"

Why? Why? Why? He drives me crazy with his whys. I've got one for him. Why didn't his mom teach him anything about women?

"Gatita."

Fine.

"I don't normally wear these."

"Wear what?"

"Pads."

"Why? You leak. You leak all over my floors. Make a big mess in my home. She said they catch the leak."

I stare at him in disbelief. Is he seriously explaining grandma pads to me? Didn't they teach him sex education in school? Or maybe a girlfriend somewhere along the way didn't want to have sex because she was on the rag? Surely, he saw her put a tampon in. He had to have seen it somehow in his life as much as he stared.

"Yes, I know that, and I'm sorry for 'leaking all over your floors', but I usually wear tampons, not pads," I explain, trying not to sound condescending, but dammit, if it isn't hard as hell with him.

Why are we even having this conversation in the first place? I should have grabbed the box, shoved one in the new underwear, and been done with it. Why don't I see these things before they happen?

"What is different?" He lowers the box to look at all four sides.

"I don't like these." I point to the box. "See the picture? I'm sitting in my blood all day. That's gross."

"You're sitting in it now."

"That's different. First of all, I didn't know I would get my period. It's late, seeing as how I have been here . . . how long?" I ask, and he narrows his eyes, refusing to answer. "Okay then, well, the second thing, when I get upstairs, I will throw away these panties and take a shower. Third, I'll be fresh and clean and not want to return to sitting in my blood. Understand?"

"And the tampads?" He pulls out a pad and tucks the box under his arm to open the little wrapper. He unfolds the pad and inspects it as if the concept is entirely foreign to him. Jeez, how is this happening?

"Tampons. They go up, you know, on the inside. No mess and no sitting in it."

"No."

I draw my eyebrows together, not sure why he's saying no. Considering the language barrier and my thinning patience, I thought I explained feminine hygiene products well.

"No, what?"

"No, inside. Not good for you," he replies swiftly, tugging on the pad's ends to flatten it before ripping off the sticky backing.

"It's fine. They are safe, and we use them all the time in America. They can't sell them if they are bad for you. And they have a string. It hangs out, so it doesn't get lost. Then you can—"

"No, nothing inside you. Only me or bebe."

Oh no. This cannot be happening. Did he say only him or a baby? No. No, on so many levels, I can't even count that high. Not to mention controlling my choice of tampons or pads. Who does that? Why does he even care?

"You're right on that one. Nothing inside me, not you and not a baby. Neither is happening."

"You no want bebe?" He gives me the pad that had his blood-crusted hands on it.

I tug the scraps of my dress tighter and then wrap my arms around myself.

"Maybe in ten years, when I'm older. Not now."

He frowns. "And me? You don't want me?"

These questions are getting harder and harder. I wish we were still talking about pads and tampons.

"Maximiliano." I take the pad and set it on the counter, resisting the temptation to look in the mirror again.

"Answer me."

"Fine, five years ago, I wanted you initially. All the time, if you remember." My face heats, remembering those steamy days in his bed.

"I do."

Choosing my words carefully, I explain, "But then I found out what you do and what you are. What you still are, only bigger now.

I don't want that. I wanted my Maxie. The Maxie that loved me, and I loved him, but he is gone. You are Maximiliano Maldonado, and I don't want him. I don't want all this. The guns, drugs, houses, and money are not what I want." I frown. The words ring truer to me than to him. If he weren't all these things, if he were different, I'd probably fall right back in love with him.

He says nothing, silent and staring as usual. I haul the box from under his elbow to grab an unopened pad before setting the crumpled box on the counter behind me.

I hate these things, but he's right, I'm leaking, and it's gross. Thank goodness I have an enormous bathtub because I see many baths in my future.

"He's here."

I stop fiddling with the wrapper to gaze at him. His eyes are blazing, and his blood-crusted knuckles hit over his heart.

"He's here. He's not gone. Maxie in here, where you left him. And he wants in here."

He points to my 'womanhood.'

"And here."

He points to my heart.

"And here."

He points to my head.

I don't know what to say. Every time I write him off, close the book on him, he rallies back. I don't understand it.

He reaches for me, intending to kiss me, and I shrink back.

"I can't," I murmur, clutching the pad for dear life. I can't fall for his pretty words. For my sanity, I must take a stand against him.

His eyes search my face, and I raise my chin in defiance. He stuffs his hands into his dress pants pockets and steps toward the door.

"No sticks inside you, only those. I wait outside." He nods at the one in my hand and slips out the door, taking another decision of mine with him—pads versus tampons are one more thing for him to control.

I clean up the best I can and vow to shower the second I'm upstairs. I have almost everything taken care of when I frown. I need clothes.

"Maximiliano?" I call, cracking the door.

"Yes."

"You ripped my dress."

"Yes."

"I need something to wear. I can't wear this. It's ruined."

"Hold it like before."

Why can't he call someone for clothes like he did the pads and underwear? If it's not his idea, it doesn't matter, and he's not doing it.

"Okay, but one of your men might see me naked." I wait, hoping to hear him call for the healer again, but hear rustling on the other side of the door.

"Wear that. No one sees what is mine." He shoves his bloodstained shirt at me, but my gaze lingers on the tattoos on his chest. The very ones I used to trace with my tongue until he'd growl with desire and bury me underneath him. "You remember, don't you?" His pecs flex over his bazillion-pack abdominal muscles, and my mouth dries out.

Then I see it. A tattoo over his heart. Script handwriting made of creeping vines covered in thorns with a single red rose. Overwhelmed by my name carved into his flesh, I raise my fingertips to touch it. He holds his breath, steeling his skin against my caress, and my eyes flicker to him, seeing brown pools of lust staring at me.

I swallow, emotion balling up in my throat due to the intimacy of this moment. We are not like this. I said goodbye, even if I failed miserably at remembering it. My hand falls away, as does my gaze. I shrink back and grip the sides of my dress around me. I want to go back to my room.

"Gatita."

He points to the box. I grab it and the dirty underwear wrapped in toilet paper to carry back to my room. Other than that, one word, he's silent, stepping aside for me to lead the way to the stairs. The walk back to my room is painfully long, with him quiet by my side.

I guess neither of us will fill the silence. Once we are at my door, he pushes through it, and I follow. He rattles the veranda door handles to ensure they are locked, glances at the camera, and checks the bathroom. I stand in the middle of the room, watching and waiting until he's satisfied.

"You will eat lunch here. I will send someone for you. You will train the animal until dinner, feed it, and return to your room. Understand?"

"Yes."

He looks at me as if trying to figure out what to say or wait for me to say more. The seconds tick by, and I clutch the box tighter, chanting for him to leave in my mind. After counting twenty seconds, he turns and walks out, locking the door behind him.

Chapter 17

I'm glad to be alone and away from him. Before, it was too much aloneness. Now, it's too much togetherness, and I welcome the solitude. Collapsing on the bed, I look at the ceiling and breathe, letting the remnants of my interactions with him fall away to think about Tiberia. My gorgeous girl is here.

Excited doesn't even describe how I feel right now. *Something to love.* He couldn't have given a more perfect gift. I practically do a happy dance lying on the bed, wiggling against the mattress and punching the air.

Tiberia is here! I've never trained a dog before, so I am unsure what I have gotten myself into, but I will love every minute I spend with her.

After another round of celebratory jiggling, I spring off the bed and take my grandma pads with me to run the bath water. While that fills, I rummage through my drawers to decide what would be best to wear to train her. Once I have pulled out my clothes, I retreat into the bathroom.

Undressing quickly, I sink into the warm bath and sigh. Since he shut off my veranda, I see hot baths being my next escape—anything to not be under the warden's watchful camera all day.

He's beyond frustrating. I grossly underestimated how controlling he can be. It's suffocating. Calling me his possession? Repulsive.

Then today, he flew in a dog for me to love. It doesn't make sense. He makes little sense. When I categorize him as the uncaring drug lord he is, he does something nice and selfless, albeit wrapped in threats of violence, to kill her or kill me. Honestly, how well do I know him anymore? Not at all.

I take all his threats seriously, but would he hurt her? After incurring the expense of the flight and his men, would he? It's a chance I can't risk. Her life is too valuable to me, not to him. Yeah, he would do it and not blink twice. I will become the best trainer possible for her so she can stay with me all the time. I trust no one here with her health and safety, that's for sure.

Sliding further into the tub to where the water line laps my mouth, I close my eyes and think of Mom. I miss her. I really, really miss her.

She must be out of her mind worrying. What did he tell her to get her to leave me? Did he threaten her? Would he kill her if she didn't go? Mom wouldn't care. She is many things, but being selfish isn't one of them. If he threatened to kill her, she would call his bluff. If he said he was going to kill me, she would leave. She would move heaven and earth to save me if my life were on the line. Maybe she's planning something now. That's my only hope.

I bet that's why he moved me out of the country. She knows where the casita is and can lead authorities right to him. She doesn't stand a chance of finding me in his country, his territory, where he owns everyone. I doubt anyone would turn against him to help her. From the little I saw today, this place is extremely remote. Like he said, sandwiched between the mountains and the sea. I need to have faith in Mom. Faith that somehow, she'll find me and rescue me.

In the meantime, I have a middle-aged Siberian to train, which brings me great happiness. Smiling, I climb out of the bathtub to dry off and prepare for her arrival. It's going to be great.

As I'm tying the laces on my shoe, I hear a loud knock on the door and see a wet Tasmanian devil pulling on the arm of the same guy from earlier. He doesn't look happy, but I don't care because she's here, and our new adventure begins.

"Tiberia!" I scream, and she lunges through the door, forcing the guard to grab the doorframe to brace himself. He snaps her leash to get her under control, but it's too much for her, and she snaps her teeth at his hand in retaliation. He looks pissed about his dog assignment, but like me, no one defies el diablo's orders.

"Are you a good girl?" I squat to baby talk in her ear while she kisses my face. Her excited howls fill the room.

"Boss said to take her out three times a day, so you're behind." His voice is deep and commanding.

Stunned, I jump to my feet. "You speak English."

Ironically, I stare at him as Maximiliano stares at me.

"Do you understand the instructions?" His expression is harsh, and his chestnut brown eyes show no emotion. His brown hair is cut high and tight, with a distinct dimple splitting his chin. He's ridiculously muscular, which would explain how easily he controls Tiberia. It must be a prerequisite to look like a murderer to work here.

"Huh? Yeah, sure. But can I know your name? No one here speaks English, well, except *him,* and I don't speak Spanish, so it's been hard and lonely."

He glares, and I would be intimidated if I hadn't grown accustomed to the master of glaring.

"Take the dog."

As he unravels her leash from his fist, I continue stroking her fur and inching the cord away from him. It takes longer than expected, and it's clear he doesn't trust me or doesn't want to get in trouble with el diablo. That much, I understand. She's woven between my legs, and I use my knees to hold her in place as I wind the leash around my hand.

"Gracias," I say, waiting for him to leave. He looks at a calm Tiberia, then me, as if sizing up my ability before deciding to go.

Once he closes the door, I bend over to love on her again. "You're a wild girl."

I press my palm against the door to ensure it is closed and then let go of her leash. She bounds over to the veranda doors and whines. Her head bucks against it, rattling the glass windows. When that doesn't work, she jumps on them, scratching deep grooves in the wood and howling as it remains closed.

"I know, Tiberia, I want out too." I walk over and sit on the floor by the doors, hoping she'll climb into my lap to snuggle.

This is why he locked it. He knew. He knew she'd be a handful and possibly try to escape over the railing. I made an absolute fool of myself and groveled on the floor at his feet over losing it. Instead of explaining the reason was Tiberia, he let me crawl, cry, and beg. He stood over me and let me carry on when he could have said he didn't want her to jump to her death. Unbelievable.

Then again, if he had told me, it wouldn't have been a surprise. Did he not want to ruin the surprise, or did he enjoy his power over me? Most likely, the latter. What if Tiberia had jumped over the edge and died in front of me? I'd be hysterical and inconsolable. He was protecting her and me without either of us knowing it.

Her whining turns into howling, and I do it too. I howl as long and loud as she does. The first time, she pauses, and I egg her on. It's excellent and fills my soul. She howls, and I laugh. She licks my face, and I howl again, waiting for her to join me. It's dumb and fun, meaningless and meaningful. For now, I am not alone. I have something to love, and love, I will.

Her crystal blue eyes catch mine, and every time they do, she walks to the door and angrily paws it. I do the same until she's annoyed with me and shakes her fur to flop by the wall.

"You're a mess. Not used to being trapped, huh? Me neither." I scratch her big mane and wonder if they kept her outside, allowing her to wander the barren desert. This probably feels like a prison if she can't come and go as she pleases.

I slide her furry body across the floor, smashing her to my side.

Even though she's still damp, I don't care. I'm so thankful to have her. I'll take her in any state. She adjusts, stretches her long limbs, and plops her head on my lap. I trace the black lines of fur on her nose, over her eyes, and down the back of her head while humming. I lean my head against the glass doors, feeling the most settled and at peace since arriving here. Soaking in this moment, we stay like this for a while until her light snores fill the quiet room.

The sunlight streaks across the floor in front of us, and I watch the dust sparkle in the air. I hear a gentle knock on the door and know it's one of the ladies bringing my lunch. I've grown so accustomed to the routine that their silent actions barely register anymore. I close my eyes, still running my fingers through her thick fur, when the door creaks open, and she bolts.

"Shit," I gasp as the sneaky beast darts past the old healer, sending the tray of food flying in the air. I scramble off the floor, trying to catch the healer's arm before she falls and breaks every bone in her delicate body. I lose my footing, my shoe sliding on the spilled soup, and I crash into her. We both tumble to the floor, her on me luckily, and I think I broke my tailbone. That's the least of my worries as Tiberia races out the door with her leash trailing after her.

"Bien? Bien?" I ask in a rush as I slide her off my lap and to the floor. Her eyes widen, her hands motioning to go, and I nod before sprinting after the dog.

Barreling down the hallway, I don't see her anywhere. Almost sure she's going to follow the hallway to get to the stairs. I call her name as I run, skidding on the carpet when I reach the staircase. A glance over the railing reveals the empty foyer, and I call her name again, running down the stairs and hearing a commotion in a hallway I've never seen.

I bolt toward the sound, and the second I round the corner, I regret what I see. Dread surges through my body when I see Tiberia being choked by the leash wound around el diablo's hand. She is coughing and hacking, and his face is murderous.

"Gatita."

It's a warning, a promise, a threat, and a guarantee of punishment later. I'd be frightened, shrinking back in remorse if I hadn't seen *her*.

She's naked beyond the open door, her tan skin flawless over her voluptuous body lying on her stomach. Raven hair tumbles across the pillow as her hand disappears underneath it. She is asleep with the sheets draped over the curve of her butt. I can't take my eyes off her.

My mind blocks out all sound and movement of the surrounding chaos, focusing solely on the gorgeous body lying in the luxurious bed. His bed. This is his bedroom. While I was trapped in my room, he was here with her, having sex. He kissed me and fucked her. I'm a prisoner, and she's peacefully slumbering without care.

"Gatita," he warns, and I ignore it.

Moving forward, I want to see her face. I need to see how beautiful she is to have this type of freedom. Does she get to come and go as she pleases? Or is she held captive like me? I must see her. I need to see her.

"No."

His strong fingers wrap around my bicep, pulling me back, and I hate the tears that spring forth. I look from the tattooed raven flying free on the back of his hand, the irony not lost on me, to the beautifully callous face of my captor.

He says nothing. He doesn't have to because he did it again. He gave me hope and immediately crushed it.

I tried not to think of his beautiful words about Maxie not being dead and that he lived in his heart. When I took my bath and laid with Tiberia, I willed myself not to think about it or draw any meaning from it. Not to make something out of nothing, but I couldn't help it. Underneath it all, I wanted it to mean something. I wanted to matter. After all the weeks of not mattering, I wanted to matter to someone, even if it was the devil incarnate.

Two of his men walk swiftly toward us, and he yells at them to take Tiberia. I should be grateful that he gives us another chance, but gratitude is the last thing I feel. The betrayal burns in my veins.

He hands the dog off to a guard, and her barks echo down the hallway while her nails grind into the carpet. El diablo shoves me away to catch the door handle and pulls it closed, sealing off her slumbering figure from my view.

"You piece of shit." My anger is palpable, and I restrain myself from carving a new scar into his face.

"You're angry?"

Yeah, let's do this.

"Damn right I am." My face is hot, and I curl my hands into fists.

"Why?" He tilts his head to the side.

"Why? Oh, I don't know. Maybe because I'm a prisoner, she's free as a bird. I'm locked in a room all day, and she's snoozing without a care in the world." I jab my index finger into his chest muscle, hoping it hurts, but he doesn't flinch.

"You no like? It makes you angry, yes?" He glances at my finger.

This again. Yeah, let's dissect every single word I say.

"Yes, it makes me very angry." Contempt and rage wrap around each word, and I jab him again. "You can't do that."

"I can do it. I do what I want."

I throw my hands in the air.

Does he want a challenge? Then let's go. "No, not anymore." My face is as murderous as he was a moment ago. To look authoritative, I plant my hands on my hips. "I'm going to figure a way out. I'm going to leave this hellhole, leave you behind, as I did five years ago. So, in the meantime, leave me the hell alone."

I wait for him to answer, and he doesn't. No quick retort, no barking commands, just his regular unreadable expression and matching stare.

"You know what, forget it. You're not worth all this." I shake my head, pressing my lips together and walking away. I almost expect him to grab my arm like he usually does, but it's his damn favorite little word that taunts me halfway down the hallway.

"Why?"

I whirl around and stomp over to him, standing even closer than before, so my yelling hurts his ears.

"Why? You're unbelievable. Because I don't want to be here. And until I can figure out how to leave your ass again, pretend I don't exist. Let's go back to you, ignoring me. Remember those weeks when you left me alone? Let's go back to that. Okay?"

"No. I no leave you alone. You no speak, no eat, sleep on the floor. No. I make you this. I fix you. You're better." His accent is harsh, barking out short sentences.

"You've got to be kidding me." My eyebrows shoot into my hair. He's delusional if he thinks I am 'fixed.'

"I no kid."

"You fixed nothing, and I'm not better." I use air quotes over his delusional word. "I don't want this, and I don't want you. I don't want to be here. I want to go home. I want to go back to my life where you don't exist. I want to wake up in my bed. Wear what I want, eat what I want, and go where I want. I want to see my mom and go back to work. I want my life back. The one where you're not in it. Do you understand?"

His eyes narrow, and he leans into my face with a sneer.

"No."

It's so softly spoken that I don't think I heard it, more like saw it.

"No?" I repeat to ensure I heard it correctly.

"No. I let you go, and you came back. You asked me for help. I helped you. I didn't look for you. I didn't come to your life and beg for help. You don't want to be here. Go. Leave." He points down the hall, and I must not have heard that last part correctly.

I stared at him as if he said unicorns were real. Did he say I am free? Leave this hellhole and never see his beautiful, betraying face again?

"Y-you're letting me leave? Do you mean it? I can go, just like that?" Confirming the inconceivable.

"Yes. Go."

He points again down the hallway. Then I realize it is all a big joke to him.

"Really? I can't cross the desert and the mountains. You know that. I need you to take me back to America. I can't walk there."

He leans back, puffing out that bare, tattooed chest with my damn name carved in it.

"Ah, you need my help again, gatita? You want my help to leave me? That's cute like puppy."

I wish I learned jujitsu because I'd have him on the ground in a chokehold faster than he could say gatita.

"It's not your help. You kidnapped me after you let Diego beat me. It's doing the right thing. Get me back to the States, and I won't even file charges." I add the sting of the beating because I'm mad at him, and it's true.

"I already told you, I no want Diego to strike you. He did it on his own. I take you here to get better, and you are angry? Makes no sense. You want to go back to America, go. Walk. I won't kill you. I tell my men not to kill you. Go." He shoos me away, grasping the door handle to show he is done with me. Probably going for another round with her, and it's so revolting. I want to murder him with my bare hands.

"One day, I will leave here, and I hope it's when someone turns you into a rotting, dead corpse. Until then, leave me the hell alone!"

I spin around and start stomping away.

"Gatita."

"What?" I scream at the top of my lungs and whirl around to face him one last time because I am done with him.

"I am rotting dead corpse when you left," he says with no anger, no malice, and no smirk. Those dark jeweled eyes and beautiful face openly stare as he did in the shade of the casita the day he kissed me.

"Yeah, right? You don't care about me. You don't even like me. It amuses you to play games with me. I didn't kill you five years ago. You must have a heart and a soul to die. The devil can't die because he's already dead. Stay away from me, or I will be the one that drives a dagger into where your heart should be."

I don't wait for any sign that my words inflict pain because I learned a long time ago that his face is made of stone. Refusing to run, I walk confidently down the hall as the tears drip down my cheeks. When I round the corner, I fall onto the stairs and bawl like a baby.

I hate him. I hate this place. I hate everything and everyone associated with him. How am I ever going to escape? No one here will help me escape him. No one will betray him. They know the consequences if they do. Death if they are lucky or tortured if they are not.

I'm never getting out of here, never leaving. I'll be his prisoner for as long as he wants until he tires of me and does God knows what to me.

Chapter 18

I cry even harder until a light touch feathers across my shoulder. My head juts up to see the old healer, her hands clasped in prayer, motioning toward the kitchen hall. I nod and dab my eyes with the bottom of my shirt. Stupid period. It is making me so emotional. Rage to tears. No, it's not my period. It's *him*.

When I stand, she makes a clapping motion and turns down the hall. She glances back several times to ensure I'm following her and pulls my arm to the kitchen table where a single place setting is waiting.

"For me?" I sit and watch her hands fly around and clap as she speaks swiftly. Her eyes follow mine to the other ladies, casting curious looks at me while they chop the vegetables and knead the dough. I smile softly and dip my head, wanting to show respect to the women that have made all the meals I had taken for granted.

I don't know why I assumed I was an island to myself. Of course, they knew I was here. They prepared three generous meals daily for me for weeks. Most went back, picked at or untouched entirely, and I never thought how that must have made them feel.

How ungrateful I am. The longer they stare, the more guilty

I feel. I look at my lap and twist the shirt hem repeatedly in my fingers. I've made a mess of everything without even realizing it.

Even if I'm being held captive and utterly miserable, I can be grateful to those taking care of me. These ladies could be in an even worse position than me, and I've only cared about my feelings and my suffering. No telling what they've gone through to wind up here.

He said he would never strike me, except that one time, but these ladies probably get hit all the time. That's precisely what he did in my presence, and they don't sit crying on staircases. I'm disappointed in myself.

"Gatita, you whisper to no one." Like the sneaky kingpin he is, I didn't even hear him come up behind me. "Why?"

Didn't I say to leave me the hell alone? I can't. I can't right now with him. Who cares if I was whispering to myself? Call it self-soothing or a tic. I don't know.

Feigning interest in the potted plants crowding the courtyard, I shake my head and look out the window. An older lady wobbles over with a steel pot in my peripheral vision, and the aroma is fantastic. She scoops a large serving of golden soup, full of vegetables, chicken, and barley, into a bowl in front of me. I hum my appreciation and smile at her.

"Gracias, *señora*."

She pats my arm, firing off something I don't understand, and my smile fades. I think señora is the correct term for ma'am. I look at my soup, biting my lip. I should read that dictionary in my drawer. It would help me communicate with them, especially after all my weeks of bratty behavior.

His presence moves around me like a dark cloud until he's opposite the table.

"She wants you to know her name is Rosa." I don't want him to translate for me even if his tone is soft, like a peace treaty. I don't want him anywhere near me.

I'm reading that book tonight.

"Hi, Rosa." I smile at her, studying the deep lines of her leathery skin and the hunch to her thin shoulders. She's had a hard life, yet she's reaching out to a stranger with kindness. What a lesson for me to learn. "Tell her it's nice to meet her too. Tell her my name is—"

"They know who you are."

I hate that I need him to translate for me.

I nod, looking down at the soup again. "Of course, they do," I murmur, wishing he would go away.

Picking up the spoon, I hear his deep voice and her light one in response as I test the temperature of the soup. It tastes more amazing than it smells, and I moan in appreciation. She pats my head, mumbling something, and hobbles to the stove.

"She's glad you eat. Said you too skinny, look sick."

"Can you leave me alone? Like I asked?" I pause my spoon between bites.

"It's my house. I go where I want. I do what I want. I talk to whom I want." He drags the chair out to sit across from me to my increasingly lousy luck. Figures, just figures he would do that.

With a snap of his fingers, a woman scurries over with a small plate of colorful bread and places it next to me.

"Eat this after the soup. It's sweet, like a treat."

"What if I don't want it?" I challenge, glaring at him.

"Then you upset Maria. Over there."

He gestures to a portly woman across the room, with a dust of flour on her cheek, indicating how freshly made these are.

"Oh."

"Keep fighting me. I told you a long time ago, I like it. That no change. You lost the fire." He reaches across the table and tugs one of my ringlets, letting it wrap around his finger. "I get it back. I keep you here, and you come back to me. Eventually."

I swat his hand away, and the corner of his mouth twitches as it used to when he was happy or entertained.

"I already told you that will never happen."

"Ah gatita, I patient man. I waited five years. Then one day, my angel ran into the desert a second time." He holds up two fingers while I continue eating. "She's different. Quiet like a nun. Hard like me. Not soft, fiery angel. She's sad. I no like it. I get a second chance. She gets second chance. I no let go of second chances. I wait for mi gatita to turn to mi angel."

He stands and walks over to me, reaching over and taking my hand in his. His thumb caresses my knuckles, and my heart thunders at his sudden compassion. I stare at it for so long that my eyes burn and close. His lips press against the crown of my head in a prolonged kiss, and then he slips away, quietly leaving as silently as he entered.

I sniff, vowing not to get tears in my soup over that man. He's not worth it. That should be my new mantra, or better, I should carve it to my forearm as a reminder I see every day. Maximiliano is not worth my tears, sorrow, or emotion, period. End of story.

The ladies return to chatting, and even though I don't understand a word they are saying, it's nice not being alone, locked in a room with my imagination as my only form of entertainment.

Quietly moving the empty soup bowl to the side, I pick up the plate of colorful bread to turn and look at the three options. The light sweet fragrance fills my senses, and I smile at the three cheerful colors of various sizes. I start with the tiny pink donut-shaped one with a dollop of strawberry jam in the center. One bite, and I am moaning again because these ladies can bake as well as cook.

I could learn from them. I'm sure they wouldn't mind, and it would get me out of my room. Would he allow it, or would he prefer to keep me locked up forever? I don't know, but he said he wants me back. This could be a way back to me, not the old version but a new one, where I cook and speak Spanish.

A glass of milk slides into my line of vision, and I look up to see Maria standing in front of me. How thoughtful. It's surprising how harsh his world is, yet these women seem to maintain their grace and generosity.

"Gracias, Maria," I whisper, giving her a soft smile. She returns my smile and says a heavily accented "de nada" before retrieving my bowl and handing it to a lady washing dishes. They watch me intently, and I awkwardly nod in acknowledgment. I don't know what to do with all this attention. Going from weeks of isolation to all eyes on me is more than unnerving, especially since they were the ones that pointed out the bloody mess earlier.

His argument that I've come back to him is delusional, not to mention the obvious fact that he kidnapped me and put me in a drug-induced coma. My finger rubs the scar on my eyebrow as a reminder of those days.

After polishing off the entire pink one, I move onto the yellow-crusted top and tear off a piece. It's as warm and heavenly as the first one, and the yellow sugar dissolves on my tongue, adding to the deliciousness.

"Gatita."

My head jerks in the direction of the doorway where he is standing.

"Why your face red? Are you ill? It is the womanhood?" he asks across the kitchen, and my cheeks heat in embarrassment. He doesn't need to keep bringing it up.

"Um?" I shake my head, putting my fingers to my lip to shush him.

"Does the bleeding make you ill? You rest. I have my men take care of the animal until I return." He pulls out his phone and hits a button on it.

Ignoring the first part, I focus on the second part, his return. What does that mean?

"You're leaving?"

"Yes."

"But . . . are you taking me, or can I go? With you?" I can't figure out what to ask. I want him to swing by the United States and drop me off. Is that possible?

"No." He puts the phone to his ear.

I stand abruptly, causing my head to swim in dizziness. I clutch the table and look down, trying to eliminate the black dots clouding my vision.

"Gatita?" He's across the room and cupping my elbow before I realize it.

"Why? I can't stay here. I don't know anyone but you. I don't know the language."

I'm mainly worried about my safety. I'm not so disillusioned that I don't know his presence protects me. If he's not here, then am I safe? Is Diego going to be here alone with me? I don't want to get beaten and suffer el diablo's brand of healing again.

"You have a book. Use it."

Releasing the table, I shake off his hand to plead my case.

"But I don't want to stay here alone. I want to come with you." It's the lesser of the two evils. With him, I am safe from everyone but el diablo himself. Here, I am safe from the devil but not his demons.

"I no go to your country. I go south, not the place for mi gatita," he murmurs, his eyes never leaving mine when he rattles off commands in Spanish into his phone.

"What if *he* comes again? Do you know? You won't be here, and he could come and hurt me. Worse than before. What if Diego . . ." I can't finish the sentence, hoping he understands my fears without having to spell it out.

"You are frightened."

"Yeah." I breathe out in relief, for he understands Diego is still a risk to me, even if he doesn't think so.

"You not be frightened. You are safe here. Not with me. South is too dangerous for mi gatita. They, how you say, like American girls. Girls, you take away from coyotes," he explains while shoving his phone in his pocket.

I already knew they liked the girls I rescued. It was all too evident in their torn lingerie and vacant eyes. Going south with him is not what I want. It's the polar opposite of what I want. I want to go north to my home where things like this don't happen.

My brain flips to the first part of what he says. Am I safe here? I doubt it, seriously doubt it. I don't have a gun, and I'm skinnier than ever. Diego could snap me like a toothpick, and the underwear incident proves he can get to me. I don't want him to go, and I don't want to stay.

"But it's not safe here. You can't keep me safe because—"

His eyes flash with anger. "No, this mi casa, and I say you are safe. No more talk." His eyes shift slightly to warn me that the ladies are listening, but I don't care. They don't speak English. They don't understand.

"I'm not safe. Don't you understand? He beat me in your house and put that underwear on me in your house. Your house isn't safe, and you can't control your men either. If you could, none of that would have happened, and now you're leaving me here. What's going to happen then? What's going—"

"Enough!" The vein on the side of his neck pulses, and his hands fly up to grip my shoulders tightly. He shakes me, forcing a gasp out of my constricted lungs, and panic rises into my chest. The sheer force of his hold pushes me onto my tiptoes, and my arms hang like wet noodles. I search his face for any sign of compassion or understanding, but it's blank as a stone as usual. "That's enough."

His voice is calm but doesn't resolve the storm brewing underneath the surface. I fight to get out of his grip, but he shakes me again. My arms are numb, and my shoulders ache from the pressure of his fingers digging into my flesh. I know I'll have bruises tomorrow.

"Y-you're hurting me."

A surge of heat rockets through my body. The black dots are back, dancing in front of his angry face.

He doesn't lighten his grip or release me. We're in a standoff, controlling eyes meeting pleading eyes until I close mine. Sweat collects on my neck, and the temperature inside the kitchen is getting to me.

"Darling."

A soft voice with a pleasant cadence rings out, and I feel him stiffen. I open my eyes, and the dots are even worse as his expression changes to a frosty icicle. His eyes stare into mine as his hands slowly release my shoulders. I'm almost free when a perfectly manicured hand with blazing red nail polish slides over his shoulder, and a stunning young Latin woman peeks from around his frame.

I blink several times, trying to get rid of the dots. When that doesn't work, I wipe my hand across my forehead and over my face. The curves of her mouth are moving, and she leans into him, displaying their closeness. This is her. She's the one. I can't help but stare at her. She's as stunning as her naked back.

She's everything I'm not. Where I'm pale, she's tanned. I have freckles, and her skin is flawless. My hair is a red mess of tired ringlets, and hers is an endless wave of thick chocolate silkiness. And her body . . . that body looks nothing like my boy body. She has curves for days on full display. She's simply magnificent.

"Maximiliano has no manners. I am Veronica, his fiancée."

Her long, naturally tan fingers extend to mine, and I feel underwater. I feel the weight of the water crushing my lungs. My ears clog because I thought I heard her say, fiancée. As in, they are going to be married. As they picked out rings, he got down on a star tattooed knee and asked her to share this life with him.

Somehow, my brain instructs my hand to shake hers. I blink and see the ladies looking everywhere but at us. I look at him, needing confirmation that I'm not high or drugged or that they didn't slip something into the sweet bread to make me hallucinate.

"I-I don't feel good."

Then darkness takes over.

Chapter 19

I gaze at the familiar ceiling above my bed. The healer is fretting around the room, and he is sitting in that armchair again. This scene is all too familiar.

"What happened?" I slide my hand into my hair to feel a knot at the back of my head. His betrayal floods back to me, and too many thoughts simultaneously push up to the surface. "You're married."

"No."

His face is still frosty. The healer drapes a cold washcloth across my forehead before patting my cheek and scurrying out of the room.

"But you will be?"

"Yes."

"Then why am I here? With all that kitten this and don't leave that. I thought you wanted me to come back to you, to be what we were?"

"Yes."

No, that won't do at all. I asked at least two questions, or maybe three, and none warrant a single-word answer.

"Look, I deserve an explanation. That's the least you can give me," I say, holding the cloth in place and switching to my side to see his face better. He mistakes my action as getting up when he jumps to his feet.

"No, you rest."

"See, that's what I don't get. You have her, not me. You should be worried about her, what she thinks, not in here telling me to rest. Why am I here?"

"You are here to heal. You are here for me. You said so."

That was too many old conversations ago to argue the merit. The most recent conversation is I want to go home, and he's engaged.

"No, I didn't say so. You kidnapped me and stuck me in this room. I'm not here for you. I don't want to be here at all. You're holding me against my will, and now you will be married?" I drag myself to sit against the pillows and throw the wet cloth into the bathroom. "Help me make sense of this."

His lips tighten, and he shoves his hands in his pants pockets. This is his telltale sign that he's closing up and unwilling to talk about it.

"My marriage is no concern to you."

Frustrated, I raise my hand and drive my fist into the soft mattress.

"Then let me go!" My scream vibrates my brewing headache. Not a smart move.

"No."

"Why?"

"You mine. I want you. I want you then. I want you now. Now, I have you," he spews more nonsense.

Why did I wake up? He's not even reasonable . . . maybe Diego could beat some sense into him instead of me.

"You're not even listening to me. You never do," I muttered, dejected.

"I hear everything you say, gatita."

"Then understand this. I already told you, you can't kiss me and screw her. And now that I find out you're going to be married, I'm not your side chick. Keep her, as you proposed, and let me go."

"No."

I scream, kneeling on the bed to throw my pillow at his head. He quickly catches it, and the second one I throw at him. I'm about to launch a third one when he grabs it and yanks me toward him. I fall into his arms with flushed cheeks, and his eyes glitter like black diamonds.

His powerful arms circle around me before we fall back onto the bed. I'm buried underneath him, and its familiarity hits me. This used to be my favorite position with him. I felt so loved and protected when his body smothered mine as if I was the only thing that mattered to him.

"Gatita."

His nickname flows into my ears, and his head lowers. I exhale in anticipation. I should fight him. This is wrong, but it's been so long. I never wanted to leave him the first time, but I had to. It wasn't my choice, but it is my choice this time. I can't stay here, and I can't give in to him.

I struggle, freeing one of my trapped hands, only for him to lace our fingers together and rest it beside my head. His strong nose traces my jaw, and my breathing becomes longer and deeper, trying to hold back the old feelings I used to have for him.

"Please don't. You have her for this, not me."

His musky fragrance swirls around my sense, and I turn my face away from his. She is his future. I'm his past.

His tongue follows the edge of my jawline, nipping at my sensitive skin and taking my earlobe between his teeth to nibble it. His warm breath fans my skin, slow and sensual. I'm losing, my resolve faltering from his teasing foreplay.

"You are beautiful. That will never change," he whispers, licking the shell of my ear and dusting soft kisses on my temple.

His words cut through the brain, and I struggle to free my other hand trapped between our bodies. He helps, partially lifting off me while those black jewels stare into mine. I push against his shoulder when my hand is free, but the most breathtaking smile forms on his lips, and I freeze. He wraps his fingers around mine, placing it beside my head and adjusting himself to align with my most sensitive part.

"I see a piece of mi angel now. You remember this."

He thrusts, bunching our clothes, and it's nearly painful how hard he is.

"Tell me you remember."

He squeezes our fingers and gives me a quick peck while waiting for my answer.

"Yes. I remember." I remember it all.

My mouth was dry, and I nervously licked my lips. I was stunned by all the intricate ink that covered most of his body. He stood naked before me. His body was on full display, proud and powerful, scars mixed with tattoos and pressed taut over ripped muscles. His erection was large and looming, the first I had seen in person, and I couldn't take my eyes off him.

"You're beautiful, Maxie." I felt overwhelmed and extremely vulnerable in my bra and panties.

His chin dropped, and our eyes aligned. "No."

He squeezed my hand and laid it on his heart, the place he said I owned.

"You the beautiful one. Pale with spotted skin. I want to taste each spot. Love each spot until you know the pleasure of a woman." His accent was heavy with desire, his intentions clear, and I could barely breathe. His heart beat strong in my palm, his muscle flexed under my touch, and I looked from those black eyes to the swaths of ink everywhere.

"Can I?" I was unsure what I was asking. This felt right, and I wanted more. I wanted all of him. I placed my other hand on his chest, splayed my fingers to cover more of his tattooed expanse, and explored. The pads of my fingers brushed his nipples, eliciting a long groan, and my eyes flickered to see him watching me.

"Keep going. Touch me. Learn," he encouraged. His flesh twitched, and his breath hallowed. Desire pooled between my legs. When my hand dipped past his abdominals, I stopped and looked into his eyes for assurance. "I like you touching me. Like you a virgin."

Uncertain, my hands fell to my sides. "I . . . um . . ."

He cupped my face, tilted it to capture my lips, and kissed me lightly before he pulled back. "Mi angel. I like you untouched. I like that no man knows you like this. I like I am first. I like you touching me. It makes me hard. I show you. We learn together. Learn each other."

Then that beautiful smile from the past appears, and I want to capture it, to hold it in my heart forever. I smile, letting the ghosts of our past dance in the forefront of my mind, bringing forward all the feelings I ever had for him.

"There you are, mi angel. I missed you."

He untangles our fingers to wind into my hair, and I lean forward, seeking his lips. His smile falters, replaced with carnal desire, as he dives into me. It's rough and raw, of teeth and tongues and quick desperation to visit what we used to be.

Our chemistry was undeniable. I know that now. I didn't understand it back then because it was all I knew. But living apart and seeing others in relationships, I knew ours was unique, once in a lifetime. That lifetime ended five years ago. I won't go back. I can't. It's wrong for so many reasons.

"Maxie, I can't do this."

He stops and gazes into my eyes for so long that I close mine to block out the intensity of his desire. He ducks his face into my neck. His breath is faint compared to mine. The sudden stillness causes reality to crash down on me.

The room is silent, eerie, and haunting. The ghosts of our memories were making promises I could no longer keep. Where he had moved on with her, I had not, not seriously, to the point of marrying someone else.

I thought it was the reverse that I had moved on, and he was left behind until I laid eyes on the sculpted body of her feminine sexiness. Then I realized I was the only one stuck in the graveyard of my old life. Disappointment settles into my gut like a block of concrete, and as justified as it is, I still hate knowing I am not completely over him.

He lifts off, setting me free, and the sudden absence of his masculine body leaves me cold and empty. By the time he makes it to the door, I'm sitting up, straightening my clothes, and watching the pulse of his jaw muscle.

He opens the door, letting a plume of cold air rush in, and I shiver. He pauses, turning to face me, and I hold my breath. I wait for him to say something, say anything, but he doesn't say a word. As expected, he's silent, his eyes raking me up and down before closing the door quietly behind him.

I don't hear the all too familiar lock. It's unnecessary at this point. He knows I won't risk going back down to see them or, more likely, him and her together. I fall back on my bed, letting guilt, shame, and regret creep in.

Chapter 20

My slumber is fitful, tossing and turning, dozing off, and then jolting awake. It's been an emotional day, full of ups and downs, and my period is not helping curtail my emotions.

There is a knock on the door, and I peer over my warm covers to see a worried Rosa bringing in a tray of food and putting it on the bureau.

"Gracious, señora."

She rattles off something, and I frown. That is too fast. I slip out of bed and pull open the drawer to get the dictionary out, holding it in the air to show her. Throwing the covers haphazardly over the pillows, I sit on the bed and pat the spot next to me, hoping she will point out her words.

I nearly clap when she sits and takes the book to flip through the pages. We take some time but work through how I feel, and I look pale through finger-pointing and pronunciation lessons.

I laugh, startling her because it's funny, and I realize she didn't mean it as a joke. After several long minutes and practicing the words slowly with a few corrections from her, I say, "I thought I always look pale," pointing to my fair skin and freckles.

She smiles politely. I think my humor is lost on her. That's okay. It's nice to interact with someone else.

We muddle through another set of her asking me if I feel ill and answering that I feel fine after a long sleep. We end with her telling me to eat so the man can bring the dog up, and I nod. She surprises me by cupping my cheek and kissing my forehead before standing to leave.

That was sweet.

I maneuver the tray to the floor in front of my veranda doors and pull the sheers apart to see outside. I miss the balcony already. I understand why he locked it, but I wish he had left me a key to open it at my discretion.

I watch the seagulls in the sky darting in and out of the water while eating another mouthwatering meal from the ladies in the kitchen. With the balcony doors locked and my escape plan thwarted, I don't know what to do now.

It's ridiculous how much I give away my power to him. That's got to stop. I welcome the break away from him. Even though I don't know how long he'll be gone, I'm taking full advantage to regroup and devise a new escape plan.

A loud banging and a whiny howl have me jumping up and throwing open the door to see my wild girl being choked by the same guard in black fatigues.

"Hola!" I chirp, glad to see her. He brushes past me and kicks the door closed with his boot. "Someone's in a bad mood."

She bucks against him like the wild bronco she is. If they understood she didn't want to be inside and wanted to roam free outside, then she wouldn't be so crazy now. I drop to my knees to hug her, and I'm assaulted with a million kisses. He snaps her leash, and she yelps but calms down immediately. Maybe he should train her.

"Do you have to be so harsh with her?"

"She's fine. A bit melodramatic." He widens his stance and props his forearm on the butt of the gun holstered at his hip.

"Hmm. Can you show me how you do that? The boss man is expecting me to train her, but I don't know how. I've never had a dog before, and she's an adult, middle-aged one. Can she even be trained?"

"Yes."

"Yes, you'll show me, or yes, she can be trained."

He scowls, and I'm tempted to say forget it, but I need his help, or else my crazy girl is done for, and it will be all my fault.

"She's sitting, right?" His sarcasm is not helpful at this point. "Then she's trainable."

"Okay."

How will I do this without experience, the internet, or even a book?

I hold his gaze for a couple of seconds and take the leash dangling in the air while I vacillate between begging him for help and figuring it out on my own.

She goes buck wild, flying, spinning, and doing donkey kicks to escape the restraints. She's so wound up that she knocks me on my butt and runs to the tray of food I left by the veranda doors.

"You let her control you. She'll do it every time if you let her."

He holds his hand out, and when I slip mine in his, he practically yanks it out of my socket to pull me to my feet. I rub my aching tailbone and then stop when I see him watching. My cheeks flush red, and I look away from his curious eyes.

Tiberia's paw clangs against the plate, and I dive under her furry face to grab the dishes she has already wiped clean. Spicy hot food in her stomach, that's not good.

"I didn't let her do anything. She's so wild."

"She not wild. She's untrained."

I roll my eyes. Semantics. Once I set the tray on the top of the bureau, I walk to where she paces like a caged animal and pick up her leash. Mimicking his hold, I try to stop her, but it's no use. She simply walks with me attached.

"See, it's not working. Maybe it's because you're all big and scary, and I'm not. She knows you mean business, and it's like playing patty-cake with me."

He sort of cracks a smile, and I stare. No one ever smiles at my jokes. No one. They usually don't understand or look away, embarrassed for me, and here . . . that's a different story. The language barrier alone is a guarantee my jokes will fail, but he sort of smiled, and it felt kind of normal. Pride swells within me, I can't even remember the last time someone smiled at my jokes, and that's what he did. He smiled, and then I smiled, and it felt good.

"You sort of smiled."

He walks over, calculated and cautious as if evaluating the enemy. I'm pretty sure the enemy isn't barefoot, wearing a tank top and pink shorts.

"You're sort of funny." He shrugs.

I blush, looking down. He thinks I'm funny, and somehow that is the best compliment I've received in this place. Forget all the beautiful words spilling out of Maximiliano. They don't count.

"You're holding her wrong. You give away control when you have slack on the leash. Move the chain up her neck, catching it at the top, and keep it tight with enough slack for her to breathe and move with you." He adjusts her chain and the leash in my hands, wrapping it around my fist and making my other hand hold the excess.

"Uh, this is—"

"Control."

"Cruel."

He towers over me, and when I look over, he motions for me to walk her around the room. Like magic, she follows. Granted, a few times, she lunged when we walked by the bedroom door and the veranda door, but mostly, I maintained control.

"I did it!" I do a happy dance and beam at him. He gives me the strangest look, but I don't care. "Wow, I did it."

"Carlos."

My head snaps up, and I mumble an unintelligent, "Huh?"

"You asked my name. It's Carlos Mendez."

"Oh, well, it's very nice to meet you, Carlos." I release my Tasmanian devil's leash and watch her awkwardly amble away. I thrust my hand out and smile at him, genuinely happy to meet him. His eyes flicker from mine to my hand, and he doesn't take it. "I'm Samantha Smith, but everyone calls me Sammie."

"Nice to meet you, but to be honest, everyone knows who you are."

"Oh," I say, feeling the air leave my body, and I flop on the bed. I don't know why he would be any different. They all know me. They all think I'm his side girl, and I hate it. It makes me furious with him. "I'm not, you know, doing anything with him. He's going to be married, and I'm not, well, I didn't agree to that, this I mean. You know, I'm not a side chick or whatever you call it here. Uh, mistress? Yeah, but no . . . I'm not his mistress. At all. I don't know what I am doing here, so yeah."

I pluck at the comforter. Hating how I feel, hating how I sound, and hating this situation.

"You don't owe me any explanations."

I must explain it because I want to set the record straight, in case he hears otherwise from his boss.

"I want you to know. It's important to me that you know the facts. I didn't agree to come here. It turned out that way. And I'm somewhat well-known back home . . ." I don't finish the rest of my thought now that it seems like someone else's life.

"We all know how famous you are. Your face is everywhere now that they have reported you missing—"

He stops, knowing he made a grave mistake telling me, but I won't say anything. Whom would I tell anyway?

"Don't worry. I won't rat you out."

He says nothing for the longest time. He stares at me as if trying to figure out where the next piece goes in the puzzle.

"Seriously, it's okay. I won't say anything to the boss. We're not exactly on speaking terms right now, but I figure, no, I knew my mom would report me missing. I don't know what he said to her to get her to go, but I'm glad she is safe. He told me that and the girls, they are safe too, so . . . I'm rambling. Sorry." I am eager to have someone to talk to, even if it's mostly one-sided.

He still doesn't move or say anything, and that's fine. I'm used to the silence. Tiberia lets out a loud howl, and I smile, getting off the bed and walking past him to retrieve her pacing figure. He's still standing like a statue, and I wrap the leash around my hands as he taught me.

"All right, let's follow those instructions you gave me. Can I take her to the beach? Is that allowed?"

He finally moves, and with a snap of his head signifying a sort of nod, I drag her over to my flip-flops lying by the bathroom door.

"You're welcome to go with us. I may never get her back if she runs away." Would she come back? If I were to escape this prison, I sure as hell wouldn't come back.

"I'll accompany you outside, and then you're on your own. Don't let yourself get killed out there," he says. *That's reassuring.* "And I shouldn't have said what I said just now."

"No biggie, Carlos." He moves to fix my hands one last time before opening the door. I express what I think. "Would it be so bad, though? If I were gone? It would be easier on everyone here."

He pauses, staring into my eyes, and I feel uncomfortable. "Easier isn't always better."

I duck my head to look at Tiberia. She hacks like I'm strangling her, and he explains she'll learn to calm herself down, that she is not choking to death. I nod and follow him out of the room.

With her trapped behind him and beside me, she behaves better. I watch his long strides and broad back twist opposite his small waist as he leads the way downstairs. He's interesting. Complex like Maximiliano and short with his words, but there is something about him I can't put my finger on. It piques my curiosity.

When we approach the kitchen, he stops and looks over his shoulder at me.

"Tighten your hold. She'll lunge when she smells the ocean air."

"Got it." I tighten to a death grip. He isn't kidding. She pulls like a sled dog in the Iditarod race, causing me to crash into his back. "Sorry."

He glares at me, and I mouth sorry again. I know I didn't physically hurt him, but I feel guilty. He snaps her leash, causing her to yelp and me to jump. His strong hand wraps around my fist, forcing a tighter hold, and now I'm the one yelping. "That tight."

"Yep." Sighing in relief when his hand leaves mine.

He silently strides through the kitchen, but when I see Rosa and Maria working, I want to practice what I learned upstairs.

"*Buenos días, señoras?*" Remembering the phrase from the little book. I am proud of my progress, which is short-lived when Rosa responds with a couple of long sentences. I furrow my brow, trying to pick out any word I understand, but there are none. This is freaking hard.

"She said good afternoon since it's after 1 p.m."

"Oh." How long did I sleep? Blame it on el diablo, learning he's getting married, my period, or fainting, probably all of it, for making me exhausted.

Without a backward glance, he exits the kitchen as if he cannot be bothered to interpret more than that short exchange. Tiberia drags me to follow him down the long hallway that leads outside. He holds the door handle, inspecting my hands to ensure I am holding her tight enough while she wiggles with excitement.

"She also asked if you would like your lunch in the kitchen or room."

"Kitchen, definitely the kitchen. That room gets too . . ." I sigh and stop. There is no need to complain. It doesn't do any good other than making me feel worse.

"I'll tell her on my way back in." He opens the door, and she lunges, almost taking me down if he wasn't there to grab the leash behind her neck. "Hold her!" he barks.

"I'm trying to, but it's like harnessing a hurricane, okay?" I bark right back.

"She's too much for you."

"Yeah, I know. I don't know why he thought I could do this. If I don't get her trained, he will kill her, and I can't have that. It's not her fault. It's my fault or will be my fault. I'm so stupid. This is another one of his games. Give me hope, kill her, and break me again. Why does he do this? Why does he hate me so much? Maybe it would be better if I died. He could kill me with one bullet. It would be faster than this slow misery."

I release Tiberia entirely, knowing he has her, and sit on a bench in the courtyard. I listen to the roar of the ocean and the surrounding seagulls calling to each other. God knows how long it took for me to finally be allowed outside, and now I'm not even happy being here. I'm angry, frustrated, and overwhelmed.

With a heavy sigh, he sits next to me on the bench and backs Tiberia to sit between his legs. Her leash wraps around his fist, and the cords of his veins pop out of his forearm, showing it takes a good bit of restraint from him to keep her in line. He doesn't say anything, and I wish he would, but I understand the silence. I've come to expect it when people around here don't want to address the elephant in the room.

"Why is it so easy for you?"

He scratches her woolly mane. It's the first bit of kindness I've seen out of him, except telling me his name, but that's not kindness, that's manners.

"I trained dogs in the military."

"Really? The Mexican military?"

His side glance cuts me in two. I almost wish I didn't ask, but I've got nothing to lose. Absolutely nothing.

"Marines."

My jaw drops for the second time today. No wonder he speaks English. He's . . .

"You're an American?" I am dumbfounded that Maximiliano employs the American military. "Holy shit, that's crazy."

"Why? Most men here are."

He thumbs through Tiberia's fur behind her ears, and she's the calmest I've seen her today.

"No way! Why? He's . . . this has to be dangerous. I mean, I don't know much, but what I do know, it's dangerous, and wow." I can't even formulate coherent thoughts.

"So is fighting for your country, and the pay here is much better than what Uncle Sam pays."

I shake my head in disbelief. "It's illegal and immoral. The drugs and the people and the violence and . . . how can you do it? How can you see innocent people get killed or tortured? The women alone, don't you have sisters or a mom? Would you want that for them?"

His jaw clenches and his fist rubs against the leash. I struck a nerve, but seriously. He used to be a Marine, one of our Marines, one of the good guys.

"Take the dog. I'm not here to babysit you."

He unwraps the leash and secures it around my palm before standing, and Tiberia lunges. I try to keep from sliding off the bench, but it takes both hands and my legs to do it. He starts walking off, and I know he's pissed at me for judging him.

"Carlos, I shouldn't have judged you for what it's worth." He turns to glare at me. "It's being here, against my will. I can relate to them, the girls, I mean."

His face twists into a scowl of disdain. "No, you can't. You're babysitting a dog, not getting raped every day."

He turns, throwing open the door to walk inside and leaving me feeling like the selfish asshole I am. He's right. I'm training a dog, something to love, not the other, more heinous thing.

Chapter 21

While I am lost in my head, Tiberia bolts, dragging me off the bench and down the path leading to the boardwalk until we hit the beach. She makes it two feet into the sand, squats, and pees a river. I mistook her exuberance for wanting to be free rather than desperately needing to pee. She trots beside me like a completely different dog once she's done.

"Thank you, Tiberia, because I don't have military dog training."

The sky is overcast and cloudy, making it rather gloomy and dark. I look out at that vast ocean and watch the waves tumble violently over each other in the distance. I've watched this ocean from my veranda so much that I know about her moods. Today is grumpy and unforgiving like she's irritated with the world by how she reaches up to hit the seagulls. They seem to duck and dart from her wrath, never daring to dive for a fish.

I sit close enough for the tide to roll in and lap at my feet, and Tiberia sits far enough away where the water doesn't touch her. The first time it hits my bare feet, I gasp. It's colder than I imagined, and I scoot back to where she sits. I shift my weight to sit on the leash and wrap an arm around her fluffy body to watch the angry ocean together. We sit for a long time until the tide inches closer to us, and I decide to walk along the beach for exercise.

The minute I stand, I forget about the leash, and she bolts down the coastline. Mounds of sand fly into the air behind her, and if I weren't petrified to lose her, I would say she looked majestic in her dead heat away from me.

"Tiberia! Come back, girl!" I scream, kicking off my flip-flops and racing after her. "Tiberia!"

I sprint the coast, screaming her name until my lungs burn and my thighs cramp.

"Tiberia! Tiberia!"

She's a spot in the distance. I fall to my hands and knees, heaving big gulps of air past the adrenaline pumping through my body. She's gone.

At the first chance she gets, she's gone, and it's all my fault. If I hadn't let go of her leash, if I hadn't sat on it, if I remembered the leash at all, she would be here. I collapse onto my stomach, crossing my arms and dropping my forehead on them.

The cold water laps at the left side of my body, and getting half drenched doesn't motivate me to move. I want to feel cold and empty physically to match how cold and empty I feel in my soul.

The angry ocean was an omen, a warning of what was to come. Here I thought sitting peacefully with Tiberia to enjoy it was a treasured gift. I finally had some freedom and a beautiful dog to share it with, and it was ripped away in a moment. The only thing he gave me to love, and she's gone, merely a bolt across the beach matching the one cutting across the sky.

I raise my head, hoping by a minor miracle that she is trotting back toward me, only for disappointment and sadness to confirm what I know to be true. She's long gone, never to return.

The longer I lie half-submerged, the colder I get until I'm shivering so badly that my teeth are chattering. I know I should get up, but a part of me also knows I deserve this. The sting of freezing water and cutting wind is what I deserve. I deserve to suffer from my sorrow and loss and everything I have been through until this point.

"Yay, I deserve this." I slide out of the wet surf to escape the rising tide and sit with my arms wrapped around my legs. Trying to become the smallest ball possible, I plop my chin on my knees and sigh. "When did I give up so easily?"

I gaze where she took off, seeing endless miles of coast and not a husky insight. I must change. Something has to give, and it definitely won't be him. It will have to be me. I used to be so . . . not nice. That's what he said all those years ago.

"I'm sorry, that was uncalled for."

"What wrong with you?" He stumbled over the words and missed some verbs, as usual.

My eyebrows bunched together, not understanding him. I need more than that to go on. "What do you mean?"

"You nice. Why?"

"What's that supposed to mean? I'm always nice." My temper rose at his insinuation that I was mean or something. I was nice all the time except with him because he pissed me off.

"No, you wild and sit on floor screaming. You talk back and throw things, but you not nice."

I stepped forward and pushed my finger into his chest to tell him off. "Look here, Your Royal Highness, I'm one of the nicest people I know. In fact . . ." Dammit, if he didn't do it again. I was about to lose my shit on him for the tenth time today. "I'm sorry, again."

I removed my finger and stepped back. Confusion wrinkled his beautiful face.

"Stop it."

"Stop what?"

"You nice, say sorry twice." He held up two fingers. It was so freaking cute. "I no like."

"You don't like it when I am nice to you?"

"No."

I was confused. Who didn't like nice people? This guy had a screw loose or something.

"Let me get this straight. You don't like me when I apologize and are nice to you?"

"No."

If he was one of those guys that liked a dominant female, I would hurl.

He sauntered forward, all sexy and masculine. His cologne hugged his body, and I leaned closer to soak it in. Had he always smelled this delicious? "I like you red, wild, like fiery hair. I like chase, like you prey. I like talk back." Backtalk, but tomayto, tomahto. "I like you. You like me—no nice. I no nice. You no nice. You fire, and I fire. Fire burns hot and bright. I like. A lot."

That's what Maximiliano was talking about earlier. He wanted the fire back, the sass, the not nice. Since I have been here, that fire was extinguished, smothered by my hopelessness and my general pity party. I don't want to be here. He knows it. I know it. That much is clear. I can leave at any time. He won't have me killed. How generous, but I wouldn't survive the terrain. What has been happening between us isn't working.

I need a fresh approach, a new angle to survive this place. Try to make the best of an awful situation.

Does Maximiliano really want the mean backtalk again? Like the old days? He struck me once, an accident, but he was hurting me in the kitchen, meant to hurt me when the backtalk became too much. Does he really want the fire back? Or just enough to entice him but still control me by force. Honestly, I don't know. He promised not to strike me again, and I'll hold him to that and throw it in his face every time. I won't let him touch me, not at all.

My goal is to survive until I can think of a way out of here. I could befriend Carlos. He said several men are former Marines, and maybe they would help me. I could pay them to help me. I doubt I can pay what el diablo pays them, but maybe one or two would be sympathetic to my plight. Help me get a message to Mom. Yes! I can't believe it. I have a plan.

As if God is sitting on the beach granting miracles, a wet, fluffy beast barrels into my side and knocks me into the sand. She whimpers, lying on top of me as I dodge her long, cold tongue that is trying to swipe across my cheek. I laugh, throwing my arms around her sand-crusted body, and release an enormous sigh.

She came back!

And I have a plan.

Chapter 22

The water from her wet fur is pooling between us, and as warm as her body is, it makes me even colder. We both need a bath. A rinse off in the ocean would help, but I already have goosebumps in my hair, and it's a fair walk back to the compound after racing across the beach.

"Okay, girl." I grasp the chain that is miraculously still circling her neck. "Let's head back."

She pops up, nearly taking my arm with her when I scold her, "No."

She wags her fluffy tail, sending clumps of wet surf around us. I laugh, knowing scolding should not elicit a tail wagging. Like Carlos showed me, I move the chain up her neck and wrap the leash around both fists for extra control.

"All right, now be a good girl." I start forward, and she lunges, causing me to fall on my knees with the heavy sand clustered around my feet. "No, bad girl."

I leverage her weight to help me up and tighten the restraint before taking a step forward. She tries to pull, and I scold her again. It doesn't matter that I am yelling at her. Her curled tail still happily swings back and forth. I drag us over to my flip-flops buried in the sand, and shake them in the air before putting them on.

It seems to take us forever to get back to the fortress, and by then, my hands are cramping from holding the leash so tight to hold her back. She's more powerful than I am. I should start working out again. It would help with Tiberia and executing my escape plan.

"Sit," I command, pulling on the leash like Carlos did, and she does nothing. I unravel one hand, adjust the chain under her neck and snap the leash again. "Sit!" I say in a deeper voice, and magic happens when her back legs squat to sit.

"Yes!" I fist pump the air, which causes her to stand, and I start again. It takes twice, and when she does it, I open the door to go inside. "Good girl, Tiberia," I say with the happiness I feel because she listened to me twice. I'll take it even if it is twice out of a zillion times.

Two breakthroughs today. She came back, and I have a new plan. I feel such hope blooming in my heart that I don't immediately snap to the commotion down the hall, but Tiberia sure does and drags me across the stone floors to investigate.

We reach the entrance to the kitchen, where I use the doorframe as leverage to brace myself from her pulling. Tiberia whines at the raised voices, wanting to dive into the mix. I peek around the corner to see Rosa and another woman running from the sink with wet towels to hunch over something on the floor.

I pause, debating how I can help them with the wild beast nearly ripping out my arms by her lunging and howling. The shouting gets louder until one lady I haven't seen before glances at me. I immediately frown. She yells something at me and makes shooing motions.

Tightening the leash on Tiberia, I creep into the kitchen to peer around the cabinetry to see Maria on the floor, sobbing, her forearm bright red, blistering, and burned. How did this happen?

"She needs a hospital," I blurt out, seeing two more unknown women bustle into the room with an older gentleman carrying a black bag. He is tall and thin, with a long, crooked nose and black rectangular glasses. His hair receded long ago, leaving stray strands flying across his aged skin.

When our eyes meet, I gasp.

I know him.

"How long?" Maximiliano paced the edge of the bed.

"Weeks," the doctor clipped when he drew a clear liquid from a small glass bottle with a syringe.

He was here with me. Maximiliano was here. But where was I? I felt so heavy, so very, very tired. I fought to stay awake, to listen.

Maximiliano grunted and glared at me while the man jabbed the needle into my skin. "I move her to the coast."

The man straightened, discarded the syringe in a black bag, and rubbed his forehead. "She shouldn't be transported. She needs to recover, rest, and heal from that beating she received. She will continue to need medical treatment."

"You come too. She's going home with me tomorrow."

Whatever he pricked me with hit like a ton of bricks, and I couldn't hear them. I blinked away the heaviness of my eyelids, which made it harder to stay awake and easier to close them. My ears listened, and home hummed through my consciousness until I succumbed to the beckoning sleep.

He knows me.

He was in America and treated me before I came here. He is an American. Oh my God, he can help me. *He* can help *me* get back to the States.

He rattles off commands to the ladies helping Maria, goes through the same motions with the bottle and syringe, and jabs her arm like my recovered memories. It takes seconds for her to fall limp beside him, and in quiet fascination and horror, I watch how fast the drugs work.

He did that to me.

That's how it happened.

One minute I'm getting beaten to a pulp by the dragon, and the next, I am here. All against my will. If that isn't like being doused with cold water, I don't want to know what is, and I tremble.

What else did he do to me? Was Maximiliano present every time? Or was I alone with this man? Utterly helpless, drugged, and vulnerable to whatever "treatment" he deemed necessary?

The more questions fall into my brain, the harder I shake until my teeth chatter.

"You smell."

I almost jump out of my skin, and Tiberia whirls around to growl at Carlos.

"Huh?"

"You both do."

I heard him both times, but I am still processing the man in the glasses.

"Come on, go upstairs," Carlos says from behind me, and like a train wreck, I can't look away even if I am horrified at what I am witnessing. "You're cold and wet and dripping all over the floor." He bumps my back, and I realize he's trying to take the leash wrapped around my hands.

I acknowledge him with a slight nod and am relieved that he will take Tiberia back with me. Careful not to slip on the tile floor, I tiptoe across the room before locking eyes with the guy again.

What did he do to me?

My actions don't go unnoticed. The man narrows his gaze when my hands sweep up and down my arms to rub my goosebumps and soothe my nerves. By the time I leave the room, I'm holding myself as tightly as possible.

"What's happening?"

"I don't know." I didn't see what exactly happened to Maria.

"You don't know what is happening with yourself?" He casts a curious glance, and I am unsure if I should tell him.

"Can I trust you? I mean, really trust you?"

"Never trust anyone."

"Oh."

I study his face to see if he is serious, and I take it seriously when he doesn't expound on it. I notice he's taking his time walking back, and I would usually hate it, but being alone in my room with that man in the house makes me uneasy.

"You really do smell."

"I know."

"Are you okay? You seem off."

I sigh. I am off. I can't trust him, so I can't tell him about the man. Then again, I need time to think about him to see if I can remember anything else.

"I'm fine."

I feel his gaze on me while I look ahead, feigning interest in the oil canvas hanging on the wall.

"Is it what happened earlier?"

It's a tough question to answer since I lost my dog and saw the man that kept sticking me with needles. "What happened earlier?"

He hesitates, his lips pursing for a second. "About rape and babysitting your dog."

I stop in the middle of the hallway. "No, you were right. There are horrible things like that happening every day, unfortunately. I needed that reminder. I am babysitting a dog, nothing more." I don't want to say it's because I don't want to be here. I've said it many times, and it doesn't matter how I feel. If I want it to change, I must figure it out on my own. He said he is not to be trusted, so why say more?

"Okay."

With nothing more to say, I walk until I see my door at the end of the hall.

"Look, I'd imagine this has to be hard on you," he says with a hint of sympathy. "Clearly, you are not used to this kind of life."

Kingpin, cartel, guns, violence, kidnapping, drugged, and a prisoner. Nope, not the life I lived in Los Angeles.

"Not even close."

"Try to make the best of it."

If this is his best chin up speech, I am correct in not trusting him. He is terrible at helping people.

"Thanks."

I push open my door and take the leash from him. He lingers a bit, looking as if he wants to say more, but I don't. I want to clean up and be alone with my thoughts.

Wordlessly, he watches me cross the threshold and close the door in his face.

Chapter 23

Locking the bedroom door, I call her into the bathroom and lock that door too. Behind two locks, I sigh in relief, knowing I am safe from that doctor guy. The memory of two locked doors hits me.

"Señorita. I have key."

"P-Please . . . n-no."

My body shook violently, and hot tears blazed down my face. I locked both doors, and I was still not safe.

"I no hurt you. It mistake."

"W-where's W-Will . . . A-Ardy?"

"We're here, darling. You can come out. It's fine. You're safe." *Will's voice was tight. His casual drawl was clipped, and I didn't believe him.*

"A-Ardy?"

"I'm here, kid."

Ardy was always the serious one and told me things I didn't want to hear, like the truth. Will sugarcoated things or omitted essential facts. Most of the time, I liked that about him. Not this time. I needed the harshness of Ardy.

"Why the guns?"

There was a long pause and a whispered exchange in Spanish between His Royal Highness and Ardy.

"For protection, similar to you."

"We're nothing alike. He and I are nothing alike," I sobbed. "Ardy, you don't carry guns and point them at people."

I heard another whispered exchange and then Will. "Ginger, of course, we carry guns. You've never seen them. They heard you screaming and thought you were being hurt. They were trying to protect you."

I loosened my arms, tucked my legs under me, and rested my back against the cool porcelain tub.

"Then why did his men point them at you and Ardy? What did Ardy say in Spanish?"

"Señorita, I use key. We talk without door."

"No! Only Ardy can come in."

More whispered words in both languages, and the door opened with Ardy charging through it. I cried in relief that neither he nor Will were hurt. I climbed out of the tub and launched myself at Ardy, grateful and happy that they were okay. His Royal Highness tried to barge into the tiny bathroom when Will pulled him back.

"I got you. You're safe." Ardy stroked my back like a baby, and I usually hated it. This time, I needed it. "This was a misunderstanding, okay? They heard you scream, and here comes the calvary."

"Are you lying?"

He never does.

"No, kid. I'm not. You're jumping to conclusions like you always do."

Ardy wasn't wrong in that I used to jump to conclusions. However, he wasn't entirely truthful about the situation either. Sure, they came running at that moment because I was hanging on Maximiliano's back, trying to hold him back when I thought he would beat Will. A complete misunderstanding.

Maxie saw Will shirtless and getting ready when I was in his room. He thought we were intimate after he banned it in his house. Granted, his protection thought I was attacking him, but I thought he was going to attack Will. I didn't have the foggiest clue what

Maxie's guys were protecting. I wouldn't dare those antics now. I'm not young, dumb, and naïve.

I twist the knobs to get the bathwater going and mentally prepare myself for a wrestling match with Tiberia. When I call her name, and she calmly walks over to clear the side of the tub, I nearly faint.

"Good girl!" My voice rises into a cartoon character cadence as I continue to praise her. "You're so good. Who's my pretty girl? Who?"

I wash her woolly fur, which is exhausting when I pour too much shampoo on her. It takes forever to get out and continues filling the tub with dirty suds. After several rounds of rinsing her off with fur-coated hands, she shakes aggressively, sending water everywhere.

"This was such a bad idea to wash you here."

All future baths will have to be outside, in the courtyard, even if that man is around. By the time she is done, I am wetter from her bath than from the beach. I grab towels to lie on the floor and then whistle for her to jump over the edge and into the open towel. She nearly knocks me over with the aggressiveness of her happiness as she buries her face in the cloth.

"You're so cute. Wild and cute." The more I baby talk to her, the more excited she gets and her wagging tail smears water across the wall. I feverishly rub her coat. Her energy is amping up, whirling around, nipping, and barking.

Pretty soon, she has me laughing at her antics, and it feels natural and normal like we are anywhere but here. For the first time since this ordeal started, I am laughing so hard my cheeks hurt, and it's bliss.

I don't care that I am soaked, hair sticking to my face with dog hair in my mouth. I don't care that the bathroom is messy and the bathtub is clogged with her fur. I feel a lightness coming from the bond I am forming with her again, and it is wonderful. A broken piece of my heart knits back together from the lovely spirit occupying this woolly mammoth. I kiss her on her head and am swiftly met with a long tongue across my face. It makes me laugh even more.

I bring you something to love.

And he did. I will never say this to him, but "Thank you." I throw my arms around her and give her the tightest hug she can stand. "Thank you for this beautifully silly girl."

She lets out a long whine, and I chuckle. She is not one to cuddle. Being left with him for the last five years would make anyone anti-cuddle.

I rise from my kneeling position to let her out of the bathroom, and a whoosh of cool air floods in. If I weren't living in such a dangerous place, I'd leave the bathroom door open. However, I am unwilling to take that risk.

Shutting and locking the door again, I work on pulling clumps of her fur out of the drain before rinsing the tub of the grit and sand. Once it is clean, I strip and take a long shower, letting the hot water pound into my fatigued muscles. I hadn't sprinted or exercised since I have been here, and the achiness can attest to that.

The freedom of going to the beach was bliss. Sitting on the sand, feeling the cold water on my feet compared to watching it from the terrace, was everything. Thinking back to how I begged at his feet for the veranda fills me with anger and resentment.

Anger at him for making me feel desperate enough to grovel. And resentment for lowering myself to him. From this day forward, I will never grovel or embarrass myself again. Add that to my plan.

As delightful as the hot shower feels, I hurry to finish so I can get downstairs to help in the kitchen since they will be shorthanded with Maria out. Once dressed in fresh clothes, I tuck the little dictionary in the back pocket of my shorts and wind Tiberia's leash around my hands before leaving. The walk to the kitchen is fast with my newfound motivation.

When I round the corner into the kitchen, I nearly stumble over Tiberia when I see Maria. Her arm is wrapped from wrist to elbow in white bandages, chopping slowly with her face grimacing in pain.

"Why are you here?" I say when four sets of eyes swing in my direction. "Oh, wait . . ." I wind the leash around my waist and tie it tight, so Tiberia can't drag me around. I pull out my dictionary and start stumbling through the words to ask what I said in English.

Either I did a terrible job, or no one wants to answer because the room is silent. After a few moments, the ladies return to work, except for Maria. Her gaze lingers on me. I flip through my book to start again. "I can help," I mutter in my language while looking for it in theirs.

"What are you doing down here?" Carlos grumbles from behind me. His expression sours as he takes in the book.

"Oh yeah, you're here," I say sarcastically to match his tone while closing my book. "Why is she here? Why isn't she at the hospital?"

"How's that any business of yours?" His hand rests on the top of his gun, and I wonder if that's a warning or something he does subconsciously. His switch-up is crazy because he was so nice to me earlier.

"Because she's hurt and needs medical attention." I throw my hand up in frustration since it's rephrasing my question.

"Again, how's that any business of yours?"

"Carlos, can you please answer my question?" I point my finger at him for emphasis.

"Why is the dog tied to your waist? That's not how I showed you." He moves forward.

"Don't worry about it. Look, I want to help her. I'm an able body, bored out of my skull, and want to help." Her eyes snap down to cut the vegetables, but the pain is all over her face.

He sighs. "If you do it, she won't get paid."

"Wait, what?" I'm stunned. "He pays them to be here? Not indentured servants working off a drug debt or something?" I shake my head in disbelief. Who would want to work here? For *HIM*?

"You're an idiot. You know that?"

Tiberia lets out a long whine, and I know she probably needs to pee, but I can't wrap my brain around being here of their own free will and being paid to work for him.

"Take your dog out." He takes a step to walk past me when I

grab his arm. He has me against the wall, his forearm across my chest and Tiberia's sandwiched behind me before I can even think.

"Holy shit." I stare at him.

"Never touch me again," he says in such a deadly voice that I nearly pee myself. It is astonishing how fast he pinned me. Not hurting me, but I couldn't move if I wanted.

"Okay."

He pauses, and I nod. Don't mess with Carlos. I get it loud and crystal clear.

"Go. Get out of here." He steps back, and everything is back to normal for him. Not for me. I knew we weren't friends, but damn, I didn't expect that. Never mind, my pulse thumping in my throat. I cautiously unravel the rope from my waist and wind it around my hands to follow his command.

When I exit the kitchen, I hear Carlos and one of the ladies conversing, unable to decipher any words because they are speaking way too fast. Golden sunlight is pouring through the large windows that run the length of the hallway, and it's relatively peaceful. The dark sky from this morning must have cleared.

Through the door, down the path, and past the boardwalk, she searches for the best spot and goes to the bathroom. I study the fortress, how high the walls are, the slope of the tiled roof, and wonder where my veranda is located. After doing her business, she kicks at the sand like male dogs do and then trots ahead of me.

"Let's go exploring, shall we?" I ask Tiberia and follow her lead. The path to the beach is carefully constructed of flagstone and a wooden boardwalk. Beyond the path is where the wind blew the sand into a ridge of dunes. Native grass grows at the top of the ridge with sticks and seaweed dotting the bottom.

Tiberia is as interested in exploring as I am. I slip the chain off her neck and watch her take off over the ridge. She marks her territory twice, and then I see it, the only balcony on this side.

The rocks were intentionally placed. Enormous boulders that were shaped by the tide, sand, and wind over time. Three elements too hard for the stones to contend with. From this angle, they are rough and ragged, jagged and misshaped into sharp points stretching to the balcony. It is not impossible to climb, but it will be tricky without the right shoes.

A long whistle cuts through the wind, causing Tiberia's head to rise from the driftwood. She drops a stick from her mouth to sniff the air and then jogs toward the boardwalk.

The sun is dipping low on the horizon, painting the sky a gorgeous pink, purple, and orange. I admire the beauty while we walk around the ridge when I see Carlos standing at its beginning. I take a mental picture of the pastel sky, hoping to see another beautiful sunset tomorrow.

Mr. I-trained-dogs-in-the-military catches Tiberia when she barrels toward him. His scowl is unmistakable, and I smile. It's the least I could do for what he did inside. As expected, he grabs her scruff, gets her under control, and completely ignores her happy howls for being momentarily free.

"Never do that again."

Always with the orders. Do this, don't do that. Am I in the military?

"Yes, sir." I snap my hand into a salute, and his face darkens. It is not as funny to him as it is to me.

"Cut that crap out." He thrusts his hand out, demanding the leash from me. I stop short, standing too far away to give it. I don't know why I am starting shit with him right now. Maybe it is because he's the only one who speaks English, or because he smiled at my joke and said I was funny, or because I don't think he'll hurt me, even if I piss him off. "Give it to me."

"Are you okay?" Asking him the same way he asked me a while ago. "You seem mad, even before I made you mad." I tuck my curls behind my ears to keep them out of my face.

"Nothing I can't handle." He takes two steps to yank the leash out of my hand.

"Well, hang in there, champ." I give him a pretend fist pump to his arm since touching him is way off-limits. It's lame, but so was his keep your chin up comment.

He slides the chain over her head and hands me the leash once it is in the proper position on her neck. I don't bother saying thanks because he didn't help me out. He killed our fun. He trails behind us, not inclined to talk to me either. That's fine.

We walk from the beach to the path. Once on it, I tie her leash around my waist and stoop to clear the sand out of my flip-flops.

"Why are you out here, anyway? I thought you had bad guy stuff to do?"

"I came to tell you that you can help Maria," he says, content to watch me get sand out of my toes. "You'll need to wash your hands before you help, though."

"Clearly," I grunt, putting them back on before standing upright. "Thanks for explaining it to them. I brought my book along." I pat my back pocket, and his eyes fall to my butt again. "Ya know, to help."

"It's good that you are trying," he says, snapping his eyes back to mine.

Wait, did he say something nice to me rather than bark orders? This switch-up is a real problem of his.

"To be honest, I should already know it. My mom is fluent in Spanish. She tried to teach me, but I didn't listen or care to learn. I miss her, and talking about her makes being here harder." I shrug, walking up the path with Tiberia in between us. "One of many regrets. So many now."

"We all have regrets." His anger from before has dissipated, and his tone sounds almost regretful.

"Yeah, I suppose. When I die, I don't want to have any regrets. I want to have done it all, seen it all, and tried it all. I mean, sure, I regret this place, but if I undo it, I undo the rescue, and that's not an option. Not that anyone's life is more important than the other, but did you know there was a little girl in our group? A little girl?" I scowl with disgust. "It's sick." Mary's fearful face flashes through my mind, and I close my eyes for a moment to say a brief prayer for her wellbeing.

"The worst of humanity."

"What those poor girls have been through, it's horrific and unimaginable." I shudder, thinking back to the night of their rescue—the wretched smell of their dungeon cells. I shake my head, refusing to be transported back to that night.

"You can't unsee it. Can't unhear it. You're left to live with it. Somehow carry on as normal when what you have experienced is the exact opposite of normal." His chestnut eyes hold so much pain that I want to comfort him when they meet mine.

I slowly reach my hand out, ensuring he sees it coming before touching his forearm. When my fingertips graze his skin, his muscles flex and then relax as if willing himself to endure it. "I don't know what you have been through, but it sounds like it's the worst of humanity. I can't pretend to understand, but I'll listen if you want to talk." I've listened to many women survive horrible abuses and life situations. These experiences taught me that most people need a listening ear and a compassionate heart. Carlos might need the same.

He says nothing. Doesn't look at me. He simply moves his arm away and clears his throat before opening the courtyard door.

I understand completely. He might tell me, and he might never. Vulnerability is hard. Trust is even harder.

A somber tension hangs over the kitchen, and I take a deep breath with a wordless Carlos beside me. There is no chatter among the ladies. All have their heads lowered, working in silence. Tonight is different.

"I'll leave you to it," Carlos mutters when passing me to exit the opposite side of the kitchen.

Tiberia lets out a long whine, and I remove her leash to collect her food bowl, fill it, and place it beside her empty water bowl. She digs in immediately while I refill her bowl from the faucet. Once she's set for dinner, I pull out my dictionary and stand in front of

Maria. With curiosity, she stops dicing the carrots and puts down her knife.

"Can . . . I . . . help?" I thumb through the pages to put it all together. She hesitates, looking over her shoulder at Rosa. "I can . . . cut." I make a cutting motion and then stop because I'm an idiot. They know what I am trying to say.

Rosa responds way too fast for me to understand, but I smile when Maria pushes the butcher block toward me. I quickly run to wash my hands before she passes me the knife and walks away. Although I am not as fast, I mimic how she cuts the carrots. I thought I would be helpful until I saw her walk back with another board and knife to continue cutting at twice my speed. I frown.

I'm not a master chef like these ladies, but I keep trying. I settle into a pattern, cutting the carrots like her, sweeping them over the edge into an awaiting dish, and starting again. Carrots turn into celery, turn into potatoes. Each time, I watch her first and then copy her actions. I pick up speed, and pretty soon, one of the ladies is humming. It's quietly comforting to be productive and not alone. Even Tiberia is calm, lying on her side, asleep underneath the table.

Occasionally, I blow my curls out of my face. They are a wild mess from getting whipped around by the ocean breeze and left to air dry, not to mention the humid kitchen adding to the frizziness. The lady kneading dough rips a dishrag in half, twirls it into a headband, and hands it to me. I thank her and put it on, securing the knot at the top. It looks cute when I catch my reflection in the silver ovens.

After messing with my hair, I rewash my hands and stop to admire the ornate sugar cookies she is piping with a pastry bag.

"Bonito." I point to them, and she smiles. I want to say more, but I already feel I am intruding on their group. Even if I think of it as helping, it doesn't mean they consider it as helping.

I return to my station, waiting for my next task since Maria has nothing for me to cut. She's bringing over an enormous pot and slams it on the counter with a loud clang that wakes Tiberia. She mutters something, and then I realize it's too heavy because of her pain. She dumps her vegetables in, so I follow, and when I see her struggle with the weight of the handles, I move to her side. Between a few words and mostly hand gestures, I move it to the stove and realize we are making soup.

We continue for a good while, her teaching me to shuck corn and me being terrible at it. This lady has the patience of a saint because, after taking nearly forever with each task, we finally have it on the fire and cooking.

The kitchen grows hotter, and all I can think of is needing a break, eating dinner, and getting off my feet. Yet, they keep going, working from one prep to another without pausing or even chatting often. I took these ladies for granted because working in the kitchen is hard work.

I wipe away the sweat and dive back in, mainly using hand motions instead of pulling out my book each time, and we muddle through. The hours pass with steaming dishes of soup, meats, potatoes, and other vegetables streaming out of the kitchen down another hall to return empty again. I never noticed the entrance tucked into the kitchen corner, but I assumed it led to his men, which is the last place I want to go. When I'm nearly dead on my feet with my sweaty clothes stuck to my back, Maria pushes a bowl of steaming soup in front of me. I beam at her.

She motions for me to sit at the table, and I thank her profusely. Tiberia jumps to her feet to smell the delicious aroma and sits beside me to beg. Crispy bread, followed by a small portion of meat and veggies, is placed on the table for me, and my stomach growls loudly.

Pulling out my book, I read through different words and sound them out between bites. Tiberia bumps my arm when it's time to share, and this is another thing that feels almost normal and something that would occur back home.

Chapter 24

"You're smiling."

I see Carlos, his green T-shirt plastered to his chest with massive sweat rings around his neck and armpits. I raise my eyebrows in curiosity. "Yeah, I guess I am."

"It was good?" He catches the sweat running down his temple with the palm of his hand.

It was great. I was productive and useful.

"Yes, they were very patient with me. Thank you for arranging it." I smile because I have a favor to ask him. "Can you ask them if I can help every day?"

His eyes narrow to the book in hand. "Ask them yourself."

He's right. I will only improve if I am forced to speak for myself.

"Why are you hot and sweaty?" His eyebrows dart up, and I realize that sounds a little sexual, although that's the last thing on my mind. "You know what I mean."

"I do."

"So?"

I motion with my hand for him to continue, and he pulls out the chair to sit across from me. He rips off a corner of my bread and drags it through the gravy as casual as if we were dating and used to eating off each other's plate.

"I went for a run." Tiberia shifts toward him to beg, and he snaps his fingers, pointing to the floor. "Down." Dammit, if that dog doesn't slither to the floor on his command. Traitor.

I lean over to see him wearing his uniform boots, which are not conducive to running. Plus, it's dark outside. "Um, you ran in combat boots?"

"Yes."

"You're not in the military anymore, so why not switch to running shoes?"

"Does it look like I have running shoes at this place you call . . . what did you call it again?" He leans his chair back on two legs and says something to one of the ladies that includes the word agua before moving my plate in front of him and finishing my food.

"Hellhole. You shouldn't eat after people. It's not sanitary."

"Why you got something?" His fork pauses midair to look at me.

"No."

"Then it's fine." He shoves the fork into his mouth.

"I thought you had eaten already. You said it was good."

"It was and is. You're done, and we don't let good food go to waste around here." He points to my bowl. I look away, thinking about all the platters of uneaten food all those weeks when I was locked in my room. That was a lot of waste.

Then it dawns on me.

"How long have you been here?"

His eyes raise to mine.

"Why?"

"Just answer the question. You seem to answer every third one I ask." I lean back in my chair, slouching to relieve my achy back.

"Wrong. I answer the ones I think are pertinent. Most are not, so I throw in a few out of pity." He guzzles the two glasses brought to him and motions for more. It irritates me how he treats them like they are at his beck and call. I can't decide if it's a male thing or a job ranking.

I sigh loudly but don't relent because I want to know. "Well, consider this a pity answer."

He stretches his long legs, bumping Tiberia and forcing her to take over my floor space. I sit cross-legged and drink the last of my water.

"I came with the dog."

"Hmm." I look at the grain of the table. He wasn't here, so he wouldn't know about the doctor or what he could have done to me. He also wouldn't know about the dragon, what he did to me in the States, or the undergarments here.

"Why?"

His question breaks my concentration. I raise my hand in a hopeless gesture because if he weren't here, he wouldn't know, and he's my only hope for answers.

A kitchen lady brings another round of everything for him, including the soup, and I perk up because I'm proud to say I helped make it.

"I helped make the soup. It is great." He sets it aside. "Too hot?"

"You probably poisoned it," he says with a serious tone, and I open my mouth to defend myself when he continues, "Answer me, why?"

My lips twitch, debating how much I trust him, and the answer in my mind is swift. Not at all.

"Doesn't matter."

"You say that more often than you mean it." He breaks the bread into pieces and throws all of it into the soup.

"You're ruining the soup. Who does that?" I protest, leaning forward to save it, and he slides the bowl out of my reach. "Well, don't waste it."

"I won't. Now answer me." He hits my chair with his boot, startling me, and I frown.

"Stop it."

He does it again and again until I explode.

"Fine! You're so annoying." I shove myself away from the table. He's unfazed and continues eating.

"I . . . I don't know." I am nervous to tell him because what if he blows me off like he has been doing? Then I'm still back at square one and feeling dumb for trusting him enough to ask. "That guy, the one with the black bag, is he a doctor or something?"

He pauses, angling his face to look around the room, and my eyes follow. Maria and Rosa are gone, and the other two ladies that I still don't know their names are washing dishes on the other side of the kitchen.

"Or something."

I immediately hate that he lowers his voice as it sends chills down my spine.

He hangs his head lower, finishing his meat and potatoes and switching it for the soggy bread bowl. The conversation dies as I watch him eat. He doesn't mind as I debate if I should ask him to come back to my room to talk or go back with Tiberia and call it a night. The day has been long and unusual, and I'm probably being paranoid from my weary mind.

"I'm beat. I'm going to take Tiberia out one last time and go to my room." I stand unexpectantly and catch him off guard. He shoots to his feet, as does Tiberia, and I stomp on the leash so she doesn't get any ideas. She's been a good girl for a long time, so she is probably ramping up to be a bad girl, or wild, or her usual husky self.

"I'll go with you." He leans over to grab her leash, and I stop him.

"That's okay. I got it." I wind her leash around my waist and tie it off, much to his dissatisfaction. My hands are achy from all the prep work. The last thing I want to do is strong-arm her outside and back in.

I'm too tired for that level of training. Plus, I want to be back in the kitchen tomorrow to help again. I glance at Tiberia's bowls, and since el diablo isn't here, I leave them on the floor for tomorrow.

"I'm going. It's dark out there."

"Suit yourself." I shrug, too exhausted to argue.

He races to finish his soup, eating it on the way to the kitchen sink while I collect the remaining dishes. The ladies are generous in taking them from me and cleaning up after us. We leave the kitchen with several "gracias" to both.

The place is tranquil as we walk down the hall, passing the long bank of courtyard windows and our reflections. Back in LA, I'd be afraid of enormous windows, for the outside shadows hold unseen threats. It's the opposite here. The threats are seen and living among us.

"Did you have a good day in the kitchen?" He pushes open the back door, and I untie the leash to release Tiberia so she can find her spot.

As we walk down the boardwalk, I slip off my flip-flops to hold in my hand.

"I did. I don't know how to cook, and my forearms are aching from chopping, not to mention standing all day. Props to those ladies. Working in the kitchen is way harder than I thought."

"You can't cook?"

"Nope." I chuckle at the surprise in his voice. Tiberia kicks at the sand, showing she is done, and when I turn to go back in, he doesn't. "What?"

"Do you want to go for a walk?"

"This late?"

I want to go to bed, yet something about the way he asked keeps me here.

"You're right. Let's go in."

He dismisses me too quickly and starts toward the courtyard. I would grab his arm, but he wouldn't see it coming, and I don't need to end up in a chokehold.

"Ya know what? Why not? It's not like I have a bedtime." I deposit my flip-flops and leash on the boardwalk's edge and step onto the beach.

Tiberia walks closest to the water, stopping to smell a piece of driftwood that has washed ashore. The moon is bright, illuminating the sand as we walk in the opposite direction of the dunes.

"I can cook," he says finally.

"Really? Where did you learn?" I pick up a piece of wood and play keep-away with Tiberia.

"In-country. We had a couple of skilled cooks in the service, and I learned from them. The time can get long over there. Your mom didn't teach you?"

I frown and throw the stick down the beach. Tiberia sprints to retrieve it. "No. Mom was always working to make ends meet. When I was in high school, she worked two jobs until she got sick."

"And your dad?"

"I don't know him. He split when I was like two or three. No memory of him at all." I watch Tiberia toss the stick in the air and then pounce on it. She's so cute.

"That's rough."

"I guess. I used to think about him a lot. What kind of man leaves his kid? Then again, I can't imagine my life with another parent. I used to hate him, not only for what he did but for what he didn't do." It feels strange talking about this after so many years.

"What didn't he do?"

"He didn't take me to father-daughter dances or take me for donuts on Saturday mornings. He didn't teach me how to ride a bike or drive a car. Didn't threaten boys that wanted to date me. I used to be jealous of my friends and their perfect families and wondered what it was like to have two loving parents." I pause, surprised at how these repressed emotions are coming up here and now. "Sorry, I don't know why I am dredging up the past like this."

I stop because we are walking further into the darkness, and it's making me uncomfortable.

"I understand. People are disappointing." He turns to face me.

"They are. I was raised to do the right thing at all costs, and it's tough. But then, other people come along and ruin it. Can we walk back now?"

"Did I upset you or something?"

I walk back, and he falls in line with me.

"No. You got me thinking, that's all." I shrug, unsure why I am spilling my guts to him. It must be my period. It always makes me melancholy and dwell on things from my graveyard of memories.

Tiberia drops her stick at my feet, and I toss it again, watching her fluffy tail bat the air as she runs.

"About your dad?"

"Sort of. Mom and I are close. No one is closer to me than her, and I love her more than life. But when I get married, I want a big family. I want Sunday dinners where everyone complains about going but enjoys being there. I want a loud and chaotic Christmas with too many gifts to fit under the tree. I want to be stressed out at Thanksgiving about how much food I must make and if I have enough chairs. Stuff like that." I gaze over at him, the moonlit casting shadows on his face.

"I get it."

"You probably think it's stupid."

"Not at all. I think I'd like something similar," he replies with such a serious tone that I wonder about his past.

We walk back in silence, each lost in our thoughts. I dust off my feet when we reach the boardwalk and slip on my flip-flops. Carlos whistles to Tiberia, and her head pops up to see where we are at before running over. She's a good girl while I put her chain on. The silence continues when he opens the back door and walks me back to my room. It's comfortable and not awkward.

"Thanks for walking us back."

He doesn't respond, and I'm not sure he even heard me when he pushes open my door and walks in.

"Whoa, what are you doing?" I barely cross the threshold when I see him rattling the veranda doors before crossing the room to check the bathroom.

He squats to look under my bed. "Always check the premises.

You've been out of this room a long time. Never know what could be waiting for you." His explanation causes me to see it in a new light.

"Well, that's unnerving." The room I considered a prison cell could actually be a threat. "Um, I know some defensive moves. I mean, I'm a little rusty at using them."

He stands, his head barely clearing the wood beam that travels the center of the ceiling. "Good, we'll start brushing up on those tomorrow."

I lean against the door, wanting to ask him three different things simultaneously, but settle on the most important one. "With the boss man gone, do you think it's safe for me to be here?"

His expression darkens. "What did I tell you earlier? Never trust anyone."

As if that's an answer at all. "Carlos, seriously."

He steps toward me, seeming to make a point of looming over me with his large stature. "Could you take me? If I were to attack you right now, what would happen?"

"Tiberia would defend me."

"Wrong. One bullet, she's done. Then it's you and me." He stands so close that I have to look up. Even Tiberia is uncomfortable and wedges her body between us.

"I run like hell. I'm faster than you."

"Possibly. But if your hair is in a ponytail, it becomes a handle to drag you back. If you waltz in here without checking and close the door, it's over."

I chew my lip. He's right. I was already beaten unconscious. "Damn."

"Precisely." He steps back to a respectable distance, and I exhale.

"So, you *do* think it's dangerous for me here?" I need confirmation after arguing this with Maximiliano. He nudges me away from the door to close it firmly.

"Depends on how loyal a man is to Mr. Maldonado." He lowers his voice as if someone is listening.

I frown. The dragon didn't seem very loyal, and nothing happened to him.

"Loyal as in?" I untie Tiberia's leash from my waist, slipping the chain over her head, and she shakes out her mane.

"Money. He'll be loyal if he needs the money until someone offers him more. The more is where you worry."

"Lovely." I collapse on my bed, another thing to worry about. "And you? Are you loyal, or are you more?" I may have gone too far with that question, but I need to know what I am up against.

"I'm loyal for now. But we're always looking for the more, especially if you support more than yourself."

I don't know what to say. This little conversation has been more than eye-opening. Don't trust anyone. Don't trust him. Anyone I trust can flip on me anytime for the right price. That's enough. Far too much to think about at this late hour.

"It's getting late." I pat the bed for Tiberia to join me.

He observes us for a few seconds, looking as if he wants to say more. Instead, he grabs the door handle to ease it open before tapping on the door frame. "Come lock this."

"I will." Not moving from my spot.

"I'll see you in the morning."

I'm so tired from this day, and my head is swimming with so much information. It's all I can do to lock the door and fall back into bed.

Chapter 25

It's too hot. I'm cooking under these covers from her furry body pressed into my side. I flip back the bedding, and she stretches with a noisy yawn.

"Glad one of us got some sleep."

I quickly shower and get ready, deciding to wear tennis shoes for better support today. Once I open the bathroom door, Tiberia stands on the bed waiting for me. Swiping the leash from the bureau, I put the chain over her head and give her a few kisses. She's so sweet and beautiful. I hope today goes better for both of us.

After pulling back my hair with the dishrag from yesterday, I stuff the dictionary in my pocket and bound out the door to see Carlos walking down the hall.

"I didn't expect to see you this early."

"I told you we'd brush up on your self-defense training. Did you forget?"

He looks like a Marine today in his tight green T-shirt and green camo pants over his usual combat boots. Not sure why he brought his gun if we are working out, but I assume he's required to carry it.

"I didn't but figured it would be later, so I could work in the kitchen." Tiberia's wiggly body bumps Carlos. I swear she has a crush on him.

"Let's do it now. You're taking her out, and we can work out there."

"Fine."

"We'll need to warm up and stretch first. Have you worked out before?" I'm surprised he is asking. He must not know about my skateboarding past.

"Yes, I worked out, even had a routine," I answer, smiling at the carpet.

"Willlll, my legs already kill from skating all day, remember?" I *groaned and sunk deeper into the squat.*

"This prevents injury." He did two squats in the time I did one. It was ridiculous how fanatical he was about fitness. "And last time I checked, you got injured. Go lower."

I wanted to punch the smirk off his face. "I can't go lower. It makes me feel like I'm going to pee myself."

"Good, that's where you should be." He showed off by squatting to the ground. "You'll thank me later for whipping your lazy ass into shape."

"I am in shape." I attempted to squat lower and fell on my butt. "What does it matter, anyway? I don't need to learn these exercises. I'm never going to use them."

"Get off your butt, Ginger, and finish your set. We're working upper after this." He did a bazillion more, and I watched. It was impressive, but I had zero desire to be like him. "Trust me, you'll use them down the line. Maybe not now, but sometime over the course of your miserable life, when you are not in shape, you'll remember this hot, sexy trainer teaching you the basics."

"Stop calling me Ginger."

"You must have liked it then," Carlos says, pulling me back to reality.

An odd thing to say. "Why do you say that?"

"Because you smiled."

We jog downstairs, Tiberia almost knocking me over at how fast she takes them. My hand skims the railing as a precaution.

"I was smiling about the trainer." My heart aches because he's no longer part of my life.

Carlos adjusts his posture and pushes his shoulders back as if I suddenly challenged his masculinity. "You dated?"

I burst out laughing, catching him off guard. My hand covers my mouth, which proves unable to block the sound. "Sorry, I'm not laughing at you, but no. If you saw us together, you'd think we were brother and sister. We bicker like the best of them." I chuckle again. Will was a good guy.

"I misunderstood." He raises his chin as if satisfied by my answer.

We enter the kitchen, and it is early because Rosa and her helper are putting on their aprons. Good. Plenty of time to practice with him and then work with her.

Breezing through the courtyard and down the path, I let Tiberia off the leash to run and be free. She's been such a good girl, and now that I know she'll come back, I don't worry.

"What are you doing?" He frowns deeply as she races off, claws ripping into the wet sand. She yaps as she runs, chasing after a flock of seagulls. "You shouldn't have let her off."

"Nah, she likes to roam. This is a prison for her, you know." I drop her leash and my dictionary on the boardwalk and watch her sprint the coast until she's a white speck on the horizon.

"You should stop calling it a prison or hellhole. Not good for your psyche. You might call it home."

I blink. I must have hallucinated or something because I didn't hear him right. "Home? Are you crazy? This will never be home. I'll keep my choice of words because they match my psyche just fine." I shake my head in disbelief. I will never call this place my home. That's way too permanent. For my sanity, I frame this as temporary. If I think about permanent, I'll plummet back into depression.

This reminds me that I need to recheck the dunes. Figure out if there is a way to escape on that side of the fortress.

"Just saying it helped me reframe things when I was in a tough place." He removes his holster, gun, and two knives from his pockets to drop beside her leash.

I consider it for a second and then decide he is still wrong. "All right, Captain, show me what you got."

"You are mixing your ranks. I was a Staff Sergeant. Watch me and follow."

"Okay." He's intriguing, and I want to know more. "How many years were you in?"

"Ten. Now let's warm up."

I don't know if I hit a nerve or not. It's hard to tell with him. Sometimes he is open. Other times, he's not. It's confusing.

He starts by running on the beach, and I hate it. The sand is slippery and heavy, trapping my shoes in it.

"I don't like this. It's making my thighs burn."

My scrawny quads are fatigued already.

"Good."

I'm glad the sun is barely over the horizon because this would be truly miserable if it were higher. "So, you retired from the military?" I try again, testing to see if he'll answer.

"Medical discharge."

"What happened?"

I need him to talk to distract me from the sweat pooling in my crevices.

"Ambushed when trying to clear a building. Surgery in Germany, stateside after that." His answers are brief and efficient. No emotion on his face or in his voice. It sounds rehearsed as if he's told this story a thousand times.

"And you're better now? Healed?"

A haunting expression flashes over his face as he gazes at the coastline. "Sure." His words indicate he is not.

"You must have been glad to be back." I try to smooth over my last question since it hit a sore spot.

"I was going to be career military." There is an inflection of anger in his voice, and I suddenly feel like I'm being too intrusive. My approach sounds like rapid-fire questioning, and I don't like it.

"Oh." I don't ask any more questions.

It's clear how much he runs this beach because he's not huffing and puffing like I am. He drops to do push-ups when I fall to my knees from leg cramps.

I marvel at the speed and fluidity at which he does them. Watching the hard plank of his body pumping up and down is getting me flushed and piquing my curiosity about other things that pump up and down. My gaze falls to his tight back and clenched buttocks, probably carved in muscle underneath his soaked clothes.

"You're supposed to be doing them too." He looks up, and I look at the ocean to hide my embarrassment at being caught thinking naughty thoughts.

Reluctantly, I sink to the sand. "This is still the warm-up? My legs hurt, though." I settle into a push-up position when he frowns.

"Off your knees."

"First time a guy has ever told me that," I smirk, and he half smiles. Once again, it makes me happy. I straighten my legs and drop to do ten push-ups before sitting back on my legs. "This is harder than I remember." My poor bicep muscles are crying in pain.

He's done too many to count by now, and I drag my forearm across my forehead to stop the perspiration from falling into my eyes.

"Keep going," he says with sweat dripping off his nose. I groan, shifting to all fours and knocking out ten more before collapsing on the sand. My arms are shaking, unable to hold my weight as I suck in precious air.

"I can't push myself up anymore." I stack my hands together and rest my chin on them, content to watch him do one-arm push-ups. "You're like a machine. Aren't you tired, or are your muscles cramping?" I can feel the sting in my shoulder blades just lying here.

"No, I do three hundred a day."

"Damn, no wonder your shirt fits like a second skin." And leaves little to the imagination. It cuts every line, mountain, and valley on his chest and stomach.

He gives me a side glance. "You checking me out?"

I roll my eyes because, honestly, I am checking him out. He's ripped as hell, has a handsome but serious face, and sometimes is nice when no one else is around. Better than some of the L.A. guys, tan, plastic, and shallow. "You wish."

His half smile remains as he jumps to his feet in one fluid movement and then offers his hand to help me up. "All right, break time is over."

Once again, he yanks my arm nearly out of the socket. "Dude, you don't need to cripple me." I rotate my elbow in large circles, which makes the spot between my shoulders hurt even more.

"Don't call me dude." His expression is serious, causing me to refrain from saluting him and saying, "Yes, sir."

Brushing the sand from my clothes, I ask, "Okay then. What are we doing?"

"Show me what you know, and we'll build on that." He cracks his neck in both ways and squares his shoulders. I mimic his actions, but they don't have the same effect of intimidation as he does.

"Well, the first thing—"

"You don't tell your attacker what you will be doing. You attack. Now go." He readies his hands in front of him. Fair point.

I launch myself at him, ending up with my back pressed against his chest and my arms hugging myself. "Wait, that didn't go as planned."

"Obviously. Try again."

He releases me. I try again, and again, and again. Become sweatier, more frustrated, and angrier each time.

"Can you let me do it once?" I curl my hands in frustration, wanting to land one punch on his stupidly smug face.

"Attackers will not let you do it once. Again." He pushes me away from him, which pisses me even off more. Switching up my moves, I go at him repeatedly. Sometimes I end up flat on my back in the sand with his hand at my throat. Other times, he restrains my hands behind my back, and I can't move. But every time, he wins, and I lose.

He tells me what I am doing wrong, pushes me away, and says, "Again."

"Don't say 'again.'" I turn away with my hands resting on my hips to catch my breath. I kick the sand, sending it flying into the wind, and cuss my life.

He sneaks up behind me and whispers, "Again" in the back of my ear. I lose it, whirling around to punch him in the face when he catches my fist and twirls my arm around my body so fast that I am pinned against him again.

"This is hopeless." I'm out of breath and lean into his frame. Mr. I-do-three-hundred-push-ups-a-day can hold me up. "I'm never going to beat you."

My hair is such a frizzy mess that I can see wisps of it in my peripheral vision. My clothes are stuck to me like a second skin, and if I weren't so frustrated and physically gross, I'd be turned on by how he holds me against him.

"That's not the point. You must catch your attacker off guard or temporarily disable him long enough to escape. Your advantage is being lithe and quick." He releases me. "Again."

"Carlos."

"Sammie."

I glare at him, returning my hands to my hips. "I'm done."

"One more, and then we'll quit." He smirks and motions for me to come at him. "Come on. You know you want to get a blow in." He stoops, sticking his face out, and that's too good of an offer to resist.

"Yeah, I do." Excited at the thought of clocking his ass, I bounce side to side and try to get an advantage before I lunge at him. I attack from his left, his wide ribcage an open invitation, and my punch lands perfectly when Tiberia attacks his right. To my horror, her jaws are snapping at his arm, and she thankfully misses.

"Tiberia! No! No! No!" I try grabbing her scruff to yank her away when her head swirls on me with those snapping jaws. I jump back in fright, watching Carlos toss her away before sprinting toward the water. She races after him, narrowly missing his leg when he dives underwater.

She's pacing the shoreline, pawing the surf, and barking at the water. I run a wide circle around her, unsure if she'll try to attack me if I pass her. He hasn't surfaced yet.

Long seconds pass, and Tiberia's barking turns shrilly. Fear clenches my chest, and panic thunders in my mind. He's been under too long. Is he in trouble? I got to help him.

The shock of cold waves hit my legs, taking my breath away as I dive in after him. The water is beautifully clear, with a brown cloud ahead of me. I'm in his wake.

My legs are toast from our workout, causing me to swim slower than the terror consuming me. I will my body to swim faster and fight the waves crashing around me. The water becomes too murky, too challenging to see, and I can't find him. I surface, gasping for air.

His head bobs twenty feet away, and I look to the sky in relief when our eyes meet. I know we've just met, but if anything happened to him because of me or Tiberia, I wouldn't forgive myself.

He cuts through the waves to get to me in seconds, and I clutch at his shoulder.

"Are you okay?" My voice is shrill.

"I'm fine." He spits out water as if he went for a casual swim. His hand holds my waist, and it immediately calms my frayed nerves.

"Are you sure?" I still cannot believe what happened. "I mean her jaws . . . and she attacked you."

His expression softens with a slightly upward turn of his eyebrow. "She didn't bite me if that's what you are worried about."

I'm worried about a bunch of things, her hurting him, him drowning in this ocean, and el diablo killing Tiberia for it. So much more than a dog bite. My throat constricts with emotion.

When I glance at the shore, Tiberia is howling and pacing, avoiding the tide rolling toward her.

"You have an advantage with her." His hand tightens on my waist as the waves push us away from each other.

"I don't understand."

"She attacked me because I was attacking you." The realization hits me. "You said yesterday that she'd attack, proving your theory."

"I guess, but I didn't think she'd go after you."

"Not my first time getting attacked."

"That's why you ran into the ocean?" I tread water while clutching his shoulder.

"Yes. I only had two options, get attacked or head for the water because I knew she wouldn't follow me in."

"That's so . . . logical. Wait, are you going to tell your boss about this?" I bite my bottom lip.

"Odd question. Why?"

"He doesn't like her, and once he hears about her attacking one of his men, he'll probably kill her," I blurt out the underlining fear I always carry with me.

"Why would he go to the trouble of flying in a dog to turn around and kill it? That makes little sense." He shakes his head, and although he thinks it's foolish, Carlos doesn't know that el diablo uses everything as a pawn to control me.

"You don't know him as I do."

"What does that mean?"

I can't get into all that with him. He said not to trust anyone, that includes him. "Are you going to tell him or not?"

His eyes narrow, searching my face for answers. "No, this stays between us."

I squeeze his shoulder in response. "Thank you."

The sun is above the horizon, reflecting in the bottom half of his brown eyes. It's beautiful. His irises are half chestnut and half golden sun, causing me to drift closer. My gaze drops to his lips, watching them mumble something and smile. His face softens when he smiles, and I like it. I am drawn to it. My lips are inches from his.

I exhale in anticipation, tilt my head to align with his, and when

I look into his eyes, they mirror my desire. His breath is mine. So close, so curious. What does he kiss like? Taste like? He feels it too. The pull between us, and when his mouth descends, I close my eyes.

A frigid blast of water rolls over my head, the wave pulling me under and tossing me to the sandy ocean floor. My ears clog from the pressure, and when I open my eyes, I can't see anything but the rotation of brown particles.

The sea tumbles around me, churning silk from the ocean floor and cocooning me. The waves are merciless, gushing in and flipping me over. With no sense of up or down, if I am close to the shore or being swept out to sea, I try not to panic. Seeing the brightest patch of light in the murkiness, I swim toward it, but the force of the current is too great, towing me to the bottom of the ocean.

Stay calm.

I chant to myself. My arms are straining to cut through the water, and my legs are pushing with all my might against the undercurrent. To no avail, the water is getting darker and colder. The riptide is too much, and panic rolls through me. The harder I try, the faster I am being hauled out to sea.

I can't die like this.

My lungs seize, trying to hold in my final breaths as the dark sea exerts pressure on my body. My face stings from the gritty sand particles, and my eyes burn, trying to see in the dirty water.

Terror shatters my mind. I am going to die. I'm drowning to death. My arms and legs are flailing to save myself when something slithers around my waist and hoists me out of the darkness. When light permeates the water, I see his heavy combat boots pummeling the water and tugging us out of the swirling mess.

With the last reserve of energy, I kick with all my might until we break through the surface together. I clutch at his shoulders, gasping for air. He lifts me further out of the water and pushes my wet hair off my face.

"I got you. Breathe." Every time I inhale, a wheeze follows, tightening my lungs. "Slow, deep breaths, like this." He models it for me, and I follow his instruction. His hand splays across my back, rubbing vigorously. "Good, like that."

I look at the sky, trying to get my mouth as far from the water as possible while still breathing. "Th-That . . . was . . ."

"Scary," he finishes.

Worry cuts across his face, and I collapse. He winds my exhausted arms around his neck and slides his hand down my spine. He repeatedly whispers that he's got me and I'm okay.

Quiet tears slide down my cheeks, falling onto his wet shirt, and I close my eyes. His arms tighten around me as sobs rack my body. He's still treading water, taking on the burden of both our body weights as I soak in his comfort.

"I'm so sorry."

All this is my fault with Tiberia, the riptide, and everything.

"Hey." He moves his neck, forcing me to stop hiding in it, so our faces are inches apart. "Don't say that. It's not your fault." Those chestnut eyes are filled with so much sincerity and kindness that it's too much, and more tears fall.

"I got you. You're okay." His deep voice vibrates into my body, and it's comforting. His index finger catches my tears, wiping them away as they fall. "How about we get out of here?"

I nod, loosening my arms, but they are weightless noodles, the same as my legs when I try to tread water. "I can't."

"Lock your arms in a loop." He shows me, and when I do it, he slides his arm in between. "Hold tight."

My hands clutch my forearms as tight as I can above my head, battling to keep my face out of the water while he tows me back to shore. I flutter and occasionally kick my legs as much as possible to help.

The power of his strokes slicing through the water with such ease is remarkable. Once he reaches shallow water, he stops and winds his arm around my waist to help me to my feet. My legs are so wobbly and fatigued that he's practically carrying me through the surf.

We collapse side by side on the sand. Tiberia steps excitedly between us, happily yapping and giving me a bunch of kisses on my face. I throw my arm up to block her, but she's undeterred, licking my arm and neck. She's happy to see me, but I am happier to see her.

"Carlos . . ." Even with my arm draped across my face, I turn my head to look at him. He's already looking at me. "I don't —"

"It's okay."

My heart is pounding in my chest, and my lungs still burn when I close my eyes to catch my breath. The ocean isn't the furious roar it was in the riptide but a gentle rolling tickling the beach—what a contrast. I might never go into the sea again.

A seagull calls in the distance, and Tiberia curls against my side to lay her head across my stomach. It's strangely peaceful after that traumatic experience.

"That's never happened to me before. Not in Texas or California. And both are known for having lots of riptides." I open my eyes to look at him lying on his back, his breathing smooth and easy, as if he didn't just save me from drowning.

"It only takes a second."

"Were you a lifeguard growing up?" I stroke the black lines of fur on her face, and she closes her eyes.

"No, I am a Raider," he says proudly, rolling to his side and propping on his elbow with his legs extended. The movement causes Tiberia to open her eyes, groan, and inch closer to me.

"I don't know what a Raider is."

"MARSOC is special operations forces. We do special reconnaissance, counterintelligence, embedded security forces, and go deep in-country. Things like that."

I don't miss the fact that he said 'we do' as if he is still in it.

"I understand the words, but I can't fathom what it means, what you did. Or what you saw."

He looks past me when answering. "I'd never want you to see what I have seen."

I've seen that look before when he talked about the medical discharge. It's as if he leaves me and returns to the time and place where those memories still live. I understand haunting recollections and ghosts that never die. I've lived among the graveyard of nightmares and their deities, dragging me through hell each night, only to return when the sun falls out of the sky. Trauma and night terrors are the worst.

I roll to my side, mimicking his position to look at him. Tiberia curls into a ball against my back. "Do you have nightmares? PTSD?"

"Sometimes." His gaze flickers back to me, and I nod. "Why?"

I don't want to tell him about the men that haunt my nights. I don't want to look in Carlos' face, tell him about my past with el diablo and the dragon, and see the repulsion. He's new and untainted by those events, and selfishly, I like how he looks at me now. If he knew, he'd never treat me the same. He'd become one of them, and I can't handle another loss as I climb my way out of the depression I was drowning in.

I think back to my therapy and the training I underwent when I talked with someone to pull me out of my nightmares and put me on the path to recovery five years ago.

"Because of the foundation and what we do, I learned long ago that trauma takes many forms, with many causes and triggers. I took some training courses to understand what it is like. Why nightmares or night terrors are so common? When people without trauma close their eyes, it's calming, and the body slows down. For those with severe or even moderate trauma, it's the opposite when they close their eyes. They are surveying for danger or threats and then fight, or flight kicks in against once real but now perceived threats." I explained it in the same manner my counselor explained it to me.

"And you took that? You volunteered to take classes for something that you don't have?" His eyebrows lift in surprise.

Not exactly.

"Something like that. Well, that's not entirely true. I tend to touch people when I talk, like when I touched your arm, and you threw me up against the wall." He opens his mouth. "I know. It was a reaction. We've been over that. But it's not the first time it has happened to me. When it happened the first time, I wondered, what the hell? It was scary. The social worker explained that what I considered 'normal' or 'comforting' touches are triggers for others, especially the sexually abused, where those were grooming or gateway touches. It's both tragic and fascinating."

He gives me a long look before responding. "That's impressive."

I draw a broken heart in the wet sand with my finger. "It's not. Like you said before, my fate is easy compared to others." My fate before this place was even easier. I wonder what he would have thought of that life.

His hand reaches for mine. "I said that before I knew you."

I snatch my hand back.

"Save your pity." I sit up and then stand, brushing clumps of sand from my soaked clothes. I'm cold and gross and need another shower. He jumps to his feet, the boots squishing from the water trapped in them.

"You'll never get it. You're strong, stronger than I thought. Stronger than you give yourself credit for."

I don't know what to say. I haven't felt very strong here, but then Maximiliano has a way of commanding all the power in the room. With him away and Carlos saying I am stronger than I think, maybe he's right. Perhaps I need to regain my confidence and be that free-spirited, fearless girl that saved some girls from coyotes.

"I know this sounds dumb, but thanks for saving my life." Yep, it sounds dumb.

"Definitely dumb." He smiles, and we slog our way back to the boardwalk. He collects his holster, gun, and knives while I slip off my shoes and socks and pick up my book. "I'll get her."

Grabbing the leash, he whistles for her since she stops to dig for a piece of wood. Her head lifts, and she jogs over to him. She must have decided he wasn't a threat anymore since she's listening to him.

With my shoes dangling from my fingers and Tiberia between us, we walk the path together.

"Sammie?"

"Yeah?"

"In truth, I should thank you. You're bringing back skills I don't use anymore. Not that I want to save you from a riptide every time. But I thought I lost those things after the injury, the teaching, and the training. It's nice to know that I still got it." The corners of his mouth turn down, not a frown but close. It took a lot of courage for him to admit that.

"I know my situation and your situation are not the same, but I know how it feels to live with doubt, regret, and guilt. And it's nice when someone comes along and unburdens some of it," I say with a long stare because if I were completely honest, he has unburdened some of my problems too.

He gives me a curt nod, and as we walk to the back door in silence, I can't help but think about our almost kiss. It seemed so natural in the moment. I wanted him. He wanted me. Now, it seems we are miles apart, lost in our thoughts. Yet a part of me wishes we had kissed because I want to know if the chemistry between us is real or if I am projecting. After all, he's the only man that has been nice to me since I got here.

"Go in and get cleaned up. I'll rinse her off out here."

"Are you sure? I don't want to trouble you with her. You have other things to do." I give him an out.

"Nah, she's a mess, and I'll rinse off too." He tosses his thumb toward the courtyard. "I'll meet you in the kitchen in twenty minutes." He flicks his wrist to look at his watch.

"I don't have a watch or phone." I shrug. Time lost all meaning weeks ago.

"Okay, then come to the kitchen when you are done." He throws open the door, holding Tiberia back when she tries to follow.

"Hey, can I ask you something?"

"Shoot."

"When I tried to grab her or intervene when she was lunging at you, she turned on me. She tried to bite me. Why? If she was trying to protect me from you, why try to attack me too?" I need to know if I can fully trust Tiberia.

He looks at her and then at me. "Dog aggression can be for many reasons. Hers seems both protective and predatory. Protective is good and what you want. However, the predatory is not good. She thinks she owns you. You'd train that out of her in a normal environment, so she knows you're the boss. But here, it seems to work for your betterment."

"Predatory?" That sounds bad, especially if she attacks Carlos, whom she likes. "How so?"

"She's not attacking unprovoked. She's a normal dog most of the time. That's good. If she is provoked, it's for a reason. It's instinctual and primal for her to attack until the threat is gone. You can't stop her, and you shouldn't try because you could get seriously hurt."

"But she was attacking you? A friend, not a foe."

"That's your assessment of the situation. She doesn't see it like that. You're being preyed upon, so she's defending her territory or what belongs to her. End of story. Instinct always prevails over rational thinking."

I nod, taking it all in.

"My advice, let her attack, don't stop her, and then deal with the aftermath." He adjusts her choke chain.

I don't like that advice at all. I don't want Carlos to get hurt if Tiberia misunderstands the situation. "I guess."

"Trust me. She can do some actual damage. You don't want to be on the receiving end of that," he says with conviction. I look into her crystal blue eyes and long tongue hanging out the side of her mouth and wonder how this sweet girl can change so fast. I wouldn't have believed it if I hadn't seen it myself. "Anyway, we're going to go clean up."

I hold his gaze for a moment, remembering how he looked at me in the water, and my cheeks heat. "Yep, see ya soon."

Chapter 26

By the time I showered and got to the kitchen, Tiberia still wasn't back, but all the ladies were. A fleeting thought crosses my mind, and I dismiss it immediately, knowing he would never hurt her after diving into the ocean to avoid her attack. Her bowls are filled with clean water and dog food, so I assume he did that for me.

"Good morning," I say to Maria, and smile when I see the cutting board and knife waiting for me. Pride swells within, knowing I did a decent enough job for them to allow me back. Maria's arm is wrapped from wrist to elbow, and she provides little instruction other than pushing mushrooms and onions toward me.

With my hair tied back and my book in my pocket, I'm happy to work again. Rosa and another lady hum a cheerful tune as sunlight floods the kitchen from the courtyard windows. I glance out there and don't see Carlos or Tiberia. Perhaps he's taking longer to bathe her, considering her thick coat. I know that battle from yesterday.

Deciding they are fine, I focus on my prep work. Like yesterday, the time passes quickly as I chop a myriad of breakfast ingredients until I hear her howling down the hallway.

Not to be disappointed, she bursts through the doorway like a whirlwind. Her nails clack and scrape against the floor, trying to pull Carlos, and I chuckle.

"She's a pain in the ass." He restrains her when she tries to jump on me. "Down." He pops the leash, and she's back on all fours but not sitting like he's trying to make her. She's too excited.

"You're not a pain in the ass, are you? You're a good girl," I coo at her. The higher my voice, the higher she howls, and I realize we can't have a howling party down here.

"Stop amping her up. I was trying to wear her out." He pops her chain again, and this time, she sits.

"I was wondering where you were."

"Running through some drills with her in the ballroom," he says, stealing a piece of chopped bacon and dropping a small amount for her. "I figured you could use the break to work."

"I wondered because her bowls were full, and someone already set the cutting board out for me."

"I can't take credit for the cutting board, but I did water and feed her." He steals more bacon and some cubed ham for the eggs.

"Well, thank you. I feel like I am always thanking you." I swat his hand when he steals more meat. Maria watches our interaction, and worry creeps in. Will she tell el diablo about me being friendly to Carlos?

"Is that bad?"

I finish cutting the last of the meat, letting him steal another bite for himself and Tiberia before handing the bowls to the cook.

"Guess not." I swipe the cutting board and knife off the counter while trying to catch Carlos' eye. When I do, I motion for him to follow me to the sink. I wash my stuff, and he leans his hip against the cabinet. I look around the room to ensure no one can hear me when I whisper, "Do you think these ladies will tell the boss man about us?"

His eyebrow pops up. "We're an 'us' now?"

I roll my eyes and then toss my head toward the cook. When his gaze meets hers, she ducks her head to appear engrossed in frying the eggs. "Ah, I see. I'll handle it."

"What does that mean?"

"It means I'll handle it. I gotta go." He unwinds her leash from his fist, and she slides to the ground at my feet. "Where do you want her?" The leash dangles from the palm of his hand while looking around the kitchen in search of something.

"She is fine here." The look of uncertainty on his face says it all. "Drop her leash, and I'll stand on it. She'll probably want to sleep under the table, anyway."

He's wary of it because it goes against all that strict military training. I'm far more laid back. When he finally drops it, I put my foot on it, and he gives me a dissatisfied look before leaving. I finish cleaning my items and dry them away before moving Tiberia under the table to nap.

The ladies go back to singing while I knead the dough and cut out circles to place on the pan. It's rhythmic and mindless, allowing me time to think.

Carlos has been a pleasant surprise, even if we got off to a rocky start. It's nice to have someone to talk to, and he's pretty handsome to stare at. And that almost kiss . . .

What if we kissed? What if one of the ladies saw? Or one of el diablo's men? I know Carlos said he'd handle the ladies, whatever that means, but the men? I don't think so. They are loyal to the boss man. Plus, Carlos is one man against however many are here. Impossible odds.

If we kissed, and they told el diablo, what would happen to Carlos? What would happen to Tiberia and me? El diablo's threats always hang over me, controlling me physically and mentally. Would he hurt Carlos in front of me? Beat him? What would my punishment be?

Goosebumps sweep up my arms and into my hair when I think of what he did to those two men. If that gruesome torture was their punishment, what was their crime? I can't think about that night.

I can't think about any of the carnage I witnessed. It makes nausea swim in my stomach.

I blink back those memories to glance over at Maria. Her face hides the pain better today. Even though I am helping, I wonder if it's enough. Deciding to find out and practice my Spanish simultaneously, I ask, "Maria, how are you?"

She looks to Rosa, talking to a guy unloading fruit boxes, before answering. "I am well."

Okay, this is going to take some work. I smile warmly, hoping to put her at ease. "And your . . ." Not knowing the word for arm, I point to it instead. Her gaze moves from my arm to my face and then to her knife. When she doesn't answer, I take that as my cue to stop asking and go about my task. I didn't think we'd gossip like old classmates, but I hoped for a little more. Maybe I offended her by asking?

Maria walks over to Rosa, and I can't hear their conversation, but when both walk over to me, I am in trouble. Rosa asks me a question, but I don't understand. I wipe the dough from my hands and reach for my book. She takes it from me, flipping through the pages and translating. "Why are you asking?"

"I was worried. I hope she's going to be okay."

"Sí, sí," Maria says, and she and Rosa go back and forth again.

"She thanks you for your help," Rosa says, and I grin.

"I am happy to help." I point to her arm and ask how it happened. They both frown, and I suddenly realize I overstepped. "No, it's okay." I shake my head and turn the pages, trying to spell out none of my business.

I am at a loss when Rosa motions to her face, tapping her fingertips against her cheeks. I hand over the dictionary. "An accident. The man with the scars hit the pot, water flying and hit Maria."

The man with the scars?

Maximiliano has a scar, but he's not here. The doctor guy doesn't have scars.

No, no, no, no, no.

"Er . . . no bueno teeth." What's the Spanish word for teeth? I open my mouth, click my fingernails against my teeth, and then make fangs from my index fingers.

"Sí, sí." Rosa flips through the book again. *"Amarillo."*

I want to faint. The dragon. She's describing the dragon, which means he's here. . . with me. And Maximiliano is not. What I feared would happen is happening. It's suddenly hot in here.

"He's here?" I point to the counter because I need a firm yes.

"No, um . . ." Rosa confers with Maria, and both gaze at me as they talk. "He here yesterday, gone today."

My breath is faint, and the room seems to sway. I fan myself not to pass out. "Is he, um, coming back."

"No. Gone." Rosa tilts her head and puts the back of her hand on my cheek. It feels cool against my clammy skin. She murmurs something and grasps my hand, leading me to the table. Stacking my arms on each other, I put my head down and close my eyes to stop freaking out.

I don't know who, but one of them places a damp towel on the back of my neck.

Don't panic.

He's gone.

I pant into the wood table. My breath fans my face as my anxiety grows. Without Maximiliano to protect me and the recovered memories of the doctor, it's too much.

Why is he here? Is he coming back? Even though I didn't see him, did he see me?

I got to get out of here now, not later. I must find a way out. After my shift, I'll look beyond the dunes because I know it was not an accident. Quiet Maria didn't do anything to provoke him, and now she's disfigured. If he finds me again, he'll beat me worse than before. No doubt about it.

With grave concerns for my safety, I pull the wet cloth from my neck, wipe my face with it and look into the courtyard, hoping to see Carlos. I'd feel safer if he were nearby. Even though he doesn't know the whole story, I'm confident he'd protect me from the dragon. Thankfully, I have Tiberia. After what she tried to do to Carlos this morning, I know she'll protect me.

She thinks she owns you.

That's okay. Let Tiberia think she owns me. He's right. Predatory is to my advantage now that I know the dragon was here. I can't wrap my mind around the fact that he was here, she got burned, and I missed everything. Fate or coincidence? I have no idea, but knowing things are going on without my knowledge makes me uneasy.

Now that I know the enemy is among us, I don't need to be complacent about my safety. I must stay vigilant, practice my self-defense moves, and watch everyone as they come and go. Carlos was right for checking my room. I will do the same and let Tiberia go in first to investigate.

Deciding I have freaked out enough and need to get back to work, I spot a breakfast taco and a glass of orange juice waiting at my station. The ladies assume it was lightheadedness from a lack of food. Good, let them think that. They are innocent of the war between the dragon and me.

The usual activity resumes, trays loaded with food going out and returning empty. Once the food is made, I revert to cleanup duty while eating and keeping an eye on the clock to count the minutes until I am done.

I work quickly, dwindling the stacks of dirty dishes until they are washed, dried, and returned to the cabinets for lunch. Even Rosa is surprised by my renewed energy and opens a napkin with two leftover biscuits for me. I thanked her and set them aside to finish cleaning as fast as possible. When she releases me from duty, I grab Tiberia and the food to race out to the beach.

Chapter 27

The sun is beating down on us, and I wish I had a hat to wear. Once Tiberia is off the leash, she runs ahead to explore. I round the corner to see the long ridge and her tail wagging like a flag in the distance.

The wind has a pleasant chill, blowing my hair back, and I relish it against the sticky heat. I eat the biscuits as I walk the endless stretch of dunes until I spot my balcony in the distance and race toward it. Sand collapses under my shoes as I climb to the top of the ridge to see a clear view of how expansive the rock formation is.

Tiberia sprints over to join me, eager to sniff and mark new territory. The boulders at the bottom are large and round, shaped to support the next row of smaller boulders stacked on top, with the crest of the rocks covered with elongated shards and intentionally jagged to discourage prisoners from escaping or risk impaling themselves. El diablo must have designed this fortress, knowing this rock formation alone can kill a man. Yet here I am, thinking of a way to use them in my escape plan. I am desperate.

I sort of map out a route to climb by surveying my balcony and comparing the dullest peaks on the spikey rocks. If I can climb up, then I can climb down at night with the help of my sheets. If I use the comforter, it could protect me from impalement. Lovely.

As I descend the other side of the ridge, Tiberia goes bounding off to the left of the formation to explore. Once I get to the bottom of the ridge and look at the boulders, I realize they are a lot more daunting than I thought. With a few more observations, I change my path and then wipe my sweaty palms onto my shirt.

The bottom layer of rocks is massive. Their roundness makes it challenging to get a foothold and a solid grip. After a few attempts, I hoist myself onto the side of a rock and hold it there for a few seconds to adjust my foot. My hands are slick with sweat again, and I brush each against my shirt before climbing higher. It takes three attempts to scale the side of the boulder, and once I get to the top of it, I have a scraped knee and elbow.

Several strands of my hair escaped the tie and are plastered to the side of my temples. I plop down and let my legs drape over the side of the rock to fix my hair and access my scrapes. Neither is too bad, but I need to remember to wash them when I get inside.

"This is harder than I thought." I look around for Tiberia, and she's nowhere in sight. I don't worry. I know she'll return when she's ready. I catch my breath, adjust my shirt, and stand, preparing to tackle the next level.

When I look up, I don't see the same vantage point I did on the ground. I'm beginning to think that nothing at this place is as it seems. The path I thought I could take doesn't have any crevices to stick my foot, and after trying to scale the side of this rock, I'm wary of falling off the higher one. I peer over the edge. It wouldn't be a backbreaking fall, but it would be a nasty one. I can't get hurt now. Breaking something will force me to stay longer to heal, and I can't have that. Being lame without Maximiliano here and the dragon coming and going as he pleases would end badly for me. That much I know.

Deciding to go left, I spot a divot in the side of the next boulder that I can tuck my fingertips into while I wedge my shoe against the adjacent rock. This one is less round and more angular. I can get good traction on the side to hoist myself up without scraping my skin. Once standing on top of it, I stretch my hands in the air to see how close I am to reaching the peak of the jagged rocks and my balcony beyond it.

Three bedsheets tied together will not be enough when I look at the ground and see how far I am. Even as I consider the shape and size of the boulders and map out two different routes down, both will be treacherous at night. I'd also have to wait for a full moon since it gets pitch black out here.

Dejected, I put my hands on my hips to reassess when Tiberia starts barking an odd, high-pitched shrill.

Crap! Someone is coming. If one of el diablo's men catches me here, they will know what I am doing and rat me out to their boss. He would know immediately that I was trying to escape, and he would lock me in my room forever.

My pulse quickens. I immediately squat, flattening my body against the boulder beside me. Her barking continues, and I cup my hands over my eyes, searching the ridge and both sides of the beach for a black-clothed figure. Seeing none, I scoot out to find her below.

"What is it, girl?" She springs back, pouncing the white sand in front of her, and continuing with that shrilly barking. Careful not to cut myself on the shale rock, I lean over the edge to get a better look. She goes berserk and bounces straight into the air. The fur on her tail is twice the size, and she is snarling so much that lines of drool hang from both sides of her mouth.

"Tiberia?" Her crystal eyes flip to mine and then drop a level below to my right to bark at a distinct spot two boulders away. "It's okay."

I climb to the adjoining rock, about to cross the crevice to the last rock, when I scream in fright. Nestled in the shade between the stones is a twisted cluster of light gray snakes, with black bands and dark gray spots. I can't hear them rattle or hiss over Tiberia's warning, but skating through America, I encountered many snakes, which look akin to rattlesnakes.

My scream draws the attention of a couple of them, and Tiberia's barking and bouncing keep the attention of the other three in the nest. Perspiration drips into my eyes, but I don't dare wipe it for fear my movement would trigger them to strike.

I'm scared to look away from them, but I need to get down. Sucking in a slow breath, I carefully slide one foot back to retreat the way I came. Ensuring I am firmly planted in the center of the boulder, I slowly lift my other foot to step back when another swivels its head in my direction. Shit!

I glance down, hoping I can jump to the sand by Tiberia, but the boulders are too wide across, and I couldn't possibly clear them without breaking my ankle or, worse, my leg. Up, I must go up and try to make it to my balcony. It's the only way. I'll risk cuts to my palms from the shale rock versus poisonous snake bites.

Leveraging one foot on the boulder behind me and the other on the sharp stone pointing to the sky, I wrap my arms around it and lift myself up. Tiberia follows my ascension, her two front paws pushing on the round boulder at the bottom.

Fear grips my chest. I can't breathe, and my hands are sweating so badly that I am losing my grip on the narrow rock. I stretch my arm up, reaching for the base of the veranda, but I am coming up short by several feet. My hand slips, and when I lower my arm to switch hands, I scream at the top of my lungs. The biggest one from the nest is creeping along the back of the rock and within a few feet of my legs.

The snake's tail curls inward, the rattle now evident as fast as it is shaking. The top half coils back, getting ready to strike, and I grab my book from my back pocket and hurl it at the curve of its body. It whacks the snake out of sight.

My chest is tight, my head is pounding, and adrenaline surges through my body. I stretch to the next pointy rock, knowing I must get out of here, but looking around, I can't figure out how. Carefully,

I lift myself to the next rock and scrape my forearm, leaving dots of blood on the white stone.

"Shit," I murmur, with sweat dripping into my eyes.

"What the hell are you doing?" Carlos hollers behind me, and I nearly cry in relief.

"Snakes!"

"Where? Where is it?" I dare a look over my shoulder to see him climbing up behind me. The bill of his hat blocks his face, but the ease with which he is scrambling over these rocks is impressive. Tiberia is still barking so loud that it is blocking out the sound of any rattling tails.

"I don't know. I threw my dictionary at it on that rock over there." I point to where I last saw it, hoping he can hear me over Tiberia's shrilling.

"Keep looking for it." I don't stop looking at all the crevices and angles it could have gone in. I hear the click of his gun before he pops up to the left of me, on the rock where the snake was. "Do you see it?"

"No . . . now—" I shriek when its head pops around the corner of the rock I am standing on, striking at me. Carlos stomps on its body, causing the snake's head to swirl and strike at him. It doesn't get a chance because he blows its head off, and the body falls limp a few seconds after.

The shot is so loud that it rings in my ears. I rest my forehead against the point of the rock to tug on my earlobe. My relief is palpable, my ears hurt like hell, and my heart is beating so fast that I can feel it in my palms, clutching the stone. Carlos fires off another shot to his left, and I need to warn him.

"There, there is a nest." I pant, realizing what a lousy idea this was. No way can I escape this place, not this way, and especially not at night. I'd be dead from snake venom before my feet hit the sand.

"We've got to get out of here."

"Yeah." Getting down is impossible. "I don't know how. It all looks the same from up here."

"Where is the nest?"

"To your left. Tiberia was warning me. I didn't understand," I say as an apology. He nods, looking to his left, where he killed the second snake.

"Then we go right." He holsters his gun to shimmy by me, jumping to the next rock and holding out his hand to help me to it. "We'll take it slow. Stay on the lookout, though."

My head bobs at his instructions. Follow him and look for snakes. Got it.

He moves first and then helps me. We zigzag at a diagonal down the side of the boulders, and I keep a vigilant watch. He jumps to the sand with his arms outstretched to catch my waist. Once I am steady on the ground, I throw my arms around his neck and thank him profusely. I'm hot and sticky, sweat coating my clothes, but he must not care because he hugs me tight against him.

Tiberia barrels into my legs, howling in excitement and ending our embrace. I pet her wiggly body, and her fur stings my torn skin.

I take several deep breaths, putting my hand to my chest to calm myself down. Almost dying in the riptide this morning and now poisonous snakes this afternoon, it's too much.

Part of me thinks I need to quit while I am behind. The other part knows I can't because I must find a way out of here. I must escape el diablo, the dragon, the doctor, and everything else awful about this place.

"Where's the nest?"

"Down there, where the rocks curve inward."

With each footstep, he sinks into the soft sand and his unbuttoned jacket flaps in the wind behind him. His pistol is pointed at each crevice he passes until he's nearly at the end of the row. He immediately squats, firing several shots, and then stands to investigate. The sound isn't as deafening, and the ringing in my ears is gone.

Tiberia tries to trot down to him when I snatch her leash from the sand to hold her back. She doesn't need to get bitten by being nosy.

He walks toward us, the black military cap shadowing the sun.

"That's the stupidest shit I've seen. What were you thinking?" he roars. Wait, he's angry? For what?

"Hey, don't cuss at me." He had no idea why I was doing it. Nor am I going to tell him now, that's for sure. "I had it under control." A lie so obvious, it's absurd to say, but my pride won't let me back down.

"You didn't and don't even start with me about how you would climb to that balcony." He lifts the bill of his cap, and I can see his eyebrows pinched together.

"Why are you so mad, anyway? It doesn't matter what happens to me." I turn away, ready to take Tiberia back inside and chalk this idiot idea up as a complete failure. His hand lands firmly on my shoulder, and I half turn to glower at him. "Get your hand off me."

"Do you know how dangerous that was? You could have slipped and hit your head, impaled yourself on a few of those rocks, or been bitten, and no one would find you. If they did, it would be too late." He drags his hand off my shoulder. "So, tell me why you are really over here?"

"Why are you wearing this uniform? Where have you been?" I give him the once over, taking in his black jacket, pants, and shiny combat boots. Compared to his usual black digital fatigues, he looks dressed for a military ceremony. He takes a few deep breaths, and I must admit, he looks smoking hot in this nice dress gear.

"Tell what you were doing?" He repeats through clenched teeth.

"Fine, whatever. I was bored. I'm on break from the kitchen and wanted to be alone with my thoughts. I saw the rocks and wanted to climb them." I shrug, hoping he believes me. "That's all."

His eyes narrow in suspicion. "In all your travels, you didn't think about snakes being in here?"

"No." I really hadn't. I was focused on how I'd get more bedding without alerting anyone.

"If I hadn't been on patrol, you could be dead by now."

I purse my lips together. Once again, he's right. I'm growing tired of him always being right.

"Patrol? For what?" My attempt to divert the conversation away from me.

He looks down his nose, the anger dissipating. "You already know the answer to that."

Drugs, threats, enemies.

I look past him toward the endless ocean that meets the horizon. "Yeah, I guess I do."

"Okay then, go back in."

Good, he believes my lie.

"What's on the other side? I mean, I've been out the front door, and the desert leads to the mountains. The back door is the courtyard and beach, but what is around this way?" I point beyond the rocks and ridge.

"More of the same."

I frown. Not what I am hoping for, but why would I expect anything different?

"Can I see?" I walk Tiberia in that direction. The breeze picks up, blowing the curls away from my face, and her snout lifts to sniff the salty air. He doesn't say yes or no. He merely walks alongside us.

When the silence gets too much, I break it.

"Maria's accident wasn't an accident." I want to pump him for information on the dragon. Did he see the dragon? Does he know who he is? Does Carlos know why he is important enough to el diablo that he's allowed to beat me to a pulp, attack Maria, and still be alive?

"Why do you say that?"

He takes the bait.

"I asked, and Rosa answered it was, but I don't think so. I think it was on purpose."

"Who would purposely maim a kitchen hand?"

The skepticism in his voice is unmistakable.

"Because the guy that did it is a cruel, sinister bastard."

"Who's the guy?"

"A vile man with scarred cheeks and decaying teeth. She said he was here yesterday, but not today?" I look at him, wanting to see if his expression changes to recognition of the dragon. Testing him will let me know if I can trust him.

"Considering I was with you or that dog most of the day. I didn't see anyone that fits that description." He cocks an eyebrow as if he caught me checking him out.

Wrong, I am seeing if he is lying, but his answer sounds sincere. The look on his face is open, no pausing before answering or squinting in suspicion.

"And you would tell me? You wouldn't lie?" I double verify because I want to ensure the dragon is gone and I am as safe as possible until el diablo returns.

"Why? What's this guy to you?" He stops, and I keep walking. I'm not going into that with him.

The longer I walk, the more disappointed I get. This damn fortress is, like Maximiliano said, desert and mountains on two-thirds of the terrain and the ocean on the other. All I see is more of this dusty, dry land and native plants dotting the landscape leading to the foothills of the mountains.

"This sucks."

I turn a full circle to see if I missed anything when Carlos joins me.

"What were you expecting?"

A city I can walk to and catch a plane home. "I don't know." I toe the dirt, disappointment settling in my gut.

"I need to finish rounds." He pauses, waiting for me to say something. I slowly gaze over the terrain and blow out an annoying breath.

"Okay."

Tiberia is exhausted. She needs a gigantic bowl of water and some cool tile to lie on.

"Go around the front, knock on the door. They will let you in." He points, and the thought of that makes me uneasy.

"Rosa or Maria will let me in?" I hope.

"No, the guards at the front." He lowers his hat over his eyes and adjusts the flap of his jacket to conceal his holster. "Go. They know who you are."

Guards that know me, but I don't know them. That's even worse and makes my stomach twist with anxiety.

"I'm good. I'll walk around back. We don't need to talk or anything. Go about your stuff."

"It's shorter around front."

I ignore him. I have already made my mind up, and it is taking the long way. Feeling bad for Tiberia and knowing I'm delaying her getting water, I slip the chain off her neck. She doesn't run far, too hot and tired, as she happily trots a few paces in front of me.

"Why don't you listen to me?"

I loosen the rag around my hair to capture the stray curls. "I don't feel comfortable. If you notice, I am only in three areas, my room, the kitchen, and the beach. I don't go wandering around this monstrosity. It's not safe for me." I phrase it as delicately as possible.

"Nothing will happen to you."

I wait for him to say more and explain how he is so assured of this, but he doesn't. We'll agree to disagree on this one since I trusted his boss man to protect me, and then the dragon beat me, under his watch and in his house.

"You avoided my question. Who is this guy?" he repeats, casting a long shadow next to mine. It's no wonder I feel safe with him. He's tall, built, and highly trained, like Will and Ardy used to be.

"I don't want to talk about him." And I don't. Diego haunted my nightmares. I don't need him haunting my days too.

The sun is high in the sky, and the heat waves from the sand have got to stifle Carlos in his fancy uniform. I'm late for the lunch prep. Once I get some water, I'll be back at my station reporting for duty.

The ridge of dunes is ahead, and the dark blue ocean beyond it bleeds into the light blue sky. The white sandy beach is beautiful and serene. Mom loved the beach and always had. The more remote and isolated, the better. If circumstances were different, I wonder what she would have thought of this one.

"You're smiling." Carlos interrupts my thoughts.

"Am I?"

"Yeah, it's rare."

"Hmm, thinking about my mom. I miss her." My eyes mist, and I sniff, but I will not cry. I decided I was done crying.

"I imagine you do."

Tiberia runs toward the rocks where the snakes are, and Carlos lets out a long whistle to call her back. She abruptly changes direction and runs to stand at the top of the ridge.

"Is she the only one you miss?"

That's an odd question.

"Uh, I guess not. I miss my friends and colleagues at the foundation, but I miss Mom the most." I'm not sure if that is the answer he is looking for.

"There's not a boyfriend or guy that you are missing?"

I burst out laughing, and he has a sheepish look.

"You're about as subtle as I am." I bump my elbow into his side, and he bumps me back.

"Well?"

"No, Carlos, there's no boyfriend or guy." My voice is higher than I intend.

"Why not?"

"That's rude. You're asking why I am single as if something is wrong with me. You don't ask married people why are you married?" I jump on my soapbox because I tire of people asking me this question back home.

"Whoa, calm down. I was curious because you run in circles that I don't. I figured you'd have your pick of men." He looks at me while I watch Tiberia dig a massive hole in the side of the dune.

It took me longer to get over Maximiliano than I care to admit. Not even Mom knows that. "Dating in LA is . . ."

"Wimpy dudes?" His chest puffs out a little, and of course, a Marine would say that. I roll my eyes, but on the inside, I like that he wants to know.

"No. I was going to say fake. You think you're on an actual date, get to a restaurant, and realize they requested a table by the windows for the paparazzi to take pictures. Or you go to a club, and they want to make their ex jealous. Or they want to pick you up in a Lambo and brag about their crypto investments. It's ridiculous." I pick up a piece of driftwood and call Tiberia. Her head pops out of the hole, and I throw it as far as I can. She races toward it, diving to scoop it up before tossing it in the air.

"That sounds awful."

"Yup."

He whistles for her, and she trots back, happy with her stick. He commands her to drop it, and right when he tries to retrieve it, she swoops in to get it and runs off.

"What about you? Do you have a girlfriend or probably a pen pal, seeing how remote this place is?" I wave my hand at the scenery. Fair is fair, he asked me and now me asking him seems fitting. I worry he might say yes for a split second, and that almost kiss floats into my brain.

"I had a girl, thought I was going to marry her, but things didn't work out," he says so matter-of-factly that I am astonished.

"Wait, what? Marry? Aren't you a little young to get married?"

I have trouble dating in LA, and this dude wants to get married. Wow. Thoughts of marriage or trusting men long enough to marry them befuddles me after the hidden life el diablo kept from me.

"I'm twenty-eight. Most of the guys in my unit had families and had been married for several years. I was one of the few who wasn't married until I met her."

"Dang." I did not know that they started so young. "What happened?" I shouldn't ask, but I can't help my nosy self.

200

"I don't know. I got hurt, and she didn't want to stick around. She split because she thought she would have to care for me." His mouth flattens into a line, and the sting of her rejection is still apparent.

Wow, again, in his darkest hour, she leaves him while he fights physically and mentally to recover. Then the ending of his career? Poor guy has had his heart ripped out and stomped on.

"I'm sorry."

"Her loss. I know there's a perfect girl for me out there that will see past all scars and love me, anyway." The conviction in his voice is admirable. El diablo demands my love. Carlos is patiently waiting for love. The difference is night and day. "You don't think so?"

I blink my thoughts away.

"No, I mean, yes. I think there is, uh, someone for everyone." An echo of an answer because I haven't heard a guy say this before. Oh sure, I hear the girls at the foundation blabber on about finding the one, but this tough Marine said it too.

"What about you? Do you believe in love?"

"Yeah, of course. But it's different. I think once you have loved and lost, you are more cautious. Like before, you free fall, but now you have a safety net." I sum up what happened to me without giving too much away.

"I like that. It's true."

I let that conversation drop because I don't want to talk about romantic love more than I must for fear he'll ask more questions and figure out it was Maximiliano. But I think about a different love that circles back to what he said.

"I wasn't always a full-time caregiver for my mom. Not at first, but toward the end, before Seattle, I was. Those were some dark days. I was juggling her being sick as a dog and going to school, trying not to fail out. It was rough. Round after round of chemo robbed me of her and robbed her of her. I saw the sadness in her eyes, and it nearly killed me. I felt guilty going to school when she was so sick, and I felt guilt at home for being healthy. It was overwhelming. I used to pray throughout the day at school that I wouldn't come home and find her . . . you know." My voice cracks, and I blink back tears. His hand rubs my back as we walk. "All I am saying is love takes many forms, and caregivers are the silent heroes."

He lets his hand fall away. "At least you stuck with her." His voice drips with venom, the hurt running deep.

"I'd like to say I did because I loved her, and most days, that was true, but I wanted to give up a few days in there. I was mad at the world. Mad at God that she got sick. Mad at the doctors when they said traditional treatments weren't working. Mad at my piece of shit dad, for not being the sick one. I was mad at everyone and everything. All those months' skating to raise money for her experimental treatments was cathartic and therapeutic because I was helping her." I don't know why I am telling him all this, but it feels good to unburden some of this, and I think he'd understand, considering what he's been through.

"Cathartic? How?"

"I used to throw rocks. Have temper tantrums in the middle of nowhere. The roads got long, my mind grew weary, and I'd ruminate on the unfairness of my life. Or perceived unfairness because, honestly, what do we know at eighteen? Anyway, it helped. I'd scream or cry or rage, whatever felt needed at the time, and it worked most of the time. One time, I forgot I was on live, which was not pretty. Luckily, I didn't cuss or say anything bad. I screamed at the mountains, knowing they could take it. That video went viral, and the money started rolling in for Mom. Odd, huh?"

"What's odd?"

"That yelling at mother nature put me on the map and started my career. I guess people resonated with my anguish."

"I think people resonated with you." When I look at him, there is a softness in his expression.

Between the ache in my heart from missing Mom, the telling of some sad times for me, and how he is looking at me right now, I can't handle it. "I don't think I want to talk about this anymore."

"All right."

The rest of the walk is silent. Neither of us starts a new conversation, and I am fine with that. In fact, I am all talked out. The kitchen will be a pleasant respite.

When we get close to the boardwalk, I call Tiberia to put her leash on. "Hey, thanks for saving me again," I say, keeping my tone lighthearted. All I end up doing is thanking him.

He touches the tip of his cap with a brief nod and then continues walking around the perimeter, leaving me to watch him go. I didn't mean to bring all that up with him, but somehow, we have a way of talking about deep things without meaning to. I've never had that with anyone but Mom, and it makes me even more homesick.

Chapter 28

Tiberia drags me down the path, and I stumble behind her. "Eager to get in?"

It wasn't fair to keep her out there that long without water. I fling open the door, and we race down the hallway to burst into the kitchen. All four ladies look up, and I wave when I drop her leash. Tiberia splays in front of her water bowl and proceeds to drink the entirety of it.

Rushing to the sink, I thoroughly wash my hands and retrieve a glass from the cupboard to get some water myself. I gulp two glasses with a loud sigh and refill it one more time to pour into Tiberia's bowl before standing at my station, ready to work. Her pants fill the room as she saunters under the table to nap.

Maria pushes a box of potatoes across the counter to me, wincing from the pressure it puts on her burn. She catches me looking at her bandage and taps my knife with hers to get started. I know my looks make her uncomfortable, but I can't help but wonder what exactly happened.

How could the dragon have been in the kitchen, and I missed him? I was outside with Tiberia and Carlos, but not that long. And why would he go after Maria? She's so quiet and such a hard worker. Then again, I don't know why he went after me. El diablo said he didn't order it and punished him, but why keep the dragon around if he hurts innocent women?

And the doctor. Even Carlos looked disturbed when I asked him. It doesn't add up. What am I missing? What is the connection between the two?

I really want to talk to Carlos. He has said not to trust anyone, but then he confided in me with some pretty personal stuff. Not to mention saving my life twice. Doesn't that make him trustworthy?

If I trust and confide in him, will he turn around and tell el diablo? Could Carlos be spying on me for el diablo while he is away? It's a possibility.

Then again, I didn't tell him the truth about why I was climbing the rocks. I don't know what to do. He's got to know more information than I do, but will knowing change my escape plan? No, because my escape plan ended in a ball of snakes and miles of desert terrain. El diablo was right when he caught me looking at the front of the land. Desert and mountain, good for him, terrible for gatita.

Would Carlos help me? He flew in with Tiberia, so he knows the flight crew. If I confided in him about my plan, would he even say yes? Would he consider it? What would it cost Carlos if he helped? He'd be risking his life. El diablo would surely torture him if we failed. Can I even ask that of him?

I don't know. The longer I stew on this, the worse it gets and the more hopeless it seems.

The hours pass quickly as I fixate on different ways to approach him. I work through lunch and take a small break to share steak, potatoes, and veggies with Tiberia.

I debated taking the food trays down the corridor to the banquet room and swiftly chickened out for two reasons. First, I'm not sure if the dragon is in there, and second, I want to propose my escape plan in private to Carlos without tipping off the other guards.

I remain in the kitchen, plating food, cleaning dirty dishes, and helping wherever I can. After everything is done and put away, Tiberia and I walk to the beach to see if he is still on perimeter duty. Looking in both directions, I don't see him or anyone for that matter.

Where is he? He didn't say he'd be gone when I left him on the beach. Unless . . . did his 'handling it' with the kitchen ladies have something to do with his sudden absence? What if they somehow got word to el diablo that we were flirty, or maybe they saw us almost kiss in the water? What if he's hurt somewhere, or they sabotaged him on the beach after we parted? What if he's being tortured right now, like those men?

No, don't think that.

Stop jumping to conclusions.

I'm overreacting.

He's a Marine and a Raider. Elite trained. He's fine.

Not wanting to sit in my room, I stay in the kitchen and help Rosa prep the meats to roast for dinner. The sunshine streaming through the kitchen windows changes to rumbling thunder and pouring rain. The kitchen lights flicker with the occasional crack of lightning, and I wonder if he is out in this mess.

The storm rages through dinner, and there is still no sight of him. My stomach is in knots, my brain is creating horrible scenarios, and my nerves are fried. Even Tiberia reacts to the energy rolling off me by lying at my feet and whining.

The longer I chant he is okay in my mind, the less I believe it. Rosa keeps a watchful eye on my fretting and helps by supplying a steady stream of tasks to keep me busy. I appreciate it because I would have lost my mind if I had to sit in my room waiting for him.

She and I are the last ones in the kitchen, making desserts that need to chill overnight. Watching the doorway too many times, she pats my hand but says nothing. She realizes whom I am looking for. We work quietly, and without my dictionary, I can't translate all her words but get the gist of it when she shows me.

The clock on the wall is nearing eleven o'clock when Carlos

walks through the doorway, looking tense. My shoulders slump in relief, releasing the tension I have held in my body from hours of worry. I stretch my neck to unwind my tight muscles.

His eyes zero in on me across the kitchen, but I am too busy surveying him from the bottom of his muddy boots to the wet, unbuttoned jacket hanging open. No blood or apparent signs of trauma, thankfully, but he looks like he's been through the dust bowl with grime smeared across his cheek and hair.

Tiberia ambles over to greet him. She sniffs his boots and licks his outstretched hand, but his eyes never leave mine.

"Are you okay?" Unable to keep the concern out of my voice. The stress from his face clears, and he scratches Tiberia behind her ear as she leans against his legs.

"Better now that I am here," he says casually, which makes me mad because I have worried all day about his safety, thought horrible things had happened to him, and that's all he says?

"Where have you been?" My temper flares now, and I don't care because he owes me an explanation.

He grins, and I stop folding in the cream cheese, waiting for an answer. "The irony."

"What irony?" I blow a curl out of my face.

"You're waiting up for me as if we lived together." He walks to the sink to wash his hands, face, and neck. When he grabs a towel to dry off, Rosa scurries over to make a plate of food for him.

"I wasn't waiting up." I take my anger out on my ingredients, whipping them so fast that the whisk clangs against the bowl. "We're making dessert for tomorrow."

Rosa is busy getting containers out of the fridge and piling heaps of food on a large platter while he watches me.

"Waiting up, baking in the kitchen, your hair is a mess. I don't know, Sammie, a guy could get used to this?" I open my mouth to object, and he winks. I stare in shock because he's outright flirting with me in front of Rosa. Is he crazy? What if she tells el diablo?

"Carlos!"

He looks at Rosa, saying something to her, and she looks at me. They go back and forth, too fast for me to translate, and then I see her taking off her apron.

"Wait, where is she going?" I watch her pack her things. "What did you say to her? We're not done."

"I told her to go home. We'd finish up."

"Gracias *señor* and señorita," Rosa says with a little bow and then piles her bags on her shoulders to leave.

"Carlos! Are you crazy? I can't do all this. There's like ten cheesecakes to make." I drop my spoon in the batter and debate on chasing after her. "We only have four done. Why would you do that?"

"She's had a long day, it's very late, and I'll help you." He puts his plate in the microwave and closes the lids on the containers to put in the fridge. "You get to stumble to bed, and she has a long drive home."

I blink and frown. It's true, but still, it should be my choice.

"Where does she live? How far is it from here?"

He stops and gives me a long look, arguing something in his head by the look on his face. "Far enough to fall asleep behind the wheel. She was dead on her feet. I didn't think you'd mind this much. I thought you liked to be helpful."

"That's a low blow. You know I do like to help, and I care about Rosa. She's been nothing but kind to me, so . . ." I shake my head, my hand cramping from beating the batter so hard. "To imply that I don't care about anyone other than myself is bullshit, and you know it."

He doesn't say anything else. He moves about the kitchen, getting his dinner ready. I spoon my batter into the pan and place it in the oven, preparing to start on the next one.

"And aren't you worried she'll tell the boss man that you are flirting with me?" I raise my chin in defiance.

"No, because I told you I'd handle it, and I did," he says, mimicking my tone. Out of the corner of my eye, he takes his jacket off and hangs it on the back of the chair when his cell phone clatters to the floor.

I turn my head so fast that my neck pops, but he picks it up and puts it away before I can get a good look at it. Our eyes meet, guilt marring his face, and I recognize that expression. It's the face of liars and cheaters.

Don't trust anyone.

He's said it too often for me not to believe him now. I can't trust him.

I don't know why I thought he didn't have a cell phone. Probably because I don't have one, the ladies don't have them, so I figured they were not allowed when working for el diablo. With one call, I could be free. He knew it too. He's one of them. Loyal to el diablo. He was befriending me to report back to him.

Wow, I am so dumb. It was all an act of telling me about himself, trying to get me to open up, and probably recording our conversations to send to the boss.

I turn away and close my mouth. The betrayal is so fresh it makes my chest ache. Here I had hoped he'd help me escape, waited all day to talk to him about it, and now it's another plan dead before it even started.

He crosses the room, retrieving his food and cutlery, and I feel him staring. "Sammie, it's not what you think."

It doesn't matter what I think. It's what I see, what I have experienced, and what I know. I don't look at him. I don't answer him. I continued mixing the ingredients because he promised Rosa I would.

"I had to run an errand today, that's all." I don't care. I don't want to hear it because it's all lies. "I didn't want to do it."

I stir faster, wanting to get these damn desserts finished as fast as possible to return to my room. I'm so done with him. I pour the ingredients into the pan and put it in the oven with the other ones. When I turn around, he's blocking my station and smelling like sweat, cheap perfume, and cigarettes.

Drawing the neckline of my shirt, I pull it over my nose and look at him in disgust. "Get away from me."

"I didn't do anything. I swear." He doesn't move.

His typically square shoulders slope forward with his fingers picking at his nails. He doesn't look innocent, he wears the face of a liar.

"Doesn't matter. Now move, you smell." Steel lines my voice. He'll get no mercy. I've been around guys long enough to know they can only go so long before they find their fun.

"But it does matter. Sam, come on."

As I walk around the countertop to my station, my shirt falls into place, and I start on another cheesecake. Reaching for the eggs, his hand covers mine, and I snatch it back. "Don't touch me. Look, leave. Get out of here. You said don't trust anyone when you should have said, don't trust me." My frustration and disappointment boil over because his night of cheap thrills is disgusting and hurts my feelings because if I were to admit it, I like him.

"You know that's not what I mean—"

"Get out!" Tiberia springs to her feet and growls. I don't even care who hears us at this late hour if anyone is still awake.

"Let me explain."

"I don't want to hear it," I emphasize each word through clenched teeth. "Now go."

I use the spatula to point toward the exit. He frowns before pushing off the counter to grab his plate and belongings from the table. With one last look at me, he walks down the same hallway Rosa did.

I place my palms on the countertop, breathing deeply to calm down when Tiberia brushes against my legs. She's the only good thing about this place. She and the ladies. Everyone else can go to hell.

After getting rid of him, I am bound and determined to get these all knocked out, cooled, and in the fridge as fast as possible. I'm angry and exhausted, but I refuse to disappoint Rosa because of his stupid ass.

It takes a couple more hours to get all the desserts done, and thankfully, I don't see Carlos again. What he did with his dinner dishes is beyond me.

Needing to take Tiberia out one more time before bed, I clean the kitchen, click off the lights and walk through the courtyard hallway to the back door. As we follow the path down to the beach, I am struck by a strong wind that chills me to the bone. I don't walk too far tonight, uneasy about how isolated it is.

Glancing at the sky, it's overcast and stealing the shine from the moon and stars. The thunderstorm cast a grayish ambiance in the kitchen until it passed, leaving a crispness to the night air. When Tiberia finally does her business, I rush back to the path and jog to the door.

The wet sand clumps on the bottom of my shoes, and I sit on the bench to scrape them against the concrete when a man's shadow appears in the courtyard windows. His face is turned away from me, but his build is slender and not one of the huge Marines employed by el diablo.

The man is dressed in a dark green suit, not the classic cut of El diablo's tuxedo, but still custom-made. His slicked back hair, trimmed beard, and manicured features, coupled with his impeccable style, scream wealth. Not to mention how out of place he looks here.

Tiberia looks at me, sitting patiently, and I scoot her between my legs as I hover over her because new faces are always bad. The dragon, the doctor. The guy in the green suit is out of sight now, but should he return and look out the window, he'd see us. Crouched, we wait several minutes, and once I think the coast is clear, Tiberia and I slip through the door and down the hall to the kitchen.

It's eerie seeing a stranger in the house this late at night. The dragon yesterday and this guy tonight. It makes the hair on the back of my neck stand on end as I tiptoe up the back staircase. Tiberia's ears are on point, and she seems aware of every creak of the old fortress as the wind howls outside.

I'd probably run back to my room if we didn't sound like a stampede of horses. Once inside my room, I make it a point to double-check that the door is firmly closed and locked. Who is that guy? Is he here with the dragon? I doubt it. They are from two different social classes. Maybe he's an associate of el diablo? If so, why is he here when el diablo isn't? The uneasy feeling settles into the pit of my stomach, making it difficult to fall asleep.

Chapter 29

A soft blue hue filters past the drapes into my room, and I groan. The sun hasn't risen yet.

"Too early." I roll over and throw an arm across Tiberia. She stretches, letting out a cute little whimper, and I smile. I love her.

My eyelids are puffy, and my eyeballs sting. I adjust my legs and get comfy against her when someone bangs on my door.

"Sam."

I groan when I hear Carlos's voice. It's too freaking early.

"I know you are in there. Open the door." He jingles the door handle, and I pull the pillow over my head. "I'm not going away until we talk about last night."

No, this is not happening. I'm so tired. I don't care about last night, today, or tomorrow. I want to sleep.

He continues banging on the door, and I sigh as I remove the pillow.

"Ugh," I grunt, dragging myself from the mattress long enough to click the lock on the door and collapse face down on the covers. I cut him a glance long enough to see him closing the door before I bury myself in the bedding. "Say your piece and get out."

I don't need to know why he smelled like cheap perfume, I deducted what happened, and it feels like a betrayal of what was building between us. His actions wiped it all away.

"I know it looks bad, but I didn't do anything. I had to run an errand, the guys wanted to blow off some steam, they drank too much, and then there were these ladies at the bar, and the—" He is repeating the same nonsense as last night, so I raise my hand in the shape of an 'L,' and then close it to say shut it. "Will you look at me?"

I flip over and peel my eyelids apart to look at him. "I know guys like you. Hell, I hired guys like you. You all go into town, get shitfaced, have sex with randos, and then come home to girlfriends begging forgiveness. I don't care, Carlos. We're nothing, so it doesn't matter." That's way too coherent of me at this early hour.

"We're not nothing. You said 'us' yesterday."

Maybe and true. I said that. "So?"

"The truth is, I was there when I wanted to be here." He squats, leveling his eyes with mine. Do I believe him? No.

"At least you don't smell anymore." I turn over and put my back to him. A book lands on the bed next to me. Reading the spine, it's a Spanish-English dictionary.

"That's the errand I went on." He walks to the other side of the bed and sits on the corner near Tiberia. She curls into a ball, hiding her snout in her tail and peeking at me. "It took me a while to find one, and by the time I caught up with the guys, they were three sheets in, and the girls, well, you're right, the guys are regulars. I left them the truck and did twenty klicks back."

I slip my hand from under the comforter to retrieve the book. Flipping the pages, it's newer with a better layout. That was considerate of him since he knows how much I rely on it. "Klicks back?"

"Twenty klicks is twenty kilometers, so I ran about twelve miles."

"You ran twelve miles in that stormy weather to get away?" I squint at him. "I don't believe you."

"It had already rained, and it was cool outside. I didn't want to be there." He tilts his head, imploring me to believe him, and I tuck the book under the covers. "Then it was nice when I saw you were waiting up and mad as hell. No one has cared about me like that in a long time." He looks at me, burrowed under the covers, and smiles. A genuine smile that gives me little butterflies.

"If I'm honest, I might have worried about you."

He chuckles, and it's such a comforting sound. "Oh, I got that message loud and clear by how upset you got."

I slide the covers down a smidge to smile at him, conveying what I find hard to put in words through actions. Then I remembered why I was distraught.

"But you have a cell phone. I saw it fall out of your jacket." I get to the point of why I felt betrayed.

He pulls it out of his pocket and tosses it on the bed between us. "This?"

I sit up and snatch it from the sheets. "This is freedom! My freedom! One call and I am out of here. Don't you understand that?" I raise my voice, anger brewing again.

An odd look crosses his face as if he hears me for the first time. "It's Beartooth. It tracks the security team, texts, or calls us. This is not a regular cell. May I?" He opens his hand, and I place it in his palm. He unlocks it, and a map with tons of dots pops up on the screen. He taps on one, and it shows their name and location on the property.

"Wow," I murmur. He's monitored as closely as I am. He taps on something else, pulling up messages about this morning's patrol and a message from him last night saying he's coming in on foot, don't shoot. I'm speechless, staring at him.

"No Wi-Fi or cellular data. Untraceable outside of the users." He continues tapping and showing, and I look away toward the veranda. Of course, el diablo would be high tech. He can afford the very best to protect himself. "There is another thing. Some guys showed up last night. I don't know who they are, and they are not on here."

This last statement has me looking back at him. He closes the tracker thing and puts it back in his pocket. "Was one wearing a fancy green suit?"

He immediately stiffens. "Did he see you?"

"I don't think so." I pause, thinking about how he turned his head but not out the window. Not at me.

"Explain."

"It was after midnight when I was finally done. Thank you very much."

"I fully intended to help you, but you kicked me out."

"Anyway. When I was taking Tiberia out for the night, it was dark, and I sat on the bench to clean the sand off my shoes. I saw him through the window, he turned to the side and was talking on a cell phone, but he didn't look out to the courtyard. You know how the bench is in the shadows, so I don't think he saw me."

"Your dog is white."

I rake my fingers through my morning curls to tame them.

"Yes, but I tucked her between my legs like you did that one time and then crouched over her to hide us."

"She didn't bark or whine?" He knows how vocal she is.

I look at the ceiling, trying to recall if she did. "No, I don't recall her making any noise."

"And when you went inside?"

"It was quiet. I was nervous because new faces are always bad for me." He frowns. "Well, except you."

"What does that mean? New faces?" He casts a curious look, causing me to look away. I haven't told him about the dragon. I'm not sure I want to, at least not yet. Because once I tell him about Diego, it will lead to Maximiliano and our relationship years ago. He admitted to liking 'us,' and I do too. I don't want to lose that once he finds out the truth. "Did anyone see you come in here?" he continues, not pressing me for answers to his other questions.

"I don't think so. I can't remember if I turned around, but Tiberia hears everything, and she didn't alert me of anything. We went straight to my room." He stands, paces a bit, and then stops.

"What is this?" He's staring at the camera.

"The boss man records me." It sounds humiliating admitting it. He looks at me over his shoulder before pulling out a huge knife and using it as a screwdriver on the plate behind the camera. "I wouldn't do that if I were you."

He ignores my warning when he severs the wires to the camera, then leans back to watch the red light die. What will happen when el diablo finds out? Will he see Carlos cut it in the last frames? What will he do to Carlos? The thought makes me nauseous.

"It's not right." He places the wall plate over the cables and screws it back into the plaster—a minor victory. I'm not on camera anymore. "And we don't know who all has access to this camera. You assume only Maldonado. It could be more."

"That's revolting." I wrinkle my nose in disgust.

"It is." He snaps his blade closed and tucks it into the breast pocket of his fatigues. When he turns around, his eyebrows pinch together, making him look furious.

"What?"

"I think it's best to stay here for a day or two."

"Here, like in my room? No." I shake my head, that's not even an option. I am not losing my freedom for a second time. "Not a chance."

"Sam, I need to figure out who these guys are and why they are here."

That's not enough of a reason.

"No, I can't. I can't go back." I take a deep breath and place my hand over my fluttering heart to stop the rising panic. "You don't understand what you are asking of me. You weren't here. You don't know."

Watching my demeanor change, he crosses the space to sit with me on the bed. His hand covers mine as his eyes search my face. "Calm down."

The room is getting hotter, and I fan myself with the book. He doesn't understand. That dark place . . . the loneliness and isolation nearly broke me. Long days of boredom, despair, and haunting thoughts. I can't do it again. I honestly don't know if I could come back from it. And el diablo is not here to force me out of it. "It was bad . . . I can't."

"Hey, look at me." His chestnut eyes are warm and understanding. "What was bad? Tell me."

My lips tremble. I fight the tears welling in my eyes and take a shaky breath. "The captivity. It was before you came and before Tiberia. I was locked in this room. Week after week. My mind . . ." I can't take the intensity of his stare. I focus on the button on his jacket. "It was haunting . . . I felt like I was losing myself."

His hand smooths back my hair and pulls me into a hug. I don't immediately reciprocate, surprised by his compassion. He doesn't falter, though, leaving his hand to rest on the back of my neck while my forehead presses into his collar. "I've been in the dark as you have. You won't go there again. All right?"

"How?" I sniff, letting a couple of tears fall onto the rough canvas of his coat. "How can you say that?"

"Because you have me now. I'll come back and tell you what I find out. In the meantime, keep yourself distracted. Practice your self-defense, workout, read your book, anything to keep those thoughts from coming." His deep voice vibrates into my body, and I want to stay in the circle of his arms where it's safe and comforting. I don't want to be alone in this tiny room. "Can you do that?"

My throat burns with emotions, and I eke out a meager, "Yeah." I finally have someone who understands how terrifying the dark thoughts can be.

His hand slips from my neck to my shoulder blades and rubs slow circles. "Let's take it one day at a time. Give me today to do some recon on these guys, and then I'll come back later. Okay? Today?"

I nod, pulling back to look at him through my watery vision. He partially smiles and wipes the wetness from my cheeks with a curved index finger.

"You'll come back? You promise?"

"I promise." He holds my hand in his and gives it a little squeeze. I exhale the tension collecting in my body.

"What about Tiberia? She'll need to go out and eat." I look at her snoozing away on the corner of the bed. "And the ladies?"

"I'll handle her. And I'll let Rosa know you have taken ill and to send up some food." He squeezes my hand again before standing and touching his pockets as if checking for something.

"My period, tell her it's my period. She'll know."

"Your period? Are you sure?" Bewilderment flashes across his face.

"A story for another time. But if it's my period, then I can return tomorrow. If I'm sick, I can't."

When he swipes her leash from the top of the bureau, Tiberia stands and stretches, then looks back at me as he slides it over her head. She seems reluctant to go with him, and I coo at her for encouragement. With his hand on the door, something else pops into my brain.

"Carlos, were both guys dressed nice, like wealthy? Because the one I saw last night was super stylish. Not like the guys around here, not like the Marines." I pause, thinking about the difference between the men. "Like upper class."

"Yes, certainly wealthy. And I suspect they buy American girls." His face is stoic when he looks at me.

"Coyotes." I instantly go numb.

"Lock the door." He taps on the doorframe before closing it behind them. I jump out of bed, bolting the lock, and lean against the door.

Coyotes.

The horror those poor girls endured . . . no, I'll stay in this room all day and night if that's what it takes to stay safe.

El diablo doesn't deal in human trafficking. Hopefully, Carlos is wrong, and they are not coyotes. Either way, I don't want to be around while they are here. Like I told him, new faces are bad for me. If Tiberia is safe, I want to stay hidden and wait for him to report back.

I hope he stays safe himself. Seeing that tracking device and how many men guard this place is concerning. How many would turn coat to help me escape? Carlos would have to convince them. Now I need to persuade Carlos.

Hearing there is a town only twelve miles away is good news. If we could use the truck he left for the men, I could hide in the back. We wouldn't have to cross the desert and mountains on foot and risk encountering the predators living out there.

Chapter 30

By the time the young girl who blushed at el diablo that one time arrived with a food tray, I had completed Will's workout routine, ran through a mix of mine and Carlos's self-defense techniques, showered, and dressed.

I thank her for the food, bolt the door, and take the tray over to the balcony doors.

The sunshine is streaming in, warming the wood floors, and it feels nice to bask in the light while I eat. My brain is a myriad of thoughts. The dragon, the doctor and his injections, the coyote from last night, Carlos holding me, escaping this place and making it back home to Mom. They run in an exhaustive loop as I eat and watch the ocean.

When I am done, I put the tray on the bureau, wash up, and lie on my stomach to study my dictionary. I work through the words, practicing tense and inflection and putting together common phrases and longer sentences. I work through so many for so long, my eyes burn, and I need a break. Closing them is a pleasant relief, and I doze off.

I wake with a start and realize someone is knocking at the door. I roll to the edge of the bed and get up to ask who it is.

"It's me."

Unfastening the bolt, I open the door in excitement and see a worried expression on his face.

"Are you okay?" He looks me up and down before stepping inside and kicking the door closed with his boot.

"Yeah, why?"

"I was knocking awhile and got concerned." Oh, he is worried because of our dark conversation. That makes sense.

"I fell asleep." I watch his expression change as I cross the room to sit on the bed and lean against the broken headboard. His eyes flicker to it.

"Compliments of el diablo."

"El diablo?"

"That's what I call the boss man since he is the devil incarnate." I sigh, tucking my hair behind my head. "Were you running again?" I glance at the sweat rings on his T-Shirt around his neck and armpits.

"Yeah." His palm sweeps the perspiration from his forehead into his hair. "I need you to tell me the truth. About the guy."

"The guy in the green jacket?"

"No, the doctor guy."

"Why?" I purse my lips.

"I saw the three of them talking when I was on patrol. I think they are working together somehow."

"Oh." That makes my skin crawl. Could he be drugging girls to get them ready to transport?

"He treated you, didn't he?"

Treated. If you can say taking advantage of a defenseless, unconscious woman by pumping her full of drugs and doing God knows what, then sure. Treated.

"Something like that."

"How do you know?"

My gaze flickers to the veranda doors, wishing they were open for the breeze to come in. I debate on this trust thing again. Carlos has been nothing but trustworthy, saving me at every turn, so I decide to go with my gut and ignore his words about not trusting anyone.

Looking him dead in the eyes, I spill my guts. "My memory is in pieces, flashes that come to me when something triggers it. I didn't know that doctor guy until I saw him in the kitchen. The minute I saw his face, it unlocked a memory of him and el diablo talking about bringing me here."

"Why here?"

"I don't know. The doctor said it was not good for me to travel, but el diablo decided otherwise. Even made that guy come with us."

"Why did you need him in the first place?"

I sigh before launching into the story, from finding the secret passageway to waking here and omitting my past with el diablo. He remains quiet. I assume adding my pieces to whatever information he has.

"Something doesn't add up. Why beat you and then drug you to get better?" Wrinkles form across his forehead as he processes.

"I know. I thought the same thing. But el diablo said he acted of his own volition, which is odd because who goes against the boss? I would think no one." Voicing my suspicions makes me feel better because I still think el diablo is lying about the dragon.

"Agree, going against Maldonado is a death sentence, and this guy isn't dead."

"I know. I can't make sense of it."

"So let me get this straight. He beats you in Columbus, slips the underwear on you here, and burns Maria. Why? It's petty stuff." His eyebrows pinch together in thought.

I glare at him because I don't find any of it 'petty.'

"You know what I mean. It's insignificant compared to his operations. Why go after innocent women? We're missing something," Carlos echoing my thoughts, validates what I had been thinking this whole time. It doesn't add up, and he's as puzzled as I am.

"Who's the third guy? You said the doctor, the green jacket guy, and there is a third guy. Who is that?" I ask, wondering if it's the dragon. "Does he have the scarred face like I described yesterday?"

"Nope, and I don't know who he is. You can't start asking questions, especially being the new guy."

I'd imagine that being true.

"You said you're mostly Marines. Does that buy you some alliance?"

"Some, but not enough to ask questions I shouldn't be asking. I'll be back. I need to figure this out." He turns on his heel, heading to the door when I decide to come clean with him about my plans. I've trusted him with some of the past, but I need to trust him more to secure my future.

"Wait!" I slide off the bed to stand next to the bureau. "Yesterday, with the snakes. I lied."

"What do you mean?" He shifts his weight to lean against the bureau.

"I wasn't climbing them for fun. I was trying to figure out a way to escape."

He twists a dark eyebrow up. I think this is probably not the right time to ask him. "How do you propose to do that?"

"Well, that's why I went on patrol with you. I wanted to look at the other side of the property to see if there were any escape routes." I lay my arm on the dresser, trying to look casual as my insides twist with anxiety.

"Impossible."

"Why? The terrain? I know it's daunting b—"

"They will kill you."

"No, el diablo said he wouldn't. He said I could try, and he would tell his guys to let me go."

"Doesn't make sense. Why would he let you go when he moved you out of the country and flew in your dog?" Skepticism mars his face, and I know it sounds unbelievable.

"He did, but I can't do it alone. What if someone helped me?" I tilt my head, and his mouth flattens into a line. I immediately know he will not help. "Hear me out. I know he pays more than Uncle Sam, but you said it yourself. I am famous and have money. Access to a lot. I could pay you more, and you can get Tiberia and me out of here."

He says nothing, just stares, and I am super familiar with this game. I always play it with his boss, so I stare back, being as expressive as possible.

"One man isn't enough." He's considering it, and a tiny seed of hope blooms.

"You'd consider it?"

"I'm not a hired gun."

"What does that mean?"

"You've had protection before. You know what it means."

"Carlos." I let out a noisy exhalation. "You said they're always loyal to the highest bidder. If I am it, why wouldn't that work?"

He doesn't answer immediately. And I have nothing more to add.

"Give me time to think." He kicks off the bureau to open the door.

"Time is all I have."

He gives me a long look before stepping into the hallway and closing the door behind him. I bolt it and walk to the veranda, wondering if he will truly consider it.

Chapter 31

Hours pass, and boredom sets in while I lie in bed staring at the ceiling. After praying, meditating, tossing and turning, and trying to sleep, I got up to sit by the veranda doors and watch the thick cloud cover float across the night sky. There is a light tap on my door, which I assume is Carlos, given it is so late. Unbolting the door, I crack it to see him in the brightly lit hallway and squint my eyes.

"You awake?"

"Yup."

"Can I come in?" He steps forward, forcing me to step back. "They left."

"The guys are gone?" I lie on the bed as he closes the door.

"Yes." His boot hits the bed by accident. "Sorry, it's dark in here."

"The moon isn't out, making the room very dark. What time is it?"

"After midnight." The bed dips. "Do you mind if I sit? I gotta get the sand out of my boots, and I can't see."

I turn on my bedside lamp and blink against the vile intrusion into my eyeballs.

"Your hair is wild."

"I'm sure it is. I laid down with it wet." I finger comb the curls and work through the knots. "How's Tiberia? I missed her today."

"Spoiled, she's sleeping with my bunkmate. He's a dog person. We've been taking turns training and exercising her." I'm not sure I like that, but I recognize Carlos can't keep towing her around while trying to do recon.

"She deserves to be spoiled. I didn't realize you share a room." I thought this place would be big enough to house everyone.

"Yeah, two guys to every room. It's not bad." He's bent over messing with his boots when he turns to face me. "Want to get out of here?" He is dumping sand all over my floor like I am a maid and will clean up after him.

"Now?" My voice is shrill, and I clear my throat to correct it. "It's late. And what do you mean 'get out of here,' like an escape?" Excitement surges through me, and I climb out of bed to get dressed in my planned escape outfit.

His boot drops, and he stares me dead in the eyes. "Escape? You need to put that out of your mind. That's never going to happen. I meant to get out of your room."

"So that's it, huh? You didn't even think it over." I stop rustling through my drawers to look at him, expecting an explanation.

"With you and I, it's impossible." He returns to dumping another load of sand from his other boot on my floor. I frown at his answers and the pile of dirt on the floor.

"What about the truck? You could take it into that town, and I could stow away in it."

"I don't have free access to the vehicles. It took a lot of convincing for me to run into town and get your book. They are suspicious of new guys here, rightfully so."

I chew on my lip, trying to think of a different approach. "Can you stop it? You're making my only living space disgusting, and who will clean it? Me? I don't exactly have cleaning products or a broom in here." I don't care if I sound grouchy. He dashed my hopes of rescuing me, so who cares?

Grabbing a change of clothes, I walk into the bathroom to brush my teeth and get ready at this Godforsaken hour. When I open the bathroom door, Carlos stands in front of it with his hand full of sand. With a raised eyebrow, I move aside and watch him flush it down the toilet. Never doubt a clean Marine, I guess.

He's out of the bathroom faster than I am, possibly uneasy about how small or close it puts us together. "Grab a sweater. The temperature has dropped."

"Okay." I exit the bathroom, slip on my sandals, and glance at the floor to see if it is spotless before rummaging through the bureau for a sweater. "Should I change out of my shorts? I have little as far as winter clothes, but . . ."

"Sweater is fine."

I grab the only sweater I can find. It's thin and made for summer, so I hope it's not too cold outside.

He opens the bedroom door, and the hallway is silent. The howling wind from the other night is gone, and the only sounds from this sleeping fortress are the creaks from our footsteps on the back staircase. The courtyard is dark, but the potted plants scrap against the windows as we pass. Once Carlos pushes open the back door, I catch my breath because he's right. The temperature is far colder.

"Damn, it's cold," I complain, and he touches the small of my back to prod me out the door. "This is a terrible idea." I hustle to put my sweater on, knowing it will not make any difference when I step away from the shelter of the courtyard walls.

"You'll be fine." He moves around my huddling self to jog down the path. "Hurry," he yells from the darkness.

I groan but jog down the boardwalk and stop when I get to the beach.

"You built a fire? How did you build a fire on the beach?"

"Easy, plenty of driftwood and seaweed." He leads me to it.

Goosebumps cover my skin, and I sit as close as possible to bask in the heat.

"Dang, this is so nice. Thank you for doing this." I smile at him, jutting my hands toward the fiery flames. He nods, looking into the fire, but does not move to sit with me. "Come on."

I pat the sand and wait. It takes a moment, and I watch the hesitation on his face until I shrug and give up. "Suit yourself."

The wind shifts, sending plumes of smoke toward me, and I choke on its intensity. "Fan it. It will dissipate," he finally squats next to me.

"You're acting odd. What's up?" I pat the sand again, trying to make this more comfortable for the both of us, and he relents, swinging to sit with his legs stretched out.

"I have a bad feeling."

I think I heard him wrong.

"You have a bad feeling?" I repeat, and his frown deepens. "That's odd because I'm the one that's all feelings, and you're the one that is all facts, I mean data, no wait, strategy . . . you know what I mean."

"Yes, that's also what is troubling me."

"That you have feelings? Yeah, I can see where that would bother you, but us normal people are used to them, as irritating as they are," I joke, and he sort of smiles, but it doesn't meet his eyes. He seems bothered about something. It's odd, and I'm trying not to freak out since I rely on his stoicism.

"Well, I have sort of confided in you. Do you want to do the same?" I offer, doubting if he will do it. He remains silent, glancing at me before looking into the fire again. I let it drop, I offered twice, and he still didn't take advantage of it.

I take off my sandals to shove my toes in the sand, wrap my arms around my legs, and prop my chin on my knee. At least it's peaceful with the crackle of the fire and the lazy roll of the ocean surf. If I could bottle this sound for later, I would.

"I have a sister. She's your age but blond. You remind me of her."

He breaks the silence, and I turn my head to rest my cheek on my knee.

"Do you talk to her?" I assumed he was a lone wolf after losing his fiancée.

"I haven't seen her in three years."

"Why not?" I don't want to be intrusive, but if this bothers him, I want to be supportive.

"She got knocked up, the guy's worthless and left them in a rat-infested apartment. Mom convinced her to move back home, help with the baby, and go to school. She blames me for running the guy off when I visited her during my last deployment."

"Did you?"

"Yeah, but he didn't need much convincing. He was staying with another girl. A real piece of shit. I send money home. My way of apologizing." He stares into the flames, and they cast an orangey hue on his tan skin.

"I'm sure she appreciates it. Being a single mom is tough."

"Yeah, I knew you'd understand. Your foundation helped her. Not directly, like you wouldn't know her name, but you guys gave the hospital a grant or something to fund her treatment."

"What hospital?" What a small world.

"St. Cecilia in Orlando."

"I was there." I smile, thinking back to that trip with fondness because we took a bunch of the kids to Disney World with their parents and caregivers. "We had the reception at the hospital and then took some kids to Disney. It was an enjoyable day. I made Ardy, my bodyguard, ride Expedition Everest. He hurled all over the place. Will chickened out. He was the loud and obnoxious one. Man, he'd let me get away with murder sometimes. But Ardy was the dad of the group. He was super serious, cautious, and always told me 'no.' I threw a temper tantrum until he agreed to go on the ride. We sat in the front, and the fact that he could see what was coming only worsened it. He hurled on the ride and then again after. His stomach wasn't right the rest of the day. It was great. I really miss those two." I chuckle, thinking back to all the good times we shared.

"What happened to them?" He stretches his arms behind him, and my laughter fades.

"Honestly, I think it was getting boring for them. Babysitting a famous kid stretched on longer than their original assignment. They were Marines, like you, wanting more action. I tried to get them for our mission, but I couldn't find them. Both went into private personal defense, I think, so I have no way of getting in touch with them. I don't even know if they work together anymore. I hope so. They make a good team. I think about them often. I don't know. Maybe it was something I did?" I shift away from him, uncomfortable at how I let two significant people slip out of my life. "Did your sister go with us? To Disney?"

"No, she was too sick. I know they wheeled some kids to the reception to meet you, but she was too sick for that too." He picks up a stick and stokes the flames.

"I'm sorry."

"Don't be. Her leukemia eventually went into remission, and when I left the first time, she was cancer-free but skinny and slightly weaker."

"And that's how I remind you of her? Skinny and weak?" I joke to lighten the mood.

"No, you're both fighters."

Fighters. He called me a fighter. I can't believe my ears because I didn't think of myself as a fighter. There are so many people that are stronger, tougher, and braver than I am. Basically, the entire world, but this Marine called me a fighter. My throat tightens, and I am glad I am looking at the fire because I couldn't look him in the face if I wanted to.

"Tell me about Maldonado. How much do you know about him?"

I slowly exhale. This is the conversation I have been avoiding. I don't want Carlos to end 'us,' but I can't keep the truth from him any longer. It was fair to keep it from him in the beginning, but now I am running out of excuses other than my whole selfish reasons.

I shift positions to mirror him. "It's a long story."

"As you said earlier, we've got time."

Yeah, we do.

I take a big breath and then talk about the man I used to love five years ago. Once I start, I can't stop. I laugh, cry, and omit the intimate details of our sexual relationship, but he gets the gist. He knows about the dragon and the doctor, but I tell him about sleeping on the veranda, the depths of my depression, and some conversations I had with el diablo before he left.

Carlos is silent for most of it, asking an occasional question to clarify, and by the time I end, I feel lighter. As if spilling my secrets, some not even Will or Ardy knew, are cathartic and healing. Only one other person in the world knows this story, and he is down south somewhere.

The fire is dying, needing more driftwood for the embers to hold on.

"It makes sense," he says after a long while.

"What does? I don't have the foggiest clue."

"Whether it be love or revenge, you're his possession."

El diablo had already called me that, and I hated it. Carlos saying it now makes it even worse.

I stare into his face, hoping to read something from his explanation. "First of all, I am not a possession. Second, I don't think he loves me, not anymore. Although ... never mind."

"He broke your headboard demanding your love." Well, yeah, that's true. "Possibly both, the more I think of it."

"He has her." I sit up.

"Doesn't matter."

"It does matter. It does because I matter!"

I throw sand at the black embers in frustration.

"Hey, calm down. I'm on your side here." He touches my forearm to stop my fit. "Plus, you're killing the fire, and it will get even colder." I throw my last handful toward the ocean. "Look, I'm telling you from his perspective."

"Fine." I rub my hands together to get rid of the excess sand. "What good does that do?"

"If you put yourself in his shoes, you can try to figure out his next moves."

"Okay, but can we go back to the fact that he has her? I know you don't care, but that's a huge deal."

"I never said I don't care. It is a huge deal, but not how you think about it."

"Carlos, spell it out because I'm tired, starving, cold, and smell like a campfire."

"Thinking strategically, he wants something from you that only you can give him. You want something from him that only he can give you."

"My freedom, yes." I pause because I don't want to give him what he wants.

"He wants your love."

Yeah. That's the problem.

I look away, watching the dark tide rolling back into the ocean. What does he want me to do? "I'm not sleeping with him." I turn back to sneer at him.

"I didn't say for you to sleep with him. But you must outwit your enemy here. You want freedom, right?" He cocks his eyebrow.

"Duh."

"Then keep your enemies closer. Convince him you want to get away with him. The two of you, a restart on a new relationship."

I want to gag.

"You want me to go on a vacation with el diablo?" Is Carlos crazy because he just said the craziest thing ever?

"Yes, if you convince him to take you to a country with an American embassy, go shopping, go to dinner, go out for any reason, you can escape him and get to the embassy. Once there, you're home free."

I pause and blink, feeling my anger dissipate because he is right. I could be free if I played the game correctly. "Holy shit, that might work." A restart vacation, could I swing it? Could I convince him? I could dredge up those feelings I used to have for him, to be the best actress in the world and pretend I am in love like my old memories. "What if he doesn't agree to a country with an embassy?"

"I might figure something out. Not saying this would work, but if I knew where you were going, maybe I could arrange something."

"What does that mean?" My breath hitches because it sounds like he's willing to help me escape. "A rescue?"

"Possibly."

"Why not rescue me now?"

"Not a chance here. His house, his land, his people. He has all the advantages. It would never work. Get him on more neutral territory where he can't control all the variables, and then we stand a chance."

I chew on my lip, mulling over everything. Both are super long shots, but it's something. Something that might work because he said 'we.' My heart warms with hope.

"But what about you?"

"What about me?" His eyebrow raises.

"How do you get out?"

"I don't want out." He throws the charred stick into the gray embers.

"What? Why not?" He's talking nonsense again. "Seriously, why not?"

He shakes his head, and I stare at every line on his face waiting for an answer. "I have nothing. I don't have a life waiting for me as you do. This is it."

That's so sad.

I scoot closer, wanting to comfort him because if this were my life and my words, I'd bawl my eyes out. "You have your sister, and you're an uncle. That's not nothing. And your mom." I place my hand on top of his. His fingers flex into the sand and then relax.

The intensity of his stare surprises me when it lifts from our hands to my face. "That's not what I meant."

"What do you mean?" Curiosity causes me to lean in. "What do you want?"

The embers crackle beside us, and the attraction burns between us. His hand slides out of mine, tracing my knuckles and caressing my arm. Chills race over my skin and into my hair. The glint in his eyes is unmistakable, matching the desire within me. His fingertips curve around my bicep, drawing me toward him, and my gaze falls to his plump lips. I don't want to taste them. I want to devour them.

I raise my hand slowly and in sight, silently asking permission to touch him. His eyes flicker to it, aware of my movement, preparing for it before returning to my face. When my hand touches the side of his neck, his skin is warm, and his jaw flexes.

Our eyes lock as he waits for me. I give him a small smile before leaning forward and brushing my lips on his. They are soft and inviting as I brush them twice before running the tip of my tongue across his bottom lip. He groans, sliding his hand to cup the back of my neck and tilting his head for deeper access.

His mouth softens, opening for me, and I moan as his tongue twists with mine. His palm cups my waist, caressing the soft skin and driving me crazy with lust. It takes everything in me not to straddle his lap.

I'm breathless as he trails kisses across my jawline, trailing his tongue down my neck and nipping at my skin. His hands knead my nape and waist, trying to hold back as the chemistry explodes between us. Ever since he saved me in the ocean, I've wondered about and wanted this kiss.

It's far more sensual than I thought it would be. His quiet patience is intoxicating, drawing me in by relinquishing control and having me initiate. He's everything opposite of el diablo, and I want more.

When he finally stops, I lean back and look into his eyes, wanting to know what this means. What does it change, if anything at all?

"Sammie . . . I didn't mean to do that."

His instant regret hits me hard. I scramble to my feet, tucking my arms across my midsection for warmth against the cold air, and start for the boardwalk.

"Wait," he hollers, and I keep walking, trying to hold it together until I get back upstairs. His hand lands on my shoulder to stop me. "I didn't mean it like that."

"It's fine." My voice cracks as I shrug off his hand, unable to look at him or I will burst out crying.

"I don't want you to think I'm trying to take advantage of you."

The wind blows my curls, and I shiver, rubbing my hands over my goosebumps.

"Come back to the fire and hear me out. Please." He touches my elbow, trying to guide me back, and I wrench it out of his touch.

"Fine."

I trudge over to the remnants of the fire to sit as close to the black embers as I can. He swings his long body to the sand and watches me.

"Well?" I gesture for him to start, seeing regret all over his handsome face.

He blows out a breath. "I'm all mixed up." He pauses, and I wait, unwilling to fill the silence like I always do. "I didn't mean what I said a minute ago. I've wanted to do that since I held you in the ocean." He shakes his head as if needing to clear his mind. "Hell, I've wanted to do much more than that."

"I get it, Carlos. Sex is all you guys think about it."

"No, it's not that. It's a bunch of stuff." He moves closer, and I shoot him a cautious look. "I came here on assignment, just another job. However long it lasted, then I saw you. I couldn't believe it that day when you opened the door. You seemed so happy. You threw your arms around Maldonado, so I thought you were a couple."

That is what I did. I was so grateful for Tiberia, and then he threatened to kill me if I tried to escape, but Carlos wasn't around for that.

"I was stumped. How is this do-gooder dating the most wanted drug lord in the world? I thought the charity was a front, and you were part of his operations, maybe laundering money through your foundation."

"Wow." I am flabbergasted.

"Yeah, I know. I'm wrong. The guys talked, and I overheard the ladies in the kitchen a few times. When I looked closer, you had bags under your eyes, skinny as can be, and then I put it all together. Hearing you fill in all the blanks made me feel sorry for you." He put his hand up when I opened my mouth. "I know you told me you don't want my pity, but I had to reframe everything. I vowed not to cross the line with you. You're here against your will. What kind of guy takes advantage of that?" He sneers in disgust.

"You're not taking advantage of me." Doesn't he know how much he has helped me? Been my saving grace to maintain my sanity? "That's the furthest thing from the truth."

He frowns, and I'm not entirely sure he believes me. "If I'm not, then what am I doing? You're going to get out of here, and when you do, you'll return to your life where everyone loves you. You'll be on every talk show about your story, and it will help more people to come forward and need your foundation. You're in a completely different world."

I search his face, my mind going a million miles an hour because I don't know whether to debate him about getting out of this place, which seems hopeless. Or argue with him about returning to a life I don't want. Or deny that I'll go on the talk show junket to relive this experience repeatedly. He takes my silence as confirmation.

"This is all I know. The military and private security are the gritty sides of what this world is, not the glitz and glamour of your world. I don't fit."

I'm confused. "You mean you've been thinking about us being an actual us?"

Tension coats his face, his jaw clenches, and he gives a curt nod. "You asked what I wanted."

I look out at the ocean, processing everything he told me, and I don't know what to say. I've been so consumed with being imprisoned and giving up hope of escaping while he's been beating himself up for wanting to date and not fitting in. How can two people in the same space live in entirely different realities?

If I ever got out of here, which seems like a long shot, could I imagine a life with him? Would he want to start a new life with me? Not my glamour world or his gritty world, but something in between? Would I?

"Let's head in, the fire is out, and it's getting cold." He stands abruptly, toeing sand onto the embers with his boot. His hand juts out to help me up, and I reluctantly take it. I'm still processing the bomb he dropped on me, and he's already moving on from this night. That is not how I work. I need time to think, pick apart every word he said, my responses, and look for hidden meanings. I can't do all that on the spot with him watching and waiting for an answer.

Chapter 32

The walk back to the fortress is silent. When we get to the kitchen, I stop and look around for anything I can grab to take back to my room with me. It's spotless as always.

"Can I get something? I'm starving." I'm not sure why I am asking him. Maybe it's how we ended it or asking to let some pressure out between us. I don't know but treading lightly seems like a good idea. "Do you mind?"

"Go for it." He leans his hip against the counter and crosses his arms. I can't decide if he is genuinely indifferent or lost in his thoughts from the campfire.

"You don't have to stay. I'll grab something quick and return to my room because this place creeps me out at night." I want him to stay, but I don't want him to feel obligated.

"It's fine. Check for leftovers or cold cuts in the fridge."

I nod, grabbing a few napkins to lie out on the counter before rummaging for bread in the pantry across from him. I rely on the light cascading in from the courtyard windows to move around the kitchen, as the overhead lights are far too bright at this hour.

"Do you want one?" I ask, pulling two pieces out for me.

239

"Sure." He doesn't move a muscle to help, and I roll my eyes when I have my back to him while getting plates out of the cupboard. "There is something I need to tell you."

That is the worst phrase in the world. Instant dread washes over me as I turn to set the dishes on the counter. "What?"

"He married her. That's where he's been."

My stomach twists.

He married her.

I am speechless. Processing the words.

"Um . . ." I can't think of what to say. She introduced herself as his fiancée. The memory is so vivid that I can remember the scent of her perfume. And el diablo? Did he stand before a priest and commit his life to her? Disbelief fogs my brain.

"Yeah," he says, his eyes never leaving mine. I tap the side of the plate. It makes sense now why I couldn't go with him. He lied to me about why. He didn't tell me it was to get married. "I meant to tell you earlier, but . . ."

I press my lips together and take a deep breath before moving to the fridge and pulling out meats, cheese, and condiments. Carlos retrieves a butter knife from the drawer and slides it across the stone countertop. "Mayo or mustard?" I open the jars and pick up the knife.

"Both. There's more."

I pause midair with a clump of mayo on the blade.

"All right." I shift, trying to steal my insides for more.

"They are having a reception, of sorts. Bringing in people for it." He frowns. "I'm not sure how to continue to hide you."

"A reception? Here?" I feel as if I am underwater, hearing the words in slow motion and taking too long for them to register. "I mean, receptions happen after weddings." I try to sound casual and convince myself that this is normal, but this is my future that hangs in the balance. "When?"

"Tomorrow."

My hands shake, and he takes the knife out of my grasp. "Tomorrow."

I look at the pattern on the tile floor. "That's . . . uh . . . fast. Tomorrow, huh?" What will happen to me? If he's back and she's here, how safe am I?

"It's why those guys were here. Maldonado is bringing in caterers, a band, staff, and extra security. All had to be cleared today."

I bite my lip, worry squeezing my guts, and when I look at Carlos, he's still watching me. "I-I don't even know what to say."

He drops the knife in the mayo jar and reaches for my hands. I wipe my sweaty palms against my shorts before placing them in his. His calloused fingers wrap around mine and squeeze.

"Why won't he let me go?" I've asked myself this question too many times, never coming up with the answer. "What am I supposed to do? Live here with him and her?" My shoulders slump in defeat. "This is so—"

"Fucked up." He frowns and pulls me into a hug. My cheek rests against his chest, his heart thumping in my ear, and I close my eyes. It is fucked up, and I have no way out. No way to escape. This means I'll be seeing el diablo tomorrow too. "We'll figure something out."

It's hopeless.

I don't voice that to him when I pull out of his arms to start on the sandwiches. He leans against the counter, content to watch me assemble them.

"More meat." He points to his sandwich, and I shoot him a look. "Ah, I hear it now."

"It sounded funny."

"No, humor is good. It's heavy tonight," he says before walking away to rummage in the pantry.

Very heavy.

My mind is so full of information to process that it's going to burst.

I pile on the meat and cheese and then add lettuce and tomatoes.

"Do you want pickles?" I ask when he passes me, holding some drinks and chips to toss on the table.

"No, let's eat here, though." He picks up both plates while I package everything and put it away in the refrigerator. He waits until I am done and pulls out my chair before pulling out his own. It's an unexpected and friendly gesture.

He sits, takes a huge bite, and dumps a bunch of chips on my plate before unloading a mountain onto his. "Tell me something."

"Yeah?" I say before starting on my sandwich.

"What happened before?"

"Before what?"

"Before you got to his casita. You told me about your relationship with him when you were skating through and the coyotes chasing you, but not the rescue itself."

Trepidation claws at my insides. I intentionally left this out. It didn't go well. I don't know what happened to them. When I woke up from my drug haze, I blocked it from my mind. I couldn't think about that while figuring out el diablo and how to handle captivity. A while back, I decided I would deal with it if I ever made it to the United States.

I pick up a chip and then drop it back onto the pile. My appetite is waning. "It's a long story."

His head tilts. "I figured since you haven't told me."

His hand comes across the table, searching for mine, and I slide it off the table to tuck in my lap. He frowns in response and goes back to eating. I don't deserve his kindness. I really don't. Not after what I did.

The feelings I had been avoiding for weeks were washing over me in waves—guilt, regret, and self-hatred.

My lip curls into a snarl as I recant my greatest failure. "That night . . . we got caught. It was all my fault." I look at my hands, remembering the dirt caked on little Mary's face.

The stench was overwhelming. I pinched the neck of my shirt over my nose as I trailed behind two armed soldiers leading our mission. With each lock they busted on the steel doors came a gaunt shadow of a soul, lost in the recesses of a dark, dank closet.

No light, no toilet, a fluid-filled mattress, an overpowering odor, and a terrified wisp of a girl. I entered their cell, assured them of their safety, and handed them to Mom. She was flanked by two men behind her, and we clustered the girls in between us as we collected them.

We were silent and stealthy, moved swiftly through the compound, and rescued six girls until we rounded a corner. I saw her. I saw Mary. The little girl was terrified. She shivered in her bone-thin clothing, standing on the platform surrounded by evil, vile men clutching fistfuls of money. I lunged against my soldiers in front, cursed at those pieces of shit, and chaos ensued.

Their captors shouted commands and scrambled to keep their buyers safe while they attempted to escape. Bullets started flying, and the men behind Mom shoved her to the floor. We all went down and took cover between rows of chairs. The leader of our mission shouted and pointed toward a door. He thrust a key into my palm and fired back.

We crawled across broken glass and overturned tables. I rushed to grab Mary. She was dazed, muted by shock, and light as a feather. When we reached the door, we sprinted down the staircase to the truck at the back of the compound. Our men kept exchanging fire until we were all loaded.

I tried to wait for them, but we were taking on too much gunfire. There were too many of them and not enough of us. I abandoned them. I left them behind when I gunned it out of there.

"I killed them," I sob, my face falling into my hands as my shoulders shake violently. A scrape of the chair and Carlos is beside me, hugging me. He clutches my hair, holding my head against his shoulder, and rubbing my back as I fist his shirt. Overwhelming guilt and regret slug through my veins, making my heart heavy and my chest ache. "And their names . . . I didn't know them . . . why didn't I know them?"

Drawing on his strength, I loosen my hands and lean back to search his face. My lip trembles, and tears stream down my cheeks. "Why didn't I learn their names?"

His knuckle wipes away my tears, watching my anguish before pulling me back into him. I sob, and his hand returns to stroking my hair. The cords of his muscular neck press into my forehead, and I feel his solid and steady pulse. Alive, very much alive when those men are not.

"In Afghanistan, an IED knocked us all over the roadside. I couldn't hear. My buddy's leg was gone, blown twenty feet away. I tried to drag myself toward it, thinking they could reattach it if I could reach it. He didn't make it. None of them did." I catch my breath and slow my tears. "Damn thing about it was I was hurt, had shrapnel in my back and abdomen, and all I could think about was his leg."

Grimacing, I lean back. "I'm sorry for your loss. I didn't know."

He tucks a curl behind my ear and says, "Save your pity."

My words are coming back to me.

"I told you that because things don't make sense at the time. We sit around after beating ourselves up about things we should have done or known. But the things you do or say make little sense in the situation. I had nightmares for months afterward about his leg. If I could have dragged myself faster, gotten on my hands and knees, and crawled, he would be here today. Know their names, don't know their names. It doesn't change that you and your team saved those girls."

I move entirely out of his embrace, suddenly needing space from the comfort and reassurance he's providing as it stands in direct conflict with the doubt and regrets I harbor.

"It cost those men their lives, I'm sure of it. And I did that. I am responsible for that." Feeling too vulnerable, I drag my legs up and wrap my arms around them to rest my chin on my knees.

He sets his jaw, scowling at me. "I know what you are thinking, and it's not true."

"You don't know." I raise my head and lower my voice because he has no idea what I think. He has no idea that I begged for my death. Even now, as my potential death seems to loom before me with all these important people coming, I want to live even though I don't deserve to.

He leans in. "It's not your fault."

"Don't say that to me."

"It's not."

"Don't compare your hero story to mine." I grit my teeth, feeling the fury and anger rise.

"I'm not, but you're wrong." He touches my knee, and I explode, standing so fast that my chair clatters against the wall. He stands too, about to say something, and I put my hands up.

"I'm right. I'm greedy, and I'm selfish. They died, and I lived, and I want to live. I want to keep on living. I hate myself for wanting to keep living, and I am the one that took their choice away. I did it. They were being overtaken while we escaped. When I threw that truck in gear, I didn't wait for them. I hauled ass out of there. I decided. I played God. I did. Me. And I fucking hate myself for it. I hate that I want to keep living. I hate myself. So, you don't know. You don't understand, okay? You don't get to say that to me." I'm heaving, the pain in my chest is piercing, and I want to cave into the mess I have made of everything.

"Don't be nice to me, Carlos. I can't handle it. I can't have you tell me lies and fill me with hope. El diablo already does that, and it kills me. Now that you know I want to live, as disgusting as that thought is, I can't fight el diablo and fight you too, okay? I can't."

"Can you listen for a minute?" I clamp my mouth closed. "It's not your fault. Marines, we chose our missions. We know some risks going in. Others we find out when we are in it. Death is a risk. Being captured is a risk. Being held hostage or tortured is a risk. Those are givens. They gave their lives for what they believed was right, is right. It's honorable what those men did. It is repugnant and self-serving that you are wallowing in guilt or hatred over their honorable deaths. If you want to hate yourself, go for it, but don't lay that crap at their feet. They completed their mission. They deserve your respect and appreciation, not your remorse."

My blood runs cold, and my stomach turns to stone. I don't want to dishonor them in any way. I'd never do that, but his concept is so foreign to me that I can't think straight. He makes it seem so clear cut when it's anything but.

"I-I don't know what to say," I whisper, blinking back more tears. I've held onto this guilt since it happened, and I can't release it immediately.

"You don't have to say anything. You need to work on reframing it for what it is. Perception of an event is not the reality of an event." He leans over to pick up my chair and motions for me to sit. He drags his back to the other side of the table and plops down.

It takes a few long minutes to calm down, and he finishes his sandwich.

"Why do you keep saying reframe it? You said that before."

He gulps his drink and then answers. "Part of the medical discharge is a psych evaluation. At first, I didn't want to go. Lots of bullshit stigma about it from how I grew up, but it helped a lot. This therapist guy was a Vietnam vet, did five tours, and saw a bunch of messed up shit, so he understood what was happening with me. So reframing is like taking the event and holding it in your hand." He picks up his empty glass soda bottle. "And you exam if from your angle, how you saw it happen, right?"

"Yeah." I'm intrigued by his demonstration.

"I see the label on this bottle. The name of the drink, the name of the company, and their tagline. What do you see from this angle?" He holds the bottle higher.

"The table of ingredients, and some super small writing under it. I can also see the label and stuff through it." He puts down his empty bottle to pick up my untouched root beer.

"Better example, now can you see my side?"

"No."

"And I can't see yours. I can only see my angle of the event, and you can only see your angle of the event. But when I twist it around, you see a new angle you have never seen before. If I keep twisting and turning, you see new angles until you finally see them all. That's what you have to do with your problems. So, in your case, you must look at the event from that little girl's viewpoint. How does she feel now that she's rescued? From those men's perspectives, when they took the job, knew the risks, and upheld the mission? It was a success. They saved those women and that little girl. And keep on going around until you have considered all angles." He places the root beer back on the table. "And that's reframing."

I open my mouth and close it, fascinated and terrified to unravel it to that depth.

"But . . ." What am I trying to say? I think for a second. "I don't know . . . that's hard, and wow, really dredging it up and then sorting through it, huh?"

"It's brutal to keep drowning in all that shit you're carrying around. Reframing is hard as hell, but it works when you wade through the sea of crap to make it to shore." He finishes his chips, then tilts the chip bag to his mouth to eat the crumbs.

I sit there dumbfounded because he blew my mind. He shoves his plate aside to rest his elbows on the table.

"You need to eat." He points to my full plate.

My food is unappealing, and I push my plate toward him, remembering he said food doesn't go to waste around here. "I lost my appetite. You can have it."

He looks from the plate to me. "It would be better if you eat it."

I shake my head and open my root beer to take a few sips.

"How is Tiberia? Can we get her now?"

"Nah, she's bedded down for the night. I'll bring her to you in the morning," he says, stuffing my sandwich in his mouth. "Well, later this morning."

"She's a good dog."

"She needs more training," he says. "Did you work out today?"

"I did. I guess we can't practice the self-defense tomorrow." I look at him, and he nods. "It's odd, right? The reception?"

"It is."

Not wanting to rehash all that, I stand and pick up his empty plate to wash it in the sink. I hear the chair scrape across the floor and the trash bin opening before feeling his presence beside me with my plate. I see a towel in his hand, ready to dry the dishes for me.

"I'm beat." I yawn, and he hums in acknowledgment. "Give me nine hours before you bring her up."

He flicks his wrist to check the time. "It's nearly 2 a.m., so you'll get a few hours. Not nine."

"Okay." I rinse the plates in the sink for him to retrieve before grabbing the disinfectant spray to wipe the table and countertops. It's rather nice to have him in the kitchen with me. Would it be like this if we could figure out a new life? Quiet evenings in the kitchen, enjoying each other's company? And long nights in the bedroom exploring each other?

That kiss. Our chemistry. He was patient, not rushed, relaxed, and let me lead. The way his fingers threaded through my hair was sexy, encouraging, but not controlling. Eager and inviting. The perfect blend of caring and desire.

"You almost done?" he asks, interrupting my thoughts, and my head snaps up.

"Yep."

My cheeks are on fire.

He is standing near the doorway that leads to the back stairs, and I quickly put away the supplies. After glancing around the kitchen to ensure it's clean, I join him as he jogs up the stairs. We walk to my room in comfortable silence. So much was said tonight. At least, he knows the entire story now, all of it.

"Thanks for tonight." The words don't do justice to the weight of everything we talked about.

"Thanks for confiding in me. I know it wasn't easy."

No, it wasn't, that's for sure.

"I'm so tired. I'm not even going to shower. I'm going to smell like a campfire." I groan as we approach my door. He's quick to disappear inside to check everything.

Once he is satisfied, I walk into my room. "I'll bring the dog by at first light. I have things to do, so I won't be around."

"Wait, what things?"

"Things. I'll be back in a few hours."

He places his hand on my waist, drawing me into his arms for a long hug. I close my eyes and rest my head against his chest, breathing in the same smoky wood scent. His forearms rest across my shoulders, and his head drops to cocoon me into his body.

I haven't felt this level of closeness, not even with el diablo. Carlos accepts me for who I was then and who I am now, and everything in between. Acceptance. I didn't even know I was looking for it, and he helped me find it. Accept all my parts, even the ugly ones that need reframing. Yes, I can see a life with him beyond this place. Tiberia and Carlos are my new vision.

With a kiss on the top of my head, his hands slide down my arms to squeeze both hands before releasing them. "Lock the door." He pulls it closed behind him, and I collapse onto the bed with a mind overflowing from tonight.

Chapter 33

I t's as if I just closed my eyes when I am greeted by fervent kisses all over my face. It takes me a second to put two and two together until a loud whine pierces my ear. Tiberia's fluffy body wiggles twice as fast with her tail slapping the air in excitement.

"Tiberia!" I pat the bed for her to launch herself onto my lap. She lands with a hard thud, rolling over onto her back so I can rub her belly. After a few scratches, she wiggles to lick my face, causing me to laugh, and I duck my head from her relentless love.

"She clearly loves you," Carlos says, and I peek over tufts of white fur to see him leaning against the doorframe. I guess I forgot to lock it last night.

"You think?" I giggle at her antics. She's rubbing her face against the shirt from last night and positioning her lower body to lie full length on me. "I missed her."

"I got to head out." He drops her leash on the bureau and opens the door. Even Tiberia perks up to watch him.

"Where are you going again?" I hug her, unsure if she'll bolt out the open door or miss me enough to stay put.

"I got to figure out today and what this means for us. See you later." He winks and closes the door behind him. He's sure in a hurry this morning, but I didn't miss the catch in his voice when he said 'us.' I like the thought of 'us' too.

"Were you good for him? I heard you were cuddling and sleeping on that guy's bed. Good girl." She yawns when I scratch behind her ear. "I feel the same way." I wonder if he had let her out yet. Let's see if she'll let me sleep a few more hours.

I slide her body to my right and shift to curl around her. She flips her head backward to give me more kisses. "Thank you for the kisses, but let's nap." I push her snout away, and she rolls into a ball, connecting her nose to her tail. I smile and close my eyes, letting sleep overtake me.

"Gatita."

I moan and roll over, reaching for that fluffy pile of fur and coming up empty. "Prob . . . floor." My eyes are plastered shut, trying to block out my bright room.

"Gatita."

My eyebrows furrow together because I thought I heard *him*, el diablo. A flash of panic shoots through my body when I realize this is not a dream.

"Are you unwell?"

A gentle hand brushes my hair and presses against my cheek. My eyes fly open to see him hovering over me. My pulse quickens at his dark, piercing eyes staring into mine. His expression softens from concern to something else. He looks different, relaxed, and even more tan.

I blink away my sleepiness and look for Tiberia. She's panting lightly by the French doors, her nose pressed against the crack of the frame but otherwise content. Am I the only one freaking out?

"You're here." I clear my throat, my heart fluttering in my chest. Does he know Carlos was in here? Did they see each other? Cross paths?

"Yes, I am home." He straightens, and I drag myself to lean

against the broken headboard. His eyes flicker to the damage he had done and back to me. "I ask you again, are you unwell?"

"Um, no." I tuck the curls behind my ears and wipe the drool from my cheek. "Why?"

"It's late, and you're still in bed." He taps his watch and grunts his displeasure. Then I see it, not a ring, but a black tattoo, winding around the third finger on his left hand.

"You're married," I blurt out. Not a question, but a statement. My eyes moved from his tattoo to his face for answers.

"Yes."

I wait, expecting more, and then realize I am a fool for expecting more. I decide to state what I know, hoping he will confirm what Carlos told me.

"That's why I couldn't go."

"Yes."

"You were marrying her." The words are still unbelievable to me, as my existence should challenge that institution. It makes me want to vomit.

"Yes."

"Uh, does your wife know what I am to you?"

I must be mental to ask, but I must know and understand how I coexist with him and her—the three of us. And what about Carlos? I want to be with him. Not here with them.

"What are you to me?" His tone is husky and challenging.

No, no, no. I glare at him. "Nothing."

It's quiet for a moment, and then he laughs. He throws his head back and laughs as if I told the funniest joke in the world. "Ah, mi gatita, I missed you too." There is a joy to his laughter and normalcy that causes me to worry. Is he unhinged? I spoke the truth, and he thought it was a joke.

"I didn't miss you. I was plotting your death in different ways while you were gone." When his gaze drops to my chest, I cross my arms over them.

"Many do. You gained weight and got some sun."

I shrugged, unwilling to discuss either with him.

"You've been busy. You damaged my camera." He walks over and taps the dead lens with his finger. I hope he didn't see that it was Carlos doing it. "I like to watch mi angel sleep and imagine how I felt when I couldn't."

"Probably fine, since you can watch *your wife* sleep next to you."

His mouth twitches as if fighting a smile, and I glance away. "I will watch you again when you share my bed."

"What?" My head swivels so fast my neck pops, and the smile he's fighting with finally comes out. "I will never share your bed or any other bed in this place. I'll sleep in the little house outside before letting that happen."

"Your cheeks are rojo." My palms fly up to cover them. "Your desire is showing. Ah, we will be good again, like we were before. I fill your heart then. I fill your heart again."

"No, not in desire, in anger." I shake my head. I cannot discuss this with him again. He only hears what he wants to hear, even though I have denied him a hundred times. It's maddening. "So, your reception is tonight."

"Ah, you heard?" He fiddles with his cufflink.

"Sure did." I like this power play, where I am not so in the dark as I was before he left.

"Yes, your dress and shoes are being brought up." The words are so matter-of-fact that I tilt my head forward to hear them again.

"Pardon?"

"Yes?"

"I thought you said my dress and shoes are being brought up?"

"Yes." He makes his way over to the door, and Tiberia stands. "*Abajo.*" He snaps his fingers and points down, and she complies.

"No, no, no, no, no." I hustle out of bed to point my finger in his face. He takes a slow assessment of the clothes I fell asleep in last night before settling on my face. "I am not going to your wedding reception like a guest. Are you crazy?" I twirl my index finger in a circle by my head. "You expect me to show up, cheer the bride and groom, watch the first dance, hear the toasts for love and happiness and babies, oh God, your babies . . . no, I'm not sitting there pretending I am happy for you, about this." My eyebrows are so high that they have probably disappeared into my hairline. "No, no way. You can forget it. You can throw that dress and shoes into the ocean like you did the other pair."

Seconds pass that feel like minutes. "You will come. I will send someone for you, dressed or not," he says quietly as his hand reaches for the door handle.

"Then what Maximiliano? Let's say I go to your stupid reception. What happens then? What happens tomorrow and the day after that and the day after that? We all live here as one big, happy polygamous family?" I throw my hands in the air because I want to know. How far has he planned this?

His face darkens in anger, and I probably should be scared, but I must know what the days ahead hold. Especially since I found a small measure of peace being with Tiberia, working in the kitchen, and spending time with Carlos. His hand rolls into a fist twice before he releases it, making me wonder if he wants to hit me.

"Tell me, el diablo. How am I to spend the rest of my days here?" I want to push him over the edge. I want him to hit me and feel like shit for it. Calling him el diablo is the linchpin.

His hand raises, and I brace myself until his knuckles caress my cheek. The kindness nearly cracks my anger. "Anger is good. You have life again. You have life, you have a dog, you have the sea, and you have me. We live here together. It's good."

He's delusional.

"It's not good. It's not. What about her? She's also going to live here, you know."

"No, she lives south, not here. Tonight, she is here, but she leaves tomorrow, and I stay." He flattens his hand against my face, sliding the palm to rest on the nape of my neck, and draws me in for a kiss on my forehead. "It's good. It's enough." The words aren't what strikes me as the oddest. It's the peaceful expression he has when saying it. He is so demented that he genuinely believes we will be together as a couple, and Carlos's words float across my consciousness 'you're his possession.'

"I send someone for you tonight. Be ready." Or else. He didn't have to say it. The threat is always implied, always hanging between us. He's done talking. Well, I am too.

Yup, definitely his possession. I nod, stepping out of this touch.

"Words, gatita." He lowers his chin in disapproval.

"I'll be ready."

He casts a long look before pulling open the door and stopping. "You don't look like a niño anymore, *mi hermosa rosa*." He turns and leaves without pulling the door closed behind him. He doesn't lock me in for the first time since I have been here, and everything about this is wrong.

Chapter 34

Before, he was unbearable and demanding, wound so tight that it threatened to choke us. Now, he's kind, softer, and laughed when I lashed out. What changed? What happened down south, aside from getting married? Where the hell even is 'down south'?

I slam the door, hoping he hears it down the corridor, and lean against it. What in the world is happening? He's back, I'm going to his reception, and my prison sentence is confirmed as his lover forever.

My shoulders sag at that depressing thought, sliding down the door till my butt hits the floor. Tiberia saunters over and flops into my lap. I rest my hand on her side, occasionally scratching up and down and sending fur floating in the stagnant air.

My hope plummets, and despair sets in. This can't be. I can't do this. I can't be his concubine. And here forever, no. I don't want him. I like what Carlos and I are building. That sensual kiss last night by the fire was everything. And I finally told him everything, all of it, and he still wanted me. The way he held me against him before he left. His acceptance, understanding, compassion, kindness, and patience filled my soul. I can't lose Carlos.

We must escape, and I need to talk to him immediately. Convince him that it's worth crossing the desert even if he doesn't think so. I don't want to play the part of a loving mistress until we can get to an American embassy in a faraway land. That will take too long.

"What are we going to do?" Tiberia's beautiful, light blue eyes meet mine. I trace the black fur lines up her nose and around her ears. "If it were you and I and Carlos . . ." I sigh, and she rolls over for me to rub her belly. As I swipe my hand back and forth, sand collects on the floor under her, and I realize she needs a bath. We both do. But hers is going to be outside this time.

"All right, let's get cleaned up." I lean forward to kiss her head before I stand to shower last night's campfire smoke off me. She pops up, stretching and letting out a happy howl. "It's so much easier being a dog. You don't worry about nothing, huh?" I kiss her again and walk into the bathroom.

She pads behind me, watching my every move, so I keep the bathroom door open, which I usually never do. It doesn't matter because el diablo left my bedroom door unlocked. He must not be concerned about my safety anymore. That or I'm no longer a flight risk. Something about his casualness bothers me.

"You'll protect me, right, girl?" I duck behind the shower curtain. Her nose pops through the corner a time or two, making me laugh. Otherwise, she settles on the floor while I work through my routine.

It takes a good while before I am ready, and once she sees me grab my sandals, she paces by the bedroom door. Her thick tail feathers the furniture and sends dust particles to sparkle in the sun.

It's peaceful to watch the warm sunlight stream across the floor to highlight her thick coat. She's such a beautiful dog and looks better with a bit of weight on her.

She jumps on the door, eager to get out, when I slip the choke chain over her snout. I aim to train her well enough to ditch the choke chain and ask el diablo for a harness. It's more humane, even though Carlos disagrees.

I swipe my dictionary off the bureau to stuff in my back pocket and grab the dishtowel hair tie to knot into a low ponytail. Now that I feel ready, I yank open the door, prepared for Tiberia to lunge, and when she does, I give her a command while pulling back. She falls in line and then walks down the hall beside me, as she does with Carlos.

"Good girl." Then I decide to do the dumbest thing ever and sprint down the corridor with her leash wrapped around my fist. She yips and barks, dragging me across the carpet until we reach the stairs. Thankfully, she stops, and we take those at a normal pace, and then I run again.

When we hit the kitchen, I stop and watch the caterers dressed in white coats scurrying around, prepping for tonight. It's an odd feeling not seeing and hearing the ladies. I'm glad they are getting the day off. They work so hard, they deserve it, but it adds to my overall uneasiness. This day is proving very strange, and I can't put my finger on why I have such a bad feeling in my gut.

Tiberia barks at me, her huge tail wagging side to side, ready to go outside. "Let's go!" I run, and she happily barks through the hallway, out the door, and down the path.

I'm out of breath by the time we hit the beach. She's excited, lunging against the chain, and once I slip it off her, she's zooming across the sand, throwing up particles as she disappears in the distance. I laugh at her exuberance.

The day is endlessly sunny, with the bluest of skies. Even the waves are calm, sliding in and out. With my back to the fortress, I could imagine myself elsewhere, on some other beach where cares are nonexistent, and peace reigns free.

I settle by the campfire remnants. The stray twig is beside the charred ashes, and I pick it up to draw in the sand. It seems the most innocent thing to do on the worst day possible.

Marrying her? What does this union do? Forge an alliance or something? More drugs, more money, more power? When is enough enough? Doesn't all this power make him a bigger target or perhaps the most prominent target? And for what? Money doesn't buy happiness. He can attest to it. He's wealthy beyond belief and still not happy.

He is right. When I left all those years ago, I never looked back. I didn't come back for him. My biggest regret is that I didn't come back for Tiberia. But I couldn't handle it . . . I couldn't.

To see all those drugs, guns, and the bloody men strung up, begging him for their lives. All I could do was shut it out. I never told Will or Ardy what I stumbled upon one sleepless night. I was too horrified. I was terrified that if his men caught me or if el diablo did, I'd be strung up. All three of us flayed as he did so relentlessly to them. I faked an emergency call of Mom relapsing, and we were out of Columbus and away from el diablo forever.

I hid behind crates of white powder packages in the dank room, desperate to crawl back to my room yet too horror-struck to move. I saw it all. Heard it all. Saw the table cluttered with so many steel knives and hatchets. It looked like a butcher's dream. Blood was everywhere, pools of it were on the floor, and bits of flesh stuck to the ceiling.

His hands dripped of their blood, it ran down his forearms, and his face was sinister. The sounds, the tearing, and cutting of flesh and their screams . . . their screams echoed against the stone walls and into my ears. Their agony was embedded in my memories and haunted me for months.

Huddled into a ball, my back jammed into a crate, I tucked my head between my knees and shoved my hands against my ears. Their muffled suffering and the bloody gore ran in a loop whenever I closed my eyes.

When the steel clanged against the cold stone floor and utter silence followed, I knew it was over. He was done torturing the two men that hung side by side, bound by their wrists. My breath was locked in my chest.

The smell . . . it was repugnant. Of piss and shit as the body lost its fluids when death finally came. I stared at the cocaine in front of me and waited. I heard Maximiliano's quiet voice, grunting sounds from his men, and the scrape of feet being dragged across the floor. It was over.

I stayed tucked into the crate until I was sure they had left. And then I waited longer. I knew I had to get out of there and return to my room, but my legs gave out when I went to stand. They were numb from being crouched for so long.

Seeing a long metal plank with a handle, I stretched and used it as leverage to pull myself up. I didn't know it was the exact escape I was looking for until a piece of the wall moved back to let the cool desert air in. I hobbled over to the opening, glanced at the gruesome scene, and vomited in the red dirt outside.

My mind was a mess, tears were burning trails down my cheeks, and I openly sobbed at the brutality of their death at my lover's hand. I propped myself up against the casita, gagged as the smell wafted past, and vomited until I had nothing left. Bracing myself against the outside wall, my fingertips settled into a crevice that slid the wall closed again. It was luck and the grace of God that I made it back to my room and out of his life within hours of that happening.

I didn't report it. I did nothing. I hated myself for a long time for being a coward and not reporting it. I never told anyone. Not a soul what I saw until last night. I was cowardly and selfish, choosing my freedom over justice for those men. It was why I tried to save so many in the following years. Every request, cause, and person who needed help got it because I was trying to fill the hole carved from my guilt.

If I did everything everyone needed, I would somehow right the wrong by not reporting what happened to those men. It's why I recklessly pursued more and more dangerous missions because, at some point, I was trying to outrun my shame and negligence.

Reframing. I've never heard of it. It's both interesting and terrifying. I don't know if I can handle picking it apart by myself. He said he had a therapist he could relate to. That's what I needed back then, but my therapist didn't talk to me about it. I need it now and will start on it tomorrow.

Tiberia dumps a dead fish in my lap. I shriek, jumping up and sending it tumbling to my feet. Her tail wags a mile a minute, proud of herself, and I wrinkle my nose. I try to fling the fish toward the water using the same twig from the fire, and Tiberia thinks it's a game.

"Shoo, girl."

I wave my hand at her while flipping the fish over, the stink hitting my nose and making me gag. Tiberia dives in, scoops it in her mouth, and sprints the coastline, never looking back. I don't even bother calling after her.

I decide to do my exercises until she wanders back, and I move into the shade of the fortress. Once I have my sandals off and drop my book next to them, I start working out.

My thoughts are circular, the end chasing the beginning in a never-ending loop. I can't escape on my own, and Carlos said he was only one man, but last night . . . everything changed. He has feelings for me, held me when I cried, and caressed my hair when I spilled my guts. He didn't judge me. He tried to take away my guilt and regret as if it were his burden. He helped me. He is always helping me.

And the kiss, it was different. He was different. He was waiting for me to kiss him, to initiate it, because he didn't want to cross a line I didn't even think existed. I saw the burning desire in his eyes, how he gripped and kneaded my flesh, conveying his want and restraining himself simultaneously. So different from el diablo.

I touch my lips while glancing at the charred remains. He built me a fire in the middle of the night, a sweet and romantic gesture. Shooting his shot, even when he can't envision a life with me in LA. He doesn't know that I can't go back there either. Too changed to return. Maybe we both don't fit. He has nothing to go back to, but neither do I. Mom would understand and wish me well in whatever my new life holds. Yes, I want Carlos. I want to start something and see where it goes.

As I huff through my last set of burpees, my foot twists in the heavy sand, and I collapse to my hands and knees. Sweat rolls down my nose and drips into the sandy white particles. My ribs are burning, my lungs are gasping for air, and I didn't realize how hard

I was pushing myself while lost in thought. I fall to my hip and drag my legs around to prop my elbows on them to catch my breath.

My energy is completely drained, and Tiberia is trotting toward me. She tries to give me slobbery kisses, and I dodge them, considering the fish from earlier. Tiberia joins me in the shade, leaning against the cool white wall of the fortress.

"It's hot already, huh? Let's go in."

I put my sandals on and stuff my book in my pocket before retrieving her leash. She trots beside me and lets me slip the chain over her head. I can tell they have been working with her because she's sweet and compliant, walking on my right side. Her energy is depleted, like mine, so I take a leisurely pace up the path to the back of the property.

The door barely closes behind me when Tiberia lunges. I can't get traction on the slick floors because the sandy residue stuck to the bottom of my sandals. It causes me to slip and fall backward. Her leash slackens, and she charges forward, growling ferociously. I open my mouth to correct her when he steps out from an adjoining hallway, and I nearly pass out.

Chapter 35

The dragon stops, looking beyond Tiberia's snarling and upright hackles to me, holding on to her for dear life. I gasp in shock.

Oh my God.

He's here.

My heart roars in my ears, beating twice as fast. Fear slides into my mind, unable to comprehend that he's feet away from me.

His head cocks to the side, unfazed by Tiberia's threat to maul him. With every lunge, I brace myself against the slippery floor to hold her back. He saunters toward us, his evil black eyes killing me with every step.

Even though I am horrified, I don't dare look away from his grotesque face for fear she'll attack.

"I wondered where he was hiding you." His sneer displays more missing teeth. Did el diablo do that? He said he handled him. "In plain sight, I see."

He's here and alive.

He stops short of Tiberia's reach, taunting her, and I strain to hold on to the leash. It cuts into my palms and rubs burn marks into the delicate skin across the back of my hands. Tiberia crouches, her shoulder blades jutting toward the ceiling, and she lunges. Her front paws claw the air, her ears pinned to her head, and salvia drips from her canines.

I can't let go of her. El diablo will kill her for sure. Probably shoot her right in front of me.

I brace my feet on the baseboard, trying to find enough leverage to haul her powerful body away from him. Tiberia and I are opposing forces working against each other, and I am losing.

"You're going to wish you were dead when I'm finished with you." He cracks his knuckles.

"He should have killed you for what you did to me." Pure loathing surges through me. "He should have flayed you as he did them."

My biceps are cramping, and my thighs are shaking, but Tiberia won't back down. Hatred flows through her too.

"Family doesn't kill family." His hand snaps back and punches Tiberia so fast we both don't see it coming. Her head absorbs the blow, flying to the right, and I scream in horror. I drop the leash and scramble to get her before she collapses to the floor.

She is not even in my arms a second before she lunges and sinks her teeth into his arm. His scream echoes after mine, trying to punch her to let go when I block it, taking the blow to my stomach, and I sway to stay upright. Pain blasts across my intestines, sending black spots across my vision as I clutch the wall.

Tiberia thrashes her head, left and right, ripping the flesh away and exposing white bone. The dragon shrieks and tries to dislodge her locked jaws. His shirt sleeve is shredded from her teeth, and blood is pumping out of his meaty flesh. Her snarls roll one after the other from the barrel of her chest, his blood soaking her mouth and dotting her face in bits of his flesh. Adrenaline throbs in my veins, screaming at her to let go while the dragon's heinous cries make me wince.

"What the hell?" El diablo tosses me away to kick Tiberia. Her jaws slack, releasing the mangled arm, and she crashes into the wall with a grotesque thud. The dragon charges forward, and I shield her body with mine, prepared to take the brunt of his fury. El diablo catches the dragon by the throat and punches him in the stomach. He crumples over, a slight reprieve as el diablo's men run down the hall.

"Get him out of here." El diablo's voice is eerily calm.

"I'm going to fucking kill her, Maximiliano." The dragon is upright and flanked by a guard on each side, holding him back. He elbows one of them in the face, and with a loud crack, blood gushes from the guard's nose. He momentarily flinches, giving the dragon a fraction of an inch to kick my side. I miss the brunt of the blow but get the steel tip of his boot in between my ribs and collapse over Tiberia.

She's panting underneath me, her blue eyes are fully dilated to jet black, and looking into mine. Instant tears rim my lower lids, and I writhe in pain from another hit to my midsection.

I can't stop moving from side to side. I can't breathe, I can't talk, and I can't assure Tiberia that she's okay. I draw my legs up, rolling into a tuck over her to allow her to breathe while protecting both of us.

"You hear me. I'm going to fucking kill you and that dog." I see the guard with the broken nose walking away and two other guards struggling with the dragon. El diablo is standing over me and roaring in heavily accented words at an untranslatable speed. "You fucking cunt. I'm going to beat that fucking mutt to death and take my time watching you die."

El diablo's temper erupts, pulling his gun from his holster and pointing it at the dragon. I can't believe it. He is protecting me as he should have last time. He's keeping his promise. El diablo is finally keeping his promise.

The dragon's threats continue as they haul him away, getting louder with more distance until they finally stop. I continue shallow breathing, knowing nothing is broken, but damn if it doesn't hurt like a mother. I coo in Tiberia's ear to reassure her.

El diablo squats, brushing back my curls to see my face. "Gatita."

One word, full of emotion. His hand slides down my back to duck under my armpit to help me sit. I immediately press my elbow into my ribs and over my stomach to soothe the pain radiating from both. When our eyes meet, I wait for his wrath, fury, and accusations of how this is all my fault if I trained her better, if I controlled her, or if I did a hundred things differently.

"Are you okay?" When our eyes meet, my lip trembles and tears spring anew for so many reasons. The dragon is here. He hit Tiberia. He hit me. He wants to kill us both. I couldn't protect myself. I couldn't protect her. This is el diablo's world, his ugly, ugly world. They spill over into unrelenting streams down my cheeks, and he pulls me against him, letting me weep.

"Don't kill her," I mumble, staring back into his eyes. He frowns. "It was . . . my fault." Trying to talk around the lump in my throat. "Punish me, n-not . . . her." I can barely make out his features through my watery gaze.

"Gatit—"

"No, no, gatita. Don't . . . don't say it." I wipe my nose on my arm and hastily dab my eyes to see him. "Don't . . . please. He punched her. He hit her when she was trying to protect me. And . . . and I slipped. I was holding her back. He punched her. It's not her fault. You do—"

He holds up his hand for me to stop, and I drop my head, blinking rapidly for my tears to fall. My throat burns, as does my nose, and his index finger captures my chin, pushing it up to look at him. "The animal attacked one of my men."

"No, no, no." My shoulders shake as I bawl again. "I-I can't . . . please." I fall to Tiberia, lying halfway across her body to cry into her fur. She curls toward me and nuzzles her nose into my face to lick my tears. "I love you, girl."

His hand lands heavy on my back, and I scoot closer into her body, figuring out what to do.

"Come off the floor." He slides his hand across my back to pull me away from her, and I flinch. I can't let this happen. I can't let him take her from me. I can't lose her. She's everything I have. She is my world. "I get you a new animal. Small, one you can control."

"I don't want another dog." I wail into her fur, bracing against his insistent tugging until he yanks me from her body. "I only want her. You promised me her."

He exhales, knowing I am right. I take advantage of his hesitancy. "Don't kill her. If you care for me and feel anything for me, you won't hurt her." I watch an emotion flitter over his face before his stone mask fastens back in place. I don't know what else to say. My mouth is working faster than my brain. "I'll come tonight. I'll go to your reception. Promise me you won't hurt her."

"You were coming anyway," he says coolly.

I search his face. He needs more, something only I can give him. "I'll be yours. No more fighting. No more arguing. I'll do it."

"You are mine."

"No, like, um, before. Like we were." Am I offering myself? Myself, in exchange for Tiberia, yes. I'll do it. "Lovers and stuff."

His eyebrow raises, the only indication from him. "Always sacrificing yourself for others. But no."

No?

I shift to sit on my legs, drawing my hands together to plead with him. Tiberia moves too, a whimper escaping as she presses against me. "Why not? Please . . . please. Why?" I scoot closer, lifting my face inches from his, imploring him with my expression.

"Not sacrifice. I want you to want me. Not for the animal, but for me." His tan fingers roll into a fist to hit the center of his chest. His gaze drops to my lips, the ones he used to suck and draw into his teeth when we made love. "Look at me like you used to. Love in your eyes, desire in your body, flush in your cheeks."

I blush at the memories, how intimate we used to be, impossible to recreate with anyone after him. He was the one. My only until he wasn't. I vowed never to fall that hard again, and I hadn't.

"Our world. You said that. Locked away, under the sheets, loving you, only you. You called it our world." His voice is raspy, mirroring emotions I didn't think he had.

My body heats, remembering those days, locked in his bedroom, laughing together, and learning how to make love from him. I rest the palm of my hands against my cheeks, hiding my embarrassment.

He falls to his knees, putting his hands over mine and staring intensely into my eyes. "I want our world. I want you like that. Not to save the animal."

I can't breathe. With this glimmer of vulnerability and intimacy, I can't think straight. It's overwhelming and unlocks a part I had imprisoned long ago. "Okay," I whisper, gazing into those dark eyes and seeing the reflection of Tiberia and me in them. My hands slip from my face, leaving his and the occasional caress of his thumb.

"Okay, what?" He focuses on my mouth. I lick my lips, my mouth suddenly dry.

"I will give you our world."

"For all our days," he whispers, inches from my mouth.

"All our days." I lean in and brush my lips on his. He growls, grabbing me with an intense hunger that has burned unabashed in him. He changes my kiss from hesitant and unsure to demanding and powerful, drawing on the heat and passion that once flowed freely between us.

He dives deeper, becoming reacquainted with all corners of my mouth. His arm locks around my shoulders, pulling me to my knees and molding me to him while he kneads my ass. He grinds himself against me, the hardness of his erection unbelievable against our clothes. I can't breathe. I'm running out of air and nudging him for a break. He sucks my bottom lip, nipping it with his teeth, and groans. I gasp for air. He's breathing hard and mutters, "Mi angel."

We were always combustion, no denying that, but as the remnants of my desire fade, logic and judgment prevail, and I sag in his arms. I sold my soul to the devil and kissed him passionately for it.

What have I done?

I traded Carlos for Tiberia. I saved her and ended it with him. I couldn't feel sicker to my stomach. If el diablo would kill my dog over her protecting me, what would he do to Carlos if he knew we kissed? Holy shit, he'd torture him in front of me. Make that sweet and tough Marine pay for my sins. That's what devils and drug lords do, torture the innocent.

Fear grips my body, bile rises into the back of my throat, and my head swims with dizziness. I can't. I can't do that to Carlos. I must find him, tell him so he can walk away. I made a mistake, but I won't let it cost him. I'll live with the devil if it means protecting my savior.

Chapter 36

"**M**aximiliano?"

His rough hands brush up my arms, sending goosebumps over my skin before slowly removing them with a warning look. My pulse quickens, caught doing something very wrong. Her seeing us in this intimate moment is downright terrifying.

Veronica is here. His bride, his wife, and his goddess. She's stunning. Standing in the middle of the hall, a white silk dress draped off her voluptuous figure, dipping and curving in all the right spots. Long, luscious hair frames her impossibly perfect face wearing a murderous expression. I'm dead from the daggers she is glaring at me. I don't blame her. He is hers, and she is his, and even though I committed to being his to save my girl, this is wrong. Horribly wrong.

"What are you doing?" Her hands are planted on her hips, and her crimson nails tap against her dress, beckoning for an explanation.

He rises from his knees to run a hand through his hair. I assume it is nervous energy, possibly a delay tactic, or maybe both. Indeed, he knew she was here, whereas I didn't. If I did, there is no way I'd have let this happen, at least not in public.

"Diego attacked her." His voice is bitter, and I'd suspect he doesn't like the position he's in. Having to justify himself is unusual and out of place. The tension between them is frightful. Her eyes flicker to mine before returning to hold his stare.

"That is a lie. That thing mauled him. Pieces are missing that cannot be stitched." She glares at me, and I am one hundred percent certain this is all my fault. "Why is it not dead? Left in the desert for buzzards to pick?"

"Go back to our room."

She ambles closer, her marble size diamond ring throwing prisms of color around the hallway. "Why is *she* not dead yet?"

I gasp, my hand covering my mouth, and I shudder at her horrible question. She wants me dead. Why dead? If he would send me back home . . . but dead?

His eyes drop to mine, taking in my small, shivering body. "Don't say that." Rage coats his face as he charges forward to grab her throat and throttle her. "You will never say that to me again."

Her eyes bug out, and she's wildly scratching at his hand to release the tightening grip that threatens to choke her unconscious. He's intentionally doing it, showing no mercy to the panic and pain he's inflicting, and she flails against him until he tosses her away.

My God.

What is happening?

They left here so loving, so happy.

Nearly falling off her towering stilettos, she recovers, settling herself, and smiles. A creepy smile full of loathing while she rubs the red ring around her neck. Her chin raises, her eyes casting down on me in victory. "Don't underestimate me, dear husband. I'll kill everything you love."

Our eyes lock, mine in terror, hers in triumph. With a raise of that perfectly manicured eyebrow, she turns and strolls down the hallway. My stomach churns with acid. Her death threats, the dragon's death threats, and both of us hurt. It's too much.

"I'm going to vomit." I crawl away from Tiberia so I don't spew in her fur. A flush of heat and nausea sweeps over my body. My stomach expels gassy burps before I hurl on the floor. He shouts for help. My body refuses to stop retching until a cold towel is placed against my forehead.

I hover on my hands and knees, spitting out strings of vomit-coated saliva. The old healer is by my side, wiping my face with the cloth and encouraging me to sit back. Her toothless smile is an echo of my drug-induced memories.

Maximiliano is still shouting, and out of the corner of my eye, I see a guard leading a limping Tiberia away.

"No, no, don't take her." I scamper off the floor, biting back the pain from my midsection to stop the guard. "Don't kill her."

"Gatita, no worry. It is filthy, covered in blood. He cleans it."

I shake my head vehemently, knowing anything can happen once she is out of my sight. Tiberia looks back at me, those crystal blue eyes begging me to save her.

"No, I don't trust him. I don't trust anyone. I will take care of her. I will clean her. I will do it." I wince, and he tries to stop me. "No, I'm fine. I'll be fine. She's mine. My responsibility, remember? I'll take care of her."

He stares at me, not wanting to show weakness to his staff, but I hobble around him to get to Tiberia. "She is my job. You said I take care of her, Maximiliano. I will do my job. Not him. He has his job. I have my job. It's not fair to him." I stand by the guard who is looking from me to el diablo. I reach for her leash, and he pulls back, waiting. It must appear as his idea to convey that he is not weak or giving in to my demands. "Right, sir? She's my responsibility?"

A nearly indiscernible nod from him, and the guy drops the leash in my hand, waiting for his next set of instructions. "Everyone has their job to do. Clean the dog, gatita. Now get out."

When the healer passes by, he catches her and says something. She bows her head and scurries down the hallway that Veronica took. I decided then and there to never, ever go down that way.

With everyone gone, it's him and me, his face unreadable and his stare as long as usual. I shrug, unsure what to say in the aftermath. I know I committed to 'our world,' a lie unbeknownst to el diablo. For now, I need solitude away from his world, if only for a few hours.

Turning my back on him and the blood-covered hallway, I look at Tiberia as she looks at me. We're both ready to leave this behind. She presses her body into my leg, and I gently stroke her head and whisper, "You'll be okay."

I breathe shallowly with my elbow pinned to my side and watch Tiberia, taking it equally slow. Together, we hobble down the hall, careful not to slip on the blood dotting the floor. I wish there were a vet here to look at my girl. She's not whimpering like before, but I know she is hurt.

"Gatita." I stop and look over my shoulder. He hasn't moved from the spot where we kissed. His eyes search mine, imploring the feelings we shared a moment ago.

The violence before and after killed the moment, yet he remains hopeful and earnest in finding love amid the savagery.

I turn to face him completely. "Would you ever leave?" Is this the life he wants? "Would you leave all this? Start over? A common man?"

He rubs his beard, the raven tattoo on his hand taking flight from the action. "No, my fate is sealed."

Those eyes pierce me anew, a deep-seated sadness within, and I look at him with sympathy.

"As is mine."

With that, I turn and take it slowly while Tiberia limps beside me. I carefully guide us through the kitchen, avoiding the catering staff, and gingerly ascend the back staircase. It takes forever to return to my room, but I bolt the bedroom and bathroom doors. The irony of bolting both is not lost on me when hours before, we felt free. We were free.

I wash Tiberia first, carefully getting her into the tub and paying particular attention to the side of her face and body, where Diego punched and Maximiliano kicked. Although she's put on some weight, I can still feel her ribs when I wet her coat.

The blood takes longer to get out of her white fur. After several rounds of shampoo, she lies in the tub, too exhausted to stand. She's in obvious pain but so calm to let me wash away the carnage. When she's done, I lift her out of the tub, ignoring my protesting ribs, and take my time drying her. I'm up next, and she settles against the cool porcelain tub while I shower.

Dread fills my gut when I think about tonight, so I push that out of my mind. Stay in the now. Think about Tiberia and what she needs to be comfortable.

Chapter 37

Once I am done in the shower, I wrap a towel around my hair and body before unlatching the door and finding el diablo and the 'something like that' doctor in my room.

"Umm . . ."

"He's here to look at you." El diablo walks over to the bureau to pull out clothes and undergarments for me to change into. He shoves them against my chest before prodding me back into the bathroom. Tiberia backs up, and I stare at the closed door.

"Okay."

I pull on my underwear, but when I get to the bra, my arm pulls against my side, sending searing pain into my lungs. I clutch my midsection, barely breathing, and fasten the bra in front to gingerly slide it up and around. I get my shirt and shorts on before the door swings open, narrowly missing Tiberia.

Tiberia hobbles past him to wait by the side of the bed. She needs help. I mumble, "Excuse me," to slip by him and lift her onto the bed, where she settles against the pillows.

"Come." He holds his hand out, expecting mine, and I wrap it against my waist instead. His eyes follow with a brief pause at my breasts, and the corner of his mouth twitches. "Oscar!"

The doctor startles and scurries away from the veranda doors.

"Please sit." He motions to the bed, places his bag on the nightstand, and fumbles through it. He retrieves his stethoscope, puts the ends in his ears, and pauses, looking at el diablo. "Maybe it's best if you step out," the doctor mutters while pushing his glasses up his nose and seeming nervous in el diablo's presence. It's the opposite of his calm and cool demeanor in the kitchen.

"No, proceed." El diablo glances at his watch and then glares at the doctor. I focus on a spot on the floor because this couldn't get more awkward.

"Uh, okay, please sit up," the doctor says, and when I do, I hold my breath. I can't look at him. He's too close. His face in my face opens the flood gates to unwanted memories and unanswered questions. "Good, now show me where it hurts."

I put the pads of my fingers into the three spots that hurt the most, and when his fingertips touch mine, I recoil. El diablo grunts at my action, yet I still don't raise my gaze from the spot on the floor.

"Can you sit a little straighter?" I turn away, deciding to look at the bureau. He's so close, it is making me anxious, and I don't like it. I comply, breathing shallow while his fingers feel my ribs and the dips in between. He hums in acknowledgment. "Nothing feels broken. Naturally, I don't have the equipment to confirm it's not a hairline fracture. This will be cold. Breathe in." He places the stethoscope inside the back of my shirt to press against my skin. El diablo moves closer. "Again," the doctor says three more times on my back before moving out of my shirt and going to the front.

"No," el diablo says, and I glance up, mouthing a silent thank you. "You have enough."

It surprises the doctor, and he mumbles something to himself before removing the black earbuds and letting the stethoscope dangle from his neck. I brace my hands on the edge of the mattress and move down the bed to put distance between us. The doctor sees my reaction and takes two steps back.

"Well?" El diablo impatiently snaps his fingers, getting both our attention.

"I'd like to look at the skin. It could be bruised," he says, removing his stethoscope and dropping it in his bag.

"No." The answer is swift and firm. "How long to heal?"

"Without a more thorough examination, one can assume they are bruised but intact. Lots of rest, nothing strenuous, and she can move around as much as can be tolerated. It would be best if she stayed in bed for a week."

"We leave in two days. Can she travel?"

My head jolts up. Did el diablo say we're leaving? Did I hear that right?

"We're leaving?" He doesn't even look at me.

"It would be better if she has a little longer, but if it's urgent and cannot be changed, yes. Two days, but not before," the doctor says, clasping his hands behind his back.

"Maximiliano?"

My brain is trying to process that my captivity is ending in two days. Where is he taking me? To another country? Will I be safe there? Does it have an embassy, as Carlos said? Could he be taking me back to the States? Back to the casita? I could escape the casita, I'm sure of it. And Tiberia? Will she come too?

"I can give her something for the pain," the doctor says, and it snaps me back to reality. He rummages through his bag, and we both say, "No" simultaneously.

Our eyes meet, agreeing not to drug me ever again. "I'll deal with the discomfort. No drugs." I shudder. "No more drugs." El diablo casts me a curious stare, and I know I should tell him about those random images, but not today.

The doctor stops digging, a look of disapproval on his face, and he opens his mouth to object before el diablo says, "You heard her."

I mouth another thank you to him, and he tilts his chin down, warning me I will have to explain myself to him.

"Okay, that's it then." He closes his bag and yanks it from the nightstand when I remember Tiberia.

"Maximiliano, I know he's not an animal doctor, but can he look at Tiberia?" I clasp my hands in front of me because I'm sure if I ask the doctor directly, he'd feel insulted and say no. I have el diablo's sympathies as I am hurt again, so why not play it up to get what I want? I'll need to learn this level of manipulation if I'm going to be his mistress. That thought is repulsive. "Pleeeeeeease?"

He stares at me for several long seconds before unfolding his arms. "Oscar, look at the animal."

"But—"

"Do it."

"Thank you!"

There is another knock on the door, and the tiny healer comes to sit on the bed beside me, saying something about water with two pills in her hand. I refuse, and she shoves them in my hand, saying something I couldn't understand.

"She says they are for the pain. Read them." They are imprinted with the name of a U.S. drugmaker, and I smile in relief. She pats my cheek as I look at her, and I take the glass of water and swallow the pills. She stands, bowing her head, and taking the glass from my hand before slipping out of the room.

"She likes you." I look at him and smile wider.

"I like her too."

A wrinkle of something crosses his face before he walks toward the veranda. I turn my attention to the doctor examining Tiberia.

"Is she going to be okay?" I scoot over to hold her paw. She's tired, resting her head against the pillow and being surprisingly good while his fingers work down her spine.

"I didn't get many details. What exactly happened?" He hits a spot that causes Tiberia to whirl around and growl at him. He jumps, hits his back on the wall, and scowls. "I don't think this is a good idea."

"Tiberia, no!" I circle her nose with my index finger and thumb so she can breathe but not bite. "Please go ahead. I'll hold her." He hesitates, glancing across the room to el diablo.

"As she says," he mutters behind me, and I refrain from smiling at how generous he is. Very unlike him, I'm sure there will be a price to pay. Or maybe he's sort of nice because he's kidnapping me again in two days.

My mind wants to comb through all the details of this trip. I want to grill him, but I know now is not the time. Tiberia needs to be well enough to travel too. There is no way I am leaving her here, and I need to talk to Carlos about everything that has transpired.

"If you will have a hold on her . . ." He proceeds with caution, his eyes darting from her teeth to the spots he is examining on her back. Tiberia whimpers when he hits another tender part. "You were saying."

"Yes, she was punched in the head and kicked in the side." I want to look over my shoulder when I say the latter part and refrain since he is to blame but is also allowing her to be examined. The duality of his conflicting actions is exhausting. "She was limping the entire way back here. She didn't whimper when I bathed her because she's a pretty tough dog."

"Hmm, how old is she?" he asks, listening to her breathing, and I loosen my ring around her nose, yet don't remove it. She paws at my hand, and I scold her before answering.

"Uh, she's . . ." Of course, I look back at el diablo, watching us and wondering if he remembers the day they found her in the truck.

He casts a disinterested look.

"A little over five years old." My fingers clamp tighter when he moves to her head and flashes his little light across her eyes. She tries to shake her head, and I chuckle. "No, be a good girl."

"Again, I'm not a veterinarian. However, I felt nothing broken, and she's responding to what I assume to be normal. She is a middle-aged dog, probably a strain or bruising across the ribcage, but no fractures. Similar to yours. And no concussion." He awkwardly pats her head and then walks to the other side of the bed to retrieve his bag. I release her nose, and she yawns noisily before rubbing her face against the pillow.

The room is silent, only the sounds of the doctor's tools scraping against his bag and Tiberia's breathing slowing into a light snore.

I pluck at the comforter, wanting to ask, needing to ask, yet hesitant that he won't answer with el diablo in the room. "Maximiliano, can you give me a minute alone with, um, the doctor?" Both sets of eyes land on me, one surprised, the other unreadable.

"Why?" He lowers his voice to intimidate me.

"I-I want to ask him some questions."

"What questions, gatita?"

The doctor looks very uncomfortable standing between us. He pulls at his shirt sleeve and fiddles with the button on the cuff. I'm unsure if he is nervous by my request to question him alone or by el diablo's presence when I ask him my questions.

"Yes, what questions?" the doctor says, attempting to deflect my attention.

"I want to know what happened in America. From there to here. I want to know who else was in this room with me. I want to know if Diego raped me, and that's why the underwear was on me. I want to know if you helped Diego somehow," I blurt out all my fears, the glimpses and pieces through all the pricks to my skin, the drugs, and the hazy memories that have haunted me since the day I got here. The information Carlos supplied about the doctor working with the wealthy guys to drug and kidnap American girls to sell to the coyotes.

The doctor blanches, his eyes wide behind his glasses, and he licks his lips before rubbing his hands together. He looks at me and then switches to el diablo, who stalks from his position by the veranda to tower over the doctor. His eyes bore into the thin man, and the scar across his face ripples when his jaw tightens.

"Gatita, stand here." His voice is dark and steely. I shake my head. I don't want to stand where he points. "Now."

His glare moves briefly from the doctor to me, and in that one second, I am off the bed and darting over to him.

I'm so uncomfortable with how this is happening that I fidget beside him. My arms wrap around my midsection, needing to hold my aching side, needing to soothe my frayed nerves, and needing to press into my stomach to control my nausea.

El diablo's heavy hand lands on my biceps, moving me to stand in front of him, exactly where he pointed. With both of his palms planted on my shoulders, the doctor is now facing both of us, and I wished I hadn't asked at all.

"Answer, Oscar."

Beads of sweat gather on the doctor's hairline, and he pushes his glasses to the bridge of his nose before clearing his throat. "As you know, you were physically attacked, and your injuries made it impossible to travel. It was against my wishes . . ." He looks from me to el diablo, and I remember that memory fragment. "But you were transported here. I intended for you to heal in the States. Circumstances made that impossible." He's choosing his words carefully, and I don't blame him. El diablo does terrible things to people.

El diablo interjects, "And the rest."

Doesn't el diablo already know? He hit the healer for it and said he would find out. Said he took care of Diego, which didn't seem to work.

"Do you not know what happened?" Confused, I glance over my shoulder. His expression is murderous, as if I am challenging him in front of his staff, and I know that's a huge mistake. My second one in a matter of hours. He grabs my chin and moves my face to look at the doctor, returning his hand to my shoulder and waiting for the answers.

"Oscar."

"You were in pretty bad shape with cuts, fractures, stitches, and bruising. The flight didn't help. You were screaming and fighting in your sleep as if reliving the attack, and you—" He motions to el diablo. "Didn't like it. He was upset at how distraught you were and ordered me to give you a sedative and something for the pain." He's visibly uncomfortable having to recant all this to me.

He takes a white cloth from his pocket and dabs it across his forehead, down his cheeks, and under his glasses. "We got you settled in here. The older women watched you around the clock, and of course, he was here. Often." He motions to el diablo again, who is silent behind me. "She took care of you, bathed you, and tried to get you to eat or drink when you were conscious, which was challenging because you were so combative."

"I thought those were his hands," I whisper, the face of the dragon always appearing in my nightmares. El diablo's grip tightens on my shoulders in response.

"I had assumed that. Everything was progressing nicely. The medicine and sedatives were working. You were less combative, and your injuries were healing faster than anticipated even though you were losing weight. It was a delicate balance of keeping you sedated, cared for, and healing."

"And not addicted," I add. Apprehension is coiling in my gut, wanting to cover my ears and pretend my version of the truth is reality, even if it might not be. El diablo wraps his arms around my collarbone and pulls me against his chest, grunting in satisfaction. Listening to the doctor becomes harder to hear as the dread builds, waiting for the answers I need.

"Well, yes." He sighs with trepidation. "Toward the end, you were coming out more and more, which showed your progress. I had sent the woman away, knowing I would be with you for a while, but I had left my bag in my room on the other floor." He pauses, his glasses fogging with the perspiration coming off him, and he slowly wipes them against his shirt. The pause allows me to exhale twice and stop holding my breath. El diablo is a rock of quiet power in all this, and I am almost glad he made me stand in front of him for this. Almost.

"When . . . when I returned, he was . . . er . . . already here w-with you." He shakily puts his glasses back on.

My head is swimming, and I start trembling. El diablo kisses the top of my head and tightens his hold on me. "And?"

"And he was hovering over you. Your, um, dressing gown was pulled up."

El diablo's arm drags across my chest at lightning speed, and before I can process what he's doing, he has a gun pointed at the doctor's head. I gasp, wanting to cry. The doctor's face is ghastly white, and his mouth is mumbling the Lord's Prayer.

"Did he rape her?" His low growl vibrates my back. I would pass out if he weren't holding me upright with his forearm.

"Maximiliano, please . . . don't do this. I-I have a family, kids. You met my wife. Please, I beg of you." His tears mix with the sweat rolling down his face and collecting at his chin.

Tears spring into my eyes. This can't happen. Regardless of what he knows or did, I can't watch him murdered inches from me. "Maxie, no . . . don't . . . don't do it . . . no."

"Answer the question, Oscar." He pushes the barrel of the gun to his head, point-blank. The doctor is a blubbering mess of crying, begging, and praying. I'm not much different when I glance at Maximiliano.

"I-I don't . . . don't know," he answers, breaking down and hysterically crying. "I'm . . . I am sorry."

Tiberia whines with him, and I sob uncontrollably for him, me, and the truth.

"You fucking piece of shit!" El diablo roars against me and starts hitting him in the head with the gun barrel. His skin breaks, blood gushes out, and it splatters my face. "You fucking let him touch her? You begged for your pathetic life when he touched her? You worthless piece of shit!"

The vengeance and brutality inches from my face are gruesome, and bile rises to the back of my throat. "Stop . . . please . . . stop. Maxie . . . N-No!" My hands cover my face, blocking out the gore and crying so hard my knees buckle. El diablo's arm tightens around my stomach to hold me. "He . . . he doesn't know. He. . . please stop."

He can't do this.

"Maxie . . ."

My heart thunders in my ears, my breath is locked in my chest, and all I see is the carnage from the two men strung up, begging for their lives. The violence, the blood, and the praying. It's the same, and it's not. I caused this. I am to blame. I had to know what happened, and now his death is on my hands.

I dig my nails into his thigh. "No, you can't . . . stop, I beg you . . . Maxie."

The doctor hunches over, blood dripping down the front of his clothes and clutching his bloody glasses. Tiberia is standing on the edge of the bed, growling and ready to pounce.

I flush with heat, sweat breaking out over my skin, and hundreds of black spots swirl closer and closer.

"Now you pay."

El diablo cocks the trigger, and darkness overtakes me.

Chapter 38

My head is throbbing, my side is aching, and I open my eyes to see Maximiliano sitting on the bed next to me. He brushes back my hair. Tiberia's head is lying across my abdomen, protecting me.

The vein in the right side of his neck is pulsing, the same pulse coming from his hand wrapped around mine. The intensity of his stare is too much. I look around the room for the doctor.

"He's gone."

I pull my hand out of his embrace to rub my head. Did I hit my head?

"Wh-What happened?" My voice is gutted from all my hysterical crying and begging.

"You fainted. I held you so you didn't get hurt." I guess I didn't hit my head. "I laid you here and cleaned you up." My blood-spattered clothes are the same. "I didn't want to change you, considering . . ." What we heard. Yeah, I get it.

"Um, what else did he say?" I try to see if a pool of blood is on the floor, but he's blocking my view with his body.

"Nothing. Pathetic. He kept begging for his life. Didn't care about your life." His voice is clipped, doused in fury that he's keeping at bay.

"So . . ." I pinch my forehead together, trying to make my head feel better. "We don't know." I look at the same ceiling and wood beams that have seen all my days and nights, all the comings and goings. If only ceilings could mirror past events, we'd know for sure.

"No. I will get it out of the doctor."

I know exactly how. Gruesomely. I close my eyes, a tear sliding down my temple to drop into the pillow. I honestly don't know how much more I can take. Madness, sadness, or a psych ward, I don't know which, possibly all three, when this is over.

"And Diego?" I open my eyes to gaze into his, which holds remorse.

"They are looking for him."

"How did you not know this, Maxie? You said you were getting answers that day when it happened. You said you were." I don't understand why this is new information to him unless he lied to me. "Did you lie to me? Say you were going to investigate it and then didn't?"

He reaches for my hand and caresses the top. "I did not lie. I was lied to. He will be taken care of, mi gatita." I search his face, taking in every scar, every stress line, and decide I believe him. I want to believe him because I want Diego to suffer. I am not sure about the doctor anymore, but Diego, yes, he deserves everything el diablo intends to do to him.

"Can I be alone?" I need time to think and space to breathe. This day will likely kill me, and it's not over yet. "Don't you need to get ready or something?" I trace the black lines on Tiberia's face, and she groans as I scratch behind her ear.

He flicks his wrist, the tiny diamonds on the face of his Rolex are too hard to distinguish the time from where I lie, but by the veranda, the sun is setting. "I have time. Why do you want me to leave? Soon, we will share a room. Then no leaving."

I sigh, forgetting my promise in the hallway. "I will always need my space. The same as you will need yours."

"No. You will be by my side always. Too many could use you to get to me."

I stare at him.

"Once we leave, it will be good."

I forgot about that too—our trip out of here.

"Back to the States? The casita?" The hope in my voice is unmistakable, and the corner of his mouth twitches as if I told a funny joke.

"Gatita, you know we are not going back there." His tone is so condescending that I look away. "We are going home."

"Home? I thought this was your home?" If 'home' is a desolate fortress by the sea.

"You cute like puppy." He stands, stretching his shoulders to look more intimidating. "My home is in this beautiful little city called Culiacan. You will like it. Eating, shopping, making love, it will be good."

My mouth opens to object when there is a light knock on the door. Oh no, is it Carlos? What will he think? What did he find out? Was he able to find a way out of here? And I need to tell him what happened to me, and Tiberia, to the dragon and the doctor. I break out in a cold sweat, anxiety clawing at my skin and my heart pounding.

"Wait." I sit up to stop him.

El diablo ignores me to cross the space in two steps and whips open the door so fast that the small woman steps back in fright. Her fear is my relief. I am so glad it's not Carlos. Even though I desperately need to talk to him, I can't do it with el diablo here. Plus, I need Carlos to hold me and tell me everything will be all right.

I lean against the headboard. Tiberia stands and stretches before rolling into a ball at the foot of the bed.

"Ah, yes. Come in."

He pushes it open enough for her to pass, carrying a long

zipped-up bag in one hand and a shoe bag in the other. She looks around the room for a place to hang it and blushes when he takes the hanger and fastens it to the top of the bathroom door. She places the shoe bag on top of the bureau and whispers something.

She's in and out of the room in about five seconds. "She will bring up some food and help you get ready." He points to the garment bag and stands in the doorway. "I know you had a hard day, but you will come tonight." He drops his chin to meet my eyes, as he always does when conveying a threat and a promise.

"Yeah."

"Good."

He closes the door, leaving me to overanalyze everything that has happened today, and my apprehension builds when I think about tonight.

Chapter 39

Needing comfort, I scoot down to curl around Tiberia. She unfurls, stretching her long limbs and swiping her tongue across my face. I snake my arm over her tender ribs and under her elbow to scratch her chest. She groans and rolls onto her back, her legs splaying to soak up the attention.

I close my eyes, the blood and violence from this day running like a movie in my mind. It's way too much. I know this is el diablo's everyday world, but I can't withstand much more of this savagery. He wants love amongst the gore, contentment amongst the carnage, and loyalty amongst the captured. He burns everything around him and then expects beauty from the ashes. I can't give him that.

The fire from last night burned the sand and left black ashes on the beach. It is temporary. The high tide will ultimately drag the ashes to their permanent resting place at the bottom of the ocean and return the beach to its pristine state. How do I do that? How am I to absorb the blood and brutality on the outside while carrying the scars of scored earth on the inside?

I can't think of Tiberia's teeth ripping his flesh when she threw her head from side to side. I can't think of her being kicked against the wall and panting with blood dripping from her jowls. I can't think of the dragon's agonizing screams ringing in my ears, the blow to my stomach and ribs, Veronica threatening my life, the doctor's blood splattering my face, and the uncertainty of being raped. I can't think about all of that. In its totality, it's far too much for me to bear.

I want quiet. The quiet in this room, quiet in my mind, and quiet in my life. Peace and quiet. Just her, Carlos and me. That's what I want. If we were to live somewhere else, I think she'd love the snow.

Deep piles of it. Where she could jump and howl, run and race as she does on the beach. I close my eyes and envision a new life in a small house tucked into the mountains of Vermont. Close enough to a quaint town for everyone to know us but far enough away from their intrusiveness.

We'd spend our days exploring nature, crossing streams, and collecting firewood for cozy nights making love. Carlos and I would rake leaves in the fall, plant pumpkins in the spring, and lead a tranquil and content life. A couple of tears slip into her fur, thinking of the life we will have far, far away from here.

I wipe the water from my cheeks, my hand coming away with blood, and my stomach turns. Slipping off the bed, I grab a towel and scrub my arms, hands, and face until no more blood is dripping into the sink. Without a mirror, it's the only way to ensure I got it all. Blood dots my shirt. I need to shower and change clothes, but I am scared to get into the shower with the dragon and Veronica here. I know el diablo thinks I am safe, but I am not. Not until those two are gone.

Walking out of the bathroom, I glance at the long garment bag. I can't believe he wants me at his wedding reception. It's absurd. This whole thing is ridiculous. The glint in her eyes, the challenge to me, and a sure guarantee that she will try to kill me at some point, although probably not at her wedding reception. She is scorched earth. Beautiful on the outside and a scarred monster on the inside.

"Damn you, el diablo."

I yank the zipper down the garment bag and push aside the

plastic to reveal an expensive black gown with a plunging neckline. It's shocking. Black for a wedding reception? Then again, it's my funeral, according to their threats today.

I don't know how I am going to do this. I wish the gown were made of armor, something to protect me from the looks, the whispers, and possibly the guns. I'm not made for this life. I don't have long stares and steely eyes to intimidate people. I don't have an iron will and guts of steel to block out the butchery and carnage of their daily life.

Grabbing the gown from the top of the door, I drape it across the bed next to Tiberia. She sniffs at it for a moment and then grows uninterested. A light knock on the door drags my attention away from the dress.

Carlos! Excitement surges through me. He's finally here.

"You will not believe—" I swing open the door and then scream.

Fear surges through my body, and I scramble to catch the edge of the door to slam it closed in the dragon's face. He throws his shoulder against it, reaching an arm through the crack to claw at me. Panic squeezes my heart, and adrenaline sizzles through my veins.

I brace my legs against the bureau for leverage. My thigh muscles bulge, and my arms strain to close the door. He rams it with his shoulder, catching an inch or two on me, and thrusting his hand through the crack to grab my curls. I clench my teeth against the violent tugging on my scalp. I scream for help at the top of my lungs, but the music from the reception is drowning me out.

"They can't hear you." He yanks harder, and the door yields another inch. Tiberia lunges through the opening, her jaws snapping and missing his arm. "Fucking beast!"

I twist my head. My scalp is in searing pain when I sink my teeth into his wrist. He curses, releasing my hair, and I ram the door repeatedly into his arm until I hear a pop. He yells and stumbles backward. I throw myself against the door to bolt it. The lock is not substantial enough. It's too old and weathered to hold back his revenge.

Tiberia claws at it, biting into the wood and getting splinters in her gums. Her eyes are black, blood dots her gums, and her vicious snarls roll one after another. I dig my hands into the scruff behind her neck and drag her hulking body into the bathroom with me.

Once inside, I slam the door, lock it, and frantically look for a weapon, anything I can use to defend us. She's on her hind legs, barking and scratching to get to him. Her nails etch into the hardwood, carving grooves in the center panel.

"You fucking bitch. I'm going to kill you!" He bellows from the other side of the door, causing Tiberia to go berserk. She crouches and attacks the bottom footplate. When that fails, she spits out the splinters and jumps up, shredding the wood with her claws.

"He loves me. You can't kill me." I try to pull Tiberia off the door, so she'll stop hurting herself when her head whips around and almost bites my hand.

"You disgrace me, my sister, and my family." He rams the door with his shoulder. It doesn't budge. This one is thicker and heavier.

Sister?

"Veronica, is your sister?" Heat crawls up my skin, and my pulse hammers in my neck. "That's why you got away with beating me." It all makes sense. He's untouchable.

"I'm going to fucking murder that animal in front of you. Finish what I started. I'm going to ruin you before I kill you. Let that bastard know I had you last before you die. My face will be the last one you see. I'll fucking enjoy it."

Finish what I started?

"Y-you didn't . . . rape me?" I pull on Tiberia's haunches, seeing blood dripping from her canine teeth, and she whirls on me again to let her go. I can't stop her. She's primal and ready to pounce on her prey.

"Fuck no, damn bastard stopped me in the States, and that fucking pussy barged in here. But we're all alone now, and I'm going to take my time, make you scream until I end you." He kicks the door with his boot, and it buckles.

He didn't rape me. I breathe at the realization, and a renewed rage explodes within me.

"You will not touch me, you piece of shit."

I grab the only thing I can find, the porcelain toilet tank lid, and position it over my head. He kicks again, and the lock buckles, sending the door flying opening.

His eyes widen in fear when Tiberia lunges. Her snarls are deep and deadly. Her long legs leap into the air, and she knocks him on his back. His arms fly up to protect his head, the bandage from earlier leaking blood and swollen with infection. Her jaws snap the air several times before finding his flesh and viciously shaking her head to rip away at the dragon.

Ear piercing screams rattle my ear drums. His torture is apparent as he flails under her, kicking the wall and the bed, everywhere but her. Guttural growls reverberate from her throat, absorbing his screams and heightening the attack. The ferociousness is predatory and primal, a wolf protecting her own.

It's grotesque and vicious, blood splattering the wall, and when she throws her head back, a strip of the dragon's skin flies into the air. Her head twists to the side for a split second, teeth solid red and bits of wood still pierce her gums, before dropping her jaws for another attack.

I am paralyzed in shock. My mouth slacks and my hands tremble as I hold the lid above my head. Her body blocks his face, where I am sure the strip of his flesh came from.

Drawn from my daze, I slam the lid against his knee as hard as possible. He howls on contact, and the impact vibrates my hands so badly that I almost lose my grip. Sweat rolls down my back as I lunge forward, dodging his thrashing boots and delivering another blow to his knee. Three blows, four, five, and then it cracks.

He shrieks and heaves his broken arm over his knee to protect it. This time, I slam the lid on his hand, shattering that too. I grunt, feeling powerful and strong. My revenge is blinding. The memories of him beating me on the floor and touching me in the bed flash before my eyes. I rain down blow after blow wherever I can until a gunshot blasts the room.

My ears are ringing, my eyes squint against the thundering loudness, and I sway, letting the lid slip from my hands. I pull at my earlobes, feeling a sticky residue on one side, and pull my fingers away to see a thin smear of blood.

Then I see my beautiful girl, her teeth embedded in his cheek and not moving. The room spins, and I stumble toward the wall to brace myself.

His panting fools me into thinking it is her breathing, and I collapse to the floor. He pries her jaws apart, writhing in pain from his cheek and ear being gnawed off, and shoves her away.

"Tiberia!" I scream in horror, soundless beyond the ringing of my ears, and crawl to her. "No, no, no . . . p-please, p-please, no!" Her gorgeous crystal blue eyes are frozen, lifeless, and staring at nothing. Her mouth is open, her tongue hanging to the side, and coated with *his* skin and blood.

"God . . . no, no, no, not her."

Tears are welling so fast that she's a black, white, and red blur. The back of my arm swipes across my eyes to clear my sight. Blood drains from her body, seeping outwards and soaking the wood planks around her.

My girl is gone. The most precious girl I have ever loved is dead in my arms. My heart breaks with sadness and guilt as I lie my head on hers. I whisper how she is the best girl in the world.

"I l-love . . . you. I . . . I'm . . . s-sorry."

I beg for her forgiveness. For leaving her behind all those years ago and failing to protect her now. I watched her attack him, defend us, protect me, and I was too shocked to stop it. I should have done everything to keep him from her. I failed her, and it cost Tiberia her life. My gorgeous girl is gone. I am devastated, wailing in her fur.

"Fucking bitch."

My head swivels to see him, barely standing, balancing on one leg, and his shin swaying from his broken knee. His shoulder slumps as his broken arm and shattered hand dangle uselessly at his side.

A tendon swings like a wet noodle outside the oozing meat of his mauled arm when he stuffs the hand holding the gun against his ripped cheek, trying to stop the bleeding. He spits chunks of bloody flesh and broken teeth toward the bed, and the black gown absorbs it.

"You murdered her!" I scream, dragging myself from Tiberia's body. "You worthless piece of shit! You murdered my girl!" Saying the words out loud makes me want to vomit, the taste of it crawling up the back of my throat to meet the lump stuck there. I choke on the toxicity of my rage. I vow to avenge her death and make his as painful as I can. If I die, so be it. I have nothing left. Carlos can't save me now as I am scorched earth.

"I'm going to enjoy killing you." His hand drops from his pox skin, his cheek missing and revealing the side of his teeth and tongue. Saliva and blood ooze over his jaw and down his neck. His earlobe is missing, and the shell of his ear is hanging by a small piece against his greasy hair. His face is grotesque and permanently damaged, a monster from Tiberia's attack. I couldn't be prouder of her.

The bed separates us. The music from the reception is loud and lively. Yeah, no one will hear us. Let's do this.

I curl my lip, baring my teeth as she did, ready to tear into him with everything I've got. "Not if I kill you first." I crouch down to touch the lip of the lid, trying to get my fingertips under it, when I hear the metal click.

"Get it. You'll be dead on your first step." He points the gun at me. My pulse quickens, and I freeze. 'Not so tough now' reverberates in my mind, unlocking the memory of when he said it to me the first time. When I was crawling away from him, trying to protect myself, and he fisted my hair to sneer in my face.

I hit the floor, flattening between Tiberia and the bed, forcing him to come to me. If he hobbles here, I can dive at his good leg and knock him down. Ground fights are never good, but it's my only advantage since he has the gun. My brain rushes through other scenarios, and this is the only one.

"Get up, *puta*."

I turn my head, looking under the bed to see a clear view of his boot. He has to balance on one leg or risk falling over since he cannot put pressure on that broken knee. Yes, this is my advantage.

"Fucking bitch. Get up!"

My pulse throbs in my skull, louder than the ringing in my ears. My body trembles with adrenaline, and my lungs burn, panting out of raspy breaths. 3 . . . 2 . . . 1.

With the lid hanging over my head, I propel myself off the floor and launch it with all my might at the gun. His eyes widen, then narrow. He has no time to fire before the lid knocks the gun out of his hand, and both clatter to the floor. The lid shatters into jagged shards, and the gun slides toward the veranda door.

He struggles to maintain his balance, trying to use his broken leg and grimacing in pain. I sprint forward, launching my feet straight into his good leg, and he collapses, his back taking the full brunt of the blow. He groans, arching his shoulders and writhing on the hard floor.

My ribs and hip bear the impact, but I shake it off, barely feeling it with adrenaline and hatred coursing through my body. My feet land atop his legs. I kick his broken knee before scrambling over to the porcelain shards.

My fingertips graze the longest piece, nearly capturing it when he traps my ankle between his upper thighs. I drive the heel of my other foot into his broken kneecap while using my upper body to lurch forward and grab the shard.

"You think you can kill me?"

His thigh muscles contract, twisting in opposite directions over my ankle and snapping the delicate bone. Shooting pain rockets up my leg and I cry out, momentarily distracted, as he drags me back to him.

"I'm going to fucking end you," he roars, compressing his legs and twisting my ankle further. My foot burns in agony, my body rages with fury, and I grit my teeth as my fist circles around to plunge the shard deep into his chest.

The force of the blow slices my fingers, and blood flows between them. He shrieks, and the veins in his neck bulge, as does the one in the center of his forehead. His legs fall limp, freeing my ankle, and I crawl to the gun on my hands and knees.

"You fucking bitch!"

I glimpse him over my shoulder, panting like a wild animal, trying to pull the porcelain out of his chest. His hand comes away bloody, and the shard remains. He groans, his eyes catching mine, and he falls to his stomach, slithering along the floor. The butt of the shard scraps the wood, pushing further into his muscle every time he uses his mauled arm to thrust forward.

"I'll kill you," he threatens, but the damage to his body and his wheezes filling the room robs him of sounding menacing. He's breaking down. He knows he will not win, and a surge of satisfaction launches me toward the gun.

My hand wraps around the grip, my finger rests on the trigger, and I flip over when he yanks on my foot. My spine digs into the floor, my neck is taut, and my arms are pinned to my body, ready to kill.

Our eyes meet, hatred in both, fear in neither. My sneer matches his. We are alike, both wanting to destroy the other, but I will be the victor this time. I will win.

"I will kill you." My voice is a whispered promise.

He surges forward, his last attempt, and there is a flicker of resignation on his face before I fire. The bullet rips through the top of his chest, blood pumps out of the hole, and his eyes widen in shock. The room is silent, his screams visible but not heard from the ringing in my ears.

His face contorts into something heinous, and his eyes trail down to the smoking hole. When they rise, I see the black depths of hell in his irises, and with one last effort, he thrusts forward, hand outstretched to grab the gun. I fire.

Brain matter and blood spray my face. The bullet blows the side of his head off, and his body slumps onto my lower half. I collapse to the floor, breathless under the weight of what happened.

My strength and resolve dissipate in seconds. My arms lie useless beside me. The gun, a terrible burden in my hand, grows heavy, and I slowly unfurl my fingers from the grip to release it entirely.

My head throbs, my heart pounds, and I stare at the ceiling. The ocean breeze drifts in under the veranda doors, carrying the faint sounds of wedding gaiety over the everlasting ringing in my ears.

I did it.

I slayed the dragon, avenged Tiberia's death, and saved myself.

Chapter 40

"Gatita, what have you done?"

His quiet footsteps stand before me, his dark eyes assessing the scene before boring into mine. I had to do it. He killed Tiberia and was trying to kill me. Kill or be killed, isn't that his world?

He's magnificent. His wedding tuxedo differs from the one he wore weeks ago. All black, fitting like a second skin on his perfect body. It looks expensive. His dress shoes are so shiny I can see the reflection of the dragon's body lying atop mine. Formed as one through hatred, betrayal, and a burning desire to destroy the other.

The brutality of the scene lies before my eyes, seeing it as he sees it, yet he doesn't understand the feeling of it. The victory of having won, having protected myself, having taken the life of my enemy, and having become like him in the process. How can I be proud and hate myself simultaneously? It's a burdensome, dreadful feeling.

He's taking it all in, slowly and meticulously, the way he always does. His guarded demeanor has kept him at the top, to become the most powerful drug lord, emotionless, calculating, and careful.

In a sudden fit of anger, he cusses, grabbing the dragon by his shirt collar and throwing his body off mine. The dragon lands with a thud beside me. His glassy eyeballs stare into mine while el diablo stomps his back. With each violent kick to his body, it flops closer toward me. El diablo is ranting in Spanish. His accent is so thick that I don't understand most words.

When the dragon's blood splatters on me, I roll to my side, putting my back to the carnage of el diablo's attack on his brother-in-law. His rage matches mine. He's beating the dragon for what he did to me. I defeated the dragon for what he did to Tiberia—rage for rage. I understand completely. Where mine has dissipated into grief for my girl, his is increasing, and the grotesque sounds of squishy flesh and squirting fluids sear it into my brain.

"Enough . . . enough, Maximiliano." Twisting against the pain in my body, I reach for his pant leg and see the bloody pulp of the dragon's unrecognizable face, caved in and flat on one side. I turn away, letting my hand fall as he continues to rail his justice on the corpse.

Wedging myself against the wall, I push against the plaster to sit, sending bolts of pain across my stomach. My ankle is on fire, my eyes burn, and my heart breaks as I look at my beautiful girl across the room.

Suddenly, he stops to straighten his jacket and runs a shaky hand through his hair to fix the pieces that fell forward. Blood and matter ruin his pants, and his shoes are no longer shiny, muted by the dragon's bodily fluids.

"Gatita." He crouches in front of me and catches my chin to hold my gaze. "Are you hurt?" He moves my face from side to side, looking for damage. Seeing none, he kisses my forehead before releasing my chin.

"He killed Tiberia." Fat tears drip down my face when I look from her at him.

He frowns, his eyes shifting to look at my blood-soaked clothes. "You killed him."

I know I did. I wanted to. He killed my beloved girl. The sound of the gun and the immediate silencing of her growling told me she was gone instantly. I had to kill him. I wanted to kill him. For her and for me. An eye for an eye.

"I killed him." I echo his words, looking at the innocent girl that died protecting me. "He killed the only thing I love." Tears flood my eyes and fall over the rim with such ease. I loved her. I had plans for her, for us, and that vile piece of shit dragon robbed me of it. He killed my desert rose and deserved to die for it—no question in my mind.

"Do you know what you have done?" His voice is low and heavy compared to the lightness of the music still floating up to us from his wedding reception below. "He was my captain and my brother-in-law."

"That's why you didn't do more when he beat me." It makes sense now. He couldn't do anything to him because of her. This marriage. Had he been planning it ever since I showed up? Or possibly before I ran back into his life in the New Mexico desert with Mom? "You knew, you and her, this whole thing . . ."

"Yes."

"You didn't . . . couldn't because you would marry her. And I . . ." I don't even know what to say. My mind is going in a million directions at once.

"A lucky inconvenience," he finishes, watching me put the puzzle pieces together.

"All this time, you knew." I shake my head. Inconvenience. Lucky inconvenience. "You kept me here all these months." My eyebrows raise into my hair as rage brews within me. I shift to my knees. His hand slides under my arm to help me stand, but I slap it away. I struggle to get my foot under me with the broken ankle. I look like the dragon, balancing on one leg and avoiding putting any pressure on the damaged one. The irony. "For nothing."

"You came back to me. I said before."

"That's not an answer! You could have freed me with Mom and the girls, and you didn't. You kept me. You knew what you were doing the whole time. You made me into this. YOU'RE A MONSTER!" I raise my hands, hoping he sees how broken I am, another useless form of life toyed and played with by his stupid game.

"You left me. Then you came back. You loved me once."

Disbelief, utter disbelief. Is he so demented that he doesn't see what he did to me?

"I know what you are. I know who you are. Why the hell do you think I left? I saw you. I saw el diablo at work." I sneer with contempt so strong that I have nothing to lose if he wants to wrap his hands around my throat and strangle me himself. I am broken and destroyed, and now a murderer like him.

"What did you say?"

"I saw you that night. Do you want to know why I left? Because I saw you that night, five years ago. What you did to those poor men." I shake my head, and he looks past me as if trying to recall what night or which event. It's disturbing. "You had them strung up, flaying their flesh and the screams . . ." I close my eyes and clutch the wall as their raw and horrendous screams haunt my mind. When I open my eyes, he's staring straight into them. "You were drenched in their blood. It was rolling down your arms and dripping onto the floor." I shudder, and he reaches for me, but I lean away. "I saw you. I saw everything. I heard everything. They begged, screamed for mercy, and you kept going. Methodically, not a word, not a pause, no mercy at all. How do I love that? How do I love the devil himself?"

I pause, offering him a chance to explain himself, even though no words will justify his actions. He remains silent, so I continue. "Damn, I was eighteen. I loved you. I loved you with everything I had. Everything I knew." I snort in contempt. "I even imagined a life with you. Getting married and having babies and living in that isolated desert land. I had dreamed of a life for us, and it was false." Saying the words aloud makes it that more sickening.

His hand hovers to touch me. Seeing how repulsed I am, he flattens his palm on the wall beside my head. "I want that too."

I don't know what to say. We stare at each other until he pulls out his phone and mumbles something into it before stuffing it back into his pocket.

"What happens now?"

I stare into those damn piercing eyes. The ones that taught me love, acceptance, understanding, and patience. The ones that made me soar and brought me to my knees. My lover and my captor. He was my everything once and my nothing now. I was his light, he was my dark, and together, we were magic. And now, here in this room, we are the same—both dark eclipsing the light and extinguishing its existence.

He pauses, drops his chin, and stares at me so intensely that my eyes burn. "I say goodbye."

Goodbye?

He said he would never say goodbye.

Panic floods my body. I look around the room for ways to escape when he pulls me from the wall and envelops me in a tight hug. I'm frozen, my arms trapped by my sides and my brain trying to process what is happening. A show of kindness, no, a display of affection. His nose nuzzles my hair, breathing me in, and I can't think.

What is happening?

"I love you, mi angel," he whispers, kissing the side of my head and holding me tightly against him. Seconds tick by. My body is tight, my mind is a wreck, and all the things I should ask him are evading my thoughts. I don't know if this is a trick or sincere. Should I fight him? Maybe I should, but he'll beat me, or even worse, kill me. Do I fake interest and hug him back? Will that send the wrong message that I want him?

My door creaks open, my pulse ratchets higher, and with such tenderness, he shifts to gaze into my eyes. His thumb pushes my chin up, dusting his lips against mine. He kisses both eyes and leaves a prolonged kiss on my forehead before stepping back.

"Goodbye, gatita."

Chapter 41

The sudden loss of his warm body sends a shiver down my spine, and then I see Carlos, watching with a hardened expression. I feel sick, wanting to vomit.

"Take her," el diablo's command is strong and confident. That intimate moment evaporates as if it had never occurred.

I break out in a cold sweat, my body shakes, and my mind realizes what is happening. I look from Carlos to him. "Take me? Take me where?" Panic shrills in my voice.

Is this it? Am I going to die? Is this how it ends? Me dying here with Tiberia and the dragon?

"Are you going to kill me?" I shriek, staring at el diablo's impassive face and then at Carlos's. "Are *you* going to kill me?" I ask Carlos and see the most indiscernible break in his gaze, and my heart thunders into my ears. "Oh my God." I cover my mouth with my hands. I can't believe I'm going to die. Today. Right now. "That's why you said goodbye." Letting my hands fall and looking at Maximiliano. "You said you would never say goodbye. But you said goodbye? Why? Why did you—"

"There are consequences to your actions, gatita," he murmurs, his eyes shifting to where the dragon lies.

Hatred fills me, and I snarl at him. "You fucking bastard. He killed my dog. He beat me twice, nearly raped me, and tried to kill me. Doesn't that matter? An eye for an eye?" I launch myself at him, wanting to add more scars to that damn face, but Carlos bear hugs me from behind. "My life for that piece of shit! You fucking bastard. I hope you burn in hell. I hope someone skins you alive like you did those men. I'll dance in your blood when they string you up and drain you dry," I scream, trying to kick at him while Carlos drags me from the room. The very last thing I see is my beautiful Tiberia, already gone. God rest her soul.

"Burn in hell, you bastard, burn in HELL," I scream down the hall, fighting, kicking, and wailing against Carlos while several other men storm past us, eager to get to their boss and captain. Fuckers will probably parade him around the compound as some fucking hero while I'm dying in a shallow grave in the desert.

The reception music gets louder and louder, vibrating throughout the house. It burns me that the bride below has no care in the world while mine is about to end. I hate them both. Let them both burn in hell.

"And you, mother—" I taunt when he dumps me in one of the hallway chairs as more guards pass us.

"Shut the fuck up." He grabs my wrists, grips them in his fist, and yanks the rope from his back pocket to tie them together. Kneeling in front of me, he leans in and whispers, "Do you trust me?"

His expression is stern and detached, but those chestnut eyes are boring into me, begging me to believe him. He's following orders. He must or at least give the appearance that he is, which is consoling. If he doesn't, we're both dead.

Yes, I do trust him.

"Want me to do it?" One of el diablo's men is standing behind Carlos, his hand on his gun. Carlos's eyes drop to the right, the pocket where he keeps his knife, and then back at me.

Self-defense. What he said on the beach, look for every available weapon to use in case you need it. I stare into his eyes and slowly raise mine to leer at the guard behind him.

"You fucking sell out. You disgust me the most." I spit in Carlos's face.

He glares at me with such hatred that it takes everything in me not to look away. He yanks on my hands to haul me to my feet. My ankle is so swollen that I hold it up to balance on one foot.

"No, I'm going to take pleasure in gutting her." His voice is so dark and deadly that a shiver runs down my spine. He is the Raider. An illusion, a shadow hiding in the night doing reconnaissance behind enemy lines. "This bitch is mine."

"Hurry. We got to dispose of the captain's body before Veronica finds out, or it will be a war between the two families," the guard says, giving me a sweeping look before nodding at Carlos.

Carlos juts his chin up in acknowledgment. He hauls me over his shoulder in one fluid motion, and his muscles dig into my injured side. I hiss at the pain. "I can't be carried like this. I'll vomit," I warn. The blood rushes to my head, making black spots dance in my vision. My bound hands are covering my mouth to keep the vomit in.

He doesn't say a word as more men run past us. When he pauses at the stairs, I warn him again. "Seriously, I'll vomit on you. My ankle is broken, but I'll hobble. Let me hobble."

"Can't. We have to get out of there. They are coming," he whispers, tightening his forearm across my thighs before jogging down the stairs. The music is blaring, and when we pass through the kitchen, it's packed with caterers. "Act dead." He jostles me to stop my squirming.

Don't throw up.

Act dead.

Don't throw up.

Act dead.

I chant in my head, knowing this is life or death.

"You got this?" a deep voice asks.

Carlos growls, "Yes," while never breaking stride as he barrels out of the kitchen and through the courtyard hallway. Black dots blanket my vision as I stare at the pattern changes of the flooring.

My mantra changes.

Don't throw up.

Don't pass out.

The night air is chilly and a welcome relief against my hot, sticky skin. I'm sweating profusely, my hair pasted to my face, and I keep repeating my mantra.

"Can you put me down?" I close my eyes because watching the sandy beach bounce around makes me more lightheaded.

"No time. We must make it." He runs, tossing me around like a rag doll, and I lift off his back to spew vomit behind us. Pain is ricocheting through my body. Everywhere hurts, and I hurl again. The long ridge and the rocks below my veranda disappear into the night at how fast he runs toward the mountains.

Carlos is spiriting over jagged rocks and rough terrain, dodging thorny bushes clustered together until the fortress is hundreds of yards away. The desert is a perfect place to dump a body.

He stops short, gently lifting me off his shoulder and holding my waist while I stand. Vomit coats my mouth, and I spit out the remnants in the brush beside us.

"It has to look real. If someone is watching."

"Make what look real?"

I look around. The shadow of the mountains is to my right, and the overly lit fortress is off in the distance to my left. Who could be out here?

"Lie down."

He helps me kneel and then eases me to the ground to lie on my back. Small rocks dig into my bones, and I wiggle, trying to move them off my spine. My ankle throbs, my ribs are excruciating, and I can't breathe.

"Legs together."

Carlos slips his hand under my knee and broken ankle, careful to cup both as he joins it to the other leg. I bear down to absorb the pain pulsing in my ankle. He carefully straddles my thighs before drawing a massive knife from this pocket to cut the rope from my hands.

"I thought you were going to kill me." My voice cracks as I look at his silhouette in the dark.

He pauses to brush his palm against my cheek before closing the knife and stowing it away. "Never."

My wrists are free, and I rub them to ease the burn. He stands, sliding a boot on either side of my waist, and draws his weapon. My heart thunders when I stare at the barrel of another gun.

Do you trust me?

Trust has been the pendulum between us, him declaring verbally not to trust while all his actions screamed to trust him. It took me time to realize that el diablo was full of pretty words and deviant actions. Carlos was the opposite, limiting his words and showing his loyalty. He asked, and I answered.

I do trust him.

"I'm going to shoot above your head, cover your ears as tight as possible, and don't move." His feet press in tighter, and I can scarcely breathe as the adrenaline races through my body. Once my hands are in place, I watch him. His stance is powerful against the night sky, glistening with bright stars. He looks like a warrior without a war.

My pulse hammers in my head, my shallow pants become white puffs in the cold air, and my ears ache from my nails sinking into them. I barely hear the trigger's click, but the gun firing is loud and unmistakable, sending a cloud of dust over me from the desert floor.

Carlos dives into a plank over me, dusting his lips to mine before tugging my hands down. He's mouthing something, but I don't understand because all I hear is a whooshing sound.

It's not the waves of the ocean, we're too far away. This whooshing is different, faster, and repetitive. Then it turns into echoes of whooshing, and when my ears pop, it becomes apparent that the sound is coming from multiple places and is getting louder.

"Don't move."

"What the . . . ?" I whisper when I see them in the cloudless sky. Silhouettes of blackbirds flying low over his head. "Carlos?"

Trepidation fills me.

"I got you." He kisses me for encouragement before burying his face in my neck. His body tightens over mine until I genuinely can't breathe. I push against his side, and he lifts a fraction for me to get one breath in before hunkering down.

His hand clamps over the top of my head until the loudest boom I have ever heard erupts behind us. A thick cloud of dust rolls over our molded bodies, and burning debris lands within inches of us.

The air is dense and poisoned with chemicals that cause me to cough. He lifts, allowing me to roll to my uninjured side to hack my guts out. The pain from my ribs while I cough, is enough to make me pass out if it wasn't for the sheer terror of what I am witnessing.

Bright orange and red flames billow out of the fortress, sending plumes of angry smoke into the night and eclipse the moon entirely.

Shouting and screaming mixes with the faint dancing music. Dozens and dozens of soldiers carrying rifles descend on the place. Some run in from the shadows, others slide down ropes from the black helicopters hovering above the fortress. It's utter chaos.

Men dressed in wedding attire spill out the doors to defend themselves, their cartel, and their leader. They are outgunned, taking on heavy gunfire before even getting a shot off. I am speechless.

If the warfare isn't enough, the fire ravages the old fortress. Age and wear are no protection against the heat and damage from the explosion. The back section crumbles, pulling at the structure until the second story craters into the first. It's dying, black soot curling the roof as the flames lick at the white stone.

The ashes float into the crisp air, and all I can think about is Tiberia. Her dazzling white coat stained red, her vacant eyes looking past me, and her exuberant spirit gone. I left her behind again. I left her behind to become part of these charred remains. They sealed her fate with el diablo. She started with him and ended with him. Ashes to ashes. She didn't deserve this. She deserved so much better.

"I love you, Tiberia." I drop my head to weep in the dirt.

"It's okay." Carlos holds my shaking body to his.

"He killed my dog." His face is inches from mine when I turn my head. "I should have saved her. I should have attacked him first, but I let her do it. The dragon killed my dog while I stood there. And now she burns with him."

He searches my face for a few long seconds, dirt and grime smeared across his forehead. "She protected what she loved. That's what dogs do. They don't think. They act. It's instinctual. You can't rationalize it. It's primal to protect those we love."

His chestnut eyes are filled with such intensity that I look away. I can't handle the comfort he is providing since my heart is destroyed, blown to bits like the fortress by the sea.

His index finger trails down my cheeks, wiping away the tears before kissing me tenderly. His soft lips slide across my cheek to rest at my temple.

"On three, we run."

He squeezes me, and I mumble my acknowledgment because I want to stay in his embrace longer. His gaze returns to the fiery fortress, and we both watch it incinerate the nightmare I had been living. More soldiers dot the ground, and there is a break in the fighting. None of el diablo's men are pouring out. The music died, and the screams ceased.

"Three."

The words enter my subconscious, and before I can react, he's pulling me from the dirt to toss me over his shoulder again. At the rate he's barreling over the terrain, ducking and dodging through the landscape, I clutch his uniform for dear life. This is what all the sweaty runs were for. He was training and preparing for this. It was going to happen, and he knew it. That's why he was gone.

I hear the whooshing again and look to see the shadow of a black helicopter. Its blades chop through the air while a rope dangles in the dark, waiting for Carlos to capture it. He carefully sets me down, and I balance on one leg, holding onto his sleeve.

He works quickly, making loops of the rope, winding it around his legs, then dipping low to see if it will hold. It is unbelievable how fast he fashions a harness out of it, and when he motions for me to sit on his lap, I scramble on. My broken ankle bobbles against his body, sending jolts of pain up my leg, and I grit my teeth while I bear hug him.

Carlos tugs on the rope, and then we are flying into the air, ascending to the helicopter. I shiver in the cold. Hope replaces the fear lashing my insides. I hope this rope holds both of us. I hope we don't get shot down. I hope we make it out alive.

Seconds feel like minutes as we dangle precariously from the rope, and I look to see how much farther until we are in the chopper's cab when one of the most wonderfully serious faces I haven't seen in a long time pops out of the metal bird.

Ardy.

I burst into tears when I see him. A mixture of happiness and relief fills me to the core when I reach him. He hooks one hand around a metal bar to hold on while reaching down to grab me when we make it to the top.

"Someone call the calvary?"

I lunge at him, ignoring my broken ankle and hurting ribs. He catches me with one arm and, with the help of Carlos, pulls me into the chopper. I bury my head in his chest and close my eyes, remembering how many times he held me like this before.

"Ardy."

"You're safe, kid."

His strength and seriousness were always comforting, but hearing him murmur those words in my ear, I know I am. Ardy always kept me safe.

Leaning back to smile at him, I see Carlos climbing in and getting a hearty handshake from the gunner on the other side. They clap each other on the back, and he turns to me with his wide, bright smile.

"You always were a pain in the ass, Ginger."

Will.

Another round of wailing bursts out of me, and I crawl to Will with Ardy's help. He grabs me when I am within reach and squeezes the life out of me. I do the same. I'm a crying mess, snot gathering under my nose and tears pooling under my chin.

"You didn't think we'd forget about you?" He chuckles in my ear, and I pull back to see that crooked smile I missed so much. "It took us some time to find you, but your momma reached out immediately."

Mom! My heart clenches, and my chest aches at the mention of her. "Oh my God. How is she?" I use the back of my hand to wipe my tears and snot. "Is she okay?"

"Your momma is fine. Aged a bit from all this." His southern drawl never sounded so comforting, and I collapse in relief. Mom is okay — aged a bit, but okay. Haven't we all aged from this? I hug him again, resting my head against his neck and letting it all sink in. It's over. Really and truly over. "All right, that's enough blabbering. Get off me so we can get out of here."

Will taps my back and gives a hand signal to the pilot. I look past him to Carlos, with his arms thrown open and the biggest smile I have ever seen on his rugged face.

"Don't tell me your ugly ass likes Ginger." Will baits him while helping me maneuver over the seat to the back of the chopper where Carlos is sitting.

"Shut up, man." Carlos takes off his jacket before lifting me onto his lap and propping up my leg for my ankle to rest on the adjoining seat.

"How do you know Ardy and Will?"

He helps me put on his jacket, and it smells like him. He closes the flaps and starts rolling up the sleeves. I stare into his face, he looks aged by all this as well, but damn if I am not falling in love with him.

"The Corps," he yells over the noise of the propeller behind us.

I look at Ardy sliding the door closed, Will adjusting his rifle out the window, and Carlos gazing at me, trying to fit them together in a unit. "They planted me with the dog to rescue you. But I didn't know you'd end up rescuing me." He tucks a curl behind my ear, his eyes shining with emotion.

I lean in to kiss him. "I think we rescued each other," I murmur against his soft lips.

Another explosion booms in the distance, and I lift my face to see clouds of black smoke roll out of the orange fire. The fortress remnants are clawing for survival. The blackened elevator shaft stands tall around the burning rubble. The lives inside are decimated, returning to the ashes from which they started. The military that stormed the building is part of the entombment. The few remaining soldiers watch it burn.

And el diablo . . .

"Goodbye, Maximiliano Maldonado."

EPILOGUE

"Can you grab more chairs from the basement?"

I carefully examine the golden-colored turkey and decide it needs more basting. His muscular arms slide around my waist, his nose nuzzles my neck, and his fresh cologne fills my senses.

"No, because they are all out. Like you asked last night." Carlos murmurs against my skin, dusting light kisses on my nape and sending goosebumps down my arm. "See, I listen to you."

Smiling, I twist in his arms, gazing into those chestnut eyes that hold so much love for me.

"Sometimes."

His hand slides up my spine to cup the back of my neck, encouraging me to kiss him.

"Give me some sugar, sugar."

"You sound like Will." I wrinkle my nose and blow a curl out of my face.

"That's a bad thing for sure." He wrinkles his nose, rubbing it against mine and gently pressing his lips to mine. I lean in, licking his bottom lip, and he groans, kneading my waist and tilting my head to deepen the kiss—the same as all those months ago.

"Get a room, Ginger," Will hollers down the hall, causing an abrupt end to our kiss. We look in unison to see his arms full of beer and ice, the only items he's responsible for bringing. Behind him trails Chelsea, the latest girl in his life. A quiet brunette that looks at him as if he hung the moon. "Damn, you made enough food to feed an army."

He dumps his armload of stuff on the counter to unwind the scarf around his neck, sending snowflakes all over the floor. Carlos kisses my head and releases me to clap Will on the back and jostle him.

"Don't say that. She's been up all night fretting and fussing about this dinner. And you're late," Carlos scolds, shaking Chelsea's hand and helping her with her coat. Will rips his jacket off and tosses it at Carlos's face, along with his scarf. Carlos shoots him a warning look before taking the coats down the hall to the front bedroom.

"Thanks, man." Will cracks open a beer to take a sip and then asks Chelsea if she wants one. No chivalry. She politely shakes her head while he helps himself to a plate of appetizers on the far side of the kitchen.

"Do you need some help?" she offers, fidgeting in the doorway and obviously conflicted between staying with me or following Will.

"Thank you, but no. Do you want a glass of wine?"

"Sure, white, if you have it," she says, walking over to place her hands on the countertop.

I set the baster down to retrieve a couple of wine glasses from the cupboard when Mom walks into the room.

She looks radiant in her white pants and cream sweater. Her brown hair has wisps of gray at the temples. She started wearing it in a bob at her shoulders due to stress-induced hair loss. Will was right in that her face had aged. The grief and worry cut new wrinkles, but the twinkle in her eyes is as bright as ever.

When we were reunited at the base the following day, she moved like an old lady. Her limp was more prominent, and she was leaning on the arm of a Marine to cross the tarmac.

My knees buckled when I saw her. I was hysterical, and Carlos practically carried me over to hug her. I wouldn't let her go, too afraid it was a dream and she would vanish. Fearful that I'd wake up and be back in that room, watching Tiberia die and killing the dragon again. I still have that nightmare. On those nights, Carlos cradles me against him and assures me that I am safe, Tiberia is in a better place, and my mom is doing well.

"Chelsea, this is the most important person in my life, my mom." I smile at her with all the love I hold in my heart as I set the glasses on the counter and open the bottle of white wine. Mom smiles graciously, holding Chelsea's hand in both of hers.

"Hi Momma," Will hollers, throwing up a hand holding a pair of tongs.

"Chelsea, so lovely to meet you. Are you keeping that one in line?" Mom jests and Chelsea's cheeks turn pink. "Because God bless you if you can."

I laugh.

"You wound me, Momma," Will bellows before shoving a hummus covered carrot in his mouth.

"Honey, do you need any help?" Mom says as Carlos reappears in the doorway with his eyebrow popping up as if asking the same question.

"All under control. Hors d'oeuvres are ready. Dinner will be another couple of hours." I hand Chelsea her drink, and I am about to lift the turkey to put it in the oven when Carlos dives in to do it for me. Chelsea joins Will, smiling at his antics when he picks up a shrimp and acts like it is swimming toward her.

"Arthur, dear, do you want some hors d'oeuvres?" Mom calls from the kitchen.

Arthur is a handsome man with caramel skin and an amiable smile that Mom met at group therapy. He was dealing with the unexpected death of his daughter from a car accident, and Mom was dealing with my loss.

She didn't tell me much of what it was like for her, always diverting the conversation back to how grateful we should be that it's all over and behind us. I suspect it was like my dark days. I am happy that she has Arthur. Their bond is strong, and their adoration for each other is admirable.

"Tell him I made his favorite, bacon-wrapped Brussels sprouts," I say to Mom. She nods before disappearing out the door.

Will and Chelsea follow, leaving us alone.

Glancing at the clock on the stove, I pour a glass of wine and offer it to Carlos, who declines. "Where is Ardy?"

Carlos leans against the counter opposite of me, crossing his arms over his chest. "He texted that he's running behind. Madeline spilled chocolate milk on her princess tutu."

"Oh, my." I chuckle.

Madeline was born four years ago, a pleasant accident for two career-oriented people. She's everything opposite of them. Maddie's a loud, sparkly, glittery girlie girl born to a Marine mom and a private security dad. She lights up a room with her mischievous energy.

"You're smiling," Carlos says under a watchful eye. The first few months were rough. I didn't leave his side. He was my shelter in the eye of the storm. He was right about the morning shows and the interview requests. With my picture plastered everywhere, I couldn't handle it. Mom dealt with it professionally, and Carlos helped me privately.

"I'm happy."

He kicks off the cabinetry to envelop me with a kiss on my head. "As am I." We watch the snowfall on the deck outside the breakfast room windows.

We didn't make it to Vermont. I couldn't after losing Tiberia. That was my dream with her. Carlos understood and suggested Grand Teton. Close to Yosemite, where we can hike and explore, but with enough privacy that the locals don't care if you are a celebrity or not.

"Auntie Sammie!" Madeline screams as she sprints down the hall into the kitchen. Snow flurries float in her wake. Carlos releases me to scoop her up and throw her into the air. She shrieks in delight and screams, "Again!"

A stressed Ardy appears in the doorway, with bags dangling from each arm and holding a brown paper bag. "Happy Thanksgiving, kid."

"Happy Thanksgiving, Ardy. You look exhausted," I say, taking a few bags off his hands to place on the counter closest to the pantry.

"I am. *Mi Amor* is driving me *loco.*" He leans in to say in my ear.

"I'm not crazy, Daddy," Maddie says when Carlos puts her down, and I laugh, picking her up and squeezing her against me. Her two little hands land on both sides of my cheeks, and we trade off, making silly faces at each other.

"I'm convinced she's Will's kid," Ardy says, dragging a wineglass off the rack and pouring a double serving. He chugs almost half before looking at me. "What?"

"I want orange hair like Sammie." Maddie pouts, crossing her arms in a huff. I laugh, Carlos smiles, and Ardy mutters in Spanish.

"Maddie, do you know who's here?" I say in an overly excited voice. "Will!"

She screams and wrestles to the ground, tearing out of the kitchen and screaming his name. It's only fair to unite the twin forces.

"Thank you." Ardy sighs.

"When is Sheila due back?"

"Four months. The last tour, she promises."

"You could always bring Maddie here. Stay with us if you need the help." I glance at Carlos, who nods in agreement. Neither of us is ready for children, as I am still healing from what happened and want to enjoy our new relationship. But Ardy needs help.

"Thank you, but we have her *abuela*. Trust me, that helps."

"I planned on taking the children sledding tomorrow." Carlos winks at me.

"Children? Something I should know about?" Ardy eyes me suspiciously before finishing the rest of his wine.

"Um, no. My sister is here and my nephew, Noah. He's almost three," Carlos says cautiously, as their reconciliation is very new. His mother died when they weren't talking, filling Carlos with guilt and regret. Two of my old demons. Her death was the olive branch that Carlos extended, and Karla agreed to. "They are in the living room."

Ardy sets his wineglass down and pulls Carlos into a bear hug, whispering something in his ear. Carlos's eyes glisten, and he sniffs when Ardy pulls away. The wound between those siblings is still open and raw, something Ardy understands from his family problems.

The doorbell rings, catching me off guard. "Who could that be?" I look at Carlos. "Oh, probably Bill, from next door. He said he would be alone for the holiday, so I invited him over."

I walk down the hallway, almost reaching the front door when Carlos blocks it. He's become an overly protective hen since we watched the fortress engulfed in flames. He had this house wired like Fort Knox, ignoring that we live in a gated and guard-patrolled neighborhood.

"Sammie, there's something I meant to tell you, and I didn't know how to bring it up." He reaches for my hands, and I put them on my hips. This is never good because he knows I hate surprises after all I have been through.

"Can we talk about this later?" I push against his shoulder, but he doesn't move.

"It's not Bill." He frowns. "I know you don't like surprises. And we talked about me going back to work in the new year." The bell rings again. He puts his hands up to block me and talks faster. "I don't like the idea of you being alone. So, I decided without talking to you. I know we agreed not to do that, but I saw this guy in town, and he had them in his truck, and—"

"Move."

He reluctantly slides to the left. "Don't be mad."

I cast him a side glance, as that's the international phrase for 'I did a dumb thing, knew you would be mad, but want you to have mercy on my soul and not hold it against me forever.'

Irritation has me yanking open the door to see an older gentleman bundled in a blue parka holding a wiggly brown and black German shepherd. The puppy is adorable, with one ear standing at attention and the other flopped forward. "Are you Samantha Smith?" he asks, with deep smile lines.

"Yes," I answer, pulling on Carlos's shirt to join me at the door. He looks at me sheepishly and then opens it wider.

"Carlos, good to see you again. Happy Thanksgiving." He offers his hand and gives Carlos a hearty shake. "I hope you don't mind me bringing him over early. He's the last one, so the wife and I thought we could head out of town tomorrow if you can take him tonight." His face is so warm and friendly that it's hard not to like him. I see where Carlos fell prey to this folksy swindler.

"Um, pardon me, Mr. —."

"Johnson, Jack Johnson. I own the ranch on the other side of the mountain. Cattle production and beekeeping. And apparently rescuing pregnant stray dogs." He hoists the dog higher.

"Mr. Johnson, Carlos didn't share this with me. And—"

"Oh, not smart. Got to run these things by the little lady first. I know firsthand. I have been married going on thirty-five years. Happy wife, happy life," the friendly farmer says, and Carlos has gone mute to the situation. "Well, he's here and all yours if you want him."

"Puppy!" Maddie screams from the space between our legs. "Can I pet her? Is she ours? I want to name her Princess. Can she sleep with me tonight? No, Noah, you can't have her." She scolds when Noah joins us at the door. Carlos wipes a hand over his face, knowing he's in deep shit.

"I want it," Noah whines, grabbing the air with his hands.

"You didn't mention you got a family, Carlos. They are a good-looking bunch. You said you didn't have a kennel, so I loaded my old one in the truck now that we're out of puppies. Also, I brought the remaining food and bowls. Got his collar on, and well, here's the leash." He flips the leash up, and it's decided between one beekeeper and two kids that are not ours.

"You know you're training him," I say when the swindler shoves the puppy into Carlos's arms. The place in my heart where Tiberia lives will never fully heal, but seeing this precious fluff ball with big, clunky paws will help with my grief. Once again, Carlos is right. This little guy will be great company.

"I know," he mumbles, worry crinkling his forehead.

"You got a dog?" Will's face is a mix of surprise and bewilderment when he sees the cute fur ball. Carlos shoves it at Will to follow the guy out to the truck to get the supplies.

"Uncle Will put her down. She's mine." Maddie stomps her foot and points to the floor.

"I need a beer." He puts the puppy on the marble floor, and it instantly pees before chasing Maddie and Noah down the hallway toward the living room. "You got that, right?" Will points to the urine and walks to the kitchen, not waiting for my answer.

I look at the puddle of pee. Look at Carlos hoisting the kennel onto his shoulder in the snow. Look down the hall to the chaos of friends and family in the living room and smile. I'm happy.

BONUS SCENE

Carlos Mendez

"Are you sure?"

I shove the phone against my ear. It's too ridiculous to believe. After weeks of reconnaissance and terrain training, our opportunity finally arrives in the most unlikely way.

"Yeah, believe it," Will growls in my ear. "Ginger was pretty torn up about leaving that dog, so if he's transporting it, that's our way to her."

Camped out at this roach motel miles from the compound prepared me well. This place is desolate, like Maximiliano Maldonado's compound. The same dusty landscape that enabled me to train under cover of darkness also allowed me to survey the drug lord's territory, acclimate to the New Mexico heat and get accustomed to the night predators that roam these parts.

"Time?" I flick my wrist to gaze at my watch. Midnight, two hours before my nightly surveillance begins.

"Six hundred hours," he says, simultaneously talking to someone else. The chatter in the background makes it difficult to hear him.

Six hours from now.

"South entrance. Black digitals."

I glance at the backpack by the door. It is packed with

duplicates of what Maldonado's men wear. I don't know how Ardy pulled it off, but he sourced my size from the same woman in Mexico that made all the private protection uniforms for the Maldonado cartel.

They were waiting in my room when I returned from one of my nightly recon missions. I donned the digitals upon arrival in the event I got caught by his ground platoon when I was conducting my patrol.

I preferred to camp in the desert as in Afghanistan, but the flat land around here made me visible for miles. The motel proved adequate cover amongst the prostitutes and their drunk customers. They didn't rat on me, nor I on them.

"Copy." I gulp down the remnants of my cold coffee and crumple the cup to toss in the trash can. "To confirm, who's vouching for me?"

"Gunner."

Gunner is Will's boy, both shit talkers that think they are water walkers. They are always trying to get laid and striking out more than they scored. Gunner and I didn't get along after I beat his ass in-country when the sweltering heat caused his rifle to slip in his sweaty palms and fire with the bullet grazing my head. Will pulled me off him and grumbled something to Gunner about wearing his mandated gloves next time.

"You sure he will not turn my ass over?" I grit into the receiver, only to be met with Will's obnoxious laugh.

"He probably would if it wasn't Sammie."

Sammie.

Fiery red hair that matched her hot temper and blunt mouth. I heard all the stories about her from the guys. She wanted to save the world, one desperate mission at a time. She had done so successfully, taking on bigger and bigger missions until she got herself in too deep on this one.

The guys hadn't seen her in a few years, but when her mom called to ask Will for help, we understood that the entire team would get involved. Ardy and Will couldn't be a mole because they knew the asshole that kidnapped her, so I volunteered. Hell, I had nothing to lose.

With my medical discharge and Casey walking out on me, my life wasn't really worth living. I'd never kill myself, but if it happened by another's hand, I wouldn't mind, so long as it was a fair fight.

"Gunner will meet you five klicks out," Will yells over the noise behind him. "And Carlos?"

"Yeah?"

"Don't fuck this up."

The call drops, and I pull my phone away to look at the 'Call Failed' screen. I lock my phone, and a smiling Sammie appears on the home screen. Like all assignments, I threw myself into getting to know the subject involved and memorizing every detail I researched. A tactic I learned from my years as a Raider.

Information on Sammie was easy to find because her life was plastered everywhere on the internet. The foundation she ran with her mom was full of stories, interviews, and posts with her hugging this girl or helping that woman. Something in those green eyes and easy smile got under my skin. I'd never admit it to the guys, but I wanted to save this girl so I could meet her. I wanted to see if she measured up to the hype because most people didn't.

Pacing the worn carpet of the motel room, I open the social media app and scroll through her wall. Knowing nothing new had been posted, I still scrolled through all her pictures and videos, having gotten to the bottom more times than I care to admit. She had even posted photos taken at Maldonado's compound years ago, which helped. In my assessment, she seemed too good to be true, and damn if I didn't have a thing for good girls.

That should have been my first clue that Casey would not work out. When she bought me a drink at the bar and asked me to go to the alley with her, I should have walked away. If that short dress, long legs, and blonde hair didn't sucker me in that night and every night until it was time to deploy, I wouldn't have fallen for such a bad person. It's what I get for being vain as hell.

But this girl, Sammie, she'd never ask a guy to go out to an alley. I doubt she'd even go to a dive bar like that. She was a celebrity, lived in LA, and dated Hollywood guys. She was in a league of her own.

Frustrated by the weeks of waiting, my veins are buzzing with adrenaline, and I swipe the app closed. Locking my phone and stuffing it in my pocket, I gaze around the room for evidence I need to wipe clean or burn in the barrel behind the motel.

Grabbing a towel and the cleaning fluid I plucked out of the maid's cart, I meticulously clean the room and bag the trash to leave nothing behind. When I am done, the place smells like a lavender forest. It's probably more suspicious to the motel staff to have it this clean than how it was when I rented it.

I load the pack on my back and use the towel to open the door before slipping into the warm night. The parking lot is half full, slow for a Tuesday night, and I round the corner to walk in the shadows behind the building. The night sky is overcast, the clouds hanging low and causing it to be darker than usual—perfect weather to jog unseen into the desert.

When I make it to the burn barrel, I quietly place the trash at the bottom, douse the towel in cleaning fluid and set it on fire with my lighter. The flames race up the tattered cotton rag as I drop it into the barrel, followed by my phone, which efficiently incinerates everything traced to me. The flames lick the top of the metal, and I step back, watching the fire for a few seconds before turning and disappearing into the landscape.

<hr />

Jogging along the patchy road to the designated meeting spot, I hear the wolves howling in the distance. The extra cloud cover in the sky blankets the desert floor, making it harder to see the rattlesnakes and coral snakes prevalent in these parts. I keep my headlamp off to avoid detection by anyone other than Gunner.

Using the compass on my watch, I slow to a walk to search

the brush and cactus landscape for him. Using satellite imagery and aerial footage, we decided long ago on the coordinates of this location. Waiting for the right opportunity to infiltrate his cartel took longer than we all wanted, contributing to the excitement surging through me.

Patience is tactical and necessary for a good plan to work. It's also frustrating planting my ass in a motel for weeks, wanting to rescue her from God knows what. I've been over this terrain more times than I can count. The restlessness in me demanded it. The more prepared I was, the better this mission would go.

I stop when movement rustles ahead. Gunner steps from the shadows, motioning with two fingers to indicate the placement of the guards on patrol. His mouth sets into a line as I draw nearer.

"Mendez."

"Gunner."

"Lose the phone. Take these, and we fly out in twenty minutes, so let's go."

He hands me a Beartooth and credentials, something I assume gets assigned to every member of Maldonado's security team.

"Phone was in the burn barrel back at the motel. What's my cover?"

I flip open the credentials to see my legal name, nothing like hiding in plain sight.

"No cover. I heard you had a death wish, so I'm glad to help you fulfill it."

With no secret identity, Gunner might finally get his payback if the cartel kills me.

"Wouldn't expect anything less." I'd clap him on the back if we weren't already racing towards the encampment.

"I stay with the plane, in and out, to avoid detection. You stay with the dog. I got your ass in as the dog trainer, said some bullshit about you doing it in Afghanistan, and they bought it," Gunner grumbles at the last part.

"They bought it because you gave them my real name, and when they did their background checks, they probably saw the picture of my unit."

"Pick up the pace."

Yep, he wants me dead.

Adrenaline pumps through my veins as the lights of the compound come into view on the horizon. I don't give a shit what Gunner says. I've got a plan for this rescue, and it's far more than being a dog trainer. It's also a recon mission for our military.

As lovely as her mom is, she'd bankrupt that girl's foundation if she tried to pull off a mission of this magnitude. Will and Ardy understood what we were up against from tracking this powerful crime syndicate for the last few years. Sammie stumbled upon his operations when she got sick from heat exhaustion while skateboarding in this remote area. The guys reported what they discovered, and the government has been after Maldonado ever since.

They've been running covert operations on his cartel and got close four years back when Will and Ardy went off the radar. It's been watching and waiting ever since until this opportunity to airlift the dog out of the country came up.

"Keep your trap shut while I get us past security," Gunner warns when we slow down at the armed checkpoint. I fall a step behind him and lower my head, appearing as nondescript as possible.

⁺⁺⁺◆◆⁺⁺

I didn't expect to travel on his private jet. I figured we'd be in the cargo hold with pallets of drugs instead of sitting in luxury with this mangy, filthy animal laying on the cream carpet at my feet. The ease and smoothness with which Gunner got me in made me wary and ready to have a gun pointed at my head at any moment.

Gunner is in the cockpit with another guard. A second guy is with me, a few seats ahead, with his eyes closed and his knee bobbing up and down. It's a short flight, less than an hour, and the sun is already shining off the plane's wings.

The windows near him are shut, mine are open, yet the view holds little interest as I run through the plan in my mind for the thousandth time. Everything is being recorded as I survey the inside of the aircraft and the cameras dotted around it. I'm motionless except for the occasional reassuring hand to the dog to maintain my cover.

I've known men to do stupider things for the love of a woman, but this is right up there with them. Looking down at the dog to inspect the blood on its ear, I wonder if we got the story right on her. I know what the guys have said, heard from her mom, and scoured my research, but this didn't add up. I don't like unknown variables in my operations.

Sammie's involvement is the biggest unknown variable. What did she do to convince one of the most powerful drug lords in the world to fly in this mutt? He could buy her a dog rescue and an entire farm, and it would still be less trouble.

As we start our descent over the mountains, I vow to get to the bottom of what is happening and report it accurately to my superiors because this do-gooder must be part of his cartel. If my suspicions are right about her, I think her foundation is a front for his drug operations, and I plan to bust them both.

ACKNOWLEDGMENTS

How do I condense all the beautiful feelings I carry in my heart into the right words that warrant the value they hold? Impossible, but I'll try.

To my beautiful Elle. God knew what he was doing when he chose me for you. I learn from you every day. Your compassion, empathy, and kindness inspire awe. Your faith, forgiveness, and mercy influence me more than you know. You are my better half, my best friend, and my love. Thank you for always supporting and promoting me, even when your classmates stop you in the hall to say, "I saw your mom on my page." I love you beyond words.

To my handsome Elkan. You have been a bundle of joy and charisma since you came into this world. Your lighthearted, worry-free outlook on life has me marvel. Your relaxed and good-natured demeanor that makes friends everywhere is something I have learned from. You are my light, my laughter, and my love. Thank you for watching and forwarding my Reels and TikToks and telling me how cringy they are. I can always count on you to be brutally honest in the best way. I love you more.

To my furry colleagues. You snore and fart most writing days, helping me remember to use all my senses when writing. You star unpaid in my videos to help build my brand. And you are always up for a walk when I get stuck on a scene and need to think it through.

Thank you for your many talents in holding down the floor, eating all the food I drop while writing, and giving me a heart attack when you bark at random animals walking by.

To my readers. I know the market is flooded with new books every month. Thank you for choosing mine to read and loving the characters as much as I do. I appreciate the support and encouragement in your emails, comments, and DMs. I read every one of them. Sharing my journey as a debut novelist on social media will hopefully inspire you to go after your dreams, big or small. Life is far too short not to live the life you want.

To Coldplay. You don't know this, but I had tickets to your concert the night Hurricane Harvey hit Houston. Along with a vast majority of Houstonians, my house sustained four feet of flood water and was unlivable for months. That same year, I got divorced and cried to Ghost Stories. Five years later, I launched my author career and danced all night at the World of Spheres concert at NRG. I wrote, edited, and rewrote this book to your library of music. I am forever grateful for your talent, perseverance, and artistry.

To Dawn Alexander. Thank you for being so supportive when we started on the other story years ago, and thank you for your help with this story. This book would not have been possible without your story coaching and developmental edits. I am proud to have worked with you and Peanut in bringing Sammie, Carlos, and Maximiliano to life. I can't wait for our next adventure.

To report suspected trafficking crimes, get help, or learn more about human trafficking from a nongovernmental organization:

- Call the toll-free (24/7) National Human Trafficking Resource Center at 1-888-373-7888.
- Text HELP or INFO to BeFree (233733).
- Submit a tip online at http://www.traffickingresource center.org/.

To report suspected human trafficking crimes or to get help from law enforcement:

- Call toll-free (24/7) U.S. Immigration and Customs Enforcement at 1-866-347-2423.
- Submit a tip online at http://www.ice.gov/tips.

To report sexually exploited or abused minors:

- If a child is in urgent need of assistance, contact law enforcement or child protective services to report abuse, neglect, or exploitation of a child. Contact the Childhelp National Child Abuse Hotline to speak to professional crisis counselors who can connect a caller with a local number to report abuse: 1-800-4-A-CHILD (1-800-422-4453).
- Call the National Center for Missing and Exploited Children's (NCMEC) hotline at 1-800-THE-LOST (1-800-843-5678).
- Report incidents at http://www.cybertipline.org.

To learn about services for victims:

- U.S. Department of Health and Human Services, Administration for Children and Families Services: https://www.acf.hhs.gov/trauma-toolkit/victims-human-trafficking

- U.S. Department of Homeland Security, Blue Campaign, Victim Assistance Resources: http://www.dhs.gov/blue-campaign/victim-centered-approach
- U.S. Department of Justice, Office for Victims of Crime, Funded Service Providers List: https://ovc.ojp.gov/program/human-trafficking/overview

AUTHOR PAGE

After retiring from a thirty-year career in corporate America, GiGi Meier is delighted to be writing romance novels about strong female characters and their complicated, swoon-worthy men. She loves telling stories and figuring out why her characters do what they do. With heartbreaking angst, panty-dropping lust, and enviable love, her stories linger long after you close the book.

When GiGi is not eating over her laptop, she likes to spend time in the pool with her children, walk her furry babies, and film videos for Instagram and TikTok. Whether attending a book club or hosting a game night, she loves connecting with new people and making friends.

www.GiGiMeier.com
https://www.instagram.com/gigimeiermedia/
https://www.tiktok.com/@gigimeiermedia1

Printed in the United States
by Baker & Taylor Publisher Services